RESERVE
STORE

GW01572036

SOMERSET COUNTY COUNCIL
COUNTY LIBRARY

SOUTH PETHERTON

	31. JUL. 1984	27. SEP. 86
28. JUN. 1983	24. AUG. 1984	25 OCT. 86
16. JUL. 1983	-7. SEP. 1984	14. NOV. 86
	-5. DEC. 1984	
20. SEP. 1983	-5. JAN. 1985	18-9-87 HB.
	-1. FEB. 1985	
-3. DEC. 1983	28. FEB. 1985	25. AUG. 1987
13. JAN. 1984	-4. JUN. 1985	20. MAY 88
14. FEB. 1984	20. SEP. 1985	28. JAN 91
-1. MAR. 1984	-1. NOV. 1985	S/L MhAR.
	-3. JAN. 1986	
-3. APR. 1984		15. OCT. 94
27 APR 1984		05. APR 97
CL/8		20. JAN 05
22. AUG. 1984		

Book No 0340459

06. MAY 08
920 COR

30105 0 03404598

latest date marked above. Normally, books
may be renewed by returning them to
the library for re-stamping.

EDWARDIAN
HEY-DAYS

THE AUTHOR IN EDWARDIAN DAYS

G. CORNWALLIS-WEST

EDWARDIAN HEY-DAYS

OR

A LITTLE ABOUT A LOT OF THINGS

SOMERSET
COUNTY LIBRARY

0340459 A

HJ | 920
CORN

LAST
COPY

EP Publishing Limited
British Book Centre, Inc.
1975

First published 1930 by Putnam, London

Republished 1975 by
EP Publishing Limited
East Ardsley, Wakefield
West Yorkshire, England

and

British Book Centre, Inc.
996 Lexington Avenue
New York, NY, USA

by kind permission of the copyright holder

Copyright © 1975 Eileen R. Quelch

ISBN 0 7158 1055 3 (UK)
ISBN 0 8277 4079 4 (USA)

Library of Congress Cataloging in Publication Data

Cornwallis-West, George Frederick Myddelton, 1874–1951.
    Edwardian hey-days.

    Reprint of the 1930 ed. published by Putnam, London.
    1. Cornwallis-West, George Frederick Myddelton,
1874–1951—Friends and associates.   I. Title.
PR6005.0675Z52   1975   823'.9'12 [B]   74–32270
ISBN 0–8277–4079–4

Please address all enquiries to
EP Publishing Limited (address as above)

Printed in Great Britain by
REDWOOD BURN LIMITED
Trowbridge & Esher

Y V L   B

FOREWORD

MANY writers of reminiscences start by apologising for having written them: to my mind fatal to the author's interests and rather hard lines on the book. I make no such apology; on the contrary, the writing of it has afforded me much amusement. The sub-title summarises the contents; it is a little about a lot of things, and, I might have added, people.

It has been my fortune to have met many interesting personalities, seen many interesting places, and done not a few interesting things, and to have been able to indulge in most forms of sport; but I have no tale of great achievements to offer, unless marrying two famous women could be called an achievement—which I doubt. Neither have I any interesting political Catherine wheels to set alight and set spinning in order that they may be displayed in their true colours. The wares I offer you are of a more humble nature, but they are displayed by one who has always tried to see the funny side, and, at the same time, to appreciate the more serious side of life.

If every writer of reminiscences who had any claim to be considered conscientious were put on oath to tell ' the truth, the whole truth, and nothing but the truth,' he would either have to forgo his claim or not write at all. ' The whole truth ': these are the words which stick in the gullet of any really conscientious writer of reminiscences. Naturally ' the truth and nothing but the truth ' is told about the various matters and incidents dealt with in this book; but no persons who have led varied, amusing lives and who have met all sorts of people, can write ' the whole truth ' without giving offence to many still living, apart from the possibility of landing themselves and their publishers in a libel action. Therefore, on any subject which might bring about this undesirable result, it is best to say nothing. The whole register of an individual's opinion and knowledge of contemporary men and matters can only be told in autobiography.

Unless a biographer has been a sort of father-confessor to his subject, much of posthumous biography can be merely surmise, and therefore probably not the whole truth. Autobiographies therefore should, I suggest, be written only from purely post-mortem philanthropical motives, as, on account of the difficulties mentioned, their authors cannot—and, indeed, should not—reap the benefits during their life-time. For instance: Mr. A. B., ex-goodness-knows-what of God-knows-where, but looked upon as a modern Pepys and known to have been the lover of a Queen-consort or of the wives of at least three different Presidents of some republic, writes his autobiography, tells ' the whole truth,' puts the manuscript into a sealed envelope upon which he writes: " To my Literary Executors, to be opened at my death," and locks up the package in the family safe. He dies. In his will he leaves the profits of the publication of the manuscript to the Impoverished Authors' Society. This alone excites the journalistic mind—an author leaving something to other authors, a rare occurrence indeed ! All the newspapers publish extracts from the said will; the manuscript is read; the literary executors, presumably doing their best for the I. A. S., let it be known that the contents are, to say the least of it, highly intriguing. Publishers from all over the world fall over each other to secure the rights. These are sold, an immense sum is realised, and Mr. A. B. smiles down—or up, as the case may be—and says, " What a noble human I was ! " If several people one could mention were to do this, and at the same time provide a fund to pay their literary executors' costs in libel actions, members of the Impoverished Authors' Society, myself included, would not have to write at all, and the general reading public would benefit accordingly.

Have I made it clear, therefore, that this is not an autobiography, but just some record of past years and friendships, and (I hope) amusing stories and anecdotes? If any of my personal friends recognise some old tales, I ask them to be lenient and not sound ' the chestnut bell,' as there may be other readers to whom they are new. My thanks are due to many friends who have lent me old photographs, and to the *Daily Telegraph* for permission to publish one or two items which have appeared in the columns of that newspaper.

G. C.-W.

London,
   July 15*th,* 1930.

CONTENTS

LIST OF ILLUSTRATIONS

EDWARDIAN
HEY-DAYS

EDWARDIAN HEY-DAYS

Chapter I

CHILDHOOD AND SOME CHILDREN

A FAIR-HAIRED boy of four years old, tall for his age, wearing
a sailor suit and bronze-leather, buttoned boots, limping as
he walked beside a double perambulator pushed by a for-
bidding-looking woman round Belgrave Square: such is
the first impression of myself which left its mark upon my
memory. It may be asked, why did I limp? The explanation is that, I being eighteen months younger than my elder
sister, it was taken for granted that her boots would fit me
as she grew out of them. The fact that a boy's feet are
usually larger than a girl's never entered into my parents'
consideration; they may not have even realised that I *was*
wearing my sister's boots—possibly it was a routine which
was in force in most families. Whatever it was, they hurt
me infernally, and I have a distinct recollection of it, especially when I was refused admission into the double pram
to sit next to my younger sister, a little girl of two and a
half.

Agricultural depression, and the consequent spending in
advance of rents which had not been collected, because the
tenants were not able to pay them, had necessitated my
father, Colonel Cornwallis-West, letting Ruthin Castle, his
Welsh home, two years after my birth; with the result that
all the early childhood of myself and my sisters—Daisy, a
little blonde, and Shelagh, a little brunette—was spent in
London, at 49, Eaton Place. I was a delicate child, as most
eight-months children are. I was born at eight months
because my mother, with the superabundance of Irish spirits

which she possessed, chose one day to chase the gardener round the garden, at the same time playing the hose upon him. This had unfortunate consequences for me, as it became evident that night that I was anxious to make my appearance into the world one month before I was due. In this emergency there was no one to look after my mother except the old Ruthin doctor, one Jenkins, a kind-hearted man who attended us all for many years. My particular recollection of him is that he always smelt strongly of some peculiar mid-Victorian disinfectant.

My mother was desperately ill. From the doctor's point of view her case was the more urgent of the two, and I therefore did not receive the attention which in ordinary circumstances I should have had, and which, being the wished-for heir, I was entitled to expect, had I been capable of expecting anything. My maternal grandmother, old Lady Olivia Fitzpatrick, was staying in the house, and she always maintained that if it had not been for her I should not have survived. She found me on a sofa, so she said, gasping like a small fish, and, after smacking some life into me, hastily administered a few drops of brandy, the first liquid that ever passed my lips.

My mother, who, as a girl of seventeen, married my father in 1871, was in many ways a remarkable woman. Not only was she noted for her beauty, but also for her wonderful spirits and for being an adept at repartee. There was at Ruthin a broad polished-oak staircase, admirably adapted to one of her favourite amusements, which was to toboggan down it on a tea-tray. We children naturally followed her example—sometimes without even a tea-tray—but our descent, in these circumstances, was not so rapid, and certainly more painful. To my father's credit be it said that, although he was brought up in the strictest Victorian school, he never appeared to be shocked by my mother's antics. I personally was very much in awe of him, although he was an exceptionally kind man. On one occasion he considered he ought to chastise me, and sent me to obtain the necessary implement from the stick-heap. I chose, as

MRS. CORNWALLIS-WEST, THE AUTHOR'S MOTHER

might be expected, the thinnest and driest I could find, which broke at the first contact. "Dear! dear!" was all he said, "what a pity! But there it is . . ." and that finished the episode. My mother, who was a great gardener, used to call him Westeria Gigantia.

My father's mother, old Mrs. Cornwallis-West, who lived at Newlands Manor in Hampshire, was typically early-Victorian. The correspondence which she had with one of her daughters on the subject of my father's marriage subsequently came into my possession on the former's death a few years ago. Like most old ladies of that period, both my grandmother and aunts kept every single letter that was ever written to them, and it was thus that I discovered the solution of the mystery which had always perplexed myself and my sisters: why I was the only one of the three who ever saw the mysterious lady known to us as Grandmama West. It appeared from these letters that old Mrs. West was very much averse to my father's marriage with a girl whom she described as "merely a beautiful Irish savage," and who was twenty-two years younger than he. However, the marriage took place, although none of my father's relatives was present. His mother subsequently gave a reconciliation party at Newlands, in the shape of a fancy-dress ball, and amongst the guests staying in the house for it was a distinguished diplomat, Lord Lyons, who at once fell a victim to my mother's charms. On the night of the ball, supper was fixed for midnight, and it was of course arranged that he should escort my grandmother in, the formalities of the day being strictly observed. Meanwhile, it appears, my mother and the distinguished visitor had ensconced themselves in a conservatory, when she, declaring that she was exceedingly hungry, suggested that a bit of supper might be a good thing. He fell in with the suggestion, with the result that they went in to supper alone, and could not be found at the time when the procession was forming up for it. After waiting a quarter of an hour, old Mrs. West took another escort and swept into the dining-room, only to find her daughter-in-law and the diplomat

3

having a good tuck-in. She was an old lady of violent temper, and apparently exploded on the spot. My parents left the next day, and my mother never met her mother-in-law again, although the latter did not die until sixteen years afterwards. The old lady never forgave her, although she was only a girl of eighteen. The episode does not say much for the domestic diplomacy of Lord Lyons.

As, however, I was the heir, Grandmama West so far relented as to have me to stay with her and one of the aunts when I was a boy of twelve. A large dinner-party was given, to which all the neighbours were invited and at which I formed the principal exhibit. Every mouthful I ate was carefully watched, to see that I did not over-eat myself, and when the meal was over I was solemnly placed at a table and told to play draughts with a young lady guest, while the rest of the party looked on. It was one of the most awful moments of my life, and of the young lady's, too, I imagine. The next morning I expressed a desire to go and fish in the lake, and after a great deal of demur, my grandmother consented, but was so terrified lest I should be drowned that she insisted on her butler accompany-ing me, and stipulated that a cord should be tied round my waist, the end of which should be firmly fastened to a tree!

Old Mrs. West was the daughter of Mrs. Whitby, that wonderful lady whom I mention in the " Life and Letters of Admiral Cornwallis," but I doubt whether she had her mother's charm.

I don't remember much about our early nurses, except one named Haig, whom I and my sisters hated. That woman frightened the life out of me when, as a boy of five, I took a small piece of bread and jam which she had left on her plate after breakfast. She told me I was a thief, and that she would give me in charge to the policeman on point duty when we crossed Knightsbridge into Hyde Park that morning. Never shall I forget my feelings as we reached St. George's Hospital, hardly able to walk from fright, and my subsequent relief when we had passed the policeman

4

and nothing had been said about it: and the cursed woman only laughed. It is one of the most vivid recollections of my life, and the reaction on my nerves was so serious that old Dr. Ticket, who looked after us in London, realised that there was something amiss, and advised my mother to make a change in the nursery staff, which she promptly did.

Children in my early days were looked upon partly as a nuisance and partly as a kind of animate toy, to be shown, if they were sufficiently attractive, to callers. We were always brought down and shown after lunch, but were never expected to utter, and were consequently all abominably shy. The first time I began to feel a little more sure of myself was when something I had said to our nurse was repeated by the nursemaid to my mother's maid. The nurse, who was an inveterate talker, had turned to me and said, " Silence is golden," when I had attempted to make a remark; and I had responded, " Talking is lead." The punishment which she promptly inflicted on me was quite outweighed by the unexpected applause I got from the visitors after lunch that day, when my mother told the story. It made me feel that I was not quite the little fool that Nanna Haig would have me think I was. As a rule, however, the maxim that " children should be seen and not heard " was thrust down our throats until we were well into our teens.

It was an unheard-of thing for children up to the age of fourteen to be allowed to eat the same food as grown-ups. The only meal we had in the dining-room was luncheon, when special but entirely unappetising food was provided for us; and I remember my own feelings—shared, I am sure, by my sisters—at seeing and smelling the delicious-looking dishes offered to the more mature humans. I confess to having appreciated good food all my life, and, looking back, can quite understand why I dissolved into tears when my governess informed me that food was totally unnecessary in Heaven.

Even at children's parties one seldom heard an animated prattle, except among the grown-ups. I remember being

5

hauled out of bed one evening to be taken to a fancy-dress ball at old Lady Conyngham's house in Belgrave Square. My sisters had dresses covered with daisies, which they had worn, as bridesmaids, at the wedding of a cousin; these were considered sufficiently fancy, and they were told to say "Spring" when asked what they represented. Presumably for economy's sake, no fancy dress had been bought for me, and I was therefore put to bed on the night of the party instead of being taken to it. We had often met Lady Conyngham's daughters in the Square, and they were always very kind to us, especially Lady Jane, then a beautiful girl of about fifteen. When my mother arrived at the house with my two sisters, she was at once asked by her hostess's daughters, "Where's George?" The result was that the carriage was sent back, and I, as I said, was hauled out of bed and dressed in the sailor suit which all small boys of that period were accustomed to wear all day and every day. To this moment I remember boys at that party asking me, with an undisguised sneer, what I was supposed to represent, and a small voice answering: "A Jack Tar."

I have a vivid recollection of the dinginess of 49, Eaton Place, and no doubt most London houses were the same. It was before the introduction of vacuum cleaners and central heating. Gas, minus the mantle, was the only illuminant; coal fires, and the appalling London fogs of those days, made everything black and grimy. The curtains, furniture and carpets were invariably dark, presumably because light colours would have made the dirt even more apparent.

There were many visitors to the house, amongst whom were the beautiful Mrs. Langtry and Mrs. Wheeler, both friends of my still more beautiful mother. I well remember their curious concertina-shaped bustles and little pork-pie hats decorated with silk pom-poms, and their tippets, either of fur or of eiderdown, which barely covered their shoulders. My mother once showed me a hat which had been sent her as a present by the late Duke of Fife: it was made of a ptarmigan, the head of which stuck out in front so that when

6

she put it on her head it gave the impression of the bird sitting on a nest.

Lord Charles Beresford was a frequent caller, who used to give us shillings and occasionally half-crowns; he had, in those days, a mass of curly hair. Sir Frederick—or rather Mr. Leighton, as he was then, was a great friend of my father. The latter, incidentally, still kept up his painting and had a large studio at the back of the house, over the stables. Another of his artist friends was Sir John Millais, who always had a great admiration for my elder sister. One day, some years later, he met her in the Park walking with her governess, and greeted her. She, being rather shy, got a bit mixed and said, " Oh, Sir Peter Lely, I am glad to see you ! "

The Prince of Wales often came, and was invariably kind to me and always asked to see me. Never a Christmas passed without his sending me some little gift in the shape of a card or a toy.

In the summer of 1880 my father took a house called The Hermitage at old Windsor, where he had a party for Ascot. It was a small place, consequently we three children were turned out and bedded down in lodgings about a quarter of a mile away, where the washing and other arrangements were nil. My recollection is that none of us had a bath until we got back to The Hermitage a week later, but nobody seemed to worry about that. I particularly remember one of the dresses that my mother wore for Ascot, as I watched her maid making it. It was of white muslin and, as was the fashion then, the waist was unhealthily waspish. What intrigued me was that, above the waistline, the muslin was gathered together to give the effect of a honeycomb, except that the holes were square instead of hexagonal ('smocking' is, I believe, the correct female term). At the angles of each square there were little blobs of red silk. Her sister, Mrs. John Brooke,* who was also of the party, had a similar dress, except that in her case the blobs were of deep yellow silk.

* The late Mrs. Guy Wyndham.

7

My mother used to tell a story of what happened that Ascot. She was seated on a coach and had just finished lunch when two men passed. One of them, whom she knew, said to the other: " That's Mrs. Cornwallis-West. Isn't she lovely? " " Yes," was the reply, " but why does she paint herself so? " (The verb " to make-up " in its modern sense had yet to be invented.) My mother overheard the remark and impulsively said to the man beside her: " Run after those two men; I want to speak to them." Then, turning to a footman, told him to bring some water and a napkin. When the two men arrived, without saying a word she took off her hat and proceeded to scrub her face with the wet napkin; then, turning to the stranger, she handed it to him, saying: " Now perhaps you'll believe I don't paint myself."

In those days rouge, powder and lipstick were not necessary adjuncts to a woman—beautiful or otherwise.

It was the custom for ladies of fashion to drive in Hyde Park in a victoria drawn by a pair of high-stepping horses, and accompanied by one—only one—of their children. To quote Max Beerbohm, " The modish appanage of Beauty in her barouche was not a spaniel now, but a little child." As I had no nose to speak of, and ' bat ' ears (over which I was made to wear a whalebone contraption) it was nearly always one of my sisters who was given the place of honour in the victoria, as they were both very pretty. One afternoon, however, Lady Dudley * appeared in her barouche with one of her six sons, and as she was a leader of society, this apparently set the fashion for mothers to produce their boys on the daily drive. One day, to my utter astonishment, I was bundled into the victoria, and afterwards drove with my mother for quite a considerable time. But the fashion waned; my sisters once more became the favourites, and I was relegated to bronze boots and Belgrave Square.

In 1880 my father took a house at Southsea for the late summer. Prince Edward of Saxe-Weimar was in command at Portsmouth. Princess Edward was very kind to me as a

* The late Georgina Countess of Dudley.

small boy, and it was at her special request that I joined my parents after lunch at Government House one day, to meet the Prince and Princess of Wales, who were going to inspect the troops on board the *Jumna* before she proceeded to South Africa, where the first Boer War had broken out. Prince Eddie * and Prince George, now His Majesty King George V, were also there. They had not been at luncheon with the grown-ups, and were in the garden when I arrived. Both were in naval uniform, and they asked me where I lived, and when and where I was going to school—all the usual sort of questions, in fact, that bigger boys ask smaller ones when they want to make polite conversation. Afterwards we all went on board the troop-ship; most of the men were lined up between decks, and I have a vivid recollection of being acutely impressed by seeing a tear coursing down the cheek of one old soldier and wondering why he was crying. I had no knowledge, in those days, of the horrors of war.

The excitement of my sisters and myself at being told we were going to leave London and return to Ruthin was indescribable. Except what we had gleaned from my father's drawings of it, we none of us had any idea of what the place was like.

The family arrived there one afternoon in May. We were met by the Volunteer Band and the Mayor and Corporation, who proceeded to present an address of welcome to my father and mother. True, they had only been absent five years, but in those days it was the custom to present addresses on every conceivable occasion and on the slightest pretext to persons who were considered worthy of them. Never shall I forget my sensations when the great gates, which opened on to a street at the end of the town, rolled back and I found myself in the grounds. It was a brilliant day; trees were just bursting into bloom. Their pale green, the red-coloured sandstone of the castle and the blueness of the sky, were in perfect harmony, and I felt I had arrived in fairyland.

* The late Duke of Clarence, elder brother of King George V.

Ruthin came to the Wests from the marriage of my great-grandfather, the Hon. Frederick West, with a Miss Myddelton, daughter and co-heiress of Sir Richard Myddelton of Chirk Castle. Sir Richard Myddelton died towards the end of the eighteenth century, leaving the whole of his estates in Denbighshire and elsewhere—which in area and value were second only to those of Sir Watkyn Wynn—to his three daughters, the eldest of whom had married a Biddulph, and the second a West; the third, Harriet, never married. Unfortunately, Sir Richard omitted to state in his will how the property should be divided.

At the time of his death, his three daughters and his two sons-in-law and their families all lived in Chirk Castle, and he was hardly cold in his grave before a quarrel broke out between the two men. This was the beginning of a feud between the Wests and the Biddulphs which lasted close on a hundred years. For hatred, rancour and folly it is on a par with the feuds which existed between certain Scottish clans.

Although the property exceeded in those days some sixty thousand acres, there was only one residence — Chirk Castle, a glorious old twelfth-century fortress, to this very day untouched and unspoilt. Built, like all feudal castles, in the form of a square, with three towers on each side and a huge courtyard in the middle, it stands some hundreds of feet above the village of Chirk and overlooks the valley of the Dee, the view extending across the plain of Cheshire right up to the Peckferton Hills, which, on a clear day, can be seen some thirty or forty miles away. This indeed was a possession worth keeping, and both men determined to strive their utmost to retain it. A law-suit was at once started, and was eventually taken, after many years of litigation, to the House of Lords.

The families, in the meantime, had separated, nominally —I say " nominally " because they each lived in separate wings of the castle. My father used to tell me how his father remembered living at Chirk as a small boy and that the children of the Wests were not allowed to speak to the children of the Biddulphs, although they constantly met in the house and grounds.

On my first visit to Chirk, as a boy of sixteen, I was given a room in one of the towers. The walls were fifteen feet thick. On one side I noticed a heavy red curtain which, with natural curiosity, I pulled aside, to discover what looked like a dungeon let into the wall; it seemed creepy and I didn't like it. At dinner that night I asked my cousin, Dick Biddulph (he had not yet taken the name of Myddelton), what it was for. His reply was characteristic: " Some damfool ancestor of ours, my dear boy, not satisfied with the castle plate closet, insisted upon having one of his own, so he hacked that hole in the wall."

During the period that the litigation lasted, the two opponents stood for Parliament, one as a Whig, the other as a Tory, each striving to become a member of the same pocket borough. Money to pay the lawyers and money to pay the electioneering expenses was poured out like water, and it is recorded that the only time the two men and their wives ever met was to sign the necessary documents to raise money jointly on the property, which up till then had not been legally divided. The only time when all parties agreed to agree was when the House of Lords' decision was made known: both thought it unfair. And after having spent the best part of a quarter of a million in ten years, they sent for the daughter of the local schoolmaster and solemnly proceeded to draw lots, having agreed that the three properties should be divided as to the estates of Chirk, Ruthin and Llanarmon. The longest straw was to retain Chirk, the second Ruthin and the third Llanarmon. There was poetic justice in the result, as the eldest daughter obtained Chirk, as she should have all along, the second daughter got Ruthin, the next in importance of the three properties, and the third, Harriet, drew Llanarmon. This lady eventually threw in her lot with the Wests and left her share to that family. Incidentally this is the property which I now own in Wales.

When the Wests were turned out of Chirk, Ruthin Castle

itself was nothing but a huge and interesting ruin; it had been destroyed by Cromwell. Inside the perimeter my great grandfather built a second edition of the castle, quite large enough and of pleasing design. My grandfather, however, when he succeeded, was not satisfied. Always jealous of Chirk, he mortgaged the property, pulled down most of the second edition and erected, in 1850, the huge mansion which now exists. He was even so foolish as to build it of red sandstone, beautiful to look at, but bad to wear and very expensive to keep up.

The feud between the Myddeltons and the Wests continued right up to my father's time. My grandmother, who was living at a place called The Quinta, near Chirk, when her father-in-law was still alive, endeavoured, about 1830, to bring about a *rapprochement*. Strictly contrary to orders, one day when her husband was away she drove to Chirk Castle. She was received by the Mrs. Biddulph of the day, and, judging from her letters to her mother, Mrs. Whitby, the two ladies must have agreed that the continuance of the family feud was idiotic, but old Mr. West at Ruthin heard about this visit and wrote a frantic and almost insulting letter to his daughter-in-law. Actually my father and the late Mr. Richard Myddelton ("Cousin Dick" to me) were the first to make it up, while the present owner of Chirk, Colonel R. E. Myddelton, is one of my oldest and greatest friends.

After having been cooped up in London for five years, the outdoor life at Ruthin was paradise. We children had perfect freedom to do what we liked and go where we liked, and our first undertaking was to explore the dungeons in the old part of the castle, of which quite a number remained. There was even an old whipping-post in a small arena, on to which the entrance to the guard-room opened. Underground passages extended for quite a distance and, although none of us would have admitted it, we were at first terrified of these dark places. The only light we had was a tallow dip or a taper, but we soon overcame our fears, and found that these relics of past ages presented marvellous oppor-

RUTHIN CASTLE AS IT WAS IN 1820, FROM A WATER-COLOUR

tunities for hide-and-seek. One of our chief amusements, whenever strange children came to play with us, was to get them lost in the dungeons. This, however, was soon stopped, as one small red-headed girl, whose name, I remember, was Violet, complained to her mother that we had treated her cruelly, and now that I come to think of it I suppose we had!

As I had been only about two years old when my father let Ruthin, at the next rent-audit dinner I was solemnly presented to the tenants as the " Mab y castell," this being the Welsh for ' heir to the castle.' I remember the function well because, much to my delight, one of the tenants presented me with a Welsh pony, which I christened May. It was a wonderful little animal, high-spirited but docile; it lived to be more than thirty years old, and practically all my nephews and nieces subsequently rode it. I having been given a pony, my sisters insisted upon having one as well, and we used to groom these animals ourselves, and ride for miles.

There were many old retainers at Ruthin in those days, both men and women, who had been employed in my grandfather's day. They and the older tenants were genuinely glad to see us back, and made a great fuss of us. On two or three days every week we would visit one or the other of them, and were always given a wonderful tea. The feudal instinct was still very much alive in Wales; whenever we walked in the town the men would touch their hats, and the women and children would stop and bob.

Our new nurse was a Welshwoman, Mrs. Evans, whom we all adored, and she us. As children we were always fond of acting or having tableaux, and on one occasion Nanna Evans was stuck in a bath and covered with an old black shawl so that only her face was showing; this was whitened with flour and she was told she was Marat, and that she was to shut her eyes and open her mouth while Shelagh, as Charlotte Corday, stood over her with the biggest carving-knife she could find!

The old woman had a marvellous-looking face, exactly

like crinkled parchment. I once asked her whether she was like that all over, and was promptly smacked.

Bolton was the family butler, who had been with my father a number of years. We children looked upon him as a personal friend, for, when there were parties in the house, instead of going to bed as we should have, we used to sit ourselves on a window-ledge outside the dining-room and be fed by him with choice morsels as the dishes were brought out, rather like three sparrows on a perch. We also looked upon him as something of a conjuror. It was the fashion to have long linen strips along and across the table instead of a table-cloth, and when I mention that the table at Ruthin would seat thirty people, the length of these strips can be imagined. When, before dessert was handed round, the table was cleared of glasses, knives and forks, etc., Bolton would go to one end of it, take up a corner of one of the strips, and whisk the whole away without any of the guests being aware of it, except for the flash of linen as it passed their eyes, leaving bare, as if by magic, the highly polished walnut table. This performance we used to watch through a crack in the screen which stood in front of the service door.

Dinner in those days, which was never later than eight o'clock, was a very elaborate affair, with many courses. The great fashion was to have the table decorated with multi-coloured Venetian glass; the wine-glasses and tumblers matched the vases and the effect was bizarre. My father invariably drank claret or sherry and so far as I know whisky was almost unheard of, but I remember my mother having one very strange drink. She had been ordered stout, as she was rather anæmic, and, to heighten its tonic effect, a poker was heated red hot in the fire and dipped into the drink. It was a matter of violent dispute among us children as to who should have the privilege of dipping the poker into the stout!

If our outdoor life was free and easy, the same could not be said of our life in the schoolroom. We had many governesses, but they never lasted long. We were inquisitive and rather intelligent children and, though we did not realise it at the time, what we subconsciously objected to

14

RUTHIN CASTLE AS IT IS, FROM A WATER-COLOUR SKETCH BY W. BUXTON

was being taught our lessons like parrots and being snubbed whenever we asked for explanations. So far as I was concerned, the climax came one Sunday morning when we were doing a Scripture lesson before going to church. We had to read aloud a chapter of the Old Testament, not one verse of which was ever explained to us. My eldest sister read aloud the third verse of the first chapter of the First Book of Kings, which gives an account of a fair damsel called Abishag, a Shunammite, who " cherished the king and ministered to him, but he knew her not." I blurted out, " I don't believe it! How could she do all that for the king if he hadn't been introduced to her? "

After this episode a family council was held, and it was decided that I should go, as a day boarder, to the Ruthin Grammar School—much to the astonishment, as I learned when I grew up, of the townsfolk and tradesmen of Ruthin, whose sons also attended that school.

At first I was treated with a certain amount of snobbish deference, but that soon wore off. I will only relate one incident which goes to show the cruelty and injustice which was often meted out to children five-and-forty years ago. Being the son of the squire, I was supposed, by my school-fellows, to have a certain amount of pocket money, whereas in actual fact I had none. Some of the bigger boys refused to believe this, and bullied me into buying sweets for them in the town on my way from the castle to the school. I bought sweets on tick up to the amount of tenpence-halfpenny, and as I could not pay the tradesman he sent the bill in to my mother. My father was away in America at the time, and she accordingly sent the bill to the head-master of the school with the request that he should inquire into the matter and take " such action as might be necessary." The only inquiry he made was to cross-question me as to why I had done it. I was far too much afraid of the other boys to tell the truth, though had I known what he intended to do I might have chosen it as the lesser of two evils. He thrashed me, a boy of eight years old, in an unspeakable manner.

I limped home, boiling with rage at the injustice of my punishment, went to the schoolroom, and found my sisters alone there. We retired under the table, where my wounds were examined—all three of us in tears—and Daisy rushed out to the nursery for the Pomade Divine, the universal salve of those days.

I have often wondered whether or not it is a sound policy to stimulate a boy's first idea of what profession he wishes to follow when he grows up. Most boys between the ages of eight and twelve are fond of things mechanical, and I was no exception; I loved railways and steam-engines. Before I went to a private school, my father asked me what I would like to be when I grew up, and I said at once: "An engine-driver." Without suggesting that he should have taken me literally, I question very much whether it would not have been wise for him—or for any father, for that matter, similarly situated—to have watched me carefully for the next five years or so to find out whether the first inclinations persisted without having, necessarily, been fostered. However, he pooh-poohed the idea of anything off the beaten track, and there and then told me I was destined for either diplomacy or the army.

One friend of mine, when only three years old, showed that he had a mechanical turn of mind. His grandmother, who was a well-known Victorian duchess, happened to be giving a large luncheon-party on his third birthday, and Tony—that is my friend's name—was brought down after lunch to be exhibited to his grandmother's guests. The old lady addressed him thus: "Now, Tony, your nurse tells me you have been a very good little boy, and, as it is your birthday to-day, anything that you choose to ask for within reason shall be granted. Think carefully before you decide."

The whole table hung on the infant's words. After a few seconds' thought, he said: "Please, Grannie, may I be allowed to pull up the plug myself?"

That boy subsequently went into a financial business. Who knows but that he might have been another Stevenson if his bent had been allowed to develop?

16

Chapter II

SCHOOLDAYS AND SCHOOLBOYS

Boys between the ages of eight and twelve are often nasty little creatures. Their minds are not sufficiently developed to have any sense of justice; with them it is purely a question of the survival of the fittest, and the supervision of older boys or masters is essential if the weaker element is to be saved from leading a life of hellish torment.

I was sent, after leaving Ruthin Grammar School, to a preparatory school at Farnborough—I refrain from mentioning which, but there are three schools there; suffice it to say that it contained so many sprigs of aristocracy that it went by the name of "the House of Lordlings." I have often discussed the past with men of my own age who were at that school, and we have all agreed that we would not go back there for a million pounds. Hardly one of the masters was a gentleman. We were taught well, I admit, but if it had not been for the fact that our parents sent us hampers of food which we were supposed to share with the other boys seated at the same table, we should scarcely have been fed at all. As it was, if one happened to be unpopular with the boy whose hamper was being shared, one got nothing at breakfast or tea but bread and butter. The only meal actually provided by the school was the mid-day meal, with its everlasting stringy beef or mutton, both invariably over-roasted.

Bullying at that school had developed into a fine art. I was a very delicate child, in fact an overgrown slab of misery, unable to take part to any great extent in games; I was in consequence made to suffer. One of the chief amusements of the bullies in our bedrooms was to tie scarves to each wrist and ankle, stretch the unfortunate victim on

17

the bed and pretending that he was 'on the rack,' only there wasn't much pretence about it. Another form of amusement was to make small boys eat flies.

The headmaster himself was, I honestly believe, a sadist; I am certain it afforded him intense pleasure to administer the severest thrashings, having first deprived the boy of any form of protection. He once, while I was there, thrashed a boy until he fainted.

Unfortunately for the bullies, I completely upset their apple-cart by attempting to commit suicide, not entirely on my own initiative, as it was suggested by one of my aggressors, who said, " Let's make young West drink ink." Before I could be prevented I had swallowed most of the contents of one of the desk inkpots. Then they really were frightened. A master came in, realised that something was amiss, saw my mouth covered with ink and was told what had happened. I was promptly given an emetic. A court of inquiry was then held and, greatly to my delight, three of the worst offenders received probably as good a thrashing as they ever had in their lives. To their credit be it said that the rest of the boys in the school realised that things had gone too far, and the known bullies were put in Coventry for the rest of the half.

At the end of my last term at a private school I developed quinsy and was a week late in returning from the holidays. Matters were not improved by an operation for tonsils, done by the local doctor in Lymington (my grandmother had died in 1887 and my father had inherited from her Newlands Manor, which he used as a summer residence) in an arm-chair in the study, without an anæsthetic. I bled so much that in the middle of the operation the doctor himself became what we should now call 'hot and bothered,' so much so that he left the other tonsil as it was, with subsequent disastrous results. However, by the time I went to Eton, at the Christmas half of 1888, I was quite all right, and looked forward with joy to the new life.

I had not been at Eton more than a day or two before I began to appreciate the comparative freedom which can be enjoyed there. After my private school, I felt as a prisoner must feel who has been released from a term of imprisonment, except that imprisonment, even in those days, did not carry with it the tortures which were inflicted on me and many others.

Boys, when they become members of a public school, appear to undergo a complete metamorphosis. They seem to shed that skin which makes them unjust, thoughtless and cruel; and gradually to assume a more generous attitude towards their fellows. They have an example set them by the older boys, who are themselves arriving at manhood and learning to appreciate the more serious side of life.

I was fortunate in being sent to Walter Durnford's house at Eton, one of the best there. My tutor was beloved by all. Scrupulously fair, he always studied the interests of the boys in his house and trusted them implicitly, with the result that it was a code of honour in the house that no one should ever let his tutor down. If anyone did, and was found out, he deservedly got a pretty bad time from the boys in the house. The following incident is typical of Walter Durnford's sense of justice. I and another boy had been for a Sunday walk in the direction of the rifle butts; on the way back we came across two others smoking under the railway arches. I happened to see two masters approaching, about three hundred yards away, from the direction of Eton, and said to the boys who were smoking that it would be better for me and my friend to go and meet the two masters, whom we now recognised as Mr. Benson and Mr. Tatham, and let the transgressors escape the other way. This we did.

Mr. Benson, whom I knew, stopped me: "West, you were smoking," he said.

"I was not, sir," I replied.

"I saw you."

"I repeat, sir, I was not, and if you don't believe me, smell my breath."

His only reply to this conclusive piece of evidence was: "Don't be impertinent. I shall report you to your tutor."

That evening, when my tutor went round the house, he came into my room. "West," he said, "Mr. Benson has reported you to me for smoking and impertinence. What have you to say?"

I told him exactly what had happened and what I had said. I heard nothing more until two days had elapsed, when I and the friend who had been with me on the Sunday received an invitation to breakfast with Mr. Benson and Mr. Tatham, who lived together. I don't know which were the shyer, the two boys or the two masters. At the end of breakfast Mr. Benson was charming, and apologised for not having believed me; I would have given anything to hear what W. D. had said to him.

It was W. D. who cured me of stammering. When I used to stare at him in pupil-room, unable to get a word out, he would say: "My dear boy, for heaven's sake sing it!"

My first summer half at Eton, the Eton v. Winchester match was played there, and I and a friend who had been at Farnborough with me and who, like me, had been bullied, went down to the playing-fields to watch the match. Lo and behold! the first person we saw was our chief tormentor, now at Winchester. He came up and greeted us effusively. I was equally effusive and, much to the astonishment of my friend, said to the Wykehamist, "Come to tea with X—— and me this afternoon." "Delighted!" he replied. I pointed across Sixpenny to the long row of Fives Courts. "You see those Fives Courts? Well, just behind them there's a tuck shop. Meet us there at five o'clock." "Right!" said he.

When he had gone, X—— said to me: "Why on earth have you asked that swine to tea? Besides, you know Jobey's * is closed in the summer half."

"Because, my friend, we're going to do what neither of us could possibly do single-handed—give him the thrashing he deserves, and get a bit of our own back!"

He met us at the appointed time, and when we told him what we proposed to do, having previously, much to his

---

* Jobey's, a well-known purveyor of refreshments at Eton.

astonishment, seized him, like all bullies he started to whine and cringe. Justice was duly administered. He showed no fight, only yelled, but there wasn't a soul about, so that did not matter. By the time we had finished with him we left him half dead behind a pepper-box in one of the Fives Courts. I tell the story against myself, and leave it for my readers to judge whether I was justified; personally, I have no regrets in the matter.

Life at Eton was to me a joy at all times, the summer half especially. I was very fond of but never, at that time in my life, much good at cricket. In those days a boy had to excel conspicuously at the game, or to be a personal friend of the keeper of the Club in which he played, according to his position in the school. Favouritism in all games was rampant, even with the master who ran the cricket— Mr. R. A. H. Mitchell. It was the common talk in the school that a boy at " Mike's," if he had the slightest pretensions to play at all, was sure of getting his eleven in preference to someone else who might be better but who was not in that particular house.

Eton cricket was at a discount in the late 'eighties and early 'nineties, and I am not surprised, considering the way it was run.

I had unfortunately strained my heart during my last Easter half at Eton, while attempting to run—I say attempting because I was a very bad runner. Consequently I was not able to play cricket during the summer half and was bored stiff. In those days the Eton Volunteers, as they were called, were armed with the Martini-Henry rifle, which kicked like a mule. I was in the Volunteers and had to do my class firing, and discovered that the insertion of a semi-inflated football bladder in the right flap of my coat gave me greater confidence, and that the discharge of the rifle had comparatively no effect. I found I shot well, and began to take up target-shooting as an amusement. To my utter astonishment I got into the Shooting Eight, but I played fair, and did not use the football bladder when I was shooting for the school.

I was also in the Band of the Corps, and played the third tenor horn parts, which consisted chiefly of *um*-pom-pom, *um*-pom-pom and an occasional long-drawn blast. It was a cause of serious disagreement between myself and my sisters when, during the holidays, they refused to allow me, when they sang, to play their accompaniments on the tenor horn.

Incidentally I may mention that through being in the band one escaped Chapel twice a week. Their friends may not know it, but the present Lord Camden was quite a good piccolo player, while the present Lord Ellesmere was a marvel on the clarionet. The band used to give a concert once a year in the drill hall, and the Precentor of Music, Dr. Barnby, actually condescended to conduct us. The programmes could not be called high-brow, the two *pièces-de-résistance* of one being a selection from ' The Gondoliers,' and ' Nazareth ' played as a solo on the euphonium by Ben Bathurst.* The first concert we gave was a great success from the performers' point of view, as we were bidden to supper by the Head (Dr. Edmund Warre) afterwards, and were agreeably surprised, not only by the excellence of the food, but also by the quality and quantity of the champagne. One is tempted to wonder what would have happened if the concert had taken place after supper and not before.

While I was at Eton the Shah of Persia visited Windsor Castle, and the Eton College Volunteers were called upon to furnish a guard of honour, complete with band. This necessitated our learning the Persian National Anthem, the most gloomy sort of nondescript dirge I have ever heard. Unkind Etonians suggested, however, that it was not the Persian Anthem at all, but merely the noise that the band couldn't help making!

It was during my second half at Eton that I first came in contact with death. Francis Wood, called by his schoolfellows " Fannie," the third son of Lord Halifax, died at my tutor's. He was a very popular boy, and I well remember the hush throughout the house when the news was

* The Hon. B. Bathurst.

conveyed to us. The morning after his death, the Dame who looked after us suggested to the Lower boys that they might like to have a last look at their friend. We felt it would be disloyal to " Fannie " to refuse, but at the same time, as I subsequently discovered, not one of us had ever seen a dead person before, and we naturally shrank from the idea. We all trooped into the death chamber, and I can see now the little white figure lying on the bed, with its hands crossed over an Easter lily, and the look of supreme and detached peace upon the features; and I remember how we afterwards discussed, in awed whispers, what we had seen. Not even contact with more violent forms of death has caused that vision to become dim in my memory.

Mr. Wintle, a master at Eton, also died while I was there, but this event has rather different associations. It was taken as a matter of course that all the boys in the school should line the route of the funeral procession, and it was a *sine qua non* that they should wear black trousers. It was therefore said of any boy who did not attend that " of course, poor chap, he hadn't got any black bags—his people couldn't afford to buy him an evening suit " !

I have often discussed with parents how much it is advisable to tell children concerning the elementary problems of sex before they are sent to school. In some ways, children living in the country are likely to become more sophisticated, surrounded, as they probably are, by animals of all kinds, than children living in towns. It is pretty certain that in any case their curiosity will be aroused, and therein lies the danger. Curiosity has far more often been the cause of children of both sexes receiving wrong ideas and impressions in sex matters than has any inherent vice. Personally, so far as a boy is concerned, given that he is normal and inclined neither to be shy nor neurotic, I think it is best to tell him everything, but it admittedly depends upon the temperament of the boy himself. Certain boys require a much more gentle and gradual introduction to the subject than do others. My father told me nothing; I was completely ignorant when I went to Eton.

There are three ways in which a boy can be made wise upon these matters. First, through his parent or guardian; and it is to be hoped, for the boy's sake, that the man who imparts the knowledge to him is not only fond of children, but a man of the world who is fully cognisant of the pitfalls into which an unsuspecting boy can stumble. Secondly, and probably the better way: that his elder brother or a clean-minded older boy should tell him, in schoolboy fashion, what to guard against. Thirdly, that he should be told by some dirty, low-minded beast, whose only object in telling is to incite erotic curiosity in the mind of his victim, in the hope thereby of satisfying his own lecherous instincts. It was my misfortune to have been told in the last way, but my guardian angel speedily came to my rescue, as, a few days later, a boy three years older than myself, who had been a friend of the family all my life, saw me in company with the other boy, whose character, although of course I did not know it, was notoriously bad. My friend sent for me and, in the nicest way possible, put me on my guard. I was ever grateful to him, and we were firm friends all our lives. When Maldwin Drummond,* for it was he, died last year, his death left a great gap in my life.

Next to Walter Durnford, the master I liked and respected most at Eton was Mr. Austen Leigh. He flogged me once, but it made no difference to our friendship. I was complained of by a master called Tuck who, when he was annoyed, used to snap out " How dare you, sir! What do you mean by it, sir! " One morning when I was a lower boy I arrived five minutes late for 7.30 a.m. school: " What are you late for, sir? " he demanded. I was feeling cold and fed up and retorted, " Early school, sir." In due course I made my appearance before Mr. Austen Leigh, who was then Lower Master. It was useless for me to protest that I had not meant to be facetious. In his curious nasal whine, he said: " You may not have meant to be comic—more than probable that was an accident on your part; but the fact

* Captain Maldwin Drummond, married to the late Mrs. Marshall Field of Chicago.

remains that it was an insulting remark, and I shall beat you," which he promptly did.

Many years later I was motoring to Lochmore in Scotland in an old eight-horse Panhard, the best paces of which were quite disproportionate to the noise it made. The road across the moor is very narrow and straight, and two miles ahead of me I observed a two-horse waggonette. It pulled up, and a man got down from it and proceeded to run towards me, waving a white handkerchief, apparently terrified lest his horses should take fright at what was still a phenomenon in the Highlands. I continued slowly, and eventually stopped at one of the passing-places. Who should come up, puffing and blowing, but Mr. Austen Leigh, who, with his brother, rented a place in Sutherlandshire. These were the early days of motoring, and, like all motorists, no matter whether their car was capable of doing twenty or sixty miles an hour, I had disguised myself with the most appalling-looking goggles. When I saw who it was I automatically became a schoolboy again, removed my mask, and said: "I'm awfully sorry, sir." When he saw who it was he, too, became the schoolmaster, and replied scathingly: "Oh, it's you, West, is it? You always were a mouldy little boy." A few minutes later his brother came up in the waggonette; the old Scottish horses were far too sensible to worry about a motor car, and after a good laugh we all three sat down on the bank and had our lunch together.

The Rev. H. Daman was a master at Eton in my day and was not very popular with some of his pupils. Two of them at the end of their last half endeavoured to get a bit of their own back. They wrote a letter to a weekly sporting newspaper more or less as follows—

DEAR SIR,

I observed this spring that a pair of partridges had nested in my orchard where I keep a cow for the benefit of my nursery. It was a source of intense gratification to me when the old hen partridge hatched out a dozen or more

25

fluffy little fellows. To my horror and amazement one day, shortly after this happened, I saw the cow proceed to devour the whole brood. Can any of your readers inform me whether they have had a similar experience of a cow eating partridges?

Yours truly,
H. DAMAN.

Eton College.

The paper published the letter, and the following week and indeed for several weeks after correspondents wrote to the editor, some to the effect that a cow eating partridges was not at all an unusual occurrence, others insinuating that Mr. Daman's imagination was—to put it mildly—devastating. It was " Hoppy " himself who scored in the end for he wrote—

" My attention has been called to a letter which appeared in your columns some weeks ago written, I imagine, by some foolish pupils of mine. Let me tell you that I have neither nursery nor orchard and that I do not keep a cow."

De Grey (the late Marquess of Ripon) to whom I related this story told me he once started a similar " hare " in the same newspaper by writing to say he had seen several snipe sitting on telegraph wires.

So far as the acquisition of knowledge was concerned, it was the same at Eton as I imagine it was, and still is, at every public school: a boy could learn just as much or as little as he chose. Provided he scraped through " Trials " and got his remove, nothing was said. If, however, he repeatedly failed to do this he was superannuated. When I was at Eton a story was told of a certain boy—incidentally now the head of one of the largest businesses in the country— to whom this would have happened but for the influence his father was able to bring to bear. When he left Eton he wrote to his tutor, and at the end of his letter asked to be remembered to his tutor's wife. He spelt ' wife ' without

AUTHOR WITH HIS MOTHER AND SISTERS, 1890

getting one letter right—YPH—which clearly shows he ought to have been superannuated.

As my father lived for nearly nine months of the year at Newlands, most of my holidays were spent there. In those days many of the old country customs were still kept up, and I well remember a Jack-in-the-Green on the first of May, and the Mummers at Christmas-time, with the quaint words of their little play, words which had been handed down from generation to generation in the same families such as " 'Ere cooms I, Beelzebub, and 'ere cooms I, King Jarge "—in the broad Hampshire dialect.

When I was sixteen I learnt to sail a boat. My mother had a little ten-ton yawl, which lay off Hurst Castle in the Keyhaven river, and I and the man who looked after it—who went by the name of Fluellen and was a first-class man in handling a boat—used to go trips round the coast. We never went further west than Dartmouth or further east than Littlehampton. What fun it was—rowing ashore in the little dinghy, going into a village, buying food and returning to cook it ourselves over the oil-stove, sleeping like a top in the little cabin and taking a dip over the side in the morning! Neither of us could read a chart or knew anything about navigation, and strangely enough we only once ran aground, but without any serious consequences.

I often spent part of my holidays at Knole, probably the most beautiful place in England, and certainly one of the oldest. Old Lord Sackville, " Cousin Lionel " as we used to call him, formerly British Minister at Washington, and famous for having got himself into trouble at the time of a Presidential election, was very kind to me. His nephew, Lionel Sackville-West,* who was like an elder brother to me, had just married his beautiful cousin Victoria, and the young couple lived at Knole.

It was these visits to Knole which created in me the love of beautiful things. The house was, and still is, crammed with every conceivable *objet d'art*—pictures, furniture, plate, tapestry—most of which have been in the house for hundreds

* Third Lord Sackville, died 1928.

of years. There is, for instance, a picture of James I, seated in a red velvet chair, by Mytyens, and beneath the picture is the actual chair.

Knole came to the Wests from the Sackvilles, and in connection with this there was another extraordinary case of litigation. The last Duke of Dorset, who was killed in the hunting field in 1826, had two sisters, who inherited all his vast possessions. One of them married the Lord Delawarr of the day, my great-great-uncle, and the other married Lord Amherst. Lord Delawarr's eldest son, Lord West, had been brought up at Knole; he loved the place and was always under the impression that he would one day succeed to it. He was a soldier of some distinction, and became a major-general during the Crimean War at a comparatively early age. During his absence from England at that time, his mother, who was a lady-in-waiting to Queen Victoria, persuaded Her Majesty to re-create the barony of Sackville, one of the titles held by the Duke of Dorset, in favour of her second son, Reginald, on the understanding that she and her sister, Lady Amherst, endowed the creation with Knole, its contents, and all the property appertaining to that part of their late brother's possessions. It was further set out in the patent that no Lord Delawarr could ever hold the title of "Lord Sackville," in fact it created two distinct branches of the family.

When Lord West returned from the Crimea and discovered what had been done in his absence, he started an action against his father and mother for conspiracy to deprive him of what he had always looked upon as his legitimate birthright. The case, however, never came into court. True, he had never been consulted in the matter and had been shamefully treated, but he did not stand the remotest chance of winning the action; as his counsel pointed out, his mother and aunt had a perfect right to do what they liked with their own property. A few years later his father died and he became Lord Delawarr. The revenge which he took upon his brother Reginald, who was then living at Knole and who, he always imagined, had

28

been the instigator of the plot, was subtle. He vowed he would never marry, and he never did; consequently, upon his death in 1871, his brother became Lord Delawarr, and had to leave Knole under the terms of the patent. The third brother, Lionel, already referred to, thus became Lord Sackville. The new Lord Delawarr was so disgusted with everything to do with the name of West that he dropped that part of the family name and retained only Sackville. It was a petty thing to do, as the family name of Delawarr is no more Sackville than mine is.

When my father died, I discovered a tin box, padlocked. I forced it open, and lying on the top of a lot of documents there was a piece of paper on which was written:

> " I bequeath these papers to the eldest son of my old
> friend and cousin, Cornwallis " (Cornwallis was also
> my father's Christian name) " to be read after the
> death of his father, in order that he may discover for
> himself how it is possible for parents to treat their
> children."

The documents in question related entirely to the case which I have just recounted. I was not born when Lord West died, but I suppose he took it for granted that my father might have a son some day.

When I was a boy, the Aquarium at Westminster used to be the great place to which to take children to be amused. It was really a sort of music-hall with side shows; there was precious little aquarium about it—its only pretensions in that direction lay in a few old pike and some odd perch in a tank. It was here that one could see Zaza shot out of a cannon twice a day, a most painful performance, I should imagine, as I believe the lady subsequently found to her cost. It was here, also, that one could see a gentleman in red tights dive from the roof into a tank in which there was about a couple of feet of water—he, too, did it once too often.

There were two side shows of which I have a vivid recollection. One was ' Doctor ' Kennedy, the mesmerist, and the other, Succi the Fasting Man. Kennedy, who I imagine must have been a student, if not a pupil, of the famous Dr. Charcot in Paris, used to mesmerise a lot of unfortunate creatures; I use the word ' mesmerise ' advisedly, but, at the same time, if they had not been mesmerised they could not have done the extraordinary things he made them do. He would take three men, sit them in front of the stage with their legs dangling over the orchestra, and tell them they were fishing. To one he would say: " You are having a wonderful day's sport," and would tell the other two that they were catching nothing. The first man went through a series of hauling in and throwing out again with the ' completely-satisfied-angler ' look on his face; the other two became more and more mournful, as they caught nothing. Then he would take another man, pour out a tumbler of oil, and tell him he was drinking a glass of beer. The wretched creature would drink it off and apparently thoroughly enjoy it. Kennedy would then get five or six of his subjects and make them bend over with their heads touching a common centre; the seventh would be told that this table of humanity was a platform in Hyde Park and that he was to mount it and address an audience. The effect was too comic for words, as, while the gentleman was addressing his Hyde Park audience, the Professor would go round and snap his fingers in the ears of one or two of the subjects who were forming the table—his method of bringing them ' to '—with the result that, as they regained their senses, the platform eventually collapsed. I remember going there one day with my sister Shelagh, then a girl of fourteen. One of the half-wits was told that he was to serenade his sweetheart; he had no voice at all, but started some ridiculous, though harmless, love-song and, with a vacant stare, proceeded to descend from the stage and walk towards my sister, who gave one yell and fled!

I have often wondered what happened to these wretched people. They were always supposed to be taken from the audience, but I need hardly say that the same ones turned up time after time. They could only have been half-witted to start with; by the time Kennedy had finished with them they must have been entirely witless.

And now for Succi, the Fasting Man. Charlie Duff, who subsequently became Sir Charles Duff-Assheton-Smith, incidentally the owner of that famous horse, Cloister, was a great friend of my father and mother. I happened to meet him at luncheon one day, and he asked me if I would like to go to the Aquarium. I accepted with alacrity. On the way there he stopped the cab outside a baker's shop and came out with a paper bag. As we had just had an enormous meal, I thought it an odd thing to do; however, I asked no questions.

" Ever heard of Succi, the Fasting Man? " he asked me, as we were approaching the Aquarium.

" Never."

" Well, you're going to see him this afternoon. He's one of the side shows, and he's backed himself to fast for forty days."

We went straight to where there was announced, on a large placard: Succi, and paid an extra sixpence to go in. Charlie Duff and I sat in the front row and there, on a slightly raised platform, we saw an emaciated creature looking at us. My companion proceeded to take two buns out of the bag he had bought, gave me one and started munching the other himself. Never shall I forget the look of yearning that came into the haggard face of the Fasting Man. When I ventured to remonstrate with Charlie Duff, all he said was: " Serve him right for making such an ass of himself! "

Another place where I constantly stayed during my holidays was Port Dinorwic, on the Menai Straits in Carnarvonshire. Walter Vivian, another friend of the family, was the manager of the famous Dinorwic Slate Quarries, which lay above the Lake of Llanberis about seven miles from the Port. The two places were connected by a private railway used for hauling slates; and it was here that the wish of my childhood was fulfilled, and I was taught to drive a locomotive. Large locomotives on the main line, small locomotives—almost toy ones—on the little quarry tramlines. How I loved it! and how useful the knowledge thus acquired has been to me on one or two occasions in later life.

My father used to entertain a great deal at Ruthin. A lover of art himself, he invited many artists to stay with him: singers, musicians, painters. Amongst the former, Signor Foli is one of my earliest recollections. He was an Irishman, and his real name was Foley. He had a magnificent baritone voice and sang " Off to Philadelphia in the morning " better than anyone else ever has or ever will sing it.

John Thomas, the famous Welsh harpist, was also a frequent visitor. With long black hair and dark eyes, he looked far more like an Italian than did Signor Foli, who affected that nationality. One day, to my horror, before my father, he seized me by the chin and said in a deep sepulchral voice: " West, your boy will be a great violinist." Not being able to read a note of music at that time, and having, in fact, no pretensions to becoming an infant prodigy, I was filled with dismay lest my father should take him literally, and foresaw an appalling prospect of the daily drudgery to which this prophecy might condemn me. I expostulated, and was relieved when my father was inclined to agree with me. John Thomas, however, was so convinced he was right that, a few days after he had left, a case arrived for me containing a violin. I am afraid I never learnt to play it.

Chapter III

STUDENT DAYS AND EARLY SOLDIERING

I LEFT Eton in 1891, as it was considered advisable that I should study foreign languages, with a view to going into the diplomatic service. Accordingly I was sent to Freiburg in Baden, on the borders of the Black Forest: a delightful town, with a trout stream flowing through the centre, and a fine cathedral having one of the most beautiful trellis-work spires in Europe. I was taken in by a family of the name of Gabler. The dear old man had been in the employ of the Eastern Telegraph Company, and could consequently speak English almost as well as I could, but, fortunately for me, his wife was conscientious, and used to rate him soundly whenever he attempted to speak anything but German to me, and so I learnt quite a lot.

I made the acquaintance of several members of the various Student Corps, Freiburg being, of course, a university town. The crack corps was the *Saxoborussen*, or White Caps. There were also the Red and Yellow Caps. The captain of the White Caps, who had been at Cambridge and was a very nice fellow, once invited me to attend one of their *Schlagerverein*, or duelling meetings. On these occasions the etiquette between the corps was very strict, and, no matter how well you knew a man in another corps, if you were the guest of a rival corps at that particular meeting you were not supposed to recognise him. As it happened, another Englishman, by name Waring, who had been at Eton with me and was also studying at Freiburg, was the guest of the Red Caps on the same afternoon. As we took our seats at the various tables allotted to each corps, he waved me a greeting, which I promptly returned, both of us being ignorant of the prevailing custom. Apparently I had offered a deadly insult to the corps whose guest I was, and I could feel by the general atmosphere that I was anything but popular. Several members came up and addressed the captain, and I knew sufficient German by then to realise that they were saying they considered they had been insulted by the *verflüchte Englander*. I explained that I was not aware of the etiquette, and apologised: I certainly was not going to fight with one of their horrible razor-like sabres, of the use of which I knew absolutely nothing. Fortunately the matter was smoothed over, thanks to the tact of my friend, the captain of the corps.

The actual duelling was the most disgusting exhibition I have ever seen. The whole of the body was swathed and padded; thick goggles were worn over the eyes and a heavy gauntlet on the sword arm. The head was the only point to be attacked. About six inches of the sabre-blade were razor-edged on both sides and were terribly whippy. The most ghastly wounds were inflicted, and it used to be the custom to endeavour deliberately to keep open the wounds and so be sure that the scars were there for life. It was said that one of the rules was that no dogs were allowed where duelling was in progress, in case a man had his nose cut off—but this I cannot vouch for.

The Black Forest, situated to the north of Freiburg, will be admitted, by those who have visited it, to be one of the beauty spots of Europe. Many were the expeditions I made in it, in summer and winter. There is a rack railway from Freiburg to Titisee, that lovely lake situated in the most gorgeous scenery; and those who wish to mountaineer can climb the Feldberg, the highest point in the Black Forest, from which the view over the Alps on a clear day is stupendous. The Forest abounds in trout streams. Badbol, a famous resort for anglers, was one of my favourite haunts, and it was there that I mastered the use of the dry fly. To the south of Freiburg, on the banks of the Rhine, is the quaint old town of Alt Breisach. The old priest there once showed me the most wonderful collection of altar plate that I have ever seen: marvellous chalices and every sort of monstrance and pyx and casket, nearly all of which dated from the thirteenth and fourteenth centuries; many were encrusted with roughly cut precious stones.

I once, while on a walking tour in the Vosges, went along a road through a long tunnel, in the centre of which was the Franco-German frontier. What struck me at the time as being remarkable was that the German half of the road, even in those days, was steam-rolled and as hard as iron, whereas the French side was all mud and slush. On the other hand, I had a perfectly poisonous lunch at a village in Alsace that afternoon, and a perfectly wonderful dinner in an equally small village on the French side, only a few miles away. I forget its name, but remember that it was a great place for making cherry-wood pipes. On my way home a couple of days later I passed through another village where a German official was haranguing the inhabitants, setting forth the pains and penalties which would be inflicted if certain regulations in force were not carried out. I mingled with the crowd, and remember well the surly faces and smothered oaths; and formed the impression that at that time the Alsatians were anything but accustomed to, or satisfied with, the German yoke.

In the summer of '91 my sister Daisy became engaged to Prince Hans Heinrich of Pless, the eldest son of the Prince —subsequently Duke—of Pless. I went to England for a few weeks' holiday, and I well remember going into my father's study one day and finding the old gentleman in a towering rage.

" What do you think of this, my dear boy? " he exclaimed. " Here are these damned Germans writing to me that it is not the custom of the house of Hochberg " (the Pless family name) " to allow the marriage of one of its members with a lady who cannot produce sixteen quarterings! "

My father certainly was no snob, and I do not suppose he had ever before bothered himself as to whether he had sixteen or sixty quarterings to his coat-of-arms, but, after all, it was only natural that he should be proud of his descent from men who had fought with the Black Prince

35

at Creçy and Poitiers. For both a West and a la Warr had been with that warrior, and it was Lord la Warr who, with a Pelham, took prisoner King John of France at Poitiers. When the former delivered the captive to the Black Prince, he said: " Monseigneur, c'est le plus beau jour de ma vie! " and ' Jour de ma vie ' had remained the motto of the West and la Warr family ever since, these two families subsequently becoming one by marriage.

Still fuming, my father went up to London the next day, and, probably for the first time in his life, visited the College of Heralds; with the result that about two months later a thing like a patchwork quilt arrived.

" That ought to satisfy them," he said when he saw it. But so loath was he to send it that it was with the greatest difficulty my mother eventually extracted it and sent it off herself to placate the susceptibilities of the Hochbergs. For a long time he refused to give his consent to his daughter's marriage. He did not approve of mixed marriages. Daisy was quite the most beautiful girl of her year, and there were many eligible young Englishmen who would have been only too pleased to marry her. As matters turned out, it was a pity one of them did not, for no woman ever suffered greater mental torture than she did, when, as an Englishwoman at heart but a German subject by marriage, she found herself an object of suspicion and dislike in Germany during the Great War.

The late 'nineties bridged the gap between the *mariage de convenance* of earlier Victorian days, where the husband was selected by the parents and the girl had no choice at all, and the twentieth-century method, whereby a girl announces her engagement to her parents and informs them, more or less politely, that if they do not like it they must lump it. In the 'nineties a girl went through a process of receiving strong recommendation as to the desirability of a certain suitor, combined with a discreet but complete schedule of the advantages to be obtained by such a marriage; and as she was accustomed to discipline and had not been encouraged to think for herself, the marriage

36

THE AUTHOR'S SISTERS, SOON AFTER THE MARRIAGE OF THE ELDER

—unless she cordially disliked the man in question—usually took place. Moreover, a father in those days considered he had every right to say to a young man, " Sir, what are your intentions towards my daughter? " and would certainly have been astonished at receiving the answer which a modern father received the other day: " Sir, my intentions towards your daughter are strictly natural."

I came back again to England for my sister's marriage, which took place that year at St. Margaret's, Westminster. It was part of my duty to show guests to their places, and for the first time in my life I was given a frock coat, in which my sisters told me, as I was so thin, I looked " like a billiard cue in a cloth cover." I found myself quite a success at a ball given previously by Pless in honour of his relations, present and future, as not only could I speak German, but could dance that ridiculous German waltz, the *deux temps*, where the man held himself erect as if on parade and tiptoed up and down exactly as though he were being pulled by strings from the top of his head like a marionette.

When I returned to Freiburg after Christmas, my sister having married a German of high rank, I found myself, to my astonishment, quite an important person among certain of the old German families who lived in the neighbourhood and who had heard that I was at the university. There was quite a colony of Englishmen and their families in Freiburg, some of whom had pretty daughters. There were also several other young Englishmen studying German, and calf love was rampant. It was more than an epidemic, it was chronic.

I returned to England finally in June 1892 and then, for the first time, learnt that, at a family conclave at which I had not been present, it had been decided that instead of going into the diplomatic service I was to go into the army, preferably into one of the regiments of Foot Guards. It was useless my pointing out that, as it had never been my intention to go into the army, I had wasted a year while I might have been working for that profession, and that it would be too late for me to go to Sandhurst. It was decided that I should get in at what was then known as ' the Back Door,' *i.e.* the Militia. As Lord Lieutenant of his county, my father was able to give me a commission in the Third Battalion of the Royal Welch Fusiliers. I went off there and then to the depot at Wrexham, and that winter had the time of my life. I rode well and got any number of mounts given me with Sir Watkyn Wynn's hounds. After passing my preliminary examinations, I was sent to Jersey to a crammer by the name of Bailey, whose sister kept house for him. He certainly was a good crammer, but the table he kept was appalling. There were twenty of us, and one day we struck. It was arranged that everyone at breakfast that morning should bring his own food, and at a given signal, potted meat, hard-boiled eggs, jam, etc., appeared from our pockets, all having previously refused the loathsome bacon and still worse tinned salmon that were offered. The result was disconcerting, as Miss Bailey, who sat at the other end of the table, promptly had hysterics. It had the desired effect, however, as the food improved.

I worked hard at Jersey, and the only recreations were golf, which I learnt there, and some sea-fishing. After passing what was then called the literary examination, it became necessary for me to cram for the technical examination, and I was sent to Colonel Fox's at Camberley, where I met many old public-school friends. It was there that a curious incident happened which is interesting from a psychological point of view. Three of us, all old Etonians, went one Saturday in August to Maidenhead, where we were met by three—shall we say—ladies? ' Perfect Ladies,' at the very top of their profession and all young and pretty. We chartered an electric launch—they were then just coming into vogue—with the intention of going down-stream to Egham, whence we intended to go back to Camberley, and the ladies to London. When we reached Windsor Bridge, about four o'clock in the afternoon, one of them suggested that we should take them over Eton College, which none of them had ever seen. We agreed, and

38

together walked down the High Street into the precincts of the old school, which, of course, was entirely deserted. We showed them round the Cloisters, the School Yard, the College Hall, Upper School and most places of interest. As we were coming out of Upper School, one of them suggested visiting Upper Chapel. I remember a slight feeling of hesitation at this suggestion; however, there was nothing for it, so we entered.

Upper Chapel at Eton, or, as it is now called, College Chapel, is a very beautiful and inspiring building; I imagine no old Etonian can enter it unmoved, or without a vivid appreciation of the days he spent at Eton surging through his mind. One of my friends suddenly made some excuse to go out, or at any rate disappeared round the back of the organ. I, thinking that he was returning, did the same thing, but, I imagined, for quite a different reason. The third man, believing, as he afterwards told us, that both of us were returning, also disappeared, leaving the three women gazing at the beauties of the building.

Some three-quarters of an hour later we three young men met at Slough Station, each with a look of blank astonishment on his face when he saw the other two—alone. The train was just coming in, and without saying a word we all got into an empty compartment. I was the first to break the silence and said to the other two: " Why did you run away? "

Almost as if by pre-arrangement, they both said: " I expect for the same reason as you did. Why did you? "

" Oh, I don't know. Somehow it seemed rather beastly —those three tarts in Upper Chapel."

" Same here," the other two replied.

Fortunately the launch had been paid for when we started; but none of the ladies ever spoke to us again.

I spent eight happy months at Camberley. I was the proud possessor of an old chestnut horse, the first I had ever owned, who, when he was not carrying me with the Staff College Drag Hounds, was being driven between the shafts of an old dog-cart.

39

When I was at Camberley I had my first experience of a run of ill luck at cards. To amuse ourselves, Osbert Molyneux * and I were playing chemin-de-fer with four packs of cards for very small points. I should be sorry to say how many times he passed, but, although we started with a modest sixpence, I found myself the loser of many thousands of pounds. I got up and started to tear my hair, thinking how I could possibly manage to raise the money, when he said: " Sit down and don't be a damn fool. You backed the winner of the Great Ebor Handicap to-day—I'll play you for the tenner you won, and we'll wash out the rest! "

Amongst those who were at Camberley with me were Dick Molyneux † and Charlie Fitzmaurice,‡ and we were all three instructed in fortifications by an old officer of the name of Firth, whose one failing was the bottle. We hit upon an idea of curing him, and one morning, having carefully scraped a hole in the end of a piece of chalk, we inserted the end of a fusee. When he came to draw a rampart on the blackboard, the chalk exploded. He dropped it and fled, and was not seen again for two days, after which he became a reformed character—we always maintained that it was due to us.

One of my mother's friends in Wales had written to old Mrs. Combe, of Pierrepont, near Farnham, that I was " at school " at Camberley, the poor lady having not the remotest idea of the difference between a crammer's and a school! Mrs. Combe, therefore, invited me over to spend a weekend, and I wrote accepting; and after work hours on a Friday I drove over, and arrived five minutes after the gong had gone for dressing. I thought the butler who opened the door looked a little taken aback, but he was too well trained to say anything. The groom took my trap round to the stables and I was shown up to my room, which, I noticed, contained a child's bed (I was then as tall as I am now, six feet three). I changed hurriedly, and appeared

---

* The late Lord Sefton. † The Hon. Richard Molyneux.
‡ Lord Charles Fitzmaurice, killed in the Great War.

just as dinner was announced. All the guests were collected in the hall, and never shall I forget the look of blank amazement on my hostess's face when she saw a young man coming down the stairs, in immaculate evening clothes. " Heavens! " she exclaimed, " I thought you were a little boy. You can never get into that bed! "

This was my first experience of a country house-party outside my own home. Whereas a few years later most of the guests would have settled down after dinner to play bridge, no one did so then. Very few women played cards, and it was only after they had retired to bed that the men, if they played at all, began. Instead, we used to dance to the strains of a pianola, if there did not happen to be a competent pianist present; and nothing more venturesome than the polka or the valse. I do remember, however, on this occasion dancing a *pas de deux* with Lady Milner, whose husband, Sir Frederick Milner, was one of the guns staying in the house. The long skirts of the period did not permit of high kicking unless they were held up, but the ladies did not seem to worry about that. It was considered bad form not to maintain a considerable gap between yourself and your partner, and no woman could complain of being ' more danced against than dancing.' Reversing, in the valse, simply wasn't done; a man who reversed his partner was considered a bounder by other men. Consequently giddiness was a common complaint among those dancing.

These were the days of long fringes and ' buns,' leg-of-mutton sleeves, and gentility. It was all up with a woman who was seen dining alone with a man at a restaurant. About the only exception, where such a thing could happen without irreparable loss of character, was the Bristol, and even that made the Dowagers sniff.

While I was cramming at Camberley I and some of my friends used to go up, whenever opportunity offered, to the fancy-dress balls at Covent Garden. Fancy dress was not necessary; masks and dominoes were allowed. The balls were very amusing, for every sort of person used to go, including most of the stage beauties of the day. On one occasion, just before our examination, Charlie Fitzmaurice came into my room for something or other and happened to leave behind him a pair of white kid gloves. That could mean only one thing: that he was going to a ball; and sure enough that evening he and several others disappeared, without saying a word to me of their intentions. I was determined to be revenged. Knowing their habits, and that there was a ball at Covent Garden that night, I caught the eleven o'clock train from Farnborough to London, procured a mask and domino from Clarkson's, and went to the ball, where I proceeded, under cover of the mask, to rag my friends about their private lives. Among the party was Dudley Marjoribanks, the present Lord Tweedmouth, who was accompanied by a good-looking actress, and, disguising my voice, I said to him: "What would the Baron say if he saw you here, and you just going up for your examination?" He was furious, and he and some others pursued me round the theatre. Eventually they got me down on a sofa and pulled off my mask, and one of them, Arthur Duff, exclaimed " My God! It's Bunnie! " (my nickname at the time). " Yes," said I, " and that'll teach you to leave your pal in the lurch when you go off to balls! " We all had supper together, and returned to Camberley in the small hours of the morning; and in spite of all this, most of us managed to pass into the army.

At another of these balls, some friends of mine dressed up a figure to look like Sir Augustus Harris, who was then lessee of Covent Garden and the promoter of the balls. Between the dances there appeared to be a devil of a row going on in one of the upper boxes and, in a loud voice, one of the disputants was heard to say: " Chuck him out! " The next moment ' Sir Augustus Harris ' was flying through the air, and landed with a thud on the parquet floor. Women screamed and a commotion ensued, until somebody proceeded to examine the corpse and discovered the joke. The perpetrators left the theatre hurriedly and were never found out.

In the modern sense of the term, there were no night

clubs in London. The Corinthian, in St. James's Square, was the nearest thing approaching one, and this, as is the way of such institutions, died a natural death. A successor —the Alsatians' Club—was started in Oxford Street. It consisted of one long room for dancing and a smaller room where a perfectly horrible supper was served at an outrageous price. The male members of it belonged to the *jeunesse dorée* of the period, while the lady members were taken from the oldest profession in the world. Amateurs never ventured within its precincts. It was both vulgar and dull, and less suited to its purpose than the old promenade at the Empire.

Plays in those days were tame affairs compared with modern productions. Although I was only eighteen at the time, I well remember the excitement created by " The Second Mrs. Tanqueray," and the artificially shocked feelings of many who witnessed it. I was taken by my father to see it, and on coming out he said to me: " We're getting on, my dear boy! I wonder what they'll give us next? " This play was discussed at every lunch- and dinner-table: acrimonious arguments took place as to whether it should have been allowed to pass the censor or not; but one and all praised the superb presentation of Mrs. Patrick Campbell's " Paula."

The lyrics for musical comedy were no worse, and no better, than the stuff dished up for public consumption to-day. Here are samples from two popular ones:

> Don't be so particular, dear,
>   Don't you be so shy!
> Kiss me perpendicular, dear,
>   With a horizontal eye!

That was harmless, but the following created quite a sensation in the Grundy family:

> " O Charles, tell 'em to stop! "
>   Such was the cry of Maria:
> The more she said " O! " they cried " Let her go! "
>   And her petticoats flew a bit higher.

Maria, it must be explained, was on a swing.

I often used to go home to my parents at Newlands for week-ends. My friend Charlie Day was the driver of the 4.55 train from Waterloo to Bournemouth; he came from my part of the world and knew me well, and I would join the express at Basingstoke, where it stopped, and travel on the locomotive as far as Brockenhurst. I generally arranged to go back on Monday morning by the early train which he was taking up, when the same thing happened. Charlie Day's favourite amusement was to take a day off in the winter and come and stand behind me when we were shooting the coverts at Newlands. One day when I was shooting badly he said to me, in his broad Hampshire dialect:

" Mr. Jarge, some o' they pheasants appear to me like reckless drivers."

" Why, Charlie? " I asked.

With a twinkle in his eye he replied: " 'Cos you puts up your gun as a signal for 'em to stop, and they don't allus do it! "

I often used to wonder what would happen if somebody pulled the communication cord, and I confess to having had longings to do this when travelling in an ordinary compartment. Many years later I was to have an experience of it. I had been to Bournemouth to recuperate from an attack of influenza, and, still having a sore throat, went up to town to consult my doctor. I caught the nine o'clock non-stop train to Waterloo, and, just as it was starting, a nasty-looking individual, smoking a cigar, got into the first-class compartment where I was. It was non-smoking. As he continued to smoke, I asked him politely to desist, mentioning that I had a sore throat. His reply was that as he had smoked a cigar after breakfast for the last fifteen years, there was no reason why he should not go on doing so. Neither argument nor abuse was of any avail, so I pulled the communication cord. The train, which was then going at some speed, pulled up in a series of jerks; heads popped out of windows, and the guard came rushing along. I requested him to remove the person from

44

the compartment. The only answer I got was that I had no right to stop the train for " a little thing like that." We proceeded on our way, and my fellow-passenger still continued to smoke his foul cigar. Next time I waited until the train was really going fast, when I pulled the cord again. Again the train came to a standstill, and it was a very hot and bothered guard who came along to expostulate with both of us. The train was not a corridor train, and a stop was made at Vauxhall to collect the tickets. My tormentor was found to be travelling in a first-class compartment with a second-class ticket. One up to me, I thought. When we reached Waterloo, a posse of the company's police, with a sergeant who knew me, was there to take the name and address of the individual who had dared to stop the Bournemouth Limited. I suggested that they should first take the name of my fellow-passenger, who was doing his best to escape in the crowd. This was done, and I went to see the general manager of the railway company, whom I knew, and told him what had happened. I promised that I would not let the company down, and would give evidence against the individual, who was indicted for

(1) Travelling in a compartment of a class superior to his ticket.
(2) Wilfully causing inconvenience to a fellow-passenger.
(3) Smoking in a non-smoking compartment.

The case subsequently came on at Bournemouth, to which place I was given a free pass. The man was defended by a solicitor from Southampton, but was fined on every count, and I calculated that that cigar cost him about fifty pounds. The case appeared in the Press, and a correspondence ensued as to when a person had or had not the right to stop an express train.

Had I wished it, it would have been easier for me to pass my examination in how to drive a locomotive than it was to pass the competitive examination in military subjects. However, I managed to get through in April, and in July of 1895 was gazetted to the Scots Guards. May and June I had spent at Chelsea Barracks, learning and passing my drills. In consequence I was considered fit to undertake regimental duty from the moment my name appeared in the Gazette.

Just before I was gazetted I attended my first really big entertainment in London, the famous fancy-dress ball at Devonshire House. My sister Daisy went as the Queen of Sheba. I have always imagined this lady to have been a petite brunette, whereas Daisy was ' tall and most divinely fair '; she had a gorgeous dress of blue silk decorated with gold braid, and was covered with diamonds and turquoises which had been given to her by her husband as a wedding present. Not having the wherewithal myself to pay for a fancy dress, I was pressed into her service, with the bribe of a free costume, as one of the *entourage* of her Court, whose dresses had been designed by a famous theatrical designer of the day. Why he should have insisted that the Queen of Sheba's male attendants were full-blooded negroes and dressed in garments like multicoloured bed quilts I have no idea, though the garments may have been inspired by his knowledge of Joseph's taste in dress. The fact remains that I hated blacking my face, and my girl friends did not in the least appreciate me in that disguise; consequently I didn't enjoy myself in the slightest, and left early, with bitterness in my heart towards the theatrical designer. I have not, therefore, a very clear recollection of the affair, but one costume I do remember standing out among the others was that of Susan Duchess of Somerset, as Queen Jane Seymour.

The first battalion parade I attended was on the occasion of the old Duke of Cambridge's last inspection of the Brigade of Guards, in Hyde Park. I being the junior ensign, it fell to me to carry the regimental colour. Although the sergeant-major of the battalion, a tall, fine-looking Scotsman named Walker, was quite aware that I knew all about drills, it did not take me long to realise that at this particular parade he was extremely nervous lest I should make a hash

46

of things. I am certain he considered that, on so important an occasion as the Commander-in-Chief's inspection, a newly-joined officer acting as colour-bearer should have had one or more full-dress rehearsals. During the march past, the sergeant-major's place was directly behind the colours, and as we were approaching the saluting base I heard a stertorous whisper behind me, breathing rhythmically in time to the music: "*Keep* the *colours* well-in-yer *for-r-k ! Keep* the *colours* well-in-yer *for-r-k !*" It struck me as being so funny that I started to giggle and turned hastily round and said: "For God's sake, shut up!"

One of society's great amusements was bicycling in Battersea Park, which was within a stone's throw of Chelsea Barracks, and we used to meet there before breakfast and solemnly 'bike' round the Outer Circle. If we happened to have a best girl, she accompanied us, dressed in a flowing skirt and short jacket, with a little plate of straw perched on her head; a shirt with a stiff collar, and a belt round a waspish waist completed the outfit. An hour's exercise, and then we would breakfast at a little restaurant in the park; afterwards, more 'biking' or a row on the lake.

I am sure many of the engagements and entanglements of that day were brought about through teaching girls and young married women how to ride a bicycle. I myself became entangled all through a 'bike,' but grew frightened and attempted to back out. My alarm increased when, as I refused to step further into the web, the lady concerned threatened to send my letters to her husband. Trembling with anxiety, I dashed off to Sir George Lewis, whose skill in dealing with affairs of this kind was already notorious. "Don't be alarmed, young man," was his reassuring comment. "They all threaten to do that, but they never do it." My case was no exception.

It may have been due to cycling that women about this time made a brief experiment in imitating men's costumes, and great excitement was caused one morning by one lady turning up in 'bloomers.' Discussions as to the best make

47

of bicycle were as acrimonious as they are nowadays as to the best make of motor-car. Like many young men of my acquaintance, I used to cycle in London as a means of getting about; the traffic offered no terrors to any of us, since we were the fastest vehicles in the streets.

My battalion was destined to take part, the year I joined, in the New Forest manœuvres, and accordingly we marched to Aldershot, where the Division was to assemble, and camped within a mile of my old private school. I could not resist the temptation to visit it; I wanted to tell them what a lovely time I had had there. So one afternoon I walked over and did so: the head master had the surprise of his life.

The life of a young officer in the Foot Guards in my time was very pleasant. Soldiering was not taken too seriously; indeed, it was purely a matter of routine, too much so if anything. Like the private soldiers, the young officers were not encouraged to think for themselves. If anyone made some mistake and started his excuses by saying, " Please, sir, I thought——" the answer invariably came out, like a rifle-shot, " You're not here to think—you're here to do what you're told! "

In all things connected with military duty, in the field or in barracks, discipline was of the strictest, as of course it should be, and discipline in the Brigade of Guards is proverbial. I am often asked by doting mothers whether I would recommend a young fellow to go for a short time into the army even if he does not intend to make it his career. My answer is always the same: that discipline is the finest training that there is for the mind and for the body. A few years' experience of it can only be good, and equip a man with that sense of order so necessary in all branches of life.

In the Mess, however, things were different. We were just a jolly family and, with the exception of the Commanding Officer, we were all equal, and called each other by our Christian or nick-names. Conversation, I admit, was not particularly intelligent. Military ' shop ' was of course taboo. The concrete subjects we discussed were almost entirely to do with sport; abstract discussions were few. I remember once starting a conversation on religion in connection with some great religious festival, the celebration of which I had witnessed in the Cathedral and streets of Freiburg. It was at dinner one night, and when I thought I was getting well into my subject I received a violent kick on the shins from my neighbour, and had the sense to shut up. Afterwards I was severely told off by the senior subaltern for daring to discuss a religious subject in the Mess, as I might possibly have said something to offend two members who were Roman Catholics.

After remaining at Aldershot a couple of days the whole Division set out by road for the manœuvres. The weather was hot, but that made no difference to our dress. It was before the days of khaki, and we marched in tunics and bearskins. The only privilege accorded to officers was that they were allowed to wear serge tunics, covered with gold braid, instead of heavy cloth ones. The latter cost thirty-five pounds and one shower of rain was sufficient to ruin them completely. Our first halt was at Alton, where we arrived, hot, tired and dusty, one afternoon in August. There was a river not very far from the camp, and two or three of us made up our minds to go and bathe. When we arrived at the banks of the river, we found it was not one of the beautiful clear chalk streams, such as we should find the other side of the ridge, between Alton and Alresford, but was sluggish and muddy, the head-waters, in fact, of the Wey. Cecil Lowther,* commonly known as " Meat " because of his beefy construction, was the first to get undressed, and he took a header into what looked like a deepish pool. After about half a minute—and fortunately before anyone else got in—he let out a yell and scrambled out. To our horror and amusement we saw that there were about a dozen leeches sticking to him. They had chosen the right subject! I don't know whether you have ever tried to get a leech off a person before it is replete; it is a

* Major-Gen. Sir Cecil Lowther.

most difficult undertaking. We eventually succeeded by holding them up with one finger and burning their tails with a match.

On the afternoon of the fourth day, we arrived at our goal, in the New Forest, a place called Godshill, having covered roughly about eighteen miles a day. The weather was glorious and manœuvres in those days were not so Spartan as in later years; we had tents to sleep in, and an enormous mess-tent run by a civilian caterer. I don't deny it—we did ourselves well.

At the close of manœuvres, which were nothing more than a series of field days, my battalion entrained for Holyhead en route for Richmond Barracks, Dublin.

Chapter IV

IRELAND AND SOME ANIMALS

I LOOKED forward to going to Ireland enormously. Being half Irish and having spent some of my boyhood staying with my grandmother and aunt just outside Dublin, I had learnt to like the country and the people. I always maintain that in order really to understand the Irish character, it is necessary that one should have a certain amount of Irish blood in one's veins. There is a great charm about the Irish, and if, when they exercise it, one is able to distinguish between blarney and sincerity, so much the better. To my mind, the principal difficulty in the Irishman's character, when you meet him as an individual, is his over-anxiety to please. For instance, a keeper awaits you at the edge of a bog on which you have been given a day's shooting. " Are there any snipe in to-day, Micky? " you ask.

" Snipe? Begob, y'r honour! they do be just jostlin' each other! "

You go into the bog and find nothing. Micky scratches his head with a look of assumed surprise: " Shure now, that's funny! There were just lashin's of 'em here yesterday."

If you take the trouble to inquire, you will probably find that he hasn't been near the place for a week and could not possibly know; but he would not mean to tell a deliberate lie, he would just say what he thought would please you.

Collectively, they are a headstrong people and yet easily led, readily influenced by the last speaker—and the Irish have a great flow of language. They are a brave race, as Irish soldiers have proved on many occasions. Their unconscious humour is, of course, proverbial. Go to America, and any thinking American whom you ask will tell you that the Germans are the best citizens and the Irish the next best (that has been said to me on many occasions); but it remains to be seen whether the Irishman, unless he happens to be a professional politician, ever will be really content with his lot so long as he remains in Ireland. He always seems to pine for something that he has not got. A year after the War, when I was Provost-Marshal in Cork, I said to a well-known Sinn Feiner in that city: "What *do* you Irish want, anyway?" His answer was typical; he knew his countrymen well: "Well, Major," he said, "it's this way. If England was to be giving Ireland what she wants, she wouldn't be wanting it."

What is it that fosters this ingrained discontent? Is it the enervating climate, combined with the curious Celtic despondency? What is it that causes that weird, fay streak in the Irish character? Why is it that they are either in the highest of spirits or sunk in the depths of despair—that such a clever race as this, who have produced so many brilliant men in all professions, should have no middle range? It seems to require some explanation. The climate itself appears to be, like the temperament of the inhabitants, all contrasts: bright, sunny days with the softest of breezes, everything that Nature can give to enhance the beauty of the scenery—and the reverse: low, threatening clouds, sudden torrents of rain, furious winds. How seldom does one experience in Ireland a sequence of dull monotonous days such as one gets in England.

As a peace-time station, Ireland in those days was the Mecca of all soldiers (I refer, of course, to the commissioned ranks). Every kind of sport was obtainable, living was cheap and the people were kind. For those like myself who were fond of hunting it was ideal, as it was possible to buy a good horse, up to fourteen stone and over, for a hundred pounds. Soldiering was by no means strenuous. The battalion arrived in Dublin after the drill season was over, and there was very little to do beyond the routine of guards and pickets, occasional battalion parades and route marches. Twice a week the Adjutant, Captain Cuthbert,* who went by the name of " Cupid," used to take the battalion into the Phœnix Park. I remember on one occasion, when we were returning from one of these expeditions, I was in command of the rear company. We were marching along the tram-lines up the Inchicore road when a tram came up behind us and was therefore obliged to go at the same pace at which we were marching. The driver and the people on the top of the car proceeded to hurl the choicest abuse at the British Army generally, and I therefore gave the command to my company " Left incline ! " which was followed in turn by the other company commanders in front. Cuthbert, who was at the head of the battalion, came galloping down, slithering on the tramlines, on his old black mare, who went by the name of " Joss "; when he reached me, both he and the mare were snorting with rage. He asked what the devil I meant by putting the battalion out of alignment, and told me to attend Commanding Officer's Orders. I was ' for it.' I attended. My C.O. was Colonel Fludyer, who went by the name of " Taddy," and when the Adjutant had formulated his complaint I was asked what I had to say. I apologised if I had done wrong and added that, as I did not care to hear the British Army abused and had had no means of retaliation, I had thought it best to allow the tramcar to pass. I was solemnly told to be more careful in future.

Many of us in the battalion had dogs, who used to accompany their masters on route marches until, one day, the General in command of the district, Viscount Frankfort de Montmorency, happened to meet the battalion accompanied by two or three dogs, which, he pointed out with a certain amount of acerbity, was contrary to Queen's Regulations, or anyhow ' not done.' The two favourite dogs in the battalion were my Irish terrier, Pat, and a poodle which belonged to Sir Cuthbert Slade and went by the name of Bingo. Everyone loved them, from the C.O. down to the

* Major-Gen. G. Cuthbert.

smallest drummer. These two dogs were inseparable; they seemed to know exactly when the battalion was going route marching, I suppose by the kit we wore. They were far too sensible to come on parade; during the preliminaries they would sit in a corner of the Barrack Square and watch and, as we marched out, join up in the ranks. After the edict was issued that no dogs were allowed on route marches, there was only one thing to do—shut them up in our rooms. They must have had a private conference about it, because one day, about three weeks later, when the battalion was going on a route march, they were nowhere to be found. As we were marching out of Barracks we saw Bingo and Pat standing a few yards away; they cut us dead as we passed. After we had gone about two miles, a distance from which they thought, presumably, that no decent-minded master would ask them to find their way back alone, they trotted up, full of conceit, and no amount of cursing could make the slightest difference to them. When we told them to go home, they followed the battalion at about two hundred yards in the rear and, after a discreet interval, joined up again. All might have been well, but unfortunately we again met the General. When we returned and had been dismissed off parade, I went to the Sergeant of the Barrack Guard, intending to curse him for allowing the dogs out of barracks when he had strict orders not to do so. He was a Scotsman, and he answered in broad dialect: " I'm verra sorry, sirr, but those dogs arre nae human, they're just deevils. They sat waitin' there for a quarter of an 'oor after the battalion had left barracks, and made nae attempt to get oot. Then, suddenly, they both made a rush together and were just gone in a flash."

As luck would have it, I happened to be dining with the General that night. I knew he would not say anything about the dogs unless I did: anything he did say would be in the nature of an official communication on the morrow. So I broached the subject, and told him what the sergeant had told me. He was a dear old man, and nothing further was said about the matter.

Pat and Bingo knew exactly to which companies their masters belonged and which barrack rooms they occupied. They never dreamed of going to visit any other company, but often went up to ours at the men's dinner hour, and generally managed to pick up something. Pat was one of the most intelligent dogs I have ever owned. His end was a sad one: he was bitten by a dog belonging to the Colonel's servant, which was proved to have dumb madness, and had to be destroyed. I heard about it one morning, and dashed into the Orderly Room so upset that I almost forgot to salute. "Taddy" looked at me, saw something was the matter, and asked what it was. I blurted out: "Your servant's dog has got dumb madness, sir, and he's bitten poor old Pat."

"Taddy" arose in his wrath. "He shall be avenged," he said, and turned to Cupid: "Issue an order that every dog in Barracks is to be examined, and that any dog found within two hours without an owner and a licence will be shot," and he added, "even if I have to shoot it myself."

Now it was a well-known fact that the one thing "Taddy" never had done in his life was to let off a gun. He loathed shooting. Consequently, when this story was repeated to Southey,* who was the best caricaturist in the battalion, and the best, in fact, whom I have ever come across, he drew the most priceless picture of the Colonel stalking dogs in barracks. Behind every pillar there was just visible either the head of a dog looking round or a tail disappearing, while terrified drummers were flying for their lives at the unaccustomed sight of the Commanding Officer with a gun in his hand. Unfortunately, as he *was* the Commanding Officer, the drawing was not allowed to be put in the book.

My brother-in-law, Prince Pless, had an Irish terrier very like Pat and as intelligent. I remember on one occasion when I was staying at Fürstenstein we were sitting talking before dinner, and Peter, the dog in question, was lying, apparently asleep, before the fire. He was getting

* Lieutenant Southey, killed in the South African War.

very old, and Hans looked down at him and said to me: "Poor old chap, he'll soon have to be put down. It's kindest, when they get as old as that." He didn't even mention the dog's name. Peter got up, looked at his master, put his tail between his legs and walked out of the room.

Dogs understand most things, especially when spoken to, or of, by their masters, and as for saying that dogs don't think, well, I just don't believe it. I had a retriever many years ago, called Beppo, whom, when he was only eighteen months old, I took with me to Scotland, salmon-fishing. One day, when alone but for him, I had fished one pool and started to walk upstream towards the next, climbing over a high sheep-fence on the way. I began to fish again, and at about the fourth cast got a salmon on; after playing it for a few minutes I realised that I had left the gaff at the pool lower down. Beppo had not followed me, he was playing about on the bank, nosing into rabbit-holes. I whistled and, when he looked up, shouted: "Seek lost!" He knew what that meant and, after a moment or two, found the gaff. Then I shouted: "Good dog! Bring it!" He carried it in his mouth until he came to the sheep-fence. He tried to get through the wire, and, every time he did so, the gaff stuck. He was there whining for three or four minutes, I encouraging him all the time. After about five minutes of vain endeavour, Beppo did a most extraordinary thing. He pushed the gaff as close as he could to the fence; he then got through himself, turned round, and, putting his head through the wire, seized the end of the gaff and slowly drew it towards him; then, picking it up, brought it to me in triumph. I thought to myself at the time, "This dog's going to be a wonder," and I was right. He was the best dog I ever owned. Many men who breed sporting dogs have told me that they consider it a great mistake to keep them in the house. I do not agree with them. I believe that the more a dog is with his master the more human he becomes and the greater is his natural wish to please. Beppo afterwards developed a form of usefulness

56

very rare in dogs. He was as fond of fishing as he was of shooting and, after he grew up, would never go to sleep on the bank when out salmon-fishing, as some dogs do; he'd watch the line the whole time, and get in a state of wild excitement when a fish was on. With trout-fishing it was the same, and, if I allowed him, he would go into the water and land a trout. I very seldom permitted it, as I was so afraid of his getting the hook in his mouth.

When I came to live in London I was afraid that Beppo might be stolen, so I had the following inscription engraved on his collar:

> DEAR STRANGER,
>
> My name is Beppo and my master's name is G. Cornwallis-West, and he lives at 2, Norfolk Street, Park Lane. He is so fond of me that if I am lost or stolen he will pay a reward to anyone who finds me and brings me back, so if you find me or steal me, please be kind and return me quickly.
>
> Yours sincerely,
BEPPO.

As a matter of fact, he was once stolen, and I got him back within three days; I shall always say it was due to the collar!

Another dog I had many years later—it died, in fact, only two years ago—a Labrador named Sambo, could be used as a stop in covert; he would lie in the middle of a ride, and pheasants and rabbits would go within a few yards of him and he would not budge. I once forgot him, and only noticed an hour afterwards; when I went back, he was still there.

One of the most remarkable instances of sagacity in a dog occurred in connection with another Labrador belonging to Lorna, Countess Howe, who is one of the best trainers of dogs in the kingdom; her influence over dogs is positively uncanny. The dog's pet name was Bolo; he is dead now, but as Banchory Bolo, his kennel name, he was well known to every lover of sporting dogs, as he won everything there was to win. I will give in Lady Howe's own words the achievement referred to:

" I never knew any dog so intelligent as Bolo was. He came to me when just over two years old, with a bad reputation as being very wild and very stupid. I can only say he became absolutely human and knew everything I said. I shall never forget how he behaved once when I had all the dogs out in the park, and amongst them a strange dog that had only been with me two days, a wild independent animal who went off into the woods to have a good hunt on his own. I could not get him back, and when eventually he did return he wouldn't allow me to catch him. Old Bolo watched me for a bit, and I gave it up, making a mental note to put a long cord on my friend next time I took him out. To my surprise I saw Bolo go up to him and herd him towards the kennels, to which he marched him exactly like a policeman, driving him just in front. I watched him go through the archway to the stable yard, and the old dog made him go into his own kennel, although the stranger had only been in it two days. Bolo then came out and sat in the archway. Presently the other dog came out. Bolo sent him in again, and whatever he said or did to him I don't know, but he evidently was quite certain that he would not come out again, as he came back to me and jumped up as much as to say ' That's settled him! ' and later, when I took the other dogs in, I found the culprit sitting in his kennel, not having moved."

Another dog now in Lady Howe's possession, called John, has also won many field trials. Of this dog she says:

" Last summer I had a fête here, and got a man called Wallace to come down from the north and give a demonstration of working sheep-dogs. For this I had to get some sheep, and bought twenty. John no doubt saw the sheep-dogs work, and appears to have taken in a good deal, as I know for the rest of the time I had them, whenever we wanted any moved from one field to another, or up the avenue, John would help us drive them through gates. He seemed to know exactly which turning they had to take, and would go on in front of them and see that they took it. I can also send him into a field where there are six hen-houses and he will bring eggs back!"

The training of dogs has always amused me, and my younger sister, Shelagh Westminster, went one better, as when quite a little girl she trained a pony, a goat and a large boarhound to every conceivable trick, the most important being the placing of a board on the pony's back and getting the goat and the boarhound to play see-saw.

A rather amusing incident once happened when I was shooting at Chieveley. One of the guns produced a nice-looking retriever, which went by the name of Flick. For some reason or other the dog took a great fancy to me, and during the week we became good friends. The man, who only had him on trial, did not like him, and said he should return him. A fortnight later I was staying in Yorkshire, and on the night of my arrival one of the other guns said, at dinner, that he had the best dog ever known; that he had bred him himself and, in fact, that there was no dog like him in England. He mentioned, incidentally, that the dog's name was Soot. The next morning when we arrived at the meeting-place, to my astonishment Soot appeared to me to be the dead spit of Flick, so I said softly: " Flick! Flick! " The dog looked at me, and was overjoyed at seeing me again. The man who had bragged about him the night before was very astonished at the dog's behaviour. " Your dog seems to like me, Ralph; I'll bet he comes to me sooner than to you," which, of course, he did. His owner was furious with me and the dog, especially when I added: " I don't think you've had that dog so long as you thought you had."

I never cared much about cats, except one, a Persian whose name was Sylvia. She used to jump from the floor on to my shoulder and never move throughout a meal, except occasionally to wave a protesting paw when a choice piece of fish went into my mouth. I believe cats' affections for human beings to be purely gastronomic or due to a love of being stroked.

When I lived in St. James's Place before the War, a lady friend came to dinner one night, and when she was shown in, she stood on the threshold, her eyes popping out of her head as if she had seen a ghost.

" Good God! " I cried, " what's the matter? "

In a low, sepulchral voice, she said: " There's a cat in the room! "

She was quite right, there was, although I did not know it. It was under the sofa.

Speaking of dogs and cats leads me on to talk about horses, which naturally played a great part in the lives of all of us who cared about hunting. When we were settled down in Ireland it became necessary to equip ourselves with a stud of hunters, each according to his means. The first animal I bought was a black mare; I never liked her, as she was not up to my weight, but she was the indirect means of my acquiring one of the best hunters I have ever owned. The transaction came about in this way. At the opening meet of the Ward Union Staghounds I had noticed a young fellow on a fine-looking black horse, and when hounds started running I saw him jump three or four fences magnificently, pull up, and jump the same fences back again, with the rest of the field going past him, until he came within a few yards of where I was struggling to make my mare get over a ditch which, in those days, looked to me the size of a young canal.

" That's a good-looking horse," said I.

" It is that, your honour."

" Whom does he belong to? "

" Mr. Mooney over at the farm yonder." He pointed to a place across a field.

" Is he for sale? "

" He is, your honour."

" Good! Let's go and see your master."

We arrived at the farm, and Mr. Mooney, the farmer, came out and greeted me. " I've been watching your horse, Mr. Mooney," I said. " What do you want for him? "

"Come inside and have a drink," was the only answer he vouchsafed.

I dismounted and went in, and tasted some of the strongest whisky ever distilled. When I asked him again what he wanted for his horse, he said: "Have another drink," and seemed quite annoyed when I refused. "Would ye like to see him lep?" he suggested.

"Thank you, no; I've seen that."

"Maybe your honour would like to lep him yourself?"

I had not become accustomed to the width and depth of Meath dykes, and still stood in awe of them; however, as I did not like to show my feelings, I agreed. Perhaps the whisky made me feel a little bolder than I otherwise might have. I got on the black horse. He gave me a great feel and he was a most marvellous jumper, even in cold blood —he seemed to love it. When I returned to the farm I once more asked his price, and was once more invited to take another drink. Eventually the old farmer said to me: "Two hundred and twenty-five pounds is that horse's price, and he's dirt cheap at it. Shure your honour can see well it's not fences he jumps—it's parishes!"

Two hundred and twenty-five pounds was more than I could possibly afford, and as he would not come down, I reluctantly rode back to Dunboyne, where I kept my horses. The next day I hankered for the black horse. I went down to the bank and I cashed a cheque for a hundred and seventy-five pounds in gold, which I had put into a sack; this I put on an outside car and drove out with a brother-officer, Cecil Elwes, to the farm. Mr. Mooney was in and took us into the parlour, where I opened the sack and poured the contents on to the table. "A hundred and seventy-five pounds, Mr. Mooney, and the gold's yours for the horse."

It was the gold that did it: he couldn't resist it. "It's a dirty trick, anyway," he said, "but ye can have the horse." We were so afraid he might change his mind that we hitched the horse to the back of the car and drove off to the stables. I forget how he was bred, but I christened him Chorister, which my brother-officers of course turned into " Choir-cad."

I had another amusing experience buying a horse called Midnight, on which I afterwards won two Point-to-Points in Ireland. He was running in a Selling Race at Baldoyle, and entered to be sold for fifty sovereigns, and, had I known then as much as I do now, I could have got a friend to claim him for me. As it was, I waited until after the race and went up to the owner and asked him what he wanted for the horse.

" A hundred and twenty pounds," he answered.

" But that's absurd, considering he was entered to be sold for fifty."

When he saw that I would not give the price asked, he admitted that he had already sold the horse to Captain Steeds, a well-known dealer at Clonsilla, for eighty-five pounds. ' Pretty hot ! ' I thought. I found Steeds and said to him : " I will give you ten pounds profit on Midnight and he needn't go into your stables."

Steeds was the essence of suavity. " Right, my dear fellow," he replied amiably, " you shall have the horse. Take him away now and send me your cheque for a hundred and twenty pounds."

" No," I corrected him, " ninety-five, you mean." He looked at me in astonishment. " You see, Captain Steeds, I've just interviewed the owner, who, after asking me a ridiculous price, admitted that he'd sold him to you for eighty-five pounds."

Steeds blustered a moment, but realised that he had made a mistake, and so I got the horse. Poor old Captain ! He never heard the end of that story, especially after Midnight won the races referred to.

As I was supposed to be a fairly good judge of a horse, one or two of my brother-officers entrusted me with the purchase of some of their hunters. There was a dealer who lived in Wexford by name Reade, a great big burly fellow who rode at least eighteen stone and was, I shall always say, the best heavy-weight to hounds that I have ever seen. I used to go there by the evening train from Harcourt Street, and, after an ample supper at his farm, we turned in at about nine-thirty and were called at daybreak next morning. I would slip on a pair of old breeches and gaiters and drink a cup of hot coffee with my host, who then took me out schooling four-year-olds over the most ghastly hairy country, such as anyone who knows Wexford must admit it to be. We would come back about nine o'clock, bath, shave and breakfast, and school another four-year-old across country to the Meet, where he used to provide me with the really finished article. I bought a good number of horses from him in this way, and he never sold me a bad one. I once saw Reade perform a feat out hunting which even for a light-weight would have been remarkable, and was still more so considering his bulk and the fact that timber is very seldom met with in the hunting field in Ireland. There was a fairly high bank out of the road, with a post and rails on top, and a biggish ditch on the far side: he jumped out of the road and in some miraculous way made his horse ' hike ' itself over the rails; the animal then kicked back at the bank and cleared the ditch on the other side.

Another well-known horse-dealer was Donovan of Cork. A friend of mine who usually bought his horses from him appeared out hunting with the Duhallow hounds mounted on an animal which he had bought from another dealer. Donovan was also out hunting, and was asked what he thought of the new purchase. As he had not sold it himself, he replied:

" Oi should call it a great big bosomy baste—a foine thing in women and turkeys, but not in horses."

I bought two horses from my Uncle Heremon Lindsay-Fitzpatrick, better known as " Pat," and quite one of the most popular characters in Ireland. He had a charming place, Hollymount, in County Mayo, and many were the stories told about him. He himself had a fund of anecdote. He told me, amongst other incidents, that on one occasion his butler came to him and said that one of the estate tenants wished to see him. "Show him in," said Pat. The man entered, twirling his hat in his hand and fidgeting in a somewhat nervous manner. As he was one of his own tenants, Pat, of course, knew him well and, as he told me, liked him. "What can I do for you?" he asked.

"Shure it's this way, Mr. Fitzpatrick. They're after holding a political meeting in the village to-night and they do be telling me that I have to take the chair. I thought that maybe your honour would help me to make me speech?"

"Of course I will," my uncle answered, "if you will tell me what you want to speak about."

"That's the delicate question, your honour, as the subject we're after discussing is—dividing up your honour's land!"

Up to the day of his death, which occurred only last year, Pat was always ready for a joke. The Christmas of 1928 he and his wife and I had lunch together at Sovrani's, and amongst other good things we ate a goulache of veal. When luncheon was over, the head waiter came up and asked him whether he had enjoyed it and whether he had found the veal tender.

"A delicious lunch!" Pat replied, adding, with a perfectly serious face, "The veal was so tender that, had I known it, I wouldn't have bothered to bring my teeth with me!" The expression on the face of the head waiter can better be imagined than described.

A friend of mine once received the following priceless letter from a man who wished to sell his horse:

"DEAR SIR,

My horse is for sale, I regret to say.

Even at £5 reduction for scrags and scars he is too much money for you, which is a pity, for I would like to see such a favourite in good hands and would have been well content to see him in yours—and the horse is 'Safety' itself. I find him so.

But if without going out of your way you could spread it that he is for sale, I should be more than grateful. I need not dilate upon him. He has spoken for himself, but his less-known qualities I will just mention.

HE is the perfectly trained gate-opener.

HE is trained too as a ' polo pony,' and it is a fine sight to see this great horse ' bending ' the trees of my avenue at a fast canter.

HE will ' passage ' and move sideways at once to the light pressure of the reins on his neck. I have ridden him over rabbit-warrens and HE jumps rabbit-holes! HE will trot at speed over long series of roadside drain cuts and never go wrong. HE will canter down impossible hillsides *and* if need be slide for yards. His ' mouth ' is perfect and he gives an extraordinarily fine ' feel '—very light, springy and easy. Lots of people would buy him if they ' got up.'

In January he was ' thrown out of work ' for three weeks and fed on bran mashes from an ' over reach,' but he is back to form. I galloped him yesterday $1\frac{3}{4}$ miles from Pickwell to Noel Arms, and ended with a spurt and itching to go on.

I have never had so big a horse of his weight with such qualities and a ' high blower.'

He is worth a lot of money, for he can ' gallop on,' though he may want one more hunt (after being laid up) as a ' finish.'

I call him cheap at £500, though I can't say I expect to get it. I am not enough in the ' Trade.'

You ought to get on him yourself one day. He would delight you and surprise you, and his great jumps are like nothing on earth; you are just lifted far to the other side, as though you didn't exist.

Yours sincerely,

F—— W——."

Chapter V

SOCIAL LIFE IN IRELAND

LORD CADOGAN was Lord Lieutenant during the time I was quartered in Ireland and, in addition to the official balls and levées which he was bound to give, many were the more informal dances and dinners that we attended at the Castle and Viceregal Lodge. He was lavish in his entertaining, and Lord Lurgan, his son-in-law, who was the steward of the household, knew exactly how things should be done.

In those days it was the custom for the Lord Lieutenant to kiss a débutante when she was presented to him. It was always said of a previous Lord Lieutenant, Lord Spencer, who wore a long red beard, that he used to retire after every fifty presentations and have that hirsute appendage scented and powdered.

One of Lord Cadogan's aides-de-camp was the late Captain Frank Wise of the 13th Hussars, an amusing Irishman and a personal friend of mine. I happened to be on Castle Guard one day during the Dublin season, and had occasion to go into St. Patrick's Hall, which was prepared for one of the huge official dinners; here I saw Frank walking round the tables with an anxious look on his face, distributing name-cards to the various places.

" What's bothering you, Frank? " I asked him.

" I can't make up my mind," he replied, " who I'll put next to His Excellency that he may play tangle-foot with."

The two Officers' Guards were at the Castle and Bank of Ireland, which used to be the old Houses of Parliament before the Act of Union. The rooms at the Castle Guard were broad and high, those at the Bank were the reverse. All were decorated by bygone officer artists, and drawings, some of them very clever, on every conceivable subject adorned the walls. The gloominess of the bank rooms must have affected the minds of some of these artists, for one or two of the subjects were gruesome and reminded one of pictures in Brussels by Wiertz. On the door of the sitting-room of the Castle Guard there was a life-size portrait of a very beautiful girl, whose eyes followed you wherever you were in the room. I always understood she was the daughter of the mess caterer at the time and that she subsequently married the officer who drew her portrait.

The levées, which we always attended *en masse*, were very ceremonious affairs. Except that it lacked the presence of Beef-Eaters and gentlemen of the Yeomen of the Guard, the setting was as elaborate as that of those held at St. James's. A story is told of Father Healey, a great wit of this period, who attended a levée, garbed, of course, in the soutane of a priest of the Roman Catholic Church. An acquaintance of his, by name Moriarty, a self-made man who had been recently created a Deputy Lieutenant of the County of Dublin, was at the same levée, dressed in his brand-new uniform. On seeing Father Healey he said to him : " Shure, Father, it's yourself that would be looking foine in a uniform, with a sword at your side, instead of that sombre garment."

" Maybe, my son, maybe I would, but since one of the aides-de-camp, by name Peter, cut off an officer's ear, we've been forbidden to wear side-arms." Then he added : " And by the way, Moriarty, is that your martial or your com-martial uniform ? "

Old Liddell, who conducted the Viceregal orchestra, was a very well-known character. I remember one night, at a state ball, one of the aides-de-camp, noticing that the numbers of the dances had not been changed, asked Liddell somewhat peremptorily why the proper number was not stuck up. The old man peered over the balcony, where his orchestra played, and replied : " There's nothing stuck up in Dublin Castle except the A.D.C.s."

A number of private dances were also given; in fact Dublin was a very gay place, and one had to be fairly fit

67

and young to keep pace with the life of it. Many's the time that we used to dance until two in the morning and catch the 8.40 a.m. hunting special. There were many race meetings within easy reach of Dublin: the Curragh, Leopardstown and Baldoyle, the last two being within driving distance. The battalion owned a four-in-hand, which was used on these occasions, and it was considered desirable that every subaltern with any pretensions to a knowledge of horse-flesh should learn to drive the team. Personally, although I was very fond of driving a trotting pony, driving more than one horse at a time always bored me; however, I was told I had to learn. The first time I attempted to take the team out of barracks I took away the sentry-box at the gate, and was never asked to drive again, for which I was profoundly thankful.

One day at a Leopardstown meeting I was standing near two men when the beautiful Lady Annesley * happened to walk past. One of the men said to the other: " Who's that foine-looking woman paycocking it about there? " " Shure that's the Countess Annesley," answered his friend; " you're right, she has a great strut on her."

I remember, on another occasion, at Baldoyle, when the numbers for a selling plate went up and there were only five starters, old James Daly, the famous horse-dealer, was standing next to me, and I turned to him and said: " What's going to win the next race, Mr. Daly? "

" Indeed," he answered, " from what I hear it may be difficult to find out which of them is really trying, so I think the best thing we can do is to go into the paddock and take a look at the reins! "

It was while I was in Ireland that the late Prince Francis of Teck, brother of Queen Mary, laid ten thousand pounds to one on what appeared to be a certainty in a two-year-old race at the Curragh. Unfortunately, like many ' certainties,' it went down.

Punchestown, from the point of view of society and, indeed, of racing, was the Ascot of Ireland. Every house

* Priscilla Countess Annesley.

in the neighbourhood was filled, and there were always crowds of English people who came over for the occasion. Betting was pretty heavy; there were many well-to-do men in the ring, and if a backer wished to place a large sum of money on a horse he had no difficulty in doing so. Richard Kavanagh and Patsy Cadogan (in order to distinguish between himself and the Lord Lieutenant there was an accent on the a—Cadogan) were the principal layers. Another curious member of the fraternity was a man of the name of James Plant, who always wore a large belt across his shoulders with his name and the words ' I'm here, I'm betting ' in silver letters. He had the reputation of having the finest flow of language of any man in Ireland. Kavanagh once told me the following story about him. There was a race meeting at Tramore, too far for the bookies to get there and back in one day; consequently they stayed at the local—and not particularly comfortable—hotel. The morning after they arrived Plant was the last to come down to breakfast, and at his place at the table was a plate upon which an egg and some bacon floated nicely in a sea of grease. He tasted the bacon, spat it out, and without saying a word to anyone went to the door and called the landlady.

" Good morning, ma'am," he said when she arrived.

" Good morning, your honour."

" Maybe you're a holy woman, ma'am? "

" I would not be saying that, sorr, but I go to Mass every Sunday."

" Then maybe ye've heard tell of Lot's wife? "

" Shure I have that. Wasn't she the woman that was turned into a pillar of salt? "

" She was, ma'am, and I'll tell you what I'll do. I'll lay you six pounds to four onst that that bacon's a cut off Lot's wife ! "

I once had a funny experience with Plant myself. I was walking in the ring at Punchestown with Lady Hesketh * when we came upon Plant having an altercation with a dissatisfied backer. The language was terrific on both sides.

* Lady Fermor-Hesketh, née Miss Florence Sherrard of San Francisco.

Suddenly, seeing Lady Hesketh, Plant took off his hat with a low bow and said: " I am not addressing *you*, milady! Is there anything I can do for you? "

A namesake of mine, who lived near Carlow, once had a horse running at a meeting there which he told me he thought was certain to win and I was to be sure to go and see it run and to keep the information to myself. The night before the race my name appeared in battalion orders as a member of a Court-martial the following day. It was too late to get anyone to take my duty for me, and I realised that even if the prisoner pleaded guilty, which would curtail the proceedings, I could not hope to catch the race special. I gambled upon being able to get away, and sent a note by my servant in the morning to the General Manager of the Great Southern and Western Railway, ordering a special train to be ready at mid-day. At the Court-martial the prisoner obligingly pleaded guilty, and I got to the station about 12.0. A special train in Ireland, when used by any other person than the Lord Lieutenant, apparently created a tremendous amount of excitement, judging by the number of officials who came to see me off. Who they thought I was, I haven't the faintest idea. We started, and I do not suppose the fifty-five miles between Dublin and Carlow were ever before, or since, covered in so short a time. When we arrived, the station-master there said to me:

" Will your honour be wanting the train back? "

" No," I answered, " I'm not going to pay for it both ways."

" Shure it has to go back annyway, and ye might as well go back in it," was the ingenuous reply. Then he added, with a wink, " And it's a foine chance for the crew to see the races."

The crew at this moment appeared, consisting of the driver, stoker and guard, the two former beautifully black.

" Would you like to go to the races? " I asked them. They beamed. Then I said to the driver: " I make one stipulation only—that as you're going to drive me back, not more than one of the engine's crew gets tight."

70

They swore by every saint in the Calendar that neither of them would, and started to thank me with the approved Irish blarney. After they had backed the train into a siding, the four of us got on an outside car, the guard sitting next to me and the stoker and driver the other side. Our arrival at the races—it was a small meeting—created quite a sensation, and I promised to put ten shillings for each man on a certain horse, without mentioning its name. The horse won at five to one; I more than paid for the special, and the crew of the train benefited accordingly. Just before we started on our journey back to Dublin, I went to the engine to pay the crew their winnings. The driver was as sober as a judge, but the stoker seemed to me a bit muzzy. "He'll be right enough by the time we get back, your honour," his mate assured me, "I'll put the hose on him as soon as we're started!"

The Curragh, as any soldier knows, used to be the Aldershot of Ireland as well as the Newmarket. I was only once quartered there, doing a short course of musketry. A story is told of a lady, the wife of a general officer holding high command in Ireland, who was entitled to an official residence at the Curragh. The lady in question, who was enormously stout, had come down to inspect the house, which was being done up by the War Department for her occupation, and on entering the kitchen she saw an engineer corporal putting in a new grate. "I don't think much of that grate, Corporal," she said.

The man looked up from his work, saw the large figure standing in the doorway, and took it for granted whom he was addressing. "Don't you worry about that, Cookie," he answered, "it'll soon sweat the belly off you."

When the figure moved, he noticed an aide-de-camp in uniform behind her, and it is said that he beat a hasty retreat through the other door and was not heard of for many days.

I mentioned that I liked to drive behind one fast horse. As I had not one of my own I engaged the services of an outside car, fitted with the recently introduced pneumatic tyres, which stood outside Richmond Barracks. This car was one of many owned by a man called Neale, but was driven by a little red-headed boy whom I christened Andy and who always referred to the owner of the car as his uncle. One day Andy came to me and asked if I could help him to get into a training stable. He knew that I knew Dick Dawson,* as he had driven me to his place on more than one occasion; Dawson was at that time training horses in Ireland and subsequently trained one or two for me. I promised the boy I would do what I could to help him, and mentioned the matter to Dawson on the first opportunity. He said: " Find out something about the lad, and if he's got a decent character send him along." Two days later I told Andy: " I have spoken to Mr. Dawson, and he is willing to take you on, but he wants to know something about you."

He interrupted me: " Shure, your honour knows all about me."

" I've only known you a short time, Andy, and I know nothing about your antecedents."

" Auntie—phwat? " he asked in astonishment.

" Well, something about your home life, who's your father, and so on."

A broad grin spread over his face. " Me father——? Glory be to God, I don't rightly know meself, but I do be thinking 'tis me uncle."

Dawson took the boy in spite of his fancy breeding, but he got bucked off and broke his wrist, and retired hurt after an innings which lasted only about three weeks.

Having made a little money racing, I thought I would embark upon a pony and trap of my own. A friend of mine told me of the most wonderful trotter, which belonged to a greengrocer on the north side of the Liffey, and accordingly I and a brother-officer went to inspect it one afternoon. The pony was brought out and trotted down the road; he was a beautiful mover. My friend, who was a cold-blooded Englishman, turned to the owner and said: " He certainly has very fine action."

* Mr. R. C. Dawson, the famous trainer.

" *Action* you call it? " the greengrocer replied with scorn.
" That's more than action; that pony is as soople as a
bloody buck! "

I bought the pony, the best I ever had. He had only
one crab—he was a bad starter, and my groom always
harnessed him with the trap against the wall so that he
could not jib. I entered him in the driving-pony class at
the Dublin Horse Show the following August, and it took
the combined efforts of my Uncle Pat, my groom and three
brother-officers to push the animal and the cart into the
ring. Eventually he started off with a bound. I was
already about three minutes late, and most of the other
competitors in the class had been called in by the judges.
I went on gaily round, in spite of the signals of the judge
calling me in, for the very good reason that, once started,
I could not stop. When eventually I did so I ranged
myself on the right of the line—in other words, the place
allotted to the first-prize winner. Colonel Tomkinson,
who commanded the Royals, was one of the judges; he
came forward with the rosettes in his hand and, seeing
me on the right of the line, gave me the first prize, much to
the annoyance of the fellow next to me. His mistake was
pointed out to him by the other judges, and the red rosette
was taken away; however, he was far too kind-hearted a
man to disappoint me, so he gave me a ' highly commended,'
with the result that I sold the pony at a good price. His
new owner subsequently told me that he cured him of bad
starting by tying him to a lamp-post for hours at a time.

I once had a glimpse of the underworld of Dublin, and of
some rough-and-ready justice, as I made friends with a
Chief Inspector of the Dublin Metropolitan Police, who
suggested that I might be amused to come to the station
onc night when the charges were being brought in. Accordingly I and a brother-officer, dressed in our shabbiest clothes,
turned up about midnight. It should be mentioned that a
certain Mecklenburg Street had the worst reputation of any
street in Dublin, being, as Miss Maisie Gay put it, in a recent
revue, full of " Mal-maisons." After one or two ' drunks '

had appeared, a burly constable marched in a man and a rather good-looking red-haired woman, and, full of judicial importance in the presence of his audience, the Chief Inspector demanded: " What is the charge, Constable? "

" I found these two creating a disturbance in the street, so I ran in both of them."

Without waiting to be questioned, the man accused the woman of having stolen his coat. She continued the argument by saying: " Oi took his coat until he pays me the money he owes me, the dirrthy dog." She was then asked her address by the inspector, and gave a number in Mecklenburg Street. This was quite sufficient and he boomed out:

" *Mecklenburg Street*, is it? Give up the coat, ye flamin' hoor! "

I used sometimes to go to England on leave, and on one occasion I was returning with my younger sister, who was going to stay with our uncle in Mayo. We didn't allow ourselves much time to catch the Irish mail from Euston, and when we were somewhere by Gower Street we discovered that the traffic was held up and diverted on account of the Prince of Wales, who was departing on a journey from the same station and was expected at any moment. I put my head out of the cab window and yelled to the policeman who was stopping us that I was one of the valets and my sister was a lady's maid; with which assurance he let us through, and we just managed to catch our train.

It was a glorious morning in May when I boarded a yacht at King's Town belonging to my friend Captain Orr-Ewing, who was one of Lord Roberts' aides-de-camp and who went by the name of " the Weasel." We were both on the way to Ruthin, where my coming-of-age festivities were to be held. There was very little wind, and we drifted slowly across the Irish Channel, arriving that evening at Holyhead. Foolishly—because the nights were cold—I took a dip over the side, and twenty-four hours later my old throat trouble started and I found myself in bed with quinsy. The house was full of visitors. Balls, presentations, etc., had been arranged, none of which I could attend. I remember having a strange foreboding at the time that I should never be able to live at Ruthin; somehow this misfortune which had befallen me seemed ominous.

" The Weasel " was a great friend of mine, and often dined on guest nights with me in Barracks in Dublin. He always said that, up to a point, alcohol had no effect on him; that point was reached, however, when the pipers, who always played round the table after dinner, began their weird music. He was in the 16th Lancers, and had broken nearly every bone in his body steeplechasing. Poor fellow! He was killed in the South African War, in connection with which unhappy event there is a curious story. In the early September of 1899 I was staying at a shooting lodge in Scotland called Glenetive, which belonged to Mrs. Greaves, a friend of mine, who is now Lady Henry Grosvenor. It was a good little deer forest, and one day " the Weasel," who was staying there at the same time, had been out stalking while I had been fishing the river with my hostess. As we were returning to the Lodge, we saw the head stalker, an old fellow by the name of Anderson, who came to meet his mistress in evident distress.

" Mistress Greaves, Mistress Greaves, a terrible thing has happened: the Captain has seen the White Pony at the head of Corrie B'hui—he'll be dead within the year."

" What does he mean? " I asked her when he was out of hearing.

" Oh, it's only one of the old man's fairy tales," she answered. Anderson had been given the name of " Old Fairy Tales " by Sir William Eden, on account of his intimate knowledge of Scottish folklore. She went on to tell me that Corrie B'hui overlooked the sinister pass of Glencoe, and that tradition had it that it was haunted by a white pony, and that anyone who saw the pony would be dead within the year. Jim Orr-Ewing was killed within eight months of that day.

Chapter VI

HUNTING—EARLY DAYS AND IRELAND

IT was a proud moment in my life when, on the eve of my eighth birthday, my mother told me she would take me out hunting the following day—not the sort of hunting I had been accustomed to up till then, my pony being led like a dog by a groom on a carriage horse; no, this was the real thing. I was to be on my own, and I saw visions of thrilling jumps and felt a vague dread of disgracing myself by falling off. I went to the stables and took down my saddle and bridle to burnish the bit and stirrup irons ready for the following day. The saddle, incidentally, was a curious affair, the leather seat being covered with seams like the pattern of a piece of needlework; some of the stitches were gone and there were signs of horsehair protruding. My request to the groom, a surly fellow named Wheeler, to be allowed to use one of the big saddles, was met with the remark that it would give the pony a sore back.

The following day I had forgotten about the shabbiness of my saddle and had not even minded when my nurse called my gaiters ' buskins '! All I knew was that my pony had been sent on to the meet and that here I was in the brougham with my mother, setting out for the great event. I can see her now, with a tall hat tilted slightly over her forehead, on which she wore a fringe; a veil with large black spots, and habit of dark blue cloth buttoned down the front, with tight waist and little tails behind. The skirt was of a newly invented safety pattern, but far longer than those used now, and not merely an apron.

The meet was at Cotton Hall, near Denbigh: the hounds, the Vale of Clwyd Harriers. The Master, old Major Birch, who had known me from babyhood, greeted me with " Off the leading-rein at last, eh, my boy? " There was a

NEWLANDS MANOR, FROM A WATER-COLOUR SKETCH BY A. BLYTH

similar congratulation from Charles Pearce, the huntsman, another old friend, who had the eyes of a bloodhound and the face of a fox, although he only hunted hares. A certain Volunteer Captain Ellis, who, when he wasn't " huntin' or shootin'," manufactured mineral waters at Ruthin, was the nut of the Hunt. Immaculately turned out in top boots and leathers, green coat, red waistcoat and shiny top hat, he looked just IT. He always had a useful horse or two, even if he did not show them off to the best advantage. Then there were the Master's good-looking daughters, Lena and Phyllis. Lena was my first love, when I was fourteen and she was twenty; I thought her divine—and no wonder! Fine riders to hounds both were, and the Vale took some getting over. A few farmers, a dozen or so neighbours, the local vet. and sometimes one or two flat-catchers from Rhyl made up what was always a small field.

We had a hunt, too, on my first real day. May, my pony, was a marvellous little jumper, and I did not fall off. We killed a hare, and I was solemnly blooded and given a pad, which I kept in the schoolroom until it became a nuisance— it having never occurred to me to have it cured.

A year or so later I was promoted and allowed to go with the fox-hounds, the Flint and Denbigh, or the old Holywell Hunt. I came across a copy of the original rules the other day; one was that any member getting married without the permission of the other members was fined twenty guineas, and another that any member proposing to increase the number of members beyond forty was fined five guineas. The members dined together four times during the hunting season, and wore full dress—red swallow-tail coat with dark red velvet collar and red satin knee-breeches with black stockings. Five guineas was the fine for not turning up in full kit at a hunt dinner.

In 1887, when my grandmother died and we went to live at Newlands, we used to go out with the New Forest Hounds, Stag and Fox. I shall always maintain that to ride to hounds really well in the New Forest requires an even better nerve than does a good hunt in the shires. Hounds go at a terrific pace, and you are either galloping through groves, dodging trees and overhanging branches—a regular Absalom business—or up rides in the enclosures where the going is so deep as to be almost unrideable. When you do get into the open, unless you know the forest well, you are apt to be bogged, and the heather is full of blind ditches where some attempt at draining has been made. The points which the staghounds used occasionally to make were tremendous. I remember once hounds finding in an enclosure some two miles east of Brockenhurst and killing in the Avon near Salisbury, a good sixteen miles as the crow flies and many more as the hounds ran.

After my elder sister married, Prince Pless invariably used to take a hunting-box somewhere near Melton, and it was there that I experienced my first thrills of galloping over grassland and jumping fly fences. Pless was a fairly heavy man, and used to ride big horses, upon which he mounted me and some of which I found great difficulty in holding. Buck Barclay, who had married a cousin of mine, was a great thruster in those days. I asked him once out hunting whether he minded my following him. " Not at all, my dear boy," he answered, but when I ingenuously said that I didn't think I could hold my horse, he wasn't quite so enthusiastic.

One season Pless took Baggrave Hall, the seat of Major A. Burnaby, now Master of the Quorn, and on a Sunday, when " Grannie " Farquhar came over after lunch, Daisy and I, who were very alike, hit upon the idea of changing clothes. The joke passed off very well, and the climax came when I danced a *pas seul* on the lawn, lifted up my skirts and showed a pair of ordinary trousers underneath. Grannie Farquhar was so pleased with the performance that, much to my delight and astonishment, he said: " I'm going away for ten days, and you can have the run of my stud till I come back! " Thank goodness I did not lame one of them, not even his favourite horse Covert Coat, which was included in the offer.

It was not, however, till some years later that I was able

to take seriously to hunting. When I was quartered in Ireland, although I was junior ensign of the battalion and consequently had no regular long leave my first year, it made no difference; one could always hunt four days a week from Dublin even when doing duty. Route marches were generally arranged when the Ward Union Staghounds met. This pack was the nearest to get to from Dublin, and they met at the convenient hour of one o'clock. The battalion generally marched out under the command of one of the captains doing duty. " Any of you boys want to hunt to-day? " he would ask in the morning. Two or three of us usually did, and at a convenient time we were allowed to fall out, with the ostensible object of doing up our boot-laces, and never appeared again. I used to have my pony-trap following behind at a discreet distance, and those of us who were hunting would jump into it, drive to the nearest ' pub,' change and dash off to the meet.

On one occasion, I remember, a bitterly cold day, the landlady suggested that we should have a drop of ' potheen.' I had often heard of this, but never tasted it, and to the uninitiated let me say that it is whisky spirit distilled privately and illegally, and about forty per cent. above proof. I only tasted it this once, and the effects were disastrous. " Quoth the Raven, ' Nevermore! ' "

One evening late in March, when the hunting season was drawing to a close and I was particularly anxious to hunt with the Ward Union the following day, a district order came up to the effect that the battalion was to provide a fatigue party to fill in trenches which had been dug by the garrison in a field near the Royal Hospital during the course of training. The order continued that the work was to be proceeded with the following day by the next battalion on the roster. The Adjutant said to me: " It takes you to command a fatigue party." I asked him how many men I could have. " A hundred if you like," he replied.

The next morning at seven o'clock the hundred men paraded. I told them what we had to do, and that if the work were completed by dinner-time each man would get a pint of beer. It is marvellous what the British soldier will do for a pint of beer! The field was as flat as a pancake by 11.50 a.m., when we marched back to Barracks. I rushed off and changed, and was met by the Adjutant, who asked me what the devil I was doing, and didn't I know that I had to fill in trenches in the afternoon as well as the morning. I replied that the job was finished, but could see that he didn't believe it. "If it isn't," he said, "you know what to expect." I heard no more about the matter and I got my hunt.

Fox-hunting days necessitated our patronising the hunting special which usually left Dublin at 8.40. This meant doing company orders at 8.0. The defaulters of our respective companies were paraded under a sergeant, and we would turn up to administer justice in full hunting kit. I believe the men rather liked it, it varied the monotony of uniform! It amused them to see an officer in a pink coat, white leathers, top boots and an immaculate silk hat; it certainly did not make them worse soldiers, nor, do I think, did it us.

We used to start out, a merry party, at about a quarter past eight, and drive in a brake to the Broad Street Station, where we met many of our friends and quite a number of the ladies, with whom we had probably been dancing the night before. The train went, as a rule, to Dunshaughlin, where the horses were unboxed. We often had to ride six or seven miles to the meet, and no one ever thought of having a second horse, for the simple reason that it was highly improbable that the second horseman would ever have found us. The hunt second horses met the Master at the afternoon draw. There were not many roads, and such gates as there were were generally locked. If you wanted to see a hunt in Meath you had to jump; there could be no shirking and, as already described, the jumps were prodigious, or at any rate they appeared so to a newcomer. In every hunt in Ireland where deep ditches had to be jumped there were always a certain number of men in attendance to help the unfortunate individual whose horse was struggling many feet below the surface of the field. These men went by the name of " Wreckers," and carried ropes and spades. Many of the ditches were so deep that it was impossible for a horse to scramble out unless some of the bank was cut away. If you had taken a fall and your horse had subsided it was amazing how, out of the blue, like vultures finding carrion, the " Wreckers " appeared and proceeded to bargain with you as to what should be the cost of extracting your wretched horse, which was very likely by now in a state of collapse.

John Watson was Master of the Meath Hounds in those days; a fine horseman and a fine huntsman. He very seldom jumped except at a stand, and, when some of us young men used to fly the narrow banks, he'd turn round and scowl and tell us we'd break our —— necks. There was a farm in the southern part of Meath known as Bush Farm, by reason of its having unjumpable bullfinches planted on the top of the banks which divided the fields; it was the only farm in the whole of the country where these horrible obstacles existed. There were only one or two places in each fence where it was possible to crawl through, and these, of course, were well known to the Master, who was thoroughly acquainted with every inch of the country he hunted. On one occasion when hounds ran across this farm from a neighbouring covert, John Watson galloped like a maniac for the spot where he knew he could get through, but he was not the first to arrive. From the top of the bank he looked down into the deep chasm below and saw a man struggling with his horse. He started to abuse him, asking him how the devil did he think any huntsman could get to his hounds when the only jumping place in the fence was blocked? The man in the ditch looked up and said: " Don't be after blaming me, Mr. Watson, there's another gentleman underneath me."

When the day was over we'd retire to the inn at Dunshaughlin, which was kept by three sisters, each prettier than the other. There we would find a marvellous tea laid out, after which we'd box our horses and the special would return to Dublin. A good dinner and a game of whist ended a perfect day—and there were many like it.

My Uncle Pat once invited me to go and have a few days' hunting with him in Mayo. My sister Shelagh was staying at Hollymount also at the time, and on the first day we went out with my uncle's Harriers. There were only about five-and-twenty people out, amongst whom I noticed a red-headed youth with staring blue eyes, who kept on looking unutterable things at Shelagh and glaring at me on every possible occasion. My uncle had some beautiful horses and I was very well mounted. We had a good hunt, and I noticed that whenever I jumped a fence my red-headed friend jumped it alongside me, giving another glare, as though he resented my being out at all. I grew rather annoyed, and it ended in our having a sort of pounding match, until we came to one enormous place where he got over and I didn't. There was absolutely no necessity for our having jumped the last three or four fences, as there was a lane running parallel down which the rest of the field were going. At the end of the hunt Pat, who had been watching the proceedings with a curious twinkle in his eyes, introduced me to the young thruster. "What, are you her brother?" he exclaimed, indicating Shelagh. I assured him I was. "And to think that I've been risking my neck for nothing!"

Two days later we had a day with the Roscommon Staghounds, the Master of which pack was a fine sportsman by the name of Balfe. The distance was a long one, and necessitated a very early start, both our horses and ourselves having to go by train. Roscommon is a wonderful country to hunt in: great big grass fields, splendid going, a few fences, but mostly stone walls. It is marvellous how a good Irish hunter will change his feet on the narrowest of banks, or 'hike' himself over a high stone wall. We were fortunate that day to come in for one of the best hunts of the season, and when it was over we went to have an early dinner with the Master and his daughter Kitty, a girl of fifteen who, despite her youth, kept house for him, as he was a widower. Mr. Balfe's house was typically Irish: square, white and ugly. Everything about it inside and out appeared dilapidated, and, as a contrast, there was the most priceless furniture in the rooms and some wonderful old silver decorated the dining-room table. The dishes were not particularly appetising, but, as another contrast, a perfect vintage claret was produced, followed by an equally good bottle of old port. Balfe himself was a fine type of Irish country squire, with a jolly face, the most notable feature of it being his nose, which was particularly red. At dinner that night he happened to mention that there were one or two cases of measles in the village. His daughter Kitty had, on account of the rough outdoor life she led, anything but a good complexion, and her father looked at her and said: " I hope *you* haven't the measles, Kitty." " Measles? I have no measles, Daddy," she retorted, with a glorious Irish brogue, " 'tis yourself that has the measles—look at your nose! "

No story of hunting in Ireland would be complete without mention of Mr. Richard Burke, Master of the Tipperary Foxhounds. I once got into hunting conversation with a stranger in the train, who turned out to be a great admirer of Burke.

" Have ye ever hunted in Tipperary? " he inquired. When I replied that I had not, he said: " Shure you don't know what hunting is till ye've seen Richard Burke and his hounds. All your Jock Trotters and your John Watsons are just sparrows! Now, sorr," he continued, " when hounds find in Tipperary, first comes the fox, then the hounds, and then the Field and lastly Burke. After a mile or so first comes the fox, then the hounds and then Burke and then the Field. A bit later on first comes the fox, then comes Burke, and then come the hounds and the Field a long way off; and at the end of a hunt first comes Burke and then the fox and then the hounds ...! I tell you, sorr, he's a grand man, is Burke."

I felt there was nothing to say, and slid into my newspaper.

It is the natural ambition of every young soldier who

hunts, to win a point-to-point, and the opportunities offered were, and still are, many. There were no flagged or cut fences in point-to-points in my day; the only flags were direction flags, probably two or three in number, round which we had to go, and those which denoted the winning-post. It was a question of having not only a good horse, but a natural eye for country on the part of the rider. My first success was in the Dublin Garrison Point-to-Point, where my horses won both the light- and heavy-weight on the same day. After the second event I went to where I had left my groom with the other horse, only to find it was in charge of a strange man. "Where's Faraher?" I said. "Shure, your honour, he's watching a bookie," and he proceeded to explain that Faraher had taken long odds to ten shillings on my winning the double event. Ten pounds meant a lot to the class of man who was making a book at this meeting; it also meant a great deal to my groom, and I rather dreaded the consequences if he were paid. He turned up about ten minutes later, and by the broad grin on his face I assumed that he *had* been. The next day when I went to the stables I found the same stranger looking after my horses, with a note from Faraher to the effect that as he was feeling rich he intended to take a few days off, but that his friend was quite a competent groom! Three days later the prodigal returned, rather ashamed of himself and a bit bleary about the eyes, but on the whole not looking so dissipated as I had expected. He was such a good groom that I said nothing; besides, I was rather touched at his having provided a locum tenens who refused to take a sixpence from me; he said that was his and Faraher's affair.

The following year I entered Midnight for the Irish Army Point-to-Point, which was held over the old Fairy House Course, the last three fences jumped being the fences on the racecourse itself. The competitors were taken up to the top of the grandstand and the course was pointed out to them by Percy Maynard, the Master of the Ward Union Staghounds. After giving us general directions he said:

84

" Ye know, boys, ye've got to jump the Poor House Drain, and if you take my advice ye'll jump it where it's been narrowed and forms part of the Fairy House Course. If ye try and jump it anywheres else ye'll probably break your —— necks." The Poor House Drain, I must mention, is one of the most noted obstacles in the whole of the Ward Union and Meath Hunts; it is very wide and in places the banks are eaten away, and, looking at it in cold blood, it appeared unjumpable except where Maynard had suggested we should take it.

We started, so far as I remember, about twenty-four of us. The obstacle described was about half a mile from the winning-post, and the leading six were racing when they came to it. They included Captain Frank Wise, Billie Lambton,* Peel, a gunner officer (also now a General), two cavalry officers whose names I have forgotten, and myself. In the excitement of the moment we entirely forgot the instructions that had been given us by Maynard, and were bent only on getting the nearest way to the winning-post. The six leaders jumped the Poor House Drain where we happened to meet it, four of us getting over. The other two fell, and one horse broke its back. The rest of the field made a slight detour and jumped the Drain in the racecourse. Frank Wise and I had a desperate finish, and his mare, Mary, beat Midnight by half a length.

When the race was over the leaders of the other contingent, who also rode a desperate finish about two minutes later, objected to the first and second as having ridden the wrong course. Percy Maynard was called in as evidence before the stewards, and I well remember what he said: " Gentlemen, I told these young officers that if they didn't jump the Poor House Drain where it forms part of the Fairy House Course they'd break their —— necks, and begob! I didn't believe it was possible for any horse to jump it where they did. But," he added, " I never told any of them they weren't to, if they were such damned fools as to try! "

The race was awarded to Frank Wise.

* Major-Gen. the Hon. Sir W. Lambton.

It was the custom to have an annual point-to-point between the Viceregal staff and whichever battalion of Foot Guards happened to be in Dublin. Amongst Lord Cadogan's aides-de-camp was Captain St. John Meyrick,* to whom, on one occasion, were entrusted the general arrangements for the race. He wrote to the battalion Mess-President, and requested that we should send in the names and pedigrees of our horses for printing on the race-cards. We had a good lot of hunters belonging to various officers, but no one had ever bothered much about their pedigrees at the time of purchase, and it is doubtful whether, with a few exceptions, the dealers themselves had any idea of them. Accordingly two or three of us thought it would be a good joke to pull Captain Meyrick's leg and invent a few. These were some:

Captain ——'s Alarm Clock, by Always out of Time.

Lieut. ——'s Eno, by Never out of Sorts.

Lieut. ——'s Prima Donna, by Sometimes out of Tune.

My animal was Never Fall, by Pulley Hauley out of The Ditch.

The evening on which we sent these in there was a ball at the Castle, and we soon found that St. John Meyrick objected to having his leg pulled; I fancy he looked upon it as *lèse majesté*. I could not resist telling Lady Lurgan about it, who promptly passed it on to her father, the Lord Lieutenant. As he was a breeder and owner of race-horses himself, he thoroughly appreciated the joke.

A rather funny incident happened in the actual point-to-point, which took place a few days later. I was lying second or third with my horse, which fell at the last fence, near where Lord Annaly and my sister were standing. Shelagh caught the horse, and between them they hoisted me back on to the saddle. I was winded and did not quite know what was happening until I found myself facing the horse's tail. Fortunately the animal was sensible and did not move on, my two friends screwed me round and I managed to finish in the first half dozen.

* Gordon Highlanders, killed in South African War.

Colonel Inigo Jones had recently succeeded " Taddy " Fludyer in command. My introduction to him was rather curious. Early one morning I came out of a block of buildings in Richmond Barracks (called the " Rookery," because most of the young subalterns lived in it) in full hunting kit, and saw a tall man in mufti walking across the Green. I had never seen Colonel Jones before, and hadn't the remotest idea who the stranger was. He stopped me and said : " What's your name ? " " West," I answered. " Oh. Well, mine's Jones." I realised that I had met my new C.O., and felt like sinking into the earth. He must have known that I was going to do company orders in hunting kit, and I naturally did not know whether he would approve of this or not. He soon eased my mind, however, by telling me that he had brought over some horses himself and wished to God he could go hunting that very day.

It was with many feelings of regret that I left Ireland when the battalion changed quarters and returned to Wellington Barracks in May of 1897. I had spent there eighteen months, which were amongst the happiest of my life, and had come greatly to love the country and the people.

Chapter VII

HUNTING IN ENGLAND

My next hunting quarters were at Compton Verney in Warwickshire, the ancestral home of Lord Willoughby de Broke, who was then Master and Huntsman of the Warwickshire Hounds and who lived in a smaller house in the village of Kineton. Compton Verney had been taken by Jim Orr-Ewing, who had left the army that year, and had invited me to spend the winter with him. I duly turned up some time in November with a stud of six horses—which, incidentally, I could not possibly afford—our old friend Faraher, and another Irish boy called Alec, who used to ride second horseman to me.

For an all-round, four-day-a-week country Warwickshire is indeed hard to beat; to my mind the Cottesmore is the only hunt that can compare with it. Great grass fields—true, most of them were ridge and furrow, a memento of the days before the repeal of the Corn Laws, and, on a horse with bad shoulders, made one feel seasick—fly fences, often protected by timber ox-rails; many small coverts situated widely apart; a few big woods, the breeding-place and often the stronghold of many a stout fox; a certain amount of light ploughland: these were its chief characteristics. From the point of view of a fox-hunter, no more glorious panorama of a perfect hunting country could be obtained than that from the highest point of the Edge Hills looking over the Kineton Vale and stretching as far as Shuckburgh.

I often used to think that people who hunted in the Shires in my day were a queer mixture. About twenty per cent., men and women, hunted for the sheer love of the sport, and knew a good deal about it; their hearts were in the right place and they were out to see a hunt if hounds ran. About

88

fifty per cent. liked the atmosphere of the hunting-field; they liked to gossip with their friends, and didn't much care whether hounds ran or not; they only jumped if obliged, and then followed each other through a gap. These comprised the ' coffee-housing ' element. The remaining thirty per cent. consisted either of middle-aged individuals, who considered that by jog-trotting their livers their capacity for eating and drinking the good things of life would be prolonged, or people who hunted simply because they believed it to be the right thing to do. Both sorts, at the bottom of their hearts, almost disliked the whole proceedings, and in this last class no one ever dreamt of jumping a fence or, indeed, of leaving the road if it could possibly be avoided.

These were the days before the advent of motor cars to any general extent. There were a few about, it is true, but they were cordially disliked by members of the Hunt, and especially by the Master. Much has been said and written about Lord Willoughby de Broke, by abler pens than mine. In my hunting experience there are four men who shine above all others in the hunting field, not only as brilliant riders, but as Masters of Hounds: they are—Jock Trotter, John Watson who succeeded him as Master of the Meath, Luke White,* and Lord Willoughby de Broke. The first named I met when I hunted as a subaltern from the depot of the Welch Fusiliers at Wrexham; he acted as a sort of master of the horse to Lord Dudley, and hunted from Malpas, in Cheshire, and it was from him that I first learnt the elementary rules of how to ride to hounds. A more fearless horseman never lived, and his chief maxims were: "Jump any fence that comes in your way when hounds first find, so as to get a good place in the hunt. When you have got your place, never take your eyes off hounds, and never jump a fence unnecessarily, as you never know how long a hunt may last, nor what you may call upon your horse to do before it is over."

Of John Watson I have already written.

* The late Lord Annaly, formerly in the Scots Guards, of Holdenby Hall, Northampton.

After Luke White left the regiment he became Master of the Pytchley, at the same time as Frank Freeman, the present huntsman, took up that post. A finer combination of master and huntsman has never been seen. Like centaurs, they seemed to be part of the horses on which they sat; both fearless riders, it was a joy to see them in a good hunt. Of Freeman it was said that when hounds failed him—and that was seldom—he must have been able to smell the fox himself, so many did he account for.

To return to Lord Willoughby de Broke. I was present at the opening meet of the Warwickshire Hounds at Compton Verney in 1897, and had been warned beforehand that he had an abrupt way with anyone who over-rode his hounds, got in his way or did not conform to the elementary ethics of hunting. I was riding an Irish mare called Carmen, upon which I had won a point-to-point in Ireland the year before, and, beyond a few fences over which she had been schooled in the autumn, she had never been hunted in England, but I was young and full of confidence. She did not disappoint me; we had a good hunt, and I remember well that we came to what was an unusual obstacle in England, a small but deep stream near Harbury Station, which ran between steep and crumbly banks. I knew Carmen was accustomed to this sort of thing in Ireland and would make nothing of it. The Master, Charlie Southampton, myself and a few others got over, some got in and the rest went round. On the way home that evening, a man whom I scarcely knew informed me that the Master wished to make my acquaintance. Lord Willoughby was a hero in my eyes, when I indulged in hero-worship, and I felt intensely proud that he should deign to take the slightest notice of a new-comer.

" Well, young man," he said, " that's a damned good mare you're riding. Where have you sprung from? "

I told him that I had been invited to hunt with ' the Weasel ' from Compton Verney that season. We rode the whole way—and it was a long way—home together in the dusk, and he told me about the country, spoke to me of his hounds, and made me feel that I had found a new friend; we remained friends always.

Some four or five years later, after illness had caused him to give up his Mastership, I was hunting that season from Broughton Castle near Banbury. I had acquired the old eight-horse Panhard already mentioned and, although I was careful not to bring it within three miles of a meet, he heard that I was using it for hunting purposes. He wrote me three pages from Egypt, where, poor man, he was endeavouring to regain some health. I wish I had kept that letter. It started by saying that the horse was the noblest animal in the world, and that nothing should be allowed to compete with its activities, whether on the farm, on the road, or in the hunting-field; it was as great an asset to man as was the dog; that motor cars were an invention of the devil and should only be possessed by *nouveaux riches* who knew no better; that in a few years the excitement of driving them would have waned and they would cease to exist. In the face of this remonstrance I had not the heart to continue using my car for the hunt, and used religiously to hack to every meet, no matter what the distance.

Many were the stories told about Lord Willoughby. Like some other Masters of Hounds, he was very fierce in the hunting-field and the mildest of men out of it. I remember on one occasion hounds were running across Charlcote Park near Stratford-on-Avon; the only way through the deer fence was by a small bridle-gate, and a certain person who shall be nameless, but who was notorious for being the biggest funk in the field, happened to be fumbling with the gate as Lord Willoughby attempted to come through it in order to get to his hounds. " Oh, it's you, is it? " he said. " Top of the hunt as usual. Here, take my horn; go and hunt hounds yourself, but," he ended, in a melancholy voice, " come back soon and tell me all about it! "

Another good story which is told about Lord Willoughby has, I believe, appeared elsewhere in print, but I shall risk repetition, as I happened to be out when the episode occurred. When hounds were running hard and for no apparent reason threw up their heads and failed to hit off the line, even with the aid of the huntsman, Willoughby would turn to a labourer in the fields or to anyone whom he happened to see near by, and say " Have you seen the fox? "

If the answer was in the negative he would exclaim: " B-r-r-r! you don't know the difference between a fox and an elephant! " On this occasion we found in Bishops Gorse near Compton Verney, and ran fast across the vale to the Edge Hills, where hounds, for some unaccountable reason, threw up their heads when they arrived at the main Banbury–Rugby road. After several futile casts, there appeared on the road an old woman—a jolly old soul she was—driving a farm cart in which was a lot of poultry.

" Hi! madam," said Willoughby, " have you seen the fox? "

" No, my lord," was the answer, " but a moment ago I saw an elephant cross the road."

It is not often, when one succeeds in pounding most of the field out hunting, that one is rewarded, as hounds invariably turn away from the person who prides himself on having jumped something rather out of the way. Only once do I remember reaping the benefit. We were running across the Kineton Vale from Farnborough, and had to get over the East and West Junction Railway which runs between Fenny Compton and Kineton. The railway gates were shut, and on both sides of them was a wire fence; the nearest bridge was a long way off. There was a screaming scent, and it looked as if we were in for a really good hunt. I was riding our old friend Chorister, who had developed into a most brilliant timber-jumper. I put him at it, and he jumped in and out of the railway, over the gates, and made nothing of it. A far finer performance was that of Freddie Freake,* who followed me on an Irish mare which had only just come over from Ireland a few days before, and which, I believe, had never been asked to jump a bit of

* Sir Frederic Freake, the famous polo-player.

timber in her life. We had the hunt entirely to ourselves for the best part of fifteen minutes.

There were several thrusters besides the Master and Freddie Freake who used to come out hunting in those days, the best of whom were Charlie Southampton and Ralph Cartwright. I once saw the latter do a marvellous thing, although it was not really necessary. Hounds found at a covert called Watergall and ran towards Kineton, over the Great Western Railway, which at that point runs on a high embankment. Most of the field went under a narrow arch, but Ralph Cartwright put his horse at the post and rails at the bottom of the embankment—and anyone who has hunted knows what a post and rails are along a railway—cleared them and the fence on the other side and landed on the embankment, up which the animal struggled. He went over the top, down the other side, and jumped the second fence and post and rails into the field beyond. As a couple, he and his wife (who was the widow of Jock Trotter) were by far the finest riders to hounds in England, and his brother Victor is probably the finest rider at the present time. Two other famous women riders of those days were my sister, Shelagh Westminster, and Miss Doods Naylor, now Mrs. Straker.

The Warwickshire Hounds did not hunt on Saturdays, and it was a question of hunting on that day with either the Pytchley or the Bicester alternate weeks. Most hunts were very kind to soldiers, and minimum subscriptions were expected. The secretary of the Bicester at that time was a gentleman by the name of Harry Tubbe, but unfortunately, when I sent my subscription, I could not remember this; I only knew it had something to do with liquid, and, without the least intent to insult him, I addressed the envelope to " Mr. Butt, Bicester "—and, alas, the postman was too conscientious; it found him. I heard afterwards that he was furious, and that old Squire Slater Harrison, a great supporter of that hunt, declared, " I won't have my Tubbe made a butt of."

Mr. Tubbe avenged himself on me many years later when

I was hunting with the Whaddon Chase. The Bicester were known to be very exclusive, and although members of that hunt had no compunction in hunting with neighbouring packs, they objected strongly to this arrangement being reversed. As, for some reason, I was unable to hunt one week on my usual days, I went out with the Bicester, which happened to be meeting near by. Tubbe came up to me and said: " Are you a subscriber to these hounds? " knowing perfectly well who I was and that I was not a subscriber. When I told him this he said: " Please understand that we do not wish strangers out, and if you come out again you will have to pay five pounds." I was very angry, and complained to the Master, Johnnie Lonsdale, with whom I had been at Eton, but the episode only seemed to amuse him. Later in the day, however, I got my own back. It was the middle of March, and we ran a fox to ground. Much to my surprise the terriers were put in, and meanwhile we went off to try another covert, which proved blank. It seemed rather late in the year to use terriers, but I certainly was not prepared for what followed, for, when we returned to the place where we had run to ground, not only was the hunted fox lying dead, but another as well, both vixens heavy in cub. I could not restrain myself—I said at the top of my voice: " Now I understand why the Bicester don't like strangers to come out with them." I was pursued round the field by two members of the hunt who, I believe, would have murdered me if they had got me.

After my marriage with Lady Randolph Churchill I hunted with the Pytchley from Ashby St. Legers, that lovely old place said to have been used by the conspirators of the Gunpowder Plot, belonging to the present Lord Wimborne. Lord Annaly had a wonderful way with his field; he never seemed to raise his voice, and yet kept them in perfect order. I remember on one occasion when hounds had been running fast and suddenly checked in a lane, we came upon a certain young man who, so gossip said, was very much *épris* with a beautiful married lady who also hunted with the Pytchley. The two were together in close proximity;

evidently it was they who had headed the fox. The sight was too much for Annaly, who groaned aloud and, rather in the manner of Henry II with Thomas à Becket, exclaimed: "If *only* someone would tell those two to get home and stay in front of a nice warm fire! They'd find it so much more comfortable!"

One day the Pytchley, after a good hunt into a neighbouring country, killed a fox close to the house of a great friend of mine, a most generous man, whose wife was notoriously the meanest woman in the land. I suggested to another friend who was with me, who also knew the owner of the house, that we should go and get a glass of port off him. He agreed, and we went and rang the bell. It was answered by our friend's wife herself, to whom we said: "Good morning, Mrs. ——, we have come to get a glass of port off Arthur."

"My husband is away, but do come in," she said; adding to the butler, who had just appeared, "Bring the port."

As we entered the hall, she followed the servant to the door leading to the back premises and we heard her say, in a loud whisper, "Kitchen port will do!"

Another story is told of the same lady. Her husband had a deer forest in Scotland, and in order to economise she served venison at table on every possible occasion, only instead of calling it venison it was described as beef. One night *filet de bœuf à la* something or other was duly inscribed on the menu and, in order to emphasise the fact that it was not venison, she turned to a lady guest and said: "How delicious Scotch beef is, isn't it?"

"Yes, my dear," the other replied, "especially when it has been fed on heather like this has."

Lady Astor, who was then Mrs. Shaw, hunted with the Pytchley in those days. She was a good horsewoman and a fearless rider, although some unkind people suggested that she didn't always allow a person jumping in front of her as much time to clear the fence as she should have. She and I once had a verbal duel. We were standing outside a

95

covert one day very late in the season, and I volunteered the remark that I intended selling my horses. " They're no use to me," she said, " I've given up keeping carriages ! "

" Never mind that," I answered, " one might serve to draw the hearse for the next man you jump on."

There was a time during my hunting career when I hunted with the Whaddon Chase and Lord Rothschild's Staghounds. The late Mr. Leopold Rothschild, who acted as Master alternately with his brother the late, or his nephew the present, Lord Rothschild, was always very kind to me, and I had a standing invitation to Ascott, the delightful place he owned near Leighton Buzzard. Once he said to me quite seriously that when he was born he was so beautiful that his co-religionists took him for the Messiah. " But," he added, " they wouldn't think so now, would they ? "

From 1910 to 1912 I hunted from Hillcrest, Market Harborough, with the late Sir Humphrey de Trafford, who was a strict Roman Catholic. Instead of having a whisky and soda as a nightcap, his custom was to drink a tumbler of vintage port. One evening, late in the season, I noticed that, instead of vintage, wood port was on the tray, and asked him casually if he had run out of the former. " No," he replied, " it's Lent."

I had tried every year to win the Army Point-to-Point, but my ambition was not fulfilled until 1898, when I won the heavyweight on a horse called Oxhill. The course was at Rugby, over four miles of fair hunting country. Here, again, there were no cut fences, but just three or four flags round which we had to go. I had ridden in the first race, the light weight, and in order to reach the weight had foolishly used webbings instead of leathers on my saddle. My horse was going well three fences from home, and it is possible that he might have brought about another double event, when, at a drop fence, both webbings broke and I ruptured a tailor muscle badly. I walked in, suffering tortures, and all the more depressed as there did not seem to be much prospect of my riding in the next race, which I knew I had a great chance of winning. In the weighing tent I found Captain Beevor, who was the doctor in my battalion. The first thing he did was to pour a large glass of brandy down my throat and then proceeded to strap up my leg so tightly that I could hardly feel anything, certainly no pain. Oxhill never made one mistake the whole way round, and I won comfortably by many lengths. He was easily the best horse I ever owned, and Dick Dawson, to whom I sent him to be wound up for a few races and point-to-points at the end of the season, always believed that he might have won a National. In addition to the Army Point-to-Point, he won the Warwickshire Point-to-Point, the Regimental race and the Household Brigade Welter Steeplechase and, but for a fall, would have won the Warwickshire Hunt Cup at Stratford-on-Avon. My chief danger in this latter event was a man with whom I had hunted all the season. Just before the saddling bell rang his sister said to me, " I do hope that you'll have a fall and that Freddie will win ! " It wasn't exactly a favourable augury with which to get up and ride a steeplechase, and as it turned out her wish was granted : her brother won the race and I broke my collar-bone.

He was a gallant horse, Oxhill. He broke down shortly after I had sold him, but after he had rested for three years he won many more races in Ireland.

One of the funniest hunts I ever attended was at Fursten-stein, my brother-in-law's place in Germany. It was a drag hunt, or *Schlepjagt*, run by the artillery officers quartered at a place called Schweidnitz. We were a party of about twenty staying in the house, mostly English and Austrians, and we commandeered every one of Pless's horses—hunters and carriage horses—and arrived at the meet. The Master, so far as his cap, tie and pink coat were concerned, was immaculately dressed, but the rest of his turn-out was a bit weird. He had large black hessian boots with long spurs, and the buttons of his white breeches, instead of being at the knee, went the whole way up the seams on both legs.

We were warned by Pless that the line would be about four miles over grass so far as possible, with small made fences at intervals; and before we started we were addressed by the Master in German. He said: " First will come the hounds, then I, and then the Frau Fürstin von Pless, and then the rest of you. Anyone who rides in front of me will be fined five marks, and anyone riding in front of Her Highness one mark!" We started off at a devil of a pace, and before we had gone half-way most of the pack were hunting hares. The fences were about three feet high.

At the end of the hunt an artilleryman—I think he must have been a bandsman, as I remember his sword had a Roman hilt—handed to the Master a bag containing broken dog biscuits; this, apparently, was the only reward the hounds got. Then the bandsman dashed into a thicket, from which he emerged carrying a sprig of young spruce. Drawing his sword, he laid it on the hilt, knelt and solemnly presented it to my sister. It was all terribly serious, and none of us dared laugh. Poor Daisy! How we chaffed her afterwards, telling her how easy it was to ride to hounds when anyone who got in front of one was fined.

My hunting career came to an end a few years ago, when I nearly broke my neck with the Blackmore Vale. Alas! hunting is a sport which, once you give up, you never take to again. When I was in that part of the world I managed to put in a day with the Cattistock, of which the well-known sportsman, Parson Milne, was Master and huntsman. It is recorded of him that when he was taking a service in the parish church during a hard frost and the congregation were singing the Benedicite, he would shut his mouth like a trap when they came to the verse beginning " O ye Frost and Cold . . ."!

Chapter VIII

ODDS AND ENDS

In the summer of 1897 I was promoted, and this necessitated my being transferred to the First Battalion, which, under Colonel Mildmay Wilson, was quartered at the Tower of London.

I rather liked being at the Tower. When I was on picket I used to amuse myself by going into all sorts of queer places not generally shown to the public, and trying to decipher the old inscriptions on the walls of the various dungeons, but whenever I thought I had discovered something of interest I found it was already perfectly well known.

An amusing episode happened there in connection with the time-honoured ceremony of the keys. For the benefit of those who have not heard it recently on the wireless, I will describe it as it was first described to me by the Sergeant of the Guard under my command. He was a Scotsman and an old soldier, and he proceeded to address the guard (most of whom were also Scots) as follows:

"Pay attention to what I'm aboot to tell ye as to the sairemony of handing over the keys. Upon the stroke of ten the sentry will hear a step approaching and he will say 'Halt! Who goes there?' and the Warder will reply 'Keys'; and the sentry will say: 'Whose keys?' and the answer will be 'Queen Victoria's keys,' and the sentry will say 'Pass, Queen Victoria's keys, and all's well!' Then the Warder will stand in front o' the Guard and remove his hat and he will say 'God Save Queen Victoria,' whereupon the whole Guard will reply 'Amen' and, mind, no laughing!"

If he had not suggested that we might laugh it would never have entered our minds—certainly not mine—but when the actual ceremony took place I felt almost hysterical.

That summer the battalion took part in lining the streets on the occasion of Queen Victoria's Diamond Jubilee in July, when that august little lady attended the Thanksgiving Service at St. Paul's. I personally was on Ludgate Hill, and have a vivid recollection of the impression made by the sight of that serene and diminutive figure who had ruled so long and so wisely over countless millions of her subjects.

The battalion was at Pirbright at the time, and had been brought up specially for this function, returning the same afternoon. That evening about a dozen of us cycled over to the residence of Colonel Godman, whose nephew, Sherard Godman, was in my battalion. We dined with him, and afterwards climbed to the top of the Nore above Hascombe on the borders of Surrey and Sussex, from which a view of the country for many miles round could be seen, and from which we witnessed that most marvellous sight, the lighting of the beacon fires to commemorate the day.

If, when at Pirbright, one wanted to attend a ball in London and to be in time for early parade next morning, one had to catch the milk-train back from Waterloo, and many a time I overslept myself and went on to Aldershot instead of getting out at Brookwood. This necessitated tipping the driver of the engine, who lived at Woking, to take me on the footplate and throw me out somewhere near the camp. Creeping down a railway embankment, through gorse, in pumps and evening dress, was not pleasant, but not nearly so bad as trying to do a tight-rope stunt across the lock gates of the canal. I never could stand height, and always used to shuffle across, sitting, with one leg on either side. One night both pumps fell into the water, and I had to walk the remaining two hundred yards to my tent in silk socks, over flints.

Manœuvres that year, which took place in Sussex, were, so far as I was concerned, a holiday, as I had been appointed galloper to General Kelly-Kenny. A few days before they began I had fallen into a bog at Pirbright while doing outpost work, and the chill which I caught kept me in bed

ROLL-CALL, FIRST BATTALION SCOTS GUARDS DONE BY AN
OLD N.C.O.

two days; consequently I was twenty-four hours late in reporting myself at Arundel, which was General Kelly-Kenny's headquarters. As I was not only the last to arrive, but also one of the junior officers on the staff, I had to put up with any accommodation that was offered me at the hotel, and found myself that night in a small room which, besides being over the kitchen, had hot-water pipes up one of the walls. The heat was insufferable. The next morning I asked the landlord if he could possibly change my room, and when I returned that night I found that my things had been moved to an attic. The hotel was an old posting establishment and, as was usual, the top floor had been used for grooms and postboys; it was now partitioned off into small rooms. That night I was woken up by the snoring of the man next to me, and as he kept on missing a snore it was impossible to get to sleep again. I threw most of the available unbreakable objects at the matchboard partition without any effect. As the weather had turned cooler, I decided that my old quarters were preferable and, lighting a candle, crept downstairs to the room over the kitchen. As I opened the door the draught blew the candle out. I felt my way to the bed, and was about to get into it, when a female in it screamed. Fortunately I had not relinquished the candlestick, and I rushed to the door and upstairs again to my attic. The following evening after dinner the senior officer present said: " The landlord has complained that someone tried to get into the barmaid's bed last night; you fellows had better warn your servants." I sat very tight, and more than a year passed before I told the story against myself.

It was while I was at Hythe doing a course of musketry, the following year, that I received an invitation from Lady Warwick to go to Warwick Castle from Friday to Monday to meet the Prince of Wales. Leave from a course was an almost unheard-of thing; on the other hand, an invitation to meet His Royal Highness almost amounted to a command. I went up to see the Commandant, Colonel Hamilton,*

* General Sir Ian Hamilton.

and he gave me leave. That visit to Warwick was a very eventful one for me, as it was there that I first met the lady who subsequently became my wife. Lady Randolph Churchill. Jennie, as she was always called by her friends —was then a woman of forty-three; still beautiful, she did not look a day more than thirty, and her charm and vivacity were on a par with her youthful appearance. I confess that I was flattered that so attractive a person should have paid any attention to me, but she did, and we became friends almost immediately.

Frances Lady Warwick was at this period at the zenith of her beauty, and Warwick Castle, one of the loveliest places in England, provided a perfect setting for its chatelaine. I went on the river with Lady Randolph, who talked to me about her son, now the famous Winston Churchill and then an officer in the 4th Hussars. He had already become notorious as the young man who had addressed the audience from a box at the Empire on the iniquity of the proposal for shutting up the promenade at that well-known music hall; and who had played polo for his regiment when it had won the Army cup in India. His mother had great faith in, and ambition for, him, and even at that time believed he would rise to great things.

I was the first person to introduce the Mauser automatic pistol to the School of Musketry. One afternoon I and another officer went down to the ranges, where firing at five hundred yards had just been completed. I asked the senior officer in charge whether I might have a shot at the target. He looked at the weapon in my hand and said: " We're not going any nearer the targets," and seemed astonished when I suggested that I should fire from the place where we were standing. " After all," I pointed out, " the weapon is sighted up to a thousand metres." He grew interested and telephoned for the target to be put up. The pistol was under-sighted, but with the sight at eight hundred metres, and using the holster as a stock, one could hit the object every time.

It was about this time that high-class French restaurants

KING EDWARD (WHEN PRINCE OF WALES) AT RUTHIN

Left to right: Hon. F. Guest, Col. Cornwallis-West, H.R.H., Mrs. Cornwallis-West, Lord Marcus Beresford, Miss Muriel Wilson, Miss Cornwallis-West, Lady R. Churchill, Author.

began to make their appearance in London. The Amphitrion, the first, had started more or less as a club some years previously, and had failed. The next to open was Willis's Rooms in King Street, St. James's, run by a famous *restaurateur* called Jules. Certain leaders of society started the fashion of lunching and dining there; other people soon followed, and the place was crowded at both meals. While I was at Hythe many of us used to come up to London at mid-day Saturday, and before leaving on Sunday night we would dine together at Willis's. Jules appropriately termed these occasions " *le dîner des mousquetaires*."

The meets of four-in-hand and coaching clubs in Hyde Park were great social events, generally followed by a drive to the Crystal Palace, where we dined and witnessed the fireworks, or to Ranelagh or Hurlingham. To a lover of horses it was a joy to be in Hyde Park on a summer's afternoon and watch the high-stepping pairs pulling gorgeous barouches or victorias, in which were seated either celebrated personages such as Theresa Lady Londonderry, or the Mrs. de Vere Robinsons who lived on the wrong side of the Park but whose husbands were very rich and were not to be outdone by anybody.

Polo was then, as now, a great attraction, the brothers Peat and John Watson being the great players of the day. As there was no room in Barracks, I lived with Arthur Peat and three other fellows in Park Street. The house was well known to the police, as never a week passed without one or other of us forgetting our latchkey. This necessitated swarming up one of the iron pillars of the verandah or doing as one member of the household did—jumping from the top of the area railings on to the ledge outside the dining-room window. The subsequent production of the latchkey, plus a whisky and soda, generally had the effect of calming the constable.

In May 1899 the Prince of Wales came to stay at Ruthin Castle for Chester Races. Lord Marcus Beresford, who managed the Prince's horses, was also a guest, together with Mr. Reuben Sassoon, whose sole job it was to make bets for

H.R.H. A curious old gentleman, Reuben Sassoon, who never opened his mouth, except to put food into it. The ladies of the party included Lady Randolph Churchill and Miss Muriel Wilson, now Mrs. Warde, who was quite one of the most beautiful girls of the day, as well as the possessor of a brilliant personality and a host of friends. It was the first time a Prince of Wales had ever visited the town, and although the visit was a private one, the excitement was intense. Filled with enterprise, the local chemist persuaded my mother to allow him to provide some toilet necessity, and promptly became a royal warrant-holder. When, two years later, the Prince became King Edward VII, the three feathers over his shop door were immediately replaced by the royal arms and a notice to the effect that he was chemist " by special appointment to H.M. the King."

Another event which shook Ruthin to its foundations was the one and only execution which ever took place in the gaol there, now closed. A wretched ex-soldier who, during a family argument, had hit his wife harder than he had intended, with fatal results, was tried at the Assizes and sentenced to death. Although there was not the slightest necessity for him to be there at all, the High Sheriff, who lived at the other end of the county, arrived at the Castle Hotel the night before the execution, and attended it in full uniform; and the local newspaper appeared heavily edged with black two days after the event.

Since July of this year the atmosphere in South Africa had been distinctly war-like, and matters had culminated in the outbreak of hostilities in October of that year. The First Battalion of the Scots Guards formed part of the first Division to be sent out, under the command of Lord Methuen. The command of the battalion itself had recently been taken over by Colonel Paget.* Arthur Paget was possessed of the true Paget manner, which unkind people described as swagger, but which was just as natural to him as it would have been unnatural to drop his aitches. His officers and men adored him. There was nothing the latter

* The late Gen. Sir Arthur Paget, K.C.B.

104

enjoyed so much as to see their C.O. clatter into Barracks in a smart brougham drawn by a pair of high-stepping horses, whose driver would take a large sweep round the barrack square and pull up in front of the orderly room, where A. P.—as he was affectionately known to his friends—would step out, immaculately dressed in a frock coat and silk hat, with a gardenia in his buttonhole, and proceed to do Commanding Officer's Orders. At that moment every man in Barracks would pop his head out of the window and take a look at what was to him one of the sights of the day.

About a week before we sailed I was sent for to the orderly room and told by my C.O. that Lord Methuen had applied for a junior officer from his old regiment to go as his aide-de-camp, that it must be someone who could ride, and that my name had been sent in. It came as a surprise to me, as I had done nothing to bring it about. The explanation was soon forthcoming, however, as I found a note from the Prince of Wales awaiting me when I went home.

October 15th, '99.

" MY DEAR GEORGE WEST,
        " I had the opportunity of speaking to Lord Methuen at the station yesterday when I took leave of Sir Redvers Bulwer, and strongly urged him to take you on his staff, so I hope it may be all satisfactorily settled.
        " I envy you going out on active service with so fine a battalion, and wish you good luck and a safe return home.
                        " Yours very sincerely,
                                " ALBERT EDWARD."

I shall never forget our march from Chelsea Barracks to Waterloo Station at about five o'clock on a dark autumn morning. There was a slight fog and, comparatively speaking, the streets were badly lighted in those days. A good many wives and sweethearts accompanied the men from Barracks and linked arms, and naturally nothing was done to prevent them. When we reached Westminster Bridge there was a large crowd, and many civilians, in mistaken kindness, broke into the ranks and pressed bottles of whisky upon the soldiers. This naturally had to be stopped, but it was difficult to prevent it in the semi-darkness. Over Westminster Bridge our ranks almost degenerated into a rabble, so great was the crush of civilians, but fortunately the Chief of Police had foreseen this, and at the entrance to the station a large number of police were posted to prevent the admission of anyone not in uniform. Some of the scenes were particularly heart-rending.

We embarked at Southampton on the *Nubia*, a small P. & O. boat of about 6000 tons. Twenty-four hours after we had sailed she was reported in one of the London news-papers as having foundered with all hands. My father, happening to see a placard, went at once to the War Office, who, of course, denied it. As a matter of fact, although the editor of that enterprising journal could not possibly have known, as it was before the days of wireless communication, we might very well have been wrecked, as the fog off Ushant was intense, and we were steaming dead slow, when suddenly it lifted, and we found ourselves not more than half a mile from the shore.

The only other excitement on the journey was inoculation against enteric, which the officers were expected to undergo first to set an example to the men. This was not done with a small hypodermic syringe; the M.O. rushed at you with what looked like a garden squirt with a spike at the end, and there was no question of the subcutaneous insertion of so many minims: it felt more like half a pint. Nor did it seem to be much good, as the casualties from enteric fever during the South African War were appalling.

The men practised firing at boxes towed astern. All went well until a shoal of flying-fish appeared, when no one paid any more attention to the boxes.

I had a pony on board called Toby, a hackney, which everybody said I was mad to take out. He was the only animal on which the voyage had no ill-effects, in spite of

"TOBY," THE PONY WHICH IN THE SOUTH AFRICAN WAR
BECAME ENTITLED TO ELEVEN CLASPS

his being cooped up in a small box; the first thing he did on landing was to shy at the men's kits. He went through the whole of the South African War, first with me on his back, and then, when I was invalided home, Colonel Paget and two subsequent Commanding Officers of the Scots Guards. He was entitled to no fewer than eleven clasps, and was shot twice through the rump, to which he paid no more attention than if he had been stung by a wasp. At the close of the war he returned home with the battalion. As he was suffering from South African horse ophthalmia, I gave him to a tenant of my father's in Hampshire. He shied more than ever when he was blind, but lived to a good old age.

The voyage was long and tedious; it took twenty-eight days to Cape Town, but the monotony was relieved, to some extent, by the fact that Alfred Rothschild had generously presented the Officers' Mess with twenty cases of 1887 Perrier Jouet.

Chapter IX

A VICTORIAN WAR

AFTER a long dusty journey the battalion arrived at Orange River, where we spent three days awaiting the arrival of the rest of the Division, which had been ordered to relieve Kimberley. It was when we were in camp there that I experienced my first African thunderstorm. A more awe-inspiring sight I have never witnessed. The lightning seemed all around one, and the drum-fire of the late war is the only thing I have ever heard since at all like the thunder. I had been sent with a message to a farm which was an outpost about three miles away from the camp, and was on my return journey when it started. My pony was terrified, and so was I. It seemed impossible that we should not be struck, and he refused to budge. A few minutes after the thunder started the rain came, and in a few seconds I had not a dry rag on me.

The Division was still a brigade below strength when Lord Methuen fought his first engagement at Belmont. On the evening before, the whole divisional staff went out to reconnoitre the Boer position. It looked impregnable, and without a preliminary bombardment of high-explosive shells it seemed a forlorn hope to attempt to take it; but we had no high-explosive shells. Lyddite, the first of its kind, was not in general use until some time after. The British artillery were then armed with the old twelve-pounder, a spade being the only method used to take up the recoil, on the same principle that old motor-cars used to be provided with a sprag to prevent them running backwards downhill.

The engagement was fought the following day and a sublime frontal attack on our part compelled the Boers to

COL. ARTHUR PAGET

retire from their positions. It was impossible to follow them up, as the 9th Lancers and Rimington Scouts were the only mounted forces with the expedition, and the horses of both units were exhausted. All his senior staff officers congratulated the General upon the great victory he had won, and then we solemnly rode back to where we had started from, and had breakfast! I confess to a feeling of bewilderment: it was the first battle I had been in, and not in the least what I had expected, which was certainly not to go back to where we had started unless we were pushed there. I was feeling depressed, as I had heard of several friends of mine in the Brigade who had been killed, so, as I was no longer wanted, I rode out to talk matters over with my brother-officers, the battalion by this time having returned to camp. The first person I met was Gerry Ruthven,* who echoed my own sentiments. It was his first engagement too, and he said: " Funny business this, George! Are all battles going to be like this—just an Aldershot field day with bullets instead of blank ammunition? "

Colonel Paget had a most extraordinary escape that day. An order had come out to the effect that as the Boers were known to be fine marksmen, all officers were to remove their medal ribbons, which presented a good spot to aim at. The Pagets did not include the word ' fear ' in their vocabulary; so the Colonel said: " I'll be hanged if I'll take off my medal ribbons! "—he had about seven— " I never heard of such damned rot! " When I saw him, there was, under his row of ribbons, a brown sear where a bullet had scorched his tunic: his guardian angel had turned him sideways as the Boer pulled the trigger. To unbelievers I may say that the Colonel's son, Captain R. Paget, still has the tunic in his possession.

That night the officers attended the burial of the men of the battalion who had been killed. There were no neat little graves with wooden crosses drawn from store, but just a pit which the Pioneers had dug. The bodies had been

* Major-Gen. Lord Ruthven.

109

collected from the battle-field and brought in on service wagons, and in South Africa bodies stiffen and decompose very quickly. The quaint positions of the limbs of some and the *risus sardonicus* on the faces of others were not pleasant to look upon.

The following day the Division started north again, and that night the General and his aides-de-camp, the senior of whom was Major Streatfield,* slept in a small deserted farm. Paul Methuen was a man of untiring energy. Four hours' sleep in the twenty-four was more than sufficient for him, and he expected the same vitality from his staff, but at the age of twenty-five it is difficult not to feel sleepy at times. That night by the light of two tallow candles, " Streattie," and I sat up and wrote out the General's dispatches on the Belmont engagement from the notes that he had himself made. There was not much sleep for either of us, as we started at dawn the following day, upon which the engagement known as Graspan was fought; another frontal attack with more heavy casualties (especially amongst the naval contingent) in proportion to the forces engaged. The Guards Brigade were in reserve on this occasion.

That day I made my first acquaintance with what was known as a Pom-pom (one-pound Nordenfeld automatic quick-firer). I had been sent with Major Streatfield with instructions to alter the direction of attack of the troops engaged on the extreme right of the line, and we were returning at a slow canter when we heard a pom-pom and realised that we were the target. We separated and increased our pace. The pom-pom's bark was worse than its bite.

On returning from carrying another message that day, when the engagement was practically over, I came across a magnificent specimen of an old Dutchman lying dead, with a look of marvellous calm upon his face, very like Rembrandt's picture of Jacob Trip in the National Gallery. For the first time it struck me that we were fighting against men of a splendid type, whose sole idea was to protect their

* Colonel Sir Henry Streatfield, Grenadier Guards.

THE MILLIONAIRE'S WAGON

SOUTH AFRICAN WAR, OFFICERS' MESS

own country from invasion. I thought of this man lying there: what did he probably know about the political intrigue at Pretoria? What did he care about the gold mines around Johannesburg or the Jews who controlled them? His certainly was a just cause. I found myself wondering whether ours was.

A few miles further on I came across my own battalion acting as outposts for the Division. There I saw what looked like an enormous gipsy wagon, and was told that the battalion had captured it and that it belonged to Cornelius Jeppe and Julius Rissik, two South African millionaires who did not want in the least to fight against the English, but who, as they had to join up like any other Dutchman, had equipped themselves with every luxury possible. They were pointed out to me, seated near their wagon, which contained every kind of tinned delicacy imaginable: tongues, chicken, *pâté-de-foie-gras*, sardines, and so on; a number of varieties of tinned fruits and, the most important of all, a quantity of Ideal milk and cases of champagne. An order had been issued that anything captured was to be handed to the Provost-Marshal immediately, and it was suggested to me that the best thing I could do was to take the prisoners into Divisional Headquarters and report the capture of the wagon, the contents of which, by the time the Provost-Marshal came to claim them, would probably have been consumed. I was particularly told to come back to supper that night!

Messrs. Jeppe and Rissik, who could speak English fluently, followed me to the station at Graspan, where I reported the facts to the General. The only water obtainable for the thirst-stricken Division was from a well near the station, and no one had dared so far to drink it, as a rumour had gone forth that the Boers had poisoned it. This I heard when I arrived with the two prisoners; and somebody made the brilliant suggestion that, as they would probably be as thirsty as we were, they should be given the first drink of the water. The suggestion was adopted, and we all sat round them, watching the effects and pretending not to. One of the prisoners noticed our restrained curiosity and asked what it meant. When we thought that a decent interval had elapsed and they were still alive and not writhing on the ground, we told them. I never shall forget the look of horror on their faces and the way each man immediately put his hands to his stomach, but no ill results followed, and the water was drunk by the rest of the Division. As a matter of fact, an empty bag which had contained cyanide of potassium had actually been found near the well, and this started the rumour. It must have been a practical joke played by a facetious Hollander, and it certainly succeeded. Throughout the war the Boers played the game, and fought in a very gentlemanly fashion. Three years later I met Jeppe lunching at the Savoy, and told him I still had his razor strop.

The following day was a Sunday, and by mutual consent was a *non dies* so far as fighting was concerned! As arranged on the Saturday night, I got leave from the Divisional Head-quarters to spend a week-end with my battalion, and arrived to find my brother-officers gorging themselves on the contents of the millionaires' wagon. I too had the best meal I had had since leaving the ship.

Arthur Paget was one of the kindest men I have ever known. "George, you're looking worn out," he said to me that night. "I am, sir." "Then you shall sleep in my tent." His tent was a little shelter which he carried on his second charger, and it just held two. I crawled into my flea-bag about nine, and remembered nothing until I was wakened by the sun the following day. Putting my head out I saw a sentry, and asked him what he was doing there. He was a man of my own company whom I knew well, and he answered with a grin: "The Colonel put me here to see you were not disturbed." It was then about two o'clock in the afternoon.

A start was made on the Monday for Honeynest Kloof on the way to Modder River, which was the next point known to be occupied by the enemy in strength. The officer who was running the Divisional Staff Mess told me that they had run out of everything except ordinary rations, and I felt rather guilty when I considered the meal I had had the previous Saturday evening. " All right," I said, " I'll do a bit of foraging on one of the flanks." On the march I got hold of a couple of mounted orderlies and went to a farm which I felt pretty certain would be deserted. It was, except for some small pigs and turkeys, all of which were running about loose. The orderlies were both Lancers: one performed a most extraordinary pig-sticking exploit and the other lassoed the turkey-cock. That night at dinner, both the turkey and the pig having been much appreciated, the General said: " To-morrow at dawn we will go out with the cavalry and artillery, the information being that the Boers are holding an empty reservoir to the right of Modder River and that the rest of the place is unoccupied." This information was supplied by Rimington Scouts; that supplied by the 9th Lancers was to the effect that the whole town of Modder River was occupied, and this subsequently proved true.

The Division had been reinforced the day before by the 9th Brigade, under General Pole-Carew.* The two other brigades were ordered to advance on Modder River, the 9th being on the extreme left flank on the far side of the railway. About seven o'clock that morning I was sent to the two Brigadiers with orders to advance in attack formation, as the General himself was more than suspicious that Modder River was strongly held. No amount of shelling had persuaded the Boers to retire from the reservoir already mentioned. After I had delivered the message to the second Brigadier, I was returning across the front of the other brigade when suddenly a terrific fire was opened all along the river-bank, which was promptly responded to by the leading battalion of the first brigade, to whom the order had been given to extend. However, I rejoined the General without having been hit by either side, though this was one of the occasions when Toby, the pony, was seared by a bullet on his quarter.

* The late Sir R. Pole-Carew.

I was sent off again immediately to General Carew at the other side of the railway with orders to him to cross the ford west of Modder River Town and outflank the Boer position, as the other two brigades on his right were temporarily held up. I was not taking any risks this time in the way of cross-fire, but went carefully round and delivered my message to General Carew, who, cheery fellow that he was, said: " Go back, my boy, and tell the General we'll turn the ——s out ! "

On my way back I had to cross the railway, and as I drew near it I saw what looked like a large grey mole-hill. When I came up to it I found it was the stomach of Mr. Bennett Stanford, the special correspondent of the *Daily Telegraph*, who was lying full length on his back in a shallow pit from which plate-layers had been taking ballast. I warned him that he was only partially under cover.

It was with difficulty that I found the General this time, and I got cursed for bringing a pony near where he was, not by him—he was another person who didn't know fear and always exposed himself unnecessarily—but by one of the senior staff officers, who asked me what the hell I meant by drawing fire on the group and risking the General's life. I fancy it was his own life he was worrying about. I gave my pony to an orderly and lay down obediently.

When we eventually moved off, the pony was nowhere to be found: the orderly had got the wind up and had gone off on it. For the first time I had forgotten to fill my water-bottle, and that was my undoing. When the General and the rest of the staff departed I had neither water nor pony, and started looking for the latter. Some hours later I was discovered by Douglas Loch * wandering about in a half-crazed condition, having been overcome by the sun.

I was sent down to hospital at De Aar the following day, where I remained ten days. When I felt better, I was bored, and determined to find my own way back to the Division, without waiting for a medical board. I walked

* General Lord Loch.

A NINETEENTH-CENTURY TRENCH

MODDER RIVER BRIDGE DESTROYED

out of hospital one morning, got on the first train I saw going north, and eventually arrived at Orange River. There was another train just starting for Modder River in charge of an Engineer officer, with whom I got into the guard's van. When we reached the Orange River Bridge the train stopped, and the stoker, a Royal Engineer, came down from the engine to tell us that the driver, evidently a Boer sympathiser, had got off and disappeared into the veldt. The stoker had done nothing but stoking before he joined the army, and then only a traction engine. Now was my opportunity. I volunteered my services as driver. The Engineer officer reluctantly took me at my word, though I am sure he felt nervous, and I boarded the locomotive. Difficulty lay in front of us, as the gradient up from the bridge was very steep and the freight train a very heavy one. There was a siding at the top of the bank into which I could put half the train, though that meant the guard's van being in the middle. Little trifles like that, however, could not be considered. After concluding the shunting operations, we started. To my horror I found, on arriving at Graspan, that there was no water to fill our tank, in which precious little was left. Up to within three miles of Modder River the climb was a steep one, after which there was a clear run down to the bridge. This bridge the Boers had demolished, and it had not yet been repaired; consequently there were a lot of trains waiting on temporary sidings until they could cross the river, and thus there were inevitably a number of what are known as 'dead' engines. I realised, therefore, that if we did not reach Modder River we should block the whole of the main line from Orange River to the Front, and it would be difficult to get supplies to the troops. The question was whether we had sufficient water to get to the highest point; after that it would be plain sailing. I decided to risk it, and started again. Freight trains in South Africa are fitted with a vacuum brake which can be operated from the guard's van; and at Honeynest Kloof the guard of the train, not realising our predicament, applied the brakes in order to drop out a bag of salt for a detachment of troops there, which he could perfectly well have done without stopping the train. Matters looked serious: there was not a drop of water in the tank and very little showing on the boiler guage. My stoker was a splendid fellow; I told him the position and all he said was: "I'm game, sir. We can only be blown up once!" Eventually we just managed to crawl to the top of the bank, and no furnace was ever raked out quicker by the driver and stoker than the furnace of that locomotive.

I little thought that the next time I should be on the footplate in circumstances of emergency would be in my own country during the General Strike of 1926, when I drove a Great Western Railway locomotive. After the strike I received an interesting letter from the Locomotive Foreman at Kidderminster, which read:

> "Now that the strike is over and we have gained such a glorious victory, I thought I would like to thank you personally and to say how pleased I am that you went through the period without mishap. Half my men are in, and it is most amusing to hear their comments on you. It was one of the biggest shocks they ever had to see you coming into Kidderminster like an old veteran. They have always thought no one could drive an engine except themselves, and to think you did so—especially passenger trains—without hitting anything, has quietened them down very much . . ."

I had only been at Modder River a few days before I became ill again. I had received a proper telling-off from the General for having dared to leave hospital without permission, and this time I was sent not to De Aar, but to Cape Town, and eventually to England. My passage home was made on the *Pannonia*, a Cunarder which had gained notoriety only a short time before, having been given up as lost for ten days. It transpired that one of her boilers had become adrift in a heavy sea. She still had the same Captain, and his accounts of the awful time he went through during that period were very thrilling.

The M.O. in charge of the sick and wounded on board was a Naval surgeon who had a passion for pulling out teeth. He never gave an anæsthetic: presumably he had none; so that the yells we used to hear most mornings were alarming until we got used to them.

When I reached home I was desperately ill, the sunstroke having in some unaccountable way affected my heart, and I was not allowed to take any exercise. I amused myself by making a miniature railway in the garden at Ruthin!

On my arrival in England, and before my illness took a serious turn, I was sent for by the Prince of Wales to Marlborough House, to whom I recounted my short but exciting experiences in South Africa. I told him that my general impression of the battles I had seen was that they were more like dangerous field-days at home, and that the British, up till then, lacked the mobility of the Boers, and were in consequence severely handicapped.

Chapter X

MATRIMONY AND BUSINESS

During the summer of 1899 Lady Randolph and I had been about a good deal together and people began to talk. It was on this account that before I left for South Africa I was asked for, and gave, a verbal undertaking to Colonel Paget that I would not marry or become engaged before leaving. In August of that year I had been invited on board the *Britannia* at Cowes, and the Prince of Wales took the opportunity of taking me aside and pointing out to me the inadvisability of my marrying a woman so much my senior. He admitted that this was the only argument against our engagement, told me that no one could possibly say what might happen within the next three months, and begged me to do nothing in a hurry. " If there *is* war," he added, " you're sure to go out. There'll be time enough to consider it when you come back."

As a matter of fact, Jennie and I had discussed it many a time, and she had always said that the difference in our ages made marriage out of the question, but after nearly a year's separation she changed her mind.

Jennie was a very remarkable woman. She dressed beautifully, and her taste, not only in clothes, but in everything, was of the best. She had a marvellous *flair* for decorating a house, and there are many houses in London which, thanks to her, have a *cachet* of their own, and which bear to this day the unmistakable proofs of her artistic talent. Like many well-bred American women, she had the will and the power to adapt herself to her immediate surroundings. She was equally at home having a serious conversation with a distinguished statesman, or playing on a golf-course. A great reader, she remembered much of what she had read, and that made her a brilliant conversationalist, but although gifted with extreme intelligence, she was not brilliant in the deepest sense of the word. She was not a genius.

Possessed of great driving force in matters which interested her, she was a good organiser, as was proved by the success she made of the *Maine* hospital ship in the South African War. Her greatest undertaking was the " Shakespeare's England " Exhibition at Earl's Court. This originated for raising funds for a National Theatre; and, as is so often the fate of schemes of this kind, artistically it was a success, financially a ghastly failure.

Her book of memoirs was a best-seller. Cleverly but cautiously written, there was not a line in it to which any of her many friends could take exception. I take it to my credit that it was I who persuaded her to write those memoirs and prophesied the success which they undoubtedly had. She also edited the *Anglo-Saxon Review*, which, from a literary and artistic standpoint, was a success, but over which she lost a considerable amount of money.

In money matters she was without any sense of proportion. The value of money meant nothing to her: what counted with her were the things she got for money, not the amount she had to pay for them. If something of beauty attracted her, she just had to have it; it never entered her head to stop and think how she was going to pay for it. During all the years we lived together the only serious misunderstandings which ever took place between us were over money matters. Her extravagance was her only fault, and, with her nature, the most understandable, and therefore the most forgivable.

During the whole of that winter she was on board the hospital ship *Maine*, and did not return to England until May 1900. By this time I had rejoined the Third Battalion of my regiment, and had been sent to Pirbright as a musketry instructor to recruits and reservists. Consuelo Duchess of Manchester * had taken a house near Windsor for Ascot

* *née* Consuelo Yznaga.

that year, and invited me there to stay; and I used to hack a pony over every morning so as to arrive at Pirbright in time for parade, and return for the races in the afternoon.

On the Thursday morning of that week my engagement was announced in the *Daily Telegraph*, and I received a peremptory order from the officer commanding my battalion, Colonel Dalrymple Hamilton, to go up and see him. He told me at the interview that if I married Lady Randolph I should have to leave the regiment. Considering that she had a host of friends, including himself, and was liked by everybody, and that there was no rule in the regiment against subalterns marrying, I considered such an ultimatum outrageous and saw red. If I had had any doubts as to the wisdom of what I was about to do they were blown to the four winds by what I considered nothing less than a piece of unwarrantable interference, and it made me obstinate. I dashed off in a hansom to the War Office and sent in my name to the Adjutant-General, who was then Sir Evelyn Wood, whom I just knew. A few minutes later I caught him going out of his office and he said: "I've no time at the moment unless you can go with me in a cab to where I am lunching, and tell me what I can do for you." On our way down Piccadilly I told him what had happened, and asked whether it was in accordance with Queen's Regulations that an officer should be told to leave his regiment because he wished to marry a woman admittedly older than himself, but of whom nothing else could be said except in her favour. Sir Evelyn reassured me, and promised to do what he could to help me.

Some three days later I was sent for again, this time to the regimental orderly room to see Colonel Fludyer, who commanded the regiment, and who poured out the vials of his wrath upon me for having dared to go to a man whom he described as " the enemy of the Brigade of Guards " —why, heaven knows! He made it quite clear to me that my presence in the regiment would no longer be desired or expected. I felt more angry than ever, and after consultation with Jennie wrote to the Prince of Wales, asking

Jennie Randolph Churchill

if I might have an interview. When I saw him and told him all about it, he came to the point at once: "Is it your intention to make soldiering your profession for the rest of your life?" he said. "If it is, then I advise you to sit tight. If, however, it is not, why make enemies of men who have been your friends and who probably will continue to be your friends after all this has blown over? My advice to you is to go on half-pay for six months or a year, look around and see if you can find something else to do, and then make up your mind at the expiration of the time."

As I had never really intended to make the army a life-long profession, I took his advice, and the following day applied to be placed on half-pay. The irony of it was that a week later I had a telegram from several brother-officers of my old battalion in South Africa, wishing me luck and telling me on no account to leave the regiment.

Jennie and I were married early in July that year. Both my father and mother had done their utmost to prevent it, which was quite natural on their part; but I well remember the feeling of intense regret at none of my family being present when I was married.

After a honeymoon spent partly at Broughton Castle, Oxfordshire, and partly in Belgium and France, and a round of visits in Scotland, we returned to London in October. Now that I had practically left the army and had only a small income, it became necessary for me to seek a new profession. The question was: which? Soon after our return I met Sir Ernest Cassel at Lady Lister Kaye's house, and found myself next to him after dinner. It was he who broached the subject and asked me what I thought of doing with myself. I told him that the administrative side of an electrical engineering concern rather appealed to me. "Not the city?" he asked. I replied that the prospect of going on a half-commission basis to a firm of stockbrokers and touting for orders from my friends had no allurements for me. He thought a moment and said: "There are many young men of your class who

121

should never go east of Temple Bar. Perhaps you are one of them." He suggested that some technical knowledge would be to my advantage, and went on to tell me that he was interested in the Central London Railway, and would put me in touch with the Managing Director of the British Thomson-Houston Company, the contractors for that line which was nearing completion.

Up to 1914 I saw a great deal of Cassel. I was friendly, but never intimate with him. I doubt whether many men ever were intimate with him; his was not a personality to invite intimacy; but with all his cold, hard-headed, hard-hearted business nature he had many kindly feelings. I believe that neither money nor social position meant anything to him beyond the power they gave him. Power meant everything to him. His friendship with King Edward was, so far as he, Cassel, was concerned, founded on his love of power; it helped to that end. In his speech he was curt and to the point. I never heard him speak on any subject with which he was not thoroughly conversant, but when he did talk he was inclined to lay down the law and resent argument. To a woman, if she were pretty and he liked her, he was suavity itself. He never forgot a slight and, like many of his race, he was extremely sensitive.

Many years after I first met him I was in Paris, and was lunching one day at the Ritz when a waiter gave me a note from a well-known and very handsome English lady who was also lunching there. In it she asked me to go to tea at her flat that afternoon, saying that it was important. I sent back a message that I would go. When I arrived, my hostess, whose husband, it must be mentioned, had recently got into serious financial difficulties, asked me to witness a document which she handed to me, telling me at the same time to read it. I found it to be a mortgage to Sir Ernest Cassel for £10,000, the security being the lady's pearls. I handed it back to her saying: "It seems perfectly in order," and added some banality about being sorry she had to lose her pearls. I confess I was rather bewildered at being asked to tea to witness a document which any servant could have witnessed equally well. "You don't understand," she said. "I want your advice. Am I to sign it?" I felt completely in the dark, and said so. "One of the stipulations Cassel makes," she explained, "is that I am to continue wearing the pearls. I don't want to bind myself to him body and soul."

"I understand," I said. "Well, if you have any qualms, get the pearls copied and put the real ones in a Bank. It will be time enough to tell him you're wearing sham ones if he suggests a *quid pro quo*." I witnessed her signature.

Three months later I saw her at Newmarket, and she was wearing pearls. She never referred to the subject, so I naturally did not ask her whether they were real or otherwise.

Soon after my first conversation with Cassel I became one of the non-paid staff of the British Thomson-Houston Company, who were also at this time contractors for the Glasgow Corporation Power Station, which was then in course of construction. I lived at Troon—I couldn't stand Glasgow—and went in every day. Looking back, I am convinced that Cassel's idea of sending me there was to find out whether I really meant to take up a business career seriously or not. Perhaps he thought that if I could stick putting on overalls and acting as a sort of unpaid plumber's mate to the highly-paid experts who were building this vast power unit, I might be worthy of help. He had been through the mill himself, and I imagine he felt that nobody could be of use unless he had some sort of similar experience. I learnt quite a lot about the technical side of commercial electricity, but it was through the late Mr. George Herring that I went into the administrative side of it.

George Herring was a very remarkable man, and made a fortune on the turf: not, it need hardly be said, by backing horses. He was one of the original promoters of the British Electric Traction Company, which had been formed for the purpose of erecting and running tramways in various large towns in the British Isles. He was also a friend of

Cassel, and between the two it was arranged that I should meet Mr. Emil Garcke, who was Managing Director of this company.

It is possible that there was no more brilliant business executive brain working in England at that time. Had he wished, Garcke could have had the various material rewards which come to many successful business men, but his was not a pushing nature; titles meant nothing to him, money less, except in so far as it brought the ordinary comforts of life. The one thing that he loathed was idleness. I shall never forget my first interview with him. He was prepared to find in me a useless sprig of aristocracy, out of a job and not particularly wanting one, who at the same time wished his friends to consider that he was ' something in the city.' Garcke looked then as he does now: his hair was quite white, and under bushy eyebrows were a pair of the most penetrating steel-grey eyes I have ever looked into. He could not afford to quarrel with either George Herring or Cassel, and therefore consented to give me a brief interview.

" Good morning. Sit down," he greeted me. " I know from Mr. Herring what you have come about. The best thing I can do is to offer you a seat on the Board of the Potteries Electric Traction Company, which operates the tramways at Stoke-on-Trent and the Potteries towns. It is one of our biggest concerns, but the fees are only £50 a year. Good-bye."

I was taken aback and replied: " It isn't a question of money, Mr. Garcke. I want to learn something about the business. Attending a Board meeting once a month would teach me nothing. I want an office in this building. Can it be arranged? "

His whole manner changed, and he at once became sympathetic. In three months' time I was chairman of the company and of several others, and was also elected a member of the Advisory Committee, and a director of the parent company itself a few years later. In connection with my election to the Advisory Committee an expensive incident occurred. There were only ten members, and competition was severe. I took it as, and it was, a compliment to have been elected after so short a probation, and therefore felt it was absolutely necessary for me to be present at the first meeting. I was motoring up from a visit to Sir Ernest Cassel at Newmarket when my car broke down, fortunately near a station. I knew that Garcke would be not only angry, but offended at my non-appearance, so I did the only possible thing; chartered a special train, which cost me about twenty-five per cent. of the year's fees.

Many years later, after I had disregarded Cassel's advice and gone into finance in the city, my firm crashed, shortly after the outbreak of the War, and I found myself in a very serious position. I had to resign my directorships, including that of the British Electric Traction Company, and I received from Garcke the most charming letter one man could write to another. At the end of it he said:

"I have suffered many vicissitudes myself, and have learned to look at the troubles of life philosophically. My view is that the best in a man is not brought out except by adversity, and that the real test of a man is how he passes through an adverse crisis, *not* in how far or how high he can scale without difficulties. And for my part I would rather trust to a guide who has climbed and fallen than to one who has never ventured."

Up to now, the only men with whom I had come in contact in subordinate positions had been those who had served under me as private soldiers or non-commissioned officers, and who, when given an order, executed it as a matter of course. I was now to come in contact with employees of the companies that I directed, and although many of them were old soldiers, it did not in the least follow that they executed orders with the same alacrity as they had in the army. I had, for the first time in my life, to deal with trade unions, and I was soon to discover that the feelings of the men towards their employers largely depended upon the local branch leader of their trade union. The first dispute I had to deal with was at Stoke-on-Trent, where the local leader was a born agitator. I had heard for some time that he had been spreading dissension amongst the men, who were receiving the standard rate of wages. He asked to see me, and I replied that I and the manager would prefer to see him with three representatives of the men themselves. At the interview he started to make a speech just as though he had been addressing six hundred instead of six men. I realised that discussion with him was useless, and that he was prepared to veto anything I suggested, so I told the three other members of the deputation that I would ask the secretary of their union, who lived in Manchester, to attend with them. This gentleman arrived a few days later, a very different type from the other. We settled the whole question to the satisfaction of both parties inside of an hour, and he subsequently came to lunch with me at the hotel. I told him I had realised that any attempt to arrive at a settlement with the local leader would have been futile, and gave my reasons. His reply was illuminating. "You see the difficulties that a union has to contend with," he said, "where the men, carried away by the verbosity of one extreme individual, elect him as their branch representative; a man whom we, at head office, know is simply out to make trouble, not so much for the benefit of the men he represents as for his own aggrandisement."

I always found afterwards that, provided one went to headquarters, dealing with a union was perfectly straightforward, and that the demands were, in nine cases out of ten, reasonable and capable of settlement.

I took more interest in the Potteries company than in any of the other companies I directed, probably because it was the first to which I had been appointed, but also because geographically it lent itself to so many interesting developments of which electric traction was capable. It was there that the carrying of parcels on the tramway system was first introduced, although so short-sighted were the officials at the Board of Trade that it was with the greatest difficulty that we induced them to allow parcels vans to be affixed as trailers to the electric cars.

It was also in the Potteries, five-and-twenty years ago, that the first attempt was made to utilise motor omnibuses as feeders to the tramway system. I had many lengthy, though friendly, arguments with my co-directors before they agreed to this experiment, and it was laughed at by many of the Boards of other companies. Garcke was with me in theory, as was his son Mr. Sidney Garcke, whole-heartedly. The latter is now chairman of the biggest motor omnibus company in the British Isles. Five-and-twenty years ago the idea was as sound as it is now, but unfortunately no motor-bus had been designed which was in any way reliable. Like most of us who drive motor-cars nowadays, I loathe trams, but I am under no delusions as to their speedy disappearance from the streets. In large cities during the rush hours they will, owing to their enormous carrying capacity, beat the motor-bus every time.

Chapter XI

EDWARDIAN SOCIETY

My wife had a host of friends in London, whom I soon got to know and who were exceedingly kind to me; and thus I became an Edwardian, in the sense that I was a member of that particular set in society with which King Edward associated himself, a set with which a young officer in the Guards or the son of a country gentleman living in the country was not likely, in the ordinary course of events, to become particularly intimate.

Those were wonderful days. Taxation and the cost of living were low; money was freely spent and wealth was everywhere in evidence. Moreover it was possessed largely by the nicest people, who entertained both in London and in the country. Dinners were Gargantuan affairs, far too long, but although there were innumerable courses, the foreign fashion of serving innumerable wines had disappeared. It was very seldom that sherry was even offered with the soup. Champagne, port and old brandy were the order of the day, or rather, night. One or two hostesses, notably Lady Hindlip,* all the Rothschilds, and Mrs. Ronnie Greville, had wonderful cooks, but on the whole the cooking was indifferent and meretricious, though the same could not be said of the wines. The champagne vintages from 'eighty to 'eighty-seven were infinitely superior to anything since produced. They were also considerably more potent.

Talking of cooking, I remember once being asked to a men's dinner-party by the late Lord Rothschild. I was in the city at the time, and the guests included all the biggest

* Minnie Lady Hindlip.

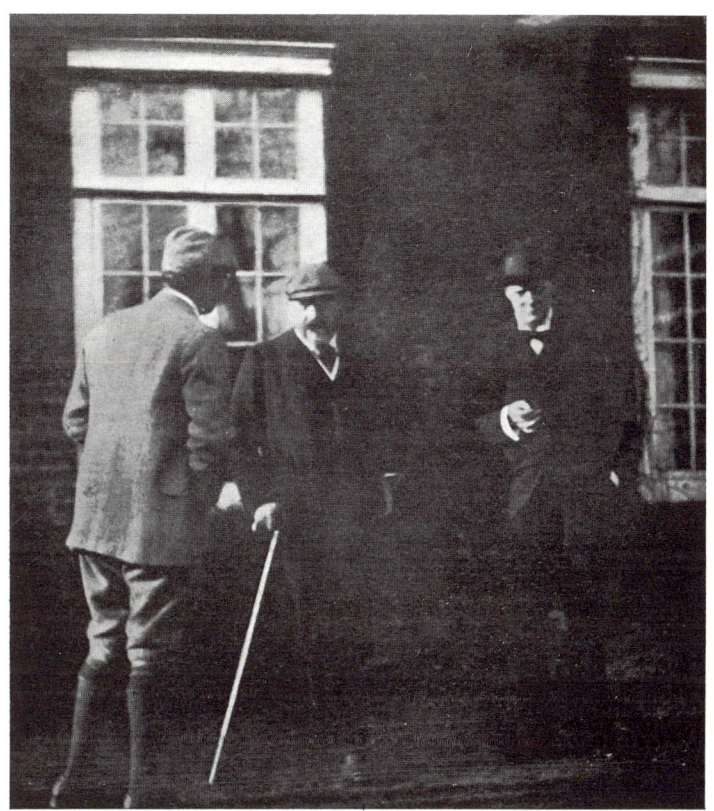
SIR E. CASSEL AND WINSTON CHURCHILL AT SALISBURY HALL

financiers, amongst whom were Sir Ernest Cassel, Lord Revelstoke and several others. To my utter astonishment I found myself seated on my host's right, and wondered why I had been given this place of honour. I was soon to discover. I noticed that in front of him were placed a plate of biscuits and a tumbler of milk. When we came to the fish, which was one of his chef's famous dishes, he asked me what it tasted like; and as I proceeded to do my best to explain, he took a bite of biscuit and a mouthful of milk with every sentence, saying: " Ah, yes, I know exactly." I then realised why I had been placed on his right: poor man, being on the strictest diet himself, he was eating by proxy, and I was his taster! He could not very well ask either Lord Revelstoke or Sir Ernest Cassel to act in that capacity: that was the task of the junior member of the company.

Jennie once had an odd conversation at a dinner-party where she found herself seated next to the Japanese Ambassador. They were discussing the literature of the two countries, and she inquired whether the Japanese had proverbs. Receiving an affirmative reply, she asked him the equivalent of ' Penny wise and pound foolish.' His Excellency thought for a moment before answering, then said: " The literal translation of the Japanese equivalent is: ' The man who goes to bed early to save candles gets twins.' "

Women's dresses at dinner-parties were very elaborate, and quantities of jewellery were worn. Those were the days of tiaras and stomachers. The blaze of jewels displayed at the opera was really amazing. My first visit to the opera had been many years previously, when I was invited to the box of the old Duchess of Montrose by a girl friend who was a relation of hers. The first thing the old lady asked me when I arrived was: " Do you like music, young man? " I said I did. " I don't," she answered—" at any rate, not this! " and promptly went to sleep.

Lady de Grey,* a great friend of Jennie, used to have

* The late Marchioness of Ripon.

parties at her house at Combe every week-end. Jean and Edouard de Reszke were also great friends of hers, both delightful fellows who used to behave like children, and loved a joke. Edouard had a long beard very carefully combed, and anointed, I imagine, with some unguent which had the effect of stiffening it. Whenever he smiled, which was frequently, his beard used to open at the bottom exactly like the claws of a lobster. One day, when it was well open, I could not resist the temptation to put my finger in and say " Casse-noisette ! " Afterwards, whenever he saw me, he used to smile, solemnly put his finger in his beard, and re-echo " Casse-noisette ! "

A friend of mine, Willie Lowe, went one evening to the service at the Carmelite Chapel. He came back to White's Club wild with excitement at having listened to what he described as the finest tenor he'd ever heard, and, full of the idea of discovering who the prodigy was, suggested that he would find any money that was necessary to have him " properly taught," and prophesied the enormous success the unknown would have at the Opera. He made inquiries, and the unknown turned out to be Jean de Reszke.

One Sunday we went to the de Greys to listen to Reynaldo Hahn, who had brought over with him a small but exquisite chamber orchestra. The only flaw, to my mind, was that he seldom played anything but his own music. On this particular occasion I had a violent fit of hay fever, and was unfortunately seated a long way from either the window or the door. I began to sneeze. After about the tenth sneeze, Hahn stopped playing and glared at me until, still sneezing, I clambered over the people next to me and made the best of my way out on to the lawn.

On another occasion a man who subsequently became a famous diplomat, but was not fond of music, was sitting in the room where Hahn was conducting his orchestra. The latter suddenly stopped and exclaimed that there was some-one in the room who was antipathetic to him. Not in the least abashed, the non-music-lover rose and went out.

Another recollection is of Kreisler playing at Combe soon

after he was married. His wife sat close to him, and he seemed to play for her alone. To him there might not have been anyone else in the room; and she, on her part, appeared hypnotised by his playing. Her eyes closed and her whole body swayed, as if she were about to faint.

The music one heard at concerts and in private houses during the season was exceptionally good, and I shall always maintain that as a drawing-room singer there was no one to touch Gilibert. He used to sing old French ballads in exactly the way they should be sung, and they formed a wonderful contrast to his singing of the part of " Danceiro " in Carmen, one of his favourite rôles.

It is said that sport and luxury flourished in the decade between 1840 and 1850; my father used to tell me that a similar state of affairs existed between 1870 and 1880; but I doubt whether in any period of history of the modern world, except perhaps that immediately preceding the French Revolution, has there been such a display of wealth and luxury as during King Edward's reign. Not even the death duties brought in by Sir William Harcourt a few years previously, or Mr. Lloyd George's rabid anti-wealth speeches at Limehouse and elsewhere, acted as a deterrent to extravagance. If Socialism was in the air, no one, in the class I refer to, bothered to think about it. The possibility of a Socialist Government was the last thing that entered into anyone's mind.

As was natural in the circumstances, money counted for a great deal, but not more than, if as much as, it does now. On the other hand, there were far fewer *nouveaux riches* in evidence. Heads of old county families were still able to keep open house and entertain their friends. Estates which had been for centuries in one family were still intact, and there were few lovely old places derelict and merely the haunts of ghosts and bygone memories, such as there are now. Life was free-and-easy up to a point, but there was much more attention paid to the idea of what people might say; perhaps, therefore, we were a little more discreet. Possibly owing to their upbringing, the young men and women of that generation had less self-confidence and, in consequence, less individuality; but we hadn't that cold-blooded wish to experiment with life in all its aspects that is so often seen now.

Although I have suggested that money counted for a great deal, it also went a great deal further. A bachelor in London with a thousand a year was comparatively well off. He could get a very good flat in Mayfair, to hold himself and his servant, for a hundred and fifty pounds per annum. Dinner at his club cost him about four shillings, and any good restaurant would have been prepared to provide an excellent dinner, if he chose to give one to his friends, at ten and sixpence a head. The best tailor in Savile Row would make a suit of evening clothes for eleven guineas, and a morning suit for about eight guineas; dress shirts could be bought for ten and sixpence. The greatest difference, however, was in the price of really good boots and shoes, which cost, roughly, half what they now do.

On the other hand, my lady friends tell me that, pro rata to the general cost of living, their ordinary clothing, apart from elaborate costumes, costs considerably less than before the War. Presumably this is accounted for by the scantiness of the amount they wear.

The servant problem was never acute, and the types of man or woman obtainable not only knew their job, but were quite prepared to carry it out for the wages they received. A first-rate cook could be got for fifty pounds a year and a butler for eighty. Service flats and living in hotels were almost unheard of, except for foreign visitors, chiefly Americans, who undoubtedly introduced the system into this country. Old family servants were the rule and not the exception, and they took a personal interest in the welfare of their master and mistress and of their offspring, if there were any. I am convinced that in many cases their wages were, to them, a secondary consideration. But I imagine that the gossip and intrigue which went on in the servants' hall and housekeeper's room then were no better than at present. A friend of mine asked his valet, who had been with him for a number of years, how they amused themselves downstairs of an evening. " Well, my lord," he answered, " one of our favourite amusements is piecing together the letters found in the wastepaper baskets in the morning—better than any jig-saw puzzle, I can assure your lordship, and much more entertaining! "

The advent of motor-cars coincided with that of the custom of week-end parties during the summer months. I worked hard all the week, and every Saturday Jennie and I used to go somewhere. We were constant visitors to Blenheim, where the Duke and Duchess of Marlborough entertained largely. It was there that I first met that brilliant person Lord Birkenhead, who was then F. E. Smith, still called " F. E." by his friends. One evening after dinner, Marlborough happened to be talking about his aunts, and mentioned Lady Wimborne,* and it was then that F. E. told us of the first job he ever had after leaving Oxford. Lady Wimborne was head of an Evangelical society whose object was to suppress anything in the nature of ' High Church,' whether spiritual or material. This society had offices in many of the big towns of England, and F. E., who was then a briefless barrister living in Birkenhead, accepted the position of secretary to the local branch which had been opened in Liverpool. Always a lover of art, he one day came across, in a picture-dealer's shop, an old Italian painting of the Madonna and Child, which he promptly bought for thirty shillings and hung up in the office. In due course, Lady Wimborne, on her annual tour of inspection of the various branches, called upon F. E. and, looking round the room, noticed the abomination. " Young man," she said, " what is the meaning of that? "

" Oh, that! " said F. E. airily. " Rather nice, isn't it? I picked it up in a dealer's here, and the experts tell me it's quite good. What do *you* think of it? "

" What do *I* think of it? " she answered, fixing her lorgnette upon him. " Don't you realise that you are an officer of a society specially ordained by Providence to

* The late Cornelia Lady Wimborne.

suppress all images and pictures of an idolatrous nature? "

For, I imagine, one of the few occasions in his life, F. E. was speechless, and he lost his job.

Another distinguished politician whom I met for the second time in my life shortly after I was married was the late Mr. Joseph Chamberlain. The first time had been when I was seven years old and he had come to Ruthin to speak on the Reform Bill of 1881 at Denbigh. I remember sitting on his knee and his telling me about a parrot, and being taken subsequently to the meeting which he addressed. It was a hot summer's day, and the stuffiness of the tent so overcame me that I was sick over my neighbour, and was put to bed at the Bull Inn.

The second occasion was at Chatsworth. One evening I came into the smoking-room and found Mr. Chamberlain alone. He asked me if I contemplated going into politics, and when I replied in the negative, he asked why, as my father had been an M.P. He seemed astonished when I said that the latter had done it more from a sense of duty than from any political ambition, and that I had gathered no encouragement from him. He asked if I played chess. " Sometimes," I answered, and then he went on to say that politics are very like chess: you are always trying to anticipate your opponent's move and counter it.

" Surely sometimes in politics," I said, " your opponent's move may be for the good of the country? " and cited his own crusade on Tariff Reform which he was just initiating. It has always been a source of regret to me that two or three other men came into the room at that moment and that my question was never answered.

As a matter of fact, my father loathed politics. He described them as a dirty game, and used to tell the story of a man who, during a General Election, had been speaking for a candidate who was a friend of his, and was asked late at night to succour a stranger whose car had broken down outside his house. The stranger in question turned out to be his friend's opponent. However, he brought him in and gave him lodging, and as they were going up to bed, said: " I wonder what —— would say if he knew I was entertaining his rival to-night? Funny, isn't it?" The other man replied: " My dear sir, if you take away the humorous side of politics, there's nothing left but the damned dishonesty!"

Another house where we often stayed for week-ends was Halton, belonging to the late Mr. Alfred Rothschild. It was more than a house, it was a palace, especially as regards the value of its contents; for it was full of the most wonderful pictures and furniture, the latter mostly French. Those who did not motor from London travelled by a special train from Baker Street to Wendover. On arriving at Halton, we found a most wonderful tea laid out, despite the fact that we were expected to eat an enormous dinner at 8.15. One dish which we were always given in July amused me by the naivety of its description; it was called *Poussins Haltonais*, and consisted of young pheasants who had had their necks wrung, quite illegal to kill, but excellent to eat.

Alfred Rothschild always had a private orchestra, which played after tea and dinner. Latterly, in addition, he provided a circus in which he used to act as ring-master, dressed in a beautiful blue frock-coat and lavender kid gloves, and armed with a whip, which he used to crack benignly. The real master of the circus was a bovine-looking individual who certainly had a knack of training animals, and who was doubtless in receipt of a high salary. There were dogs and ponies and—a thing which I had never seen before or since—trained cocks and hens.

The routine of Sundays at Halton never varied. We saw little of our host in the morning, as, despite the fact that they saw each other every day in the week, he was usually closeted with his elder brother, Lord Rothschild, who rode over from Tring. After a huge luncheon, those who were capable of it played tennis, and at about half-past four tiny carriages drawn by dear little ponies, each attended by a diminutive groom in blue livery, were brought round for the use of the ladies, while the rest of us walked up a steep hill to a châlet, from which there was a glorious view. There was another sumptuous tea spread out, and we were shown the pack of black-and-white King Charles's spaniels. After tea, the more sensible members went for a walk to overcome the effects of lunch and prepare for dinner; those less sensible walked down the hill and played bridge till dressing time.

One day Sir Edgar Vincent * said to his host: " Alfred, you ought to have a golf course here." " My dear Edgar," was the reply, " it shall be done." About a month later I was again at Halton, and on my way up from the station noticed, in some uncut hay-fields near the house, nine round mowed patches, each with a red flag stuck in the middle. Poor Alfred! He had no idea of golf, nor, apparently, had his bailiff, and he seemed quite hurt when no one volunteered to go out and play.

I am sure Alfred Rothschild had not an enemy in the world, and his friends were legion. He was one of the most generous men I have ever known. One evening after dinner I was playing bridge, and he was standing behind my chair. I happened to say: " What an excellent cigar this is, Mr. Alfred."

" You smoke cigars, George? "

" Yes, indeed I do," I replied, and thought no more about it. A few days later a parcel arrived from New Court † containing three hundred of the largest and choicest cigars.

Another delightful place to which we used to go for week-end parties was Reigate Priory, which was at that time leased to Mr. and Mrs. Ronnie Greville. Their parties were always amusing, as they contained a leaven of interesting intellectual people as well as those who moved in Edwardian society. One of the most entertaining of them, though I doubt very much whether the guests looked upon him as such, was Mrs. Greville's father, old Mr. McEwan, a Scottish millionaire. A little frail old gentleman with a beard, he gave one the impression that his one idea

* Lord D'Abernon. † The office of the house of Rothschild.

was to obliterate himself, although it was indirectly through him that such luxury as one experienced there was possible. I liked the old man immensely, and often used to go for walks with him. One day I was explaining to him that my sole motive for having gone into business, apart from having something to do, was to endeavour to make sufficient money to pay off the mortgages on my family estates. He stopped in his walk and looked at me with his head on one side, and, in the Scottish accent which was natural to him, he said: "A most praiseworthy object, young man. I hope ye'll succeed, but I doot ye will."

"Why?" I asked.

"Some men are born to make money, it just comes natural to them; others never will. Maybe ye're one of the latter."

I felt rather crestfallen.

"I've worked hard all my life," he went on, "but it's been an easy thing for me to become rich, I just couldna help it; and the only pleasure it gives me is the thought that I'm able to give pleasure to others. But money doesn't necessarily come from hard work."

I thought of Cassel's remark about men who should never go east of Temple Bar, and thought how strange it was that two millionaires should have said practically the same thing. I realise now how true it is that in order for a man to make money he must have a natural *flair* for it.

As chairman of the Potteries Electric Traction Company, my visits to Stoke-on-Trent were naturally frequent. The Grand Duke Michael of Russia was at that time living at Keele Hall, about three miles from Newcastle-under-Lyme. Both he and his wife, Countess Torby, were extremely kind to me, and I had *carte blanche* to go there whenever I had to visit the Potteries. Although situated within a short distance of the manufacturing district, Keele Hall itself, which belonged to Mr. Ralph Sneyd, might have been miles away, so entirely was it in the country.

The Grand Duke was a born autocrat, and never forgot the respect which was due to his rank. In many ways he was an absolute child. Once he got an idea into his head,

137

no matter how wrong it was, nothing in the world would ever get it out. It will be remembered that owing to his morganatic marriage he had been forbidden access to Russia, and it had become an obsession with him that, although he was allowed a large income from his own estates in that country, its Government did everything it could to make life as unpleasant as possible for him in the country which he had chosen as his domicile. As a matter of fact, beyond his exile, the only stipulation the Russian Government made was that he should not wear his Russian uniform at Court, and this was subsequently rescinded through the intervention of King Edward.

On one occasion when I visited Keele, he took me into his room and proceeded to explain to me how he had been the recipient of further insults from his country. It seemed that the post of Lord High Steward of Newcastle-under-Lyme had become vacant. Newcastle-under-Lyme is one of the oldest boroughs in the kingdom, and this office is a relic of bygone days. What the Lord High Steward's duties were in the past I have no idea, but so far as the present is concerned they are *non est*, and the position is purely a sinecure. The appointment is made by the Mayor and Corporation, who, doubtless appreciating the honour of having so notable a resident near by, and mindful of possible pecuniary advantages from the point of view of subscriptions to local charities, had offered the post to the Grand Duke, who accepted it. About a fortnight after his acceptance, he told me, he received an intimation from the Town Clerk that he regretted it was not in their power to offer the post to a foreigner, which was undoubtedly the case. The Grand Duke, however, was convinced that the Russian Government, hearing of, as he put it, " the important post " which had been offered him under the British Government, had put a spoke in his wheel and requested that the offer should be withdrawn. I explained to him that I was certain that what the Town Clerk had written was correct, and that the offer had been made without proper consideration; but he was obdurate, and was in fact extremely annoyed with me for having dared to question his view of the matter.

Although he lived in England upwards of thirty years, and played golf for the same period, it was curious that he never improved in either the game or the English language. He had his own way of thinking out and doing things in life, and no amount of argument or teaching could alter it.

A few months after the death of Queen Victoria, the Grand Duke gave a large week-end party for King Edward, to which Jennie and I were invited. We all arrived in the deepest mourning. The whole party returned on the Monday afternoon by special train. The train itself was elaborate, and what struck me particularly was that the guide to the journey, printed by the Railway Company, not only showed the stations through which we passed, but also the gradients which the train went up or down! As it was soon after the King's accession, it was arranged that the train should proceed slowly through big stations like Crewe and Stafford, in order that the populace might get a glimpse of their new sovereign. He was playing bridge to pass the time, and as the train slowed up at each station an equerry-in-waiting politely reminded His Majesty that it would be as well to show himself at the window, which he did, the cards being hastily put away. It was a very hot afternoon, and we were all perspiring freely; and one lady as we neared London produced some *papiers poudrés* and began to whiten her nose and generally clean up her face. The King asked what it was she was using, and, on being shown, took two leaves himself and proceeded to powder his nose. The result was comic, but was duly rectified before he stepped out of the train at Euston.

I remember being brought into the rubber of bridge that afternoon, as one of the men who usually played high points, a diplomat, had been obliged to leave on the Sunday. I won quite a considerable sum, about thirty pounds, entirely from His Majesty, who produced an enormous roll of notes from his pocket from which to pay me. I had always understood that kings never carried money, which shows how mistaken one can be.

Balls in London during the Edwardian period were very elaborate affairs. There were a number of large houses where notable hostesses entertained on a vast scale. A sight never to be forgotten was the beautiful Duchess of Sutherland * receiving her guests at the top of the staircase at Stafford House. If royalty happened to be present, as was generally the case, a quadrille was invariably danced. Very few knew the steps and the rest floundered through it as best they could.

Another hostess was my sister Shelagh, Duchess of Westminster. The ballroom at Grosvenor House—since, alas! pulled down—was magnificent and, with the exception of Bridgewater and Dorchester Houses, very few collections of pictures in London could vie with those belonging to the Duke. At one ball given in honour of the Crown Prince of Germany, when all the guests had departed except his equerry, the Crown Prince himself was nowhere to be found. My sister was furious when eventually he was discovered closeted (not in a sitting-room) with a beautiful but rather rapid lady of title.

Lady Tweedmouth † and her husband used to entertain lavishly at Brook House. She was a great friend of Jennie, being, of course, her sister-in-law, and was one of the bravest women I ever knew. We dined there one night before a ball, late in July 1909, and when we came away, Jennie was terribly depressed, almost in tears. I asked her the reason, and she told me that her hostess had confided to her that she had received her death-warrant from the doctor that afternoon, and could not live more than three months: she was suffering from an incurable disease. She had been the life and soul of the evening, and nobody would have guessed that this terrible sentence was hanging over her. She died not many weeks later.

The Tweedmouths had a most beautiful place in Scot-

* Millicent, Duchess of Sutherland.
† Fannie Lady Tweedmouth, *née* Churchill.

land, Guisachan, which we visited every summer. It was there that I first met the late Lord Rosebery. On one occasion when he was staying there another visitor in the house happened to be a youth of about seventeen, who had arrived at the 'spotty age.' After dinner, when the ladies had left the dining-room, Rosebery uttered some marvellous epigram, and the youth at once suggested that he had seen him studying Marcus Aurelius before dinner. Rosebery looked at him with those curious, cod-fish blue eyes of his, and said: " All my life I've loved a womanly woman and admired a manly man, but I never could stand a boily boy."

Another statesman whom I met at Guisachan was the late Lord Haldane, at the time when he was perfecting his reorganisation of the British Army. We occasionally went for walks together, and he, knowing that I had been in the army, was kind enough to discuss one or two minor details with me. I remember pointing out to him of how little use the then Corps of Reserve Officers was, instancing that I had left the army as a lieutenant, and if there were a war within the next ten years or so should return to my regiment as a lieutenant probably older than the senior officers in it, having forgotten everything I knew about soldiering. I suggested that a certain number of reserve officers (as apart from special reserve) should be called up every year for ten days' training with their regiments. " I am entirely in accord with you," he said, " but I don't suppose reserve officers would agree or would volunteer for service unless they were paid, and that is where I am up against the Treasury."

I never knew a man smoke so many black cigars as Lord Haldane. He formed the habit of retiring into a summer-house in the grounds, where he worked, and the whole place was littered with cigar ends at the end of the day. Once, when he saw that I noticed it, he said: " It's a bad habit, my dear boy; I wish I could break myself of it, but I can't work unless I smoke."

Jennie and I were invited to spend one Whitsuntide at

Hackwood, the place leased to the late Lord Curzon of Kedleston. Amongst the guests were many distinguished men, including the late Lord Balfour, and Sir Edgar Vincent, now Lord D'Abernon. The first night, after dinner, I expected to hear a brilliant conversation on some absorbing topic of the day, and was prepared to listen with both ears fully pricked. I did hear a very interesting discourse, but it was a monologue on the part of our host. Several attempts were made by other eminent members of the company to interlard his opinions with some expression of their own, but they soon gave it up as futile. Of all the brilliant men I have ever met, Lord Curzon was the most egotistical, but he was always worth listening to. His knowledge of the English language and his powers of phraseology were phenomenal. He was also one of the pluckiest of men. He once told me that he practically never knew what it was to be out of pain, and yet, meeting him in private life, whether in his own or other people's houses, one would never have guessed it.

Clubs in London have not changed much since my young days. The Turf Club is still the most select. White's used to be equally so; it is, and always has been, a cheery place in which to pass a couple of hours. Of White's it is said that it is the only club in London where any member can make use of a certain expression not used in polite society and nobody look up to see who said it. Once when I was there, a friend showed me an ingenuous letter which he had received from the sister of a one-time lady friend of his; it read as follows:

> " DEAR CAPTAIN ——
>
> " I know you will be glad to hear that your little friend Jasmine is going to be married, and you might like to know that she is still seeing a few friends to help her to pay for her trousseau. . . ."

The Garrick Club has always been a combination of wit and intellect, not entirely Bohemian, as it comprises members of all professions. One of my sponsors at my election to it was the late Robert Marshall, the playwright. My first day there I was seated at lunch at the big table, hardly knowing a soul, when he came in and, seeing me, said at the top of his voice: "Hallo, there's my candidate! I can't tell you, my dear fellow, how much money you owe me for the hire of motor-cars to bring the Committee to the poll!"

Robert Marshall became a playwright under rather fortuitous circumstances. He was quartered with his regiment in Belfast, and, accompanied by several brother-officers, went to see a play given at the local theatre. When they returned to Mess, Marshall declared that he had never seen a worse play, and that he'd eat his hat if he couldn't write a better one. One of his brother-officers took him up, and bet him fifty pounds that he would not write a play within six months which would be accepted and produced. He took up the challenge, and within the specified time had written and placed "The Second in Command," a play which had a long run and was one of Mr. Cyril Maude's greatest successes. A great raconteur, one of his favourite stories was that of an artisan returning home about 3 a.m. and meeting a rather worn-out lady in Piccadilly. "Good-evening, Miss," said the artisan. "You look cold; can I offer you a drink?"

"Well," she replied, her accent being the perfect genteel Cockney, "I don't mind if I do."

"I'm afraid I've only got cold tea in my can."

The lady glared at her would-be friend. "*What !*" she said, "*tea fer me?* Young man, you've hintirely mistaken the situation! I'm the daughter of a clergyman, and my brother is a brigadier-admiral who goes out hunting every day and brings home such beautiful dead rabbits—you dirty little tea-toper!"

Which reminds me of an experience of my own the other day. I was on the point of driving up to the entrance of a big store, the commissionaire outside having beckoned me on, when a taxi-driver with his flag up deliberately crossed me and forced me to pull up short; whereupon the commissionaire addressed the driver of the cab: "Where the 'ell do you think you're coming to, you lousy swine?" Then, turning to me, he said: "Some of these 'ere taxi-drivers seem to 'ave forgotten one of the first rules in life—that manners maketh man!"

The late Joe Comyns-Carr was one of the most amusing members of the Garrick. He was never at a loss for an answer, and used to keep us in fits of laughter. There happened to be two members of another club to which he belonged, both of the name of Smythe; one of them, however, declared that the other had no right to spell his name with a 'y' and that he was merely Smith. Both were unpopular with the other members, and Joe Carr made the following rhyme about them:

> "Two Smythes there were of equal birth,
> Though not, alas, of equal worth;
> But the Smythe who said his blood was blue
> Was far the bloodier of the two."

In those days supper after the theatre was one of the particular attractions of the Garrick, especially after a first night of a play. There one used to meet all the famous actors and playgoers of the day. Many plays were pulled to pieces; a few were praised. The late Sir Herbert Tree was a constant visitor. He was a brilliant conversationalist, but, like many men of that type, he preferred to monopolise the conversation. Also, although no man was better than he at pulling somebody else's leg, he never could bear to have his own pulled. One night at supper he was giving a dissertation on the great lovers of the world, and when he had finished I said that he had left out two of the most important. "Have I, my dear boy? To whom do you refer?"

"Crippen and Miss Le Neve," I answered; but he didn't like it, especially when the others laughed.

The late Colonel Claude Lowther was another amusing member of the Garrick Club. He and I once went together to see a play called "In Dahomey," in which all the actors and actresses were coloured. It was the first experiment with a troupe of coloured artistes that was made in London. We were both bored stiff with the play, and in the middle of the second act Claude started a political argument. As his conversation was conducted in anything but a whisper, two ladies sitting in front of us became annoyed, and turned round and " Shushed " violently at him. " My dear George," he said, without modulating his tones, " we mustn't talk; we're annoying the relations of the actors."

Another member of the Garrick, whose caustic wit spared no one, was the late Sir W. S. Gilbert. He once told me of a correspondence he had with Mr. Blackwell, of the firm of Messrs. Crosse and Blackwell, who had a considerable property near Harrow Weald, upon which game was preserved, and which joined Gilbert's small estate. The latter's dog had been caught poaching, and his owner received an irate letter from the game preserver, who, in his turn, received the following reply from his neighbour:

> " DEAR MR. BLACKWELL,
>
> " I am sorry you are so ' cross ' with my ' Pickles ' for trespassing on your ' preserves.' Please accept my apologies.
>
> " Yours   "

In 1906 the Atlantic Club was promoted. It was purely a gambling club, and one night there I had the horrible experience of seeing a man cheat at cards. The game was poker and the stakes were high. I was merely an onlooker, standing behind and rather to the side of the man who cheated. He was dealt king, queen, knave and ten of a suit: obviously he had the chance of drawing to a flush or a straight. He had raised the pool on his hand and was the last to take cards. The discard from the other players was in the middle of the table. The card given him was of no use, and he deliberately threw it on the discard and drew another. To my amazement, not one of the players noticed it. This time his hand was successful. One other man was looking on, and I strolled casually round the table, took him aside and asked him if he had noticed anything odd. He replied that he had, and we discussed what was the best thing to do. We knew that the member who had cheated was a rather popular ne'er-do-well, who had got away with a good many queer things in his life, and whose reputation was not of the best. We decided that nothing should be done until I had spoken to the member who was the principal sufferer, who, having had three aces, had lost a big coup which otherwise he would have won. I sat up till three o'clock in the morning waiting for the game to finish, and then walked down St. James's Street with the man who had been cheated, who was a personal friend of mine. I told him what I and the other member had seen, and he said he would think it over and let me know what to do. I realised that, as he was attached to a royal household, the last thing he wanted was a public scandal. The next morning he rang me up and told me to do nothing; that he himself would deal with the cheat. The latter left London shortly afterwards, and died a few months later on the Riviera.

Very high gambling used to take place at White's Club in those days. Shouette Ecarté was the game played. One or two rich men used to take the bank, and others, who were called 'the Villagers,' used to punt against them. Many thousand pounds changed hands in a week, and it soon developed into a farce, as it was a question of dog eat dog. Providentially, it died a natural death,· as what was going on got to the ears of King Edward, who, it was said, made some very trenchant remarks to the chairman of the committee.

At a certain large club in London, of the caravanserai type, a member brought a well-known demi-mondaine to lunch in the ladies' annexe. Two stuffy, and perhaps envious, members saw her, and complained to the secretary. As the latter was about to proceed on his holidays, he left the matter to his junior to attend to, and this resulted in the following notice appearing on the notice-board:

146

SALISBURY HALL

" Members are requested not to bring their mistresses into the Club, unless they happen to be the wives of other members."

In 1905 Jennie and I decided to live in the country some-where near London, and she sold her house in Cumberland Place. After searching for weeks we discovered an archi-tectural gem of the Jacobean period. Salisbury Hall—that was the name of the place—is situated between Barnet and St. Albans, and stands on the site of an old castle, which accounts for the moat surrounding it. The house itself was built by Sir Thomas Salt, a city magnate in the time of Charles II, and there is no doubt that it was used as a ' Petit Garçonnière ' by Charles II, and that Nell Gwynne lived there from time to time. In fact it was there that the first Duke of St. Albans was born, and the existence of the moat gives credence to the story of his mother having said at the time of his birth : " Throw the little bastard into the moat," and the King's reply : " No, spare the first Duke of St. Albans ! "

King Edward once came to spend Sunday with us, and when I recounted to him this story he said quickly : " You're wrong. If Charles II said anything, he said ' Spare the first Earl of Burford,' which was the title first given to Nell Gwynne's child before he was made Duke of St. Albans." I was astonished at His Majesty's knowledge of the details.

It will be remembered that Charles II gave Nell Gwynne the right to levy dues on every ton of coal brought within a certain area round London, a stipulation being made that the area must be defined by her in one day. She started from and finished up at Salisbury Hall, and the road she took now forms the boundary of the Metropolitan Police Area. It also accounts for the curious pear-shaped forma-tion of the latter, of which London Colney, a village near Salisbury Hall, is the apex. It was a coincidence that Jennie and I should have gone to live there, as it was her first husband, Lord Randolph Churchill, who, when

Chancellor of the Exchequer, compounded these dues with the then Duke of St. Albans.

We used to entertain there at week-ends, and I remember two distinguished foreign actresses paying us a visit. The first was Jeanne Granier, then at the zenith of her fame. Speaking in French, she greeted me: " What is the meaning of your railway companies being so religious? " I failed to understand what she was driving at, and asked her. " *Mais écoutez,*" she answered, "*je suis partie de Saint Pancras et je suis arrivée à Saint Alban—deux saints, et je n'ai voyagé que ving-cinq kilometres !* "

The other guest was the famous Duse. It was at the time of her parting with D'Annunzio, and she was a very unhappy woman. Poor lady! She arrived in tears, and was taken into the drawing-room by Jennie, where she remained the whole day, visited at intervals by the lady members of our party. Personally, although I was her host, I never saw her, let alone spoke to her—nor did any of the male members.

Clare Frewen, now well known as Clare Sheridan, was a niece of Jennie's, and was a constant visitor at Salisbury Hall. An amusing, wayward girl, I always thought that one day she would strike out a line of her own. Her father, the late Moreton Frewen, possessed a beautiful old fourteenth-century manor-house in Sussex called Brede Place. When Clare got engaged to Wilfred Sheridan she was asked by a friend what she intended doing during the honeymoon. " We are going to Brede," was the reply. " Possibly," her friend retorted. " But where are you going to stay? "

148

DRAWING-ROOM AT SALISBURY HALL

Chapter XII

RACING IN ENGLAND AND ELSEWHERE

RACING in England in the Edwardian period was not the expensive amusement it is nowadays. For instance, admittance to the Royal Enclosure at Ascot, for a man, instead of costing six pounds, cost two pounds for the week. In addition, one was able to race more or less in comfort. If one was jostled it was at least by one's own friends, and not by the curious people that are now met with there. Ladies' milliners and writers of the society articles in daily and weekly newspapers were not given tickets. They were certainly not, as now, taken from the class of people who would ordinarily get into the enclosure. Subscriptions to the various racing clubs in London were less, as were the crowds, but for really comfortable racing nothing could beat Newmarket, especially the July meetings. A few of the habitués there always had large parties for each meeting. Jennie and I used frequently to stay there with Mr. and Mrs. Rochefort Maguire. There was a big dinner-party most evenings at one house or other in the neighbourhood, and I remember finding myself on one occasion next to Theresa Lady Londonderry, when dining at Palace House, the Newmarket residence of Leopold Rothschild. Lady Londonderry, who was known to her friends as Nellie, had been one of the most beautiful women of her day, as well as being very intelligent. That night we got on to the subject of cruelty, not cruelty to animals, but mental cruelty as between men and women. She elaborated an argument which at the time was new to me: " It is as cruel," she said, "to be too kind, as it is to be too hard-hearted. I could mention one or two disastrous marriages where a man and woman had become engaged and one or the other, although still caring, realised that

149

marriage would probably not be a success because of temperamental or other difficulties, but from a mistaken kindness, a wish not to inflict pain on the person who cared for him or her, allowed matters to take their course, with the result that both suffered far more in after life than the momentary pang of a broken engagement."

Among the best-known men in the racing world was Marcus Beresford, who looked after the King's horses. For many years King Edward had refused to allow his horses to be entered in handicaps, his idea being that he bred only for classic events: praiseworthy in theory, but difficult in practice, although he was, on the whole, very successful. One year he had a number of very indifferent three- and four-year-olds and, after a great deal of persuasion, allowed Marcus Beresford to enter one for a big handicap at Newmarket. The weights appeared one evening, and the King's horse was in his opinion unfairly handicapped. He was furious with his manager, and rated him soundly in the rooms before everybody for having allowed the horse to be entered, saying: " I told you what would happen, and I was right." All the answer he got was: " Well, sir, if you were King Henry the Eighth no doubt you could have the handicapper beheaded, but you can't do that now."

Another story is told of Marcus Beresford and Sir Ernest Cassel. When the latter was made a K.C.M.G. he consulted Lord Marcus as to whether it was advisable to have the lettering of his new title painted after his name on his private horse-boxes. The reply was: " Well, Sir Ernest, you can put the K.C.M. outside, so long as you put the Gee inside! "

Another great personality of the turf whom I just remember was the late Captain Machell, about whom many people have written, but I do not think one particular interview of his with the late Mr. Warren De la Rue, whose horses he looked after, has ever been recorded. For some reason De la Rue's wife decided to leave him, and wrote him a note telling him that she had done so. Her husband was very much upset and sent for Machell, whom he considered one of his best friends and whose advice he wanted. The latter, however, did not in the least relish being drawn into other people's domestic affairs, and, while De la Rue was telling him chapter and verse of his matrimonial difficulties, Machell fell asleep. In a final frenzy De la Rue thumped the table, upon which Machell woke up, and the only words he heard were: "Tell me, my friend, what am I to do with her?"

Machell, whose thoughts ran only on race-horses, and who, in his comatose condition, assumed that they were the subject of the conversation, answered: "Do with her, my dear fellow? Why, put her in a selling race and let her go for what she'll fetch!"

In all the years I went racing I never heard of more than half a dozen really big coups coming off. Personally I was only in one, to a small amount, and that was when Demure, belonging to a friend of mine, Mr. Lionel Robinson, won the Cesarewitch.

Another friend of mine, Graham Prentice, brought off a big coup over a horse called Booty at Liverpool. He was staying at the time with the late Mr. H. J. King, who had taken a box, and provided a sumptuous lunch. When lunch-time came, neither Graham Prentice nor his friend and trainer, Captain Bewicke—the owner of Booty—who had also been invited, appeared; and it was only when the latter's horse had won at a long price that he turned up, all smiles, to be met by Mr. H. J. King, all frowns, for he realised why his guests had failed to put in an appearance before the race. He said nothing at the time, but subsequently at Epsom the same year he had another box and another lunch. Prentice had a horse called Pekin running, and again he was King's guest and Bewicke had been invited. Neither appeared, but this time King was not to be done. Well primed with his own champagne, he went down the ring and backed Pekin to win thousands. The horse started a hot favourite, and won. Prentice turned up, as before, after the race, this time without a smile, for he had backed the horse in London at starting price, and hoped to get good odds, as it was before the days of " the blower." His host, however, met him, beaming, and said: " I wasn't caught twice, Graham my lad. I won a packet over your horse."

The biggest coup that Prentice ever attempted to bring off was in 1905, when he had a mare called Little Eva, which was tried, a practical certainty, to win the Cambridgeshire. O. Madden, the jockey engaged, went to London a few days before the race and spent his time in taking Turkish baths and dosing himself with Epsom salts, but failed to reduce himself to the necessary weight by three pounds. That night a friend of mine who was sleeping next door heard Bewicke and Prentice having a heated argument as to whether they were to declare three pounds over-weight or put up a boy named Winter. Prentice wanted Madden, his trainer the other. Finally, Winter was put up. He did not possess the strength which the other jockey had, and failed to manage the mare at the starting-post; she became unruly and was kicked so badly that she took no part in the race.

On one occasion at Newmarket I overheard a funny conversation between Leopold Rothschild and a bookmaker of the name of Benjamin. The former wanted to back his horse, which was running in the next race, and naturally wished to obtain the best price. He asked Benjamin what he was laying the animal, and, upon hearing the odds, said: " What a pinching Jew price! " A look of pained astonishment came into the bookie's face as he exclaimed: " That from you, Mr. Rothschild? "

We used sometimes to go to France for the Grand Prix. Paris on these occasions was, and still is, a very cosmopolitan city, as sportsmen of all nations in Europe go to see this celebrated race. A story is told of a well-known Irish sportsman of the name of Fraser who went over, one year, with the late Mr. Gubbins, owner of Galtee More, a Derby winner. Recounting his adventures, Fraser said: " When the race was over we were that thirsty we decided to go and have a drink, so we went into one of those greenhouse-looking places in the Bois de Boulogne. Not one of us could speak a word of French, so I got up and I said in a loud voice: 'If there's any gentleman here will tell me the French for a whisky and soda I'll stand him one'; and, would you believe it, the whole Kāfe rose to a man!'' His subsequent adventures were even more amusing, as he got lost that night, forgot his address and was taken to the police station. The only way he could get to know where he was staying in Paris was to telegraph to his wife in some out-of-the-way spot in Roscommon, asking what address he had left her!

I shall never forget the Derby of 1909, when King Edward won it with Minoru. The enthusiasm of the crowd was tremendous. They not only all won money—or nearly all—but the fact that a truly British sportsman, who was also their reigning sovereign, should win the great classic race of the year and be sufficiently democratic to lead his horse into the weighing-in enclosure, appealed to them enormously.

The greatest tragedy that has ever happened in racing was when Craganour won the Derby in 1913 and was disqualified for bumping. It will be remembered that no objection had been made either by the owner, trainer or jockey of the second horse, Aboyeur, to whom the race was awarded, but the stewards took it upon themselves to take this extreme measure. I remember the race well myself; I had every reason to, and, as many onlookers said at the time, if there was any bumping it was done by the horse to whom it was awarded. I was then in partnership with a man called Wheater, and we had recently lost a great deal of money owing to the general slump caused by the Balkan War. Wheater was a great race-goer and a very good judge of racing. He had backed Craganour to win the Derby when he was a two-year-old the previous autumn, and stood to win fifteen thousand pounds, all of which, had the horse been given the race, was to go to resuscitating the fortunes of the firm of Wheater, Cornwallis-West & Co.

Craganour belonged to Mr. Bower-Ismay, who was so disgusted with the action of the stewards that he sold practically the whole of his stud, including the real Derby winner. In August of that year I was in Buenos Ayres, and happened to be present at a race meeting there when Craganour, who had been bought by a rich Argentine, was displayed to the racing public of that country. The horse was slowly led up the course between the races, and no reigning sovereign could have received a greater ovation. The applause which started when he first made his appearance gradually increased in volume as he approached the grandstand, and became so overwhelming that he grew frightened, and it looked as if he were going to break away from the man who was leading him. It speaks well for the sporting instincts of the Argentines that directly they realised what was happening the noise stopped as if by magic. He was a beautiful-looking horse, but, I understand, never did much good at the stud.

Racing at Buenos Ayres is the acme of comfort. When I was staying there with my elder sister, we arrived at the race-course about 12.30, and were taken up in the lift to the top of the members' stand, where there was a huge restaurant, and, after an excellent lunch, were escorted to our arm-chairs—for this is what they were—two tiers lower down, where coffee and liqueurs were served. If one wished, one could watch every race as comfortably as if seated in the stalls of a theatre. Not only that, but the horses in the paddock could be examined through a pair of race-glasses, and if one wanted to bet, all that was necessary was to ring a small bell, when a boy in uniform appeared, to whom one handed the amount to be wagered and a slip upon which was written the name of the horse chosen. This he took to the Tote, and brought back a ticket. If the horse was successful, one again rang the bell and told the boy to go and collect the winnings.

The Jockey Club itself at Buenos Ayres is a wonderful place, luxuriously, if somewhat vulgarly, decorated, and supplied with every conceivable amenity for sport and comfort.

Some of the Edwardian bookmakers were very well-known characters, many of them exceedingly rich men. Fry was always considered to be one of the richest, until the arrival of

Tod Sloan, the American jockey, who was the first to introduce into this country the American seat on a race-horse:
short stirrup leathers and practically the whole weight
carried on the horse's withers. Sloan's success was phenomenal. In 1897 and 1898 he won no fewer than sixty-three
races out of one hundred and fifty-one mounts. His backers,
amongst whom were many Americans, won large sums, and
it was always said that Fry was one of the heaviest losers.

Another well-known bookmaker was Charlie Hibbert. He
would form his own views of a race and very often lay the
favourite heavily at a longer price than would his *confrères*.
It used to be said that if Charlie Hibbert was laying the
favourite it was a good thing not to back it, though this was
by no means a safe rule, as very often he was wrong.

Two other big firms were Cooper & Rowson, and Pickersgill, whose successors still operate on the rails. Pickersgill
was a very remarkable man. He not only made a large
fortune laying horses, but he conducted a big business in his
own city of Leeds, took an active part in municipal government and was, as well, a most charitable person.

Perhaps the greatest proof of the futility of trying to make
money backing horses was the case of the late Sir Patrick
Blake, an impoverished Irish baronet. He had the sense to
see that the only way to make money racing was by laying
the odds, and not taking them. He started in a small way,
operating among his personal friends in the various members'
enclosures at race meetings. This was allowed for a time,
until other bookmakers became aware of it and complained
to the authorities that Blake had an unfair advantage over
them, for, whereas they were confined to one stand during
the day, he was allowed to move about anywhere. His
activities were therefore stopped, and he was told that if he
wished to lay horses he must conform to the rules which
governed all bookmakers. Nothing daunted, he took his
place on the rails, and in a few years he had amassed
sufficient money to retire with a comfortable income.

A friend of mine, who knew what he was talking about,
assured me that, before the late Government introduced the

betting tax, they were given access to the accounts of one or two of the best-known turf commission agents in the kingdom, including a big London firm, whose books showed that at the end of the year only three per cent. of their many thousands of clients were winners.

The Household Brigade used to, and still hold their annual steeplechase meeting at Hawthorne Hill. In 1899 I ran a horse—the same Oxhill mentioned in a previous chapter—in a welter steeplechase, one of the most important races in the meeting. Several well-known amateur jockeys were riding in the same race, including Reggie Ward * who was considered one of the best. I told a brother-officer, Hugh Fraser † (known in the regiment as " the Bo'sun " because of his rolling gait), that I thought my animal was sure to win, and asked him to put me a hundred pounds on and to help himself afterwards. It was the custom for the officers of the Brigade to give luncheon tickets to any well-known bookmakers whom they happened to know, and amongst the fraternity on this occasion was a man of the name of Gurney, who wore a long beard and looked far more like a highly respectable Methodist parson than a bookmaker. Hugh Fraser and Gavin Hamilton,‡ another brother-officer, happened to look into the luncheon tent just before the race in which I was riding, and saw Gurney having a good tuck-in, with liberal potations of champagne. When the numbers went up he was back at his place on the rails. There were eight starters, and my two friends approached him : " What will you lay the Field ? " they asked. He knew them both well and, feeling very pleased with himself, he just glanced at the number-board and answered : " Two to one to you, gentlemen."

" I'll take two hundred to one about Oxhill."

" Certainly, Mr. Fraser ; twice if you like ? "

" Done ! " answered the Bo'sun.

Harry Marks, another bookie, who was standing next to

* The late Hon. Reginald Ward, of the Blues.
† Major the Hon. Hugh Fraser, Scots Guards, killed in the Great War.
‡ The present Lord Hamilton of Dalziel.

Gurney, turned to him and said: " You blinkin' old fool! What's the matter with you? Don't you know as 'ow this 'orse won the Army Point-to-Point? 'Ere, I'll take six to four!" and six to four was the price at which Oxhill started. Fortunately he won.

Many years ago, when on my way back from Lingfield, I fell into the hands of a three-card-trick gang. After racing I followed a benevolent-looking old gentleman into a first-class compartment and sat down opposite him; two others followed, and just as the train was leaving a fifth man took one of the remaining corner seats and put up a newspaper. After a few minutes one of the occupants of the centre seats suggested a game of cards. It looks so easy to spot the queen, but trying to do so cost me a tenner plus another fiver lent me by the benevolent one, who had also (apparently) lost, and whom I promised to repay on our arrival in London. Two of the sharpers got out at Clapham, at Victoria " Grey Whiskers " and I drove in a hansom to the Guards Club, where I was to hand over the fiver he'd lent me. When I got back into the hall, after cashing a cheque, I found him in the hands of the man behind the newspaper, who had followed us, and who turned out to be a detective. " We've been on the look-out for this gang a long time, sir," he informed me. The benevolent one got his deserts all right.

This is a short chapter, but my chief recollection of racing in Edwardian days is wondering how I could pay the bookies on Monday morning.

Chapter XIII
UNSUCCESSFUL ENTERPRISES

I HAVE referred to Wheater. After four years' work with the British Electric Traction Company, although I was earning quite a good income from directorships and various other fees, I was anxious, for the reasons explained in a previous chapter, to make capital, and was not satisfied with income; and with the position I occupied there was no prospect of doing this. Wheater was a north-country-man, clever, but a born gambler (which I only found out later), and in touch with many rich men in his part of the world. He had recently migrated to London and, ambitious like myself, was anxious to start a financial business—a sort of minor issuing house, in fact. Instead of going to Cassel, who had always befriended me, or to other rich City men I had met in London society, I, to my cost, sought no advice, but decided to go into partnership with Wheater, who had a glib tongue; the pill which I after-wards had to swallow was richly covered in gold. He was clever enough to know that, with the connections I had, there was hardly an office in the City that I could not walk into and expect—and indeed did receive—not only atten-tion, but the most courteous civility. Thus the firm of Wheater, Cornwallis-West & Co. was founded.

At the beginning everything prospered. In the first year, merely operating in large lines of the shares in north-country steel and iron works controlled by the late Lord Furness, we made over twenty-three thousand pounds. A curious incident arose in connection with the shares in one of these companies, by name the Cargo Fleet Steel Company, then considered the most up-to-date steel works in the United Kingdom. My partner pointed out to me that if we could get the house of Rothschild interested in this company, other concerns in the City would follow like sheep. I appreciated that what he said was true, and decided to make an attempt, and, with that idea in my mind, visited New Court and asked for an interview with Lord Rothschild. He could not see me, but I was shown into the big room—my first visit to that august apartment—and there interviewed Mr. Leopold Rothschild, who was of course an old friend. He listened patiently to what I had to say and, as was always the case in those days when one wished to do business with the house of Rothschild, he said he could do nothing without consulting his brother Natty. He was kindness itself and, leading me out of the room, on our way to the main door went to the cashier's desk and muttered a few words in the ear of an old gentleman, who handed him a banknote. As I was leaving the office, Leopold put this into my hand and said: " Here's a little present for you, my dear George, with my best wishes for your future in the City." I was so dumbfounded that I did not entirely realise what I was doing, and stuffed it into my pocket. When I got back I discovered that he had given me a note for one hundred pounds. My feelings were mixed: I was furious at not being taken seriously, but treated like a boy who expected to be tipped, yet at the same time I appreciated that he meant it as an act of kindness. I knew that if I *was* to be taken seriously the last thing to do would be to accept it, and wrote him a letter pointing this out, while, of course, thanking him. This I sent, with the note, by hand to New Court. That afternoon I received a telephone message: would Mr. Cornwallis-West go to New Court immediately to see Lord Rothschild? On my arrival I was conducted to his table without a moment's delay. Natty Rothschild, one of the kindest men in the world, was gruffness itself, and this was often mistaken for bad manners. " Um! " he said. " What was it you came to see Leo about this morning? " I told him all I had said to his brother. Without making any remark or asking any questions he said: " I'll take five thousand Cargo Fleet shares. Good-bye." Through that deal alone, we succeeded in placing over fifty thousand shares within the next fortnight.

Looking back, I realise that possibly the greatest misfortune which can happen to any firm in the City is to start by making a large amount of money in the first year of its existence. Money-making seems such an easy affair that one is apt to work by Rule of Three and argue that, if it is possible to make twenty thousand in one year, obviously in three years it will be sixty thousand, and then the thought arises as to how many years it will be necessary to stay in the beastly place before one can retire with a large fortune.

We were not members of the Stock Exchange, but naturally had a good deal to do with members of that body, as we were what is called the ' shop ' in the shares before mentioned. Close and constant contact with both jobbers and brokers necessitated our being given innumerable tips as to how to get rich quick. I am convinced that if we had sold a bear of every share we were advised to buy, the dream of retiring in a few years with a large fortune might have materialised. A friend of mine who went into the City a few years before I did told me that the first piece of advice he ever got, from a man who really knew what he was talking about, was that there is ' never a tip without a tap.' " You can be perfectly sure," said my friend, " that if ever you are advised to buy certain shares it is because somebody or other wants to sell them, and once the tap is turned on, the market is likely to become flooded."

My first interview with one of the general managers of the bank with whom we had just opened an account was rather curious. It happened to be Parr's Bank, now amalgamated with one of the ' Big Five.' We had just made an issue of the debentures in Pinner's Hall, one of the most prosperous office buildings in the City of London, and were desirous of an advance against a certain number which we had failed to place. The manager in question was not an encouraging individual. When I explained to him the object of my visit, he said to me, with a sort of pompous facetiousness: " My dear sir, you have made a mistake. We want your money: we don't want to lend you ours!" I happened to recollect that Parr's Bank was originally founded in Warrington, so I replied: "Well, Mr. ——, if that had always been the policy of Parr's Bank they would never have got further than Warrington." I expected to be politely shown the door, but to my astonishment the loan was granted.

Of all the stony-hearted individuals I have ever had to deal with, those connected with life insurance offices are the worst: many could give points to money-lenders. During my youth I raised a certain amount of money on my reversion, the interest upon which had been actuarially calculated; a certain fixed sum therefore became payable upon my succession to the family estates. The office concerned was the Phœnix, and when this happened I went to interview the gentleman who had charge of the matter. My poor old father was hardly cold in his grave at the time, yet this individual's comment was: "Ah, let me see. . . . Cornwallis-West . . . yes. Your father lived too long. The Company lost money over the transaction."

Amongst the many prominent men whom I met in business was Mr. Hoover, now President of the United States, who was then with Messrs. Bewicke Moreing, the big Australian mining house: a quiet, capable man, but the last person I should have imagined would have sufficiently interested himself in politics to come to fill so high a position.

A man whom I knew very well and with whom my firm had some business transactions was Graham Prentice, whom I mentioned in connection with racing. In his way he was quite a personality. Almost the biggest jobber in the Kaffir market, he made a large fortune in the first South African boom, though, as a matter of fact, it was not anything like so large as people imagined. About five feet ten in height, he weighed eighteen stone, but his agility was remarkable, and he was quite a good squash-racket player. He used to tell me that one of the reasons for his success as a bidder was his voice, which, when bidding for shares, would rise to almost falsetto heights easily heard above the din of the market.

I once sold Prentice a picture which I came by through an extraordinary coincidence. All my life I have been interested in collecting prints, and one day I bought an engraving of a Morland picture at Christie's for thirty-five shillings. I was astonished at the cheapness of it, and asked the auctioneer afterwards whether it was a stumer. He assured me it was not, and the only reason he could give for the small sum it fetched was that none of the dealers knew the picture from which it was taken. That same evening I walked into Robinson & Fisher's opposite, where there was a picture sale the following day, and in a corner I noticed a picture which was catalogued as " ascribed to Morland." It was so dirty that the subject was indistinguishable, but a dog's tail and a child's arm reminded me of the mezzotint I had bought that afternoon. I left a commission for ten pounds, and two days later the picture arrived, having been knocked down to me for eight guineas. I had it cleaned, and found it to be a genuine Morland, signed and dated, and the actual picture from which my print had been taken. I did not care much about it, but Graham liked it and bought it from me.

Wheater and I had an interest—far too large an interest— in a copper mine in Spain. Like the race-horse whose owner said it might win a good handicap if only it could gallop faster past trees, the Cerro Muriano would have been an excellent mine if only there had been more copper in it. The best part about it was its situation in the middle of the Sierras, near Cordova. The country was certainly lovely: in the spring every hillside was covered with white, sweet-smelling gumcistus, just as if there had been a fall of snow. Owing to our large holding in the concern I was elected a director of the company, and frequently visited Spain on this account. It was in this mine that I had one of the narrowest escapes from death that it is possible to imagine. I was walking along one of the levels and had not noticed that the mine captain, who, of course, should have been in front, had remained behind for something or other. The person following immediately behind me was Fred Carr, the British Consul at Cordova, who was also a director of the company, and suddenly, without any alteration of his voice, he said to me: " Have a look at the vein above your head, West; there's some fine ore in it." I stopped, and when my head was up he took me quietly by the shoulder and pulled me back. My feet had been actually on the brink of a winze—a sheer drop of a hundred and twenty feet; and had he lost his head and shouted in alarm I should not be writing this now.

One enterprise with which I was indirectly connected, and which lost a huge sum of money, was the Shakespeare's England Exhibition referred to in Chapter X. The models of the old Tudor houses, the Globe Theatre, the Mermaid Tavern and other buildings were exquisitely designed by Sir Edward Lutyens. No money was stinted to make the exhibition an artistic success, and it undoubtedly was. The fact that too much money was spent originally was the cause of its financial failure. My wife had approached Cox and Co. with a view to their backing the project: every sort of investigation was made as to the number of people likely to pass through the turnstiles, the results of previous exhibitions were compared, and they consented to do so to the tune of thirty-five thousand pounds. Another fifteen thousand pounds was necessary, and Jennie asked me to approach Mrs. W. B. Leeds,* a great friend of mine and the widow of an American millionaire, who had left her everything he possessed, with a view to her undertaking the remaining liability. I was loath to do so, as I knew that money transactions between friends are, to say the least of it, undesirable. However, I thought it over, studied the figures carefully, and came to the conclusion that, although there was an undoubted risk, if it was good enough for the bank, with whom it was arranged that she should stand upon an equal footing, she might be justified in assisting my wife, whose friend she also was. I happened to be going to Paris, where

* The late Princess Christopher of Greece.

she was staying, and I put the proposition before her. She at once asked me if I advised her to take it up. I replied that I could not advise her; that there must be a certain amount of risk attached to it, but that I had promised Jennie I would ask her though I would not try to persuade her in any way. She consented to do it, and I am sorry to say she lost every penny, but she paid her liabilities without a murmur, and never once did she reproach me for the part I had played in the matter.

Amongst the entertainments given at the Exhibition, towards the end, was the Tourney, founded on the famous Eglinton Tournament. Why that was a failure I shall never understand: it was well advertised, but when the night arrived the great arena at Earl's Court was nearly empty. Heads of famous houses, clad in armour *cap à pied*, with their arms emblazoned on their breast-plates, jousted in the orthodox fashion, and many lances were broken—though, as these were made of papier mâché, no one was hurt. After the Tourney, which was won by the Duke of Marlborough, there was the Mêlée, in which I took part, also clad in armour, and these events were followed by a ball, at which, I regret to say, there was more than enough room to dance.

The Mermaid Tavern in the gardens was run as a club, and Jennie had roped in all her friends and her friends' friends to become members; it contained a very good restaurant and a room where one could read the papers and write. It was well patronised, and ought to have been a great success, but, like everything else connected with this ill-fated exhibition, it seemed cursed by bad luck and resulted in a heavy loss. The day before it was opened, my wife gave a huge luncheon-party to celebrate its inauguration. She drew upon her friends from all classes of society: the ' idle rich,' the Corps Diplomatique, the Bar and the Stage were all represented. Amongst the guests was a certain well-known actor who, the whole world was aware, had been living apart from his wife for a number of years. He was much attached to a charming and beautiful lady of foreign extraction by whom he was said to have already had two children. Two days before the party Jennie received a letter from him asking whether he might be allowed to bring a lady friend with him. Not realising, or perhaps not caring, whom he was likely to bring, she replied that she would be delighted, and he arrived, when a number of the guests had already assembled, in company with the lady referred to. Making a somewhat theatrical bow to his hostess, he said—or rather declaimed: " May I be allowed to present to you the mother of my children! " I happened to be standing near the Marquis de Soveral, the Portuguese Minister, at the time, and he turned to me and said : " *Tiens ! ça c'est magnifique !* " adding that it was far the best British dramatic effort he had ever witnessed.

Soveral was a man who had a host of friends, including the King. He very often lunched and dined with us, and it was he who told me the origin of dark port as compared with light port from the wood, such as he declared was solely drunk in Portugal. It appeared that during the Peninsular War the Portuguese were anxious to sell their wines to the British army; and as they realised that claret had been, up till then, the wine principally drunk in England, they thought it advisable to make their wine look as much like claret as possible, even if it did not taste like it. The only way to achieve this was to bottle it almost immediately instead of keeping it in the cask.

A wet summer largely contributed to the failure of Shakespeare's England. In those days Earl's Court and the White City were amusing places in which to spend a hot evening; some of the side-shows were very entertaining and there were quite good restaurants. During the Eton and Harrow match both places were crowded every evening, and yells of " E-e-e-ton! "—" H-a-a-rrow! " could be heard everywhere. Boats full of Eton boys and their female relations, all waving light blue flags, would dart down the water-shoot, followed by an equally enthusiastic crew of the opposition waving dark blue banners.

Not very long before the outbreak of the War, the *Daily*

Mail started a sort of buying and selling agency in stocks and shares usually dealt with on the London or provincial stock exchanges: in other words, the scheme was that the buyer and seller should be put into immediate contact and that the broker's commission should be avoided by both. I believe Mr. Duguid, who was then city editor of the *Daily Mail*, inspired the scheme. It was necessary that a firm accustomed to this sort of transaction, and with an adequate clerical staff, should be appointed to give effect to the contracts entered into, and Wheater, who knew Duguid, was sent for and asked by him whether our firm would undertake the job and accept some fixed remuneration for doing so. When the scheme was first proposed to me I was dead against it; we were not a bucket shop in any sense of the word and, as I pointed out to Wheater, it looked very much as if we should be considered as such if we undertook to do what had been suggested. The brokers were our friends. The whole of our business was conducted through them, and we dealt with a considerable number. Any issuing house—and we were an issuing house in a small way —must of necessity employ stock-brokers; why, I asked, did he want to go out of his way to antagonise them, as he certainly would? However, he decided to proceed. A few days later I met the late Lord Northcliffe in the foyer of the Carlton Hotel. " We are doing business with you, I hear? " he said to me. " Not with me," I answered, " with my firm if you like; I personally am dead against it. Any honest broker is entitled to earn his commission; why should the *Daily Mail* want to take the bread out of his mouth? "

If he had spoken the truth he would have said it was merely an attempt to increase the circulation of the *Daily Mail*; as it was, he said nothing. He just gave me a look as if to say: " Poor fool! One of those people who can't take advantage of an opportunity when it's offered to them . . ." and stalked into the restaurant. When war broke out shortly after, the scheme died a natural death.

One of the most interesting, if unsuccessful, ventures I ever went into was in connection with the scientific cultivation of pearls. I happened to go to Newlands for the week-end, and on my mother's table saw two huge pearl-oyster shells, on which were beautiful black baroque pearls. She told me that a gentleman by the name of Mr. Savile Kent, who had been an inspector of fisheries under the Australian Government, had given them to her and had stated that they were the results of his own experiments in pearl cultivation. I knew that the Japanese had already succeeded in doing this to a certain extent, but nothing I had ever seen equalled these. The next morning I interviewed Mr. Savile Kent, who showed me further specimens and said he believed that, if sufficient money were forthcoming, he could scientifically irritate the fleshy folds of the oyster sufficiently to cause it to produce a perfect sphere. I took some of his specimens with me to London and showed them to several friends of mine, one of whom, Joe Laycock,* said he would come into a syndicate, but would first like the opinion of some well-known expert. Accordingly one afternoon he and I went round to Welby's in Garrick Street, produced one of the shells with a baroque pearl attached, and asked them what they considered to be the value of the pearl. The answer was " Anything from fifty to sixty pounds." As it had probably not cost more than a few shillings to produce, it seemed worth while going on, and Laycock became one of the members of the syndicate. Mr. Savile Kent was sent out to an island off the north coast of Australia, near the Torres Straits, with sufficient money to continue his experiments. He maintained that it would take at least three years to produce entirely satisfactory results. A year later he sent us back some marvellous specimens so far as they proved the possibility of creating the actual floating pearl. After two years he himself returned home on sick leave, and the specimens he brought with him were still better, and made us all enthusiastic. Our hopes were dashed, however, when a few weeks later he became seriously ill and died.

When the syndicate was formed he had declined to

* Sir Joseph Laycock, K.C.M.G.

167

acquaint the board with his actual secret. We all knew enough about the formation of a pearl to realise that he must have discovered some way of opening the oyster without killing it, but what that method was, and what was the irritant used to start the formation of the pearl had remained a secret. The only way in which he had met us had been by depositing in the Bank an envelope which he said contained the whole secret of the process, and with this we had to be content. When, after his death, the envelope was opened, we found nothing intelligible, and it seemed fairly obvious that he meant to carry the secret with him to his grave. We all lost our money, but it was exciting while it lasted.

Quite the most expensive unsuccessful venture in which I was ever involved was in connection with a patent. I had always been interested in rifle-shooting, and for this reason an Australian, by the name of Ashton, approached me in 1905 about an automatic rifle which he had constructed. It is not often that the patentee produces the finished article, and I was full of enthusiasm—until I tried to fire the rifle. It was a recoil-operated weapon and it jammed persistently. I told him that I was not prepared to finance it, and suggested that the only satisfactory automatic rifle would be one operated by a minute portion of the gas formed by the explosion of the cartridge. He became quite keen about the idea, and some months later produced the blue prints of what looked like a very simple method of operation. What with patents and manufacture it cost me the best part of five thousand pounds, and after many attempts spread over two years the perfect weapon was produced, and was called the West-Ashton rifle. Lord Tweedmouth was then First Lord of the Admiralty, and I had no difficulty in getting it tried at Whale Island; nor did I meet with any opposition from the War Office, who were quite willing to experiment with it.

After some months' delay I was informed that so far as the Navy was concerned it was felt that, considering how seldom a blue-jacket had reason to use a rifle, an automatic one appeared unnecessary for that Service. The War Office had no fault to find with the weapon, and the Small Arms Committee only turned it down because, in their opinion, " an automatic rifle would encourage the waste of ammunition by the soldier," and it would be " an impossibility to supply ammunition to an army in the field armed with automatic rifles "—and this only seven years before the Great War! Alas, I was so disgusted that I did not even keep up the master patents. Gas operation is, of course, the method used for the Lewis gun, of which hundreds of thousands were made and used between 1914 and 1918.

Chapter XIV

SHOOTING

My first recollection of firing off a gun is vivid, as the recoil knocked me flat on my back. My father had a shooting party at Ruthin and, as a boy of ten, I was standing next to one of the guests in the old deer park. It was a rabbit shoot, and the rabbits were being driven downhill to be shot by the guns as they ran down the wall of the park. The guest in question was waiting for the beaters to come up when, all of a sudden, an old cock pheasant flew up from the bracken and perched himself on top of the wall about five-and-twenty yards away. " I'd love to shoot that pheasant! " I exclaimed. Colonel Howard, affectionately known to his friends as ' the Pieman,' handed me his gun, saying: " Go ahead! " I killed the pheasant and thought I had killed myself until I was picked up and reassured that I was still alive.

As was natural, I was rather afraid of guns for a year or two afterwards, and it was not until I was fourteen, and just going to Eton, that I was allowed to shoot. My father had a queer notion about boys handling guns, and suggested to the head-keeper, Hurst, an old family servant, that during my preliminary instruction I should use only blank cartridges. As black powder was in general use in those days, I should not have known—except by the results—whether I had been firing a charge of shot or not. A more foolish way of teaching a boy how to shoot it is difficult to imagine, as the one thing necessary to instil into him is confidence in himself, and if he keeps loosing off his gun and hitting nothing he naturally becomes down-hearted. Fortunately for me, Hurst did not carry out my father's proposal, and I never forgot the latter's look of astonishment when, after a few days' tuition, I came home and announced that I had shot rabbits running. However, he was too wise to remonstrate with his old servant, and it was not until some years afterwards that I discovered that the plot had miscarried. I cannot say that Hurst was a good instructor—certainly not when one compares modern methods of tuition—and his appreciation of one's prowess was usually damned by faint praise. All he said when I had shot my first flying pheasant was: "Very good, sir, but the birds do fly in the shot sometimes!"

My father was a good shot of the old school. I remember going out with him soon after I had started to shoot, walking up partridges. He had a habit, when he brought off a good right and left, of hitting the butt of his gun violently with the palm of his hand as he said "By Gad! That was good!" Curiosity overcame me, and I asked him why he did it. "You see, my dear boy," he replied, "when I was your age, and for a good many years after, I shot with a muzzle-loader, and after each discharge we had to slap the butt of the gun in order to shake out the unburnt powder, so that even now I forget that I'm shooting with a breech-loader—force of habit, my dear boy, force of habit!"

He had some funny old cronies who used to shoot with him in Hampshire, one or two even older than himself. Their get-up was marvellous: not exactly a tall hat, but something very near it, make of brown felt, square cut-away whipcord coat with huge game-pockets and enormous buttons, tight breeches—plus fours and stockings were, of course, unheard of—funny old-fashioned leggings, and stout hobnailed boots. Two dear old gentlemen by the name of Jennings, who, I well remember, were members of the party on the occasion of my memorable visit to my Grandmama West at Newlands, were always my father's guests on rough days' shooting. They were very poor, and used to load their own cartridges and make the cases do over and over again. Consequently, after a drive was over, one used to see them surreptitiously picking up all the empty cases they could find and stuffing them into their pockets.

A great friend of my father, with whom he used to shoot, was old Squire Morant of Brockenhurst Park. Shooting here always started late in the day and finished when it was far too dark to see, let alone hit, anything. My father once asked the head keeper why Mr. Morant persisted in doing this. This worthy, almost as old as his master, answered in broad Hampshire dialect, " Well, sir, it be this way, Mr. Morant 'ee do love to see the fire a-coming out o' the guns."

If there was any type of person in the world whom my father disliked it was the rich *parvenu*. Such a person happened to take a place near Ruthin, where he had very good shooting and turned down a lot of pheasants. He asked my father on many occasions to shoot with him, but he always refused. One day, however, he accepted, more out of curiosity, as he subsequently admitted, than for any other reason—a curiosity which nearly cost him his sight, as his host shot him just beneath one eye. My father was not a man who was easily roused, but this was too much, and he proceeded to expostulate in terms not exactly polite to his host. All the latter said was: " Sorry, Colonel! Lucky I didn't let off the other barrel, wasn't it? "

Dangerous shots are a curse out shooting, but fortunately they are not often met with nowadays. Still, accidents do happen: the late King Edward was certainly not a dangerous shot, but I once saw him shoot a beater. We were staying with Sir Ernest Cassel at Newmarket for one of the October meetings. The King was at the end of a small spinney, I was on his left, and an equerry, the late Sir George Holford, was on the other side of him. It was almost the end of the drive and, as the beaters were approaching, an old hare popped out of the spinney. The King had been having an animated conversation with a lady friend, who unwisely pointed out the hare to him, and he, not realising that the beaters were so close, shot at it. There was a piercing yell, and an aged beater, who evidently knew perfectly well who had shot him, came out of the spinney holding his knee. His Majesty, not realising what had happened, had turned aside and resumed his conversation, and George Holford went up to him and said: " Do you know, sir, you've shot a beater? "

The beater, who, it was subsequently discovered, was very little hurt, but doubtless saw prospects of a life annuity, continued to moan. The King was much upset, and the man was removed and no doubt received adequate compensation.

Never a good shot at taking birds in front of him, King Edward used to make some marvellous long shots at birds behind.

It was at a shooting-party in Norfolk that there happened one of the few occasions when I saw the King really annoyed. One of the guests was Mr. Smith-Dorrien, who owned a beautiful place in the Scilly Islands and was known as ' the King of the Scillies '; and he and the King were deep in conversation after luncheon one day out shooting when they should have been taking their places for the next drive. Our host, a famous yachtsman, and a wild and thoughtless Irishman, put his head into the marquee where lunch had been served and had the bad taste to say: " Come on, you two kings! The beaters are ready to start."

King Edward looked daggers, and for the moment we all expected an outburst, but soon afterwards he had apparently forgotten all about the incident, and was his usual cheery self again.

The first shooting-party I was ever asked to was when, as a young man of eighteen, I received an invitation from the late Ralph Bankes, the squire of Kingston Lacey, a beautiful place in Dorsetshire, containing some wonderful pictures and incidentally a marble staircase. Concerning the latter there was a notice pinned up in the bedrooms advising guests not to go down it in nailed shoes in the morning or to go up it after dinner!

A very funny thing happened during this visit. When we arrived our host remarked that his butler had been taken ill, and that he had been obliged to have a temporary man. At dinner that night there was a haunch of venison on the menu, and this, as was often the custom in those days, was placed on the table and carved by the host himself. I noticed the temporary butler swaying slightly and looking oddly at the haunch during the process of carving; suddenly he made a lurch forward, seized the dish and said thickly: "You've got about as much idea of carvin' a haunch of venison as a rabbit 'as—let me 'ave a shot!" He attempted to stagger to the sideboard, dropped the dish, and fell on top of it.

I was too busy hunting to pay much attention to shooting before the South African War, but I do remember a visit to Abbotsbury, a place belonging to Lord Ilchester. It was the only occasion when I have ever shot driven coot. There is a long inland lagoon behind the gravel spur known as Chesil Beach, where, at a certain time of the year, thousands of coot congregate. We were eight guns, two forward, four in boats and one on each shore. The coot at first started to go forward, where they were shot by the two guns ahead; the fun began when they came flying back over the boats and the two shore guns. They were high and looked to be going at quite a moderate rate; in reality they were flying very fast. We shot over eight hundred that afternoon.

After I was married I could, had I wished, have shot every day in the season, but was obliged to refuse owing to business ties. It was about this time that many men, who had never dreamt of it before, began going into business, with the result that hosts, in order to obtain guns, were compelled to have shoots at week-ends. Big *battues* were the order of the day. Landowners could afford to run their own shoots, and syndicates were the exception. The advent of shooting schools produced better shots, and really bad shots, which were common in the days of my boyhood, became fewer and fewer. Shooting is a game of skill, and there is much to learn before any man can expect to become a really fine shot; it was the technique of shooting that was taught at the various schools round London.

The best all-round shot I have ever seen in my life was the late Lord Ripon, whom I knew as Lord de Grey, though in my opinion there was not much to choose between him and

Teddie Oakley.* On one occasion when I was shooting with Lord Howe at Gopsall, soon after I was married, Lord de Grey, who was one of the guns, said to me on the evening of the first day's shooting: " I've been watching you, young man; you shoot quite respectably, but I could improve your shooting thirty per cent. if you let me." I was not only flattered, but felt it was extremely kind of him, and said that I should be more than grateful if he would tell me how. He asked me to meet him on the lawn the following morning before breakfast with my gun, and, when I did so, explained what had never been pointed out to me before: the importance of footwork when shooting. Any novice who may happen to read these lines and is not already cognisant of the fact can try it himself. Let him take a gun and aim at a moving object at an angle of forty-five degrees, follow the object round without moving his feet, and he will find that, if it is going to the left, the more he brings his gun round to the left the more the barrels will be tilted. Let him move his left foot back or his right foot forward, and the barrels will automatically become horizontal. The same rule applies, of course, with an object moving to the right. The result is that if the feet are not moved when swinging on an object before shooting, the shot is always low, and nine people out of ten, when they miss a bird, shoot underneath it.

For three mornings running Lord de Grey schooled me in this exercise. He was quite right in what he said: my shooting did improve enormously. Unlike many brilliant shots, he was not a jealous shot, although he was very careful of his reputation, and for this reason I imagine was sometimes inclined to exaggerate his performances. At the same party at Gopsall an unfortunate incident happened. After dinner one night he told his host that his servant had been taken ill, and that he would like a loader for the following day. Sir John Willoughby,† another guest, remarked that as he was obliged to go to London for the day to attend a board meeting he would be unable to shoot, so

* The late E. de C. Oakley.
† Sir John Willoughby, of Jameson Raid fame.

his servant, who was an excellent loader, would be available. The next evening, when the ladies had left the dining-room, the day's sport was discussed, and George Howe asked de Grey how many birds he had killed.

"A hundred and twenty-four," he answered, "and I fired a hundred and twenty-seven cartridges."

Johnnie Willoughby was no respecter of persons, and blurted out: "That isn't correct, for my servant told me that you fired over a hundred and fifty."

There was a dead silence, broken only by our host hastily rising and suggesting we should join the ladies.

To my mind, a really good shot is a man who is not afraid of blowing off a great number of cartridges, certainly not one who takes the trouble to count them. A good shot should fire at anything he thinks within range and not care if he misses. Several men I know who have the reputation of being brilliant shots never shoot at a bird which there is the slightest chance of their being unable to hit. Possibly their average is exceptionally good, and that is all they seem to care about.

The Barkers, especially Frank, and the Hambro family are and always have been brilliant shots, but I do not believe any one of them has the faintest idea of how many cartridges he has fired at the end of the day. Their average may not be so good as that of others I could mention, but they have probably succeeded in killing more stuff.

In Edwardian days it was usually the practice for the host to place the guns for covert shooting. Except for grouse and partridge driving, the use of numbers and moving up two after each drive were unheard of. The frequency of syndicates running pheasant shoots has brought this about. At one or two places where I used to shoot it was the practice of the host to allow his head-keeper to place the guns, a most undesirable state of affairs, as it often meant that the guests whom the keeper thought would tip him heaviest at the end of the day got the best places. Many years ago I was invited to stay with a certain noble lord for covert-shooting in Nottinghamshire, where this was the custom. There were

176

three other lords and two maharajahs there, and I was the only commoner—besides being far and away the poorest. The result was that I went with the beaters every drive. I didn't risk this experience a second time.

There is a story told of the late Lord Portsmouth and Lord Hardinge when shooting at the former's place, Hurstbourne. He went up to his keeper and said: "Jones, where is the best place this next drive?" It was pointed out to him.

" Very well, I'll go there."

" Punch " Hardinge was not to be done. " Where's the next best place, Jones? " he said. " Because I'll go there! "

I was once honoured by an invitation to shoot at Sandringham for both covert shooting and partridge driving. We were nine guns, including King Edward and the Prince of Wales, now H.M. King George V. The last two mentioned did not, however, allow themselves to count as guns, inasmuch as they did not move up after each drive, and consequently always took the outside, and generally the worst, places. The bags on that occasion were prodigious. We got over two thousand pheasants in one day, but, like all Norfolk pheasants, they did not fly particularly high. At many of the stands there were two rows of guns, and at one time I found myself behind the Marquis de Breteuil, who said to me, before the birds started to come out: " I'll shoot all the cocks and you shoot the hens or any cock that gets past me." It was a good arrangement, and one I have often since adopted, as the cocks always fly higher to start with than the hens.

One of the best covert shoots in England was at West Dean in Sussex, which belonged to the late Willie James. I often shot there, and one year I was invited to a shooting party when King Edward was also staying in the house. Everything was magnificently done, and a private orchestra was an added attraction. This particular one was run by a man named Cassano. One evening, coming down to dinner, I met His Majesty on a landing, and he said: " What are you going to play to-night? "

" Bridge, I suppose, sir," I answered.

He looked round quickly, and then burst out laughing and said: "I took you for the man who conducts the band."

Curiously enough, I remember on another occasion, at the Marlborough Club, when I was waiting for my brother-in-law, Prince Pless, with whom I was going to dine, King Edward came into the room, shook me warmly by the hand and, much to my astonishment, started talking in voluble German—until he found he had mistaken me for Hans. Beyond the fact that Pless, Cassano and myself were all tall and fair, there wasn't much resemblance.

The Duke of Westminster for many years leased Llanarmon, my place in Wales, where the pheasants fly notoriously high. There are not many places outside that little country where pheasants fly as high. A few years ago before the Duke gave up the lease I had occasion to visit the place and saw his head-keeper. I asked him why his master wanted to turn down the enormous quantity of pheasants that he did, and whether he really enjoyed shooting. "Well, sir," was the answer, "what the Duke really enjoys is to ask the best shots in England up here, stand behind them, and laugh at them when they miss."

I used to shoot a lot at Eaton * in the old days, but as the ground was not adapted to it, the birds did not fly very high. The keeper, by name Garland, had been in the Grosvenor family for over forty years, and consequently was *persona grata*, and allowed to say things which no other servant would dare to. On one occasion Prince Francis of Teck was one of the guns, and after a stand where the birds had flown particularly low, he proceeded to explain to Garland what he ought to do to make them fly higher. The old man listened attentively, with his hat in his hand, and when the lecture was finished he said: "Well, your 'Ighness, if I *was* to do it, you wouldn't 'it 'em."

It isn't five-and-twenty years ago since I formed one of six guns who killed three hundred and thirty-seven brace of partridges within sixteen miles of Marble Arch. This was at a place called Mimms, which belonged to the late Mrs.

* Eaton Hall, Chester, the seat of the Duke of Westminster.

Burns. The ground shot over lies halfway between Barnet and St. Albans on the right-hand side, but what with the new Hatfield by-pass and the general encroachment of London in that direction I very much doubt whether it would be possible to shoot twenty brace there to-day. When I was quite young the late Duke of Westminster told me that he remembered as a boy shooting snipe in what is now Belgrave Square.

The biggest and most tiring shoot in which I ever took part was in Ireland, at a place called Kylemore, on the west coast, which belonged in those days to the Duke of Manchester, who had reared thousands of tame wild duck. The formation of the ground was curious: there was a loch about four miles long, on one side of which was a wooded slope, Above the slope was a sort of terrace in which were innumerable small ponds where the duck were fed; their natural flight was to the lake below. It had been the Duke's intention to have three days' shooting, but the first two days it rained as it only can rain in that part of the world, and shooting was impossible. Falconer,* another guest, himself a brilliant shot, suggested that we might go for a record in wild-duck shooting, and accordingly a programme which had been intended to last three days was condensed into one. We killed over two thousand duck in the day. My shoulder was raw, my head ached, and at the last beat of the day I was obliged to shoot off my left shoulder, with indifferent results.

I have often heard it debated as to which is the most enjoyable form of shooting: driving grouse or partridges. It is difficult to say. On a bright day in October, with the leaves turning, the stubble still a pale yellow and the turnip fields brilliantly green, the surroundings are truly fascinating, and, from the point of view of sport, the partridge is a most satisfactory bird to kill. When he comes over a fence and sees the guns his sharp cry seems to say: " Good God! What's that? " and he alters his flight; and that is where the skill of the shooter comes in (I speak, of course, of English partridges; a French partridge never alters his flight and is

* The present Lord Kintore.

179

very easy to hit). It is amusing, too, to find a few odd pheasants in a turnip field, anxious to get back to the covert from which they have strayed and very often flying far higher than they do later in the year.

On the other hand, there is no denying the extreme attraction of grouse driving. The purple heather, the patches of bracken, the rowan trees in the burns, covered, as the season progresses, with vivid red berries: the whole often accompanied by a distant view of the sea or high mountains, or of a river winding its way through green valleys amid fields of ripening corn, form a setting which can hardly be surpassed. So far as the sport itself is concerned, a grouse, being the bigger bird, flies faster than the partridge, but seldom swerves and, in my opinion, is easier to hit. Two of the most difficult birds to hit when driven are his cousins, one twice and the other four times his size: the black cock and capercailzie. Being so large, both birds appear to be flying very slowly, whereas the contrary is the case. I have many times seen a good grouse shot miss what looked like a perfectly easy black cock over his head.

I was eighteen when I received my first invitation to shoot driven grouse, at a place called Bodydrys in the Ruabon Hills, belonging to Sir William Williams. The other two guests were Walter Chetwynd and a Captain Everett. I remember the day well, as it was the only occasion in my life when I killed five driven grouse with two shots: three with the first barrel and two with the second. My butt was on a knoll, the birds came round it and I actually shot downhill at them, and thought how easy it was to shoot driven grouse—an impression which was soon to correct itself.

Sir William had once been in the First Life Guards, and was known as " the Wild Welshman." Anyone less like a Life Guardsman it was impossible to imagine: with bright red face and beard, and eyes like blue flannel, he was just a bluff country squire. That evening as we sat down to dinner he said to Everett: " What would you like to drink? " Everett, hoping, like the rest of us, for a glass of champagne, did not dare to suggest it, and mildly replied that either white wine, claret, or whisky would do equally well. Old Bill Williams turned on him and said: " I suppose you're one of those rotten-gutted fellows who can't drink beer for dinner! " and beer was all we got.

There are many sportsmen, including myself, who are very fond of shooting grouse over dogs. True, the actual shots are easy, but there is no more interesting form of sport than to see really good dogs working.

Many years ago I was invited to shoot grouse on the 12th with my friend Captain Combe at Strathconon. I had been given a Browning self-loading gun, from which it was possible to fire five consecutive shots as quickly as one could pull the trigger. From the point of view of the true sportsman it is not a satisfactory weapon; moreover it is clumsy and badly balanced; however, that particular year I took it up with me as well as my other guns. I asked my host's permission, which was readily granted, to take it out and try it, and I arranged a plot with his brother, Captain Boyce Combe, who was also staying in the house. It was settled that when we arrived at the meeting-place on the hill, directly he saw the gun taken out of its cover, he was to say to me "What a fool you are to come out shooting grouse with a single-barrel gun!" I was to say nothing, but, at the first point, was to loose off all five barrels as quickly as I could, while he was not to fire at all. We were anxious to see the effect of this performance on the Scottish keepers, who had never even heard of a self-loading gun, let alone seen one. All went beautifully. At the very first point an old cock grouse got up, and I fired off five barrels in about four seconds. The man who was working the dogs fell back in the heather in pure surprise; the other ghillies sat down. The head-keeper's remark was: " Eh gosh! What a terrible weepon! " As a matter of fact it *was* a terrible weapon, and very effective on coveys getting up near. I never used it again except when going out by myself for a rough day.

Rough shooting, in the sense of a varied bag, has always appealed to me. The first day's rough shooting I ever had was in Anglesey, a veritable paradise for this form of sport.

I was staying as a boy of sixteen with old Lady Vivian at Glyn, and was sent out with a keeper. My total for the day was fifty-three head, including twenty-seven snipe. From the point of view of variety the best day I ever had was many years ago in the Isle of Mull, at Duart Castle, which belonged to the late Murray Guthrie. I had been out one day by myself and had done extraordinarily well. This fired my host, who suggested that he and I and another man staying in the house, named Norton, should go out the following day, starting at daybreak, and try to make a record. It was a glorious morning late in September when I was called, and I well remember seeing the sun rising over Ben Cruachan. It had been decided, after consultation with the head-keeper over-night, that the first things to try for were a red deer and a roe deer. Accordingly a large wood was driven, and we were lucky. I got a roe deer and my host got a stag. True it was not a large one—it only just had horns—but it counted all the same. We then walked in a line for miles over heather, through bogs, scrub, turnip and stubble fields, and drove one or two small woods, with the result that by lunch-time we had killed grouse, black game, partridge, pheasant (it was out of season, but that didn't matter), woodcock, full snipe, jack snipe, golden plover, green plover, brown hare and rabbit.

We were somewhat tired at half-past one, but lunch revived us—though not the head-keeper, who, we discovered afterwards, perhaps owing to his excitement at our having killed a stag, had been taking surreptitious pulls at the whisky flask; by the time we were ready to start again he was completely incapacitated. We were on a moor and looked up apprehensively at a peak many hundred feet above us, where we knew we should find ptarmigan. It had to be faced, and at half-past two we started again, leaving the keeper snoring peacefully in the heather. On the way up we shot some more grouse and one or two blue hares, and succeeded in getting a brace of ptarmigan. By the time we got back to where we had left the keeper it was nearly five o'clock; he had disappeared, and we subsequently discovered

A TYPICAL SCENE ON A SCOTTISH MOOR

he had slunk home, thoroughly ashamed of himself. Murray Guthrie then decided to try for duck in a small loch above the house. On the way there we got a pigeon and the loch produced three sorts of duck: mallard, teal and widgeon. This made nineteen different varieties of game in one day. I shot a moorhen near the loch, but as nobody volunteered to eat it we didn't count it. We were all dead beat when we got back, and I recollect Murray saying to me: " The best thing to do is to get into bed, even if it's only for half an hour—it's wonderful how it refreshes you." I followed his advice, and the next thing I was aware of was the butler asking me if I was coming down to dinner. When I discovered that they had sat down to it ten minutes ago I replied that I had better stay where I was, so was sent up a pint of champagne and a grouse, and that was the end of a perfect day.

Every man who has shot a great deal has some record of curious " rights and lefts " and single shots. Some years ago in Scotland I did the keeper a good turn with a right and left by shooting two sorts of vermin. I happened to be standing near the river when a hawk flew over me, which I shot, and directly I had fired a cormorant got up from under the bank, which I also killed. I brought off a curious single shot at the same place, on the moor. A wild duck got up out of a burn and, when rising, flew up the face of a hill; I shot it, and when I went to pick it up heard something fluttering near where it lay, and found a grouse.

The price of guns and cartridges nowadays is very high. Cartridges which used to cost eleven shillings per hundred now cost twenty-two; and it used to be possible to buy a pair of guns at a well-known London maker's for one hundred and ten pounds, whereas more than two hundred pounds is now asked for the same article.

I often used to shoot with my brother-in-law at both of his places in Germany, Pless, in what is now Polish Silesia, and Fürstenstein, which lies some five hours' journey further north and is still in Germany. Pheasants at Fürstenstein flew well. At Pless, although there were thousands of them, they flew very badly in most places. The parties at the latter were enormous, and we were seldom less than ten guns, mostly Austrians and Germans, many of whom, including Pless himself, shot with the Browning self-loading gun as a matter of course: why, I could never understand. It is a heavy and badly balanced weapon, and they certainly did not kill any more than if they had shot with a pair of double-barrel guns, although it is true they loosed off a great many more cartridges.

After each beat, the head *Jäger*, a dear old gentleman in a green uniform covered with gold braid, used to ask each gun how many birds he had shot, with the unfortunate result that at the end of the day a great many more birds were claimed than were gathered. The man who shot the most was congratulated by the others as being the *Jagdkönig*, and, by way of recognition of his prowess, he was entitled that evening to wear, pinned on the lapel of his dress-coat, a gold badge in the form of a stag's antlers, between which was the Croix de S. Hubert. Pless's half-brother, Count Wilhelm Hochberg, then a youth of nineteen, being one of the family, was naturally not accorded the best places, but in spite of this fact he was *Jagdkönig* the first day. The same thing happened on the second day, and I began to get suspicious. The third day I watched him, and noticed that he listened attentively to what everyone else had said they had shot, and invariably arranged that he was the last to be asked, when he always went one or two better than the highest number given. On the fourth and last day, I determined that something should be done about it, and that I would be *Jagdkönig*, so I kept aside and listened to what he said, and then came forward with my number, which was always two better than his. That evening before dinner, when we were assembled in the drawing-room, all the ladies came forward and said: " *Congratulieren, Herr West ! Sie sind heute der Jagdkönig ! *"

I had taken my sister into the plot, and also one or two of the other guns, who were very annoyed with the young Count for his behaviour, and it was agreed that it would be a good thing to teach him a lesson. I now took off the badge with which I had been decorated and handed it to Daisy, saying: " I'm no *Jagdkönig*, any more than Willusch is! I just went one or two more than he did after each stand— I got so tired of his being *Jagdkönig* every night! "

The Count was furious, but all Pless said was: " That just shows what rot it is to count birds before they are gathered. I'll never allow it again," and he never did.

There was something picturesquely mediæval about shooting abroad in those days. All the old customs of venery were kept up. Every *Jäger* carried a bugle, and over each species of game after it had been laid out on the ground a different form of ' Last Post ' was played by the buglers, who lined up in front of the stricken corpses and were conducted by the head *Jäger*. Even when one went out alone after roe deer, and was successful in killing one, the *Jäger*, on arrival at the gate of the Castle, would stop and blow a blast announcing the death of the roe deer.

Walking up partridges at Fürstenstein was amusing; it was not done in the ordinary way, with two or three beaters and perhaps the same number of guns walking in line. I was sent out once with Prince Linyar for this form of sport and, to my astonishment, when we arrived at the meeting-place I discovered what looked like half the population of the neighbourhood awaiting us. We proceeded to form a huge horseshoe, the ends of which were at least half a mile apart and the total perimeter quite a mile, the beaters being about fifty yards apart. Linyar was on one side of the horseshoe and I on the other. Keeping our formation correctly, under the guidance of the *Jägers*, we proceeded to beat in a whole country towards a large field of maize. The nearer we got to the maize field, the closer was the formation of the horseshoe. At first the partridges got up and flew ahead; then they began to fly back over the line and offered very sporting shots. When we arrived at the field, thirty or forty coveys must have gone into it, besides innumerable hares. Linyar and I were posted, and the beaters were sent round and began to walk slowly through the maize. Instead of getting up in coveys, most of the birds started to go back in two and threes. There were three operations of this kind during the day, and the ground covered each time was considerable. We killed over eighty brace and innumerable hares, and for two guns it was a wonderful day's sport.

Another enjoyable day I had at Pless was shooting hares in the winter when the snow was frozen hard. Here again an army of beaters was employed, at least three hundred, and to every ten a *Jäger* was allotted, whose duty it was to see that his squad kept their line. We were four guns: my brother-in-law, self, and two officers from the garrison, who were not particularly good shots. When we arrived at the meeting-place we found the beaters already in formation. A line about six hundred yards wide had been made, the men abreast facing in the direction in which we were going; at each end of this line was a gap of about fifty yards, after which, at right angles to the front line, was another line of beaters extending for about five hundred yards on each flank, one man behind the other. To ensure that this formation should not be broken, young spruce trees had been cut down and placed at two-hundred-yard intervals, all in perfect alignment, one line for each gun; so that all one had to do was to walk up one's own particular row of spruce trees. The beaters, ignorant Polish peasants, typical ' *Kanonenfutter*,' were kept in their places by the *Jägers* with oaths and often kicks.

At a signal given by the head *Jäger* on his bugle, the whole line advanced. The spruce trees extended for about three miles, and at the end of this distance a huge net was spread across the plain. Behind the net were shelters, in which were other *Jägers* whose duty it was to drive the hares back as soon as they approached the net. At the first start the hares got up and ran in front of the guns. Pless and I, one on each flank, were near the gaps, and as the flank beaters approached the ends of the net the hares started to double back and make for the gaps. The flank guns, of course, had by far the best shooting. I have never seen hares run faster, nor would I have believed it possible for hares to have hidden in the snow in the way they did and only jump up and dart off when the beaters approached. We had four drives of this description during the day and killed over eight hundred hares, of which more than three-quarters were shot by Pless and myself. The arrangements were perfect and were a striking proof of German efficiency.

The best way to get to Pless was to go via Vienna. One night I found myself at a loose end in that city and, on the recommendation of the porter of the Bristol hotel, I visited the Horseshoe restaurant, where there was a cabaret. After I had been there a short time, the waiter came and informed me that Fräulein Mitzi would like to make my acquaintance; and a few yards away I saw a much-made-up blonde ogling me. I politely informed the waiter that I was not one of the gentlemen who prefer blondes. Three minutes later he came back and told me that Fräulein Anna had an equal desire to make my acquaintance. This time a decided brunette was indicated, and again I declined the invitation. Nothing daunted, the waiter returned a third time and drew my attention to the most appalling-looking, painted youth. 'Good Heavens!' I thought, 'this is no place for me,' and, placing a twenty-crown piece on the table, left hurriedly.

Chapter XV

DEER-STALKING

FOR a man who is fit, able to walk, climb and sometimes even run, there is no finer sport than deer-stalking. Should he be lucky enough to own a deer forest himself, he can, if he wishes, do his own stalking, which is more than half the fun and excitement of the game. A good shot is always a good shot and pleasing to the man behind the rifle; but to have successfully pitted your brains against a stag's power of sight and smell and to have arrived within a hundred and fifty yards of him unperceived is by far the more satisfactory achievement. Were it not for the fact that venison is food and that deer have to be kept down, I have often thought that I would just as soon snap the animal with a Kodak as shoot him.

In one or two forests which I have stalked all my life, I have been allowed the privilege of stalking for myself, and know what a difference it makes to the day's enjoyment. Speaking generally, most stalkers object to an amateur doing his own stalking; it is his, the stalker's, business to bring the man out with him up to the stag, hand him the rifle and tell him which stag to take. I have met a few stalkers, dour Scotsmen, who carry out the letter of their task admirably, but fail to enter into the spirit of the sport, and discuss matters with the guest who has been sent out with them. It was with such a man that I had my first day's stalking at Invercauld, many years ago: his name was McHardie, a curious old fellow who always wore trousers on the hill instead of the orthodox knickers and stockings. On that memorable day, full of excitement, having hardly slept the night before, I made an early start. McHardie, who was head-stalker and lived near the house, was waiting

188

for me in the yard with two ponies. When he saw me he just grunted " Good morning," and evidently took me for a young ignoramus unworthy of his skill as a stalker. One of the main points in deer-stalking is to have the right-coloured clothes, of a tone which blends with the surroundings, and I noticed that he studied mine, which, fortunately, were all right. Followed by two ghillies, we rode about six miles to the spying-place, where McHardie dismounted, put a quid of tobacco into his mouth, and took out his spy-glass. I followed his example (except for the tobacco), but never having spied before, I failed to pick up any deer. After a silence of about ten minutes, broken only by the expectorations of the stalker, he shut up his glass. " Can't you see any deer? " I asked. " Nothing worth a shot," was the answer.

I explained to him that, never having seen deer on the hill in Scotland before, I should like to have a look at them, even if these were too small to shoot.

" It's just a waste of time," was his comment. However, I insisted on his pointing out to me where they were. Then began the most extraordinary sort of negative explanation I have ever heard, which went something like this :

" Ye see yon craggie on the skyline? "

" Yes," I said, looking where he pointed.

" Weel, if ye cast your een doon the side o' the hull ye'll come to a big black hag. If ye look to the west o' that a wee bittie " (no self-respecting stalker ever says ' right ' or ' left '; he always mentions the points of the compass) " ye'll see a green patch."

" Yes, yes ! I see," I answered, becoming more and more excited.

" Weel, they're no there." Another pause, and a spit; and I felt inclined to say : ' Where the hell are they, then? '

" If ye carry your een a wee bittie further doon the burn," the monologue continued, " which runs oot o' the green patch, ye'll come to some burnt heather : weel, there's twa beasts lying doon on the edge o' the burnt heather—but I doot ye'll see them ! "

I did see them eventually, and realised for the first time the difficulty of picking up deer when they are lying unless one's eye is accustomed to it.

We got up and proceeded to climb for about a mile. No word of explanation as to where we were going or what was likely to happen was forthcoming; he just plodded on like a machine, and gave me the impression that he was bored with the whole affair. Suddenly he flopped down as if he'd been shot, and I had the presence of mind to do likewise. He turned round and in a stertorous whisper said: " I see some beasts."

" Where? where? " I said, and started to get up.

" Lie doon."

Crawling on his stomach for about fifty yards, he got behind a knoll and took out his glass. The sun was shining and I could see, about a quarter of a mile away, a herd of deer. I could not understand how they could possibly have seen us from that distance, and did not realise that we were on the skyline, until one of the ghillies who were close behind explained to me. I took out my glass and crawled up alongside McHardie, and, seeing that there were one or two good stags, promptly developed the first symptoms of stag fever. I ventured the remark that these were certainly shootable.

" Can ye see them? " he asked me.

" Of course I can," I answered indignantly. " I saw them with the naked eye."

At this I seemed to go up a point or two in his estimation, and, as I was evidently looking in the right direction, he believed me. Without taking me into his confidence as to how he intended to stalk the deer, he started off again. He was a fine stalker, and by observing everything he did, even to taking up little bits of heather and throwing them in the air to see which way the wind was blowing, and often standing and watching the scud on the side of the hill, I learnt quite a lot.

Suddenly he stopped, took the rifle out of its case, and asked me if I had often shot with one. I assured him that I knew all about that. He then instructed me to crawl beside him up to a stone about twenty yards in front of us, whence we peered over and saw the deer about a hundred and fifty yards away.

" Take the nearest light-coloured beast standing," were his instructions.

Much to my relief I found that the symptoms of stag fever had passed away. I took a careful aim, and killed my first stag. The rifle I was using, which had been lent me by Cecil Lowther, was a ·450 single-barrel which kicked like a mule, so there was no chance of getting another stag, as the whole herd went off like a flash.

I was delighted, but I think McHardie was astonished. I was duly blooded, and we sat down and ate our lunch. I tried my utmost to pump him as to the why and wherefore of all we had done, but could get nothing but monosyllables out of him, and it was not until some years afterwards, when I really knew something about the game, that he condescended to discuss with me some of the interesting features of deer-stalking.

I am glad to say that that type of stalker is the exception rather than the rule: most of them are the most charming class of men I have ever come across—Nature's gentlemen, in fact. If they are out with a man who is keen and active they will take him into their council of war and discuss every detail before the commencement of a stalk, and explain exactly the route to be taken, and even show the point where it is intended to get into the deer.

Another stalker at Invercauld was a very different type from McHardie. His name was Macpherson, a sinewy giant of about six feet three, with a flowing beard and whiskers; he looked a true Highlander, the sort of man who had fought at Culloden, which battlefield could be seen through a glass from the highest point of his beat. One day in 1899 when I was out with him we had had a long disappointing morning and seen nothing worth a shot, and were having lunch together on the side of a hill. Opposite us was another face, about a mile away. War was in the air, and, like most Highlanders of his type, he took an intelligent interest in what was going on in the world. Suddenly he said to me:

" Supposing the Boers (he pronounced it ' Boors ') were on yonder hull, what would Mr. West be doing? "

The question was so unexpected that for the moment I was at a loss for an answer, but, with the slight military knowledge that I possessed, I tried to explain to him the procedure of an artillery preparation followed by an infantry attack; and he kept saying " Eh, ah! Eh, ah! " After a pause he continued:

" I've been wanting for a long time to tell a gentleman from London aboot an idea I have in ma heed."

" What is it? "

" Weel, I'm thinking that if a man in a balloon were to go above the Boors and if he were to drop bullets shaped like arrows upon their heeds, it would be doing them grievous bodily haarm! "

He little realised that in another sixteen years what he suggested would actually be carried out, only by aeroplanes instead of balloons.

Macpherson had a little Skye terrier called Toddles, the only creature that lived with him. He explained to me that he had tried a housekeeper, but that she had left him as she found the place lonely. As he lived in a cottage on the hills, with not another living soul within miles, I was not surprised. Then he added that he wasn't sorry: women worrited him. Another day when I was out with him we were after a very fine ten-pointer, which had a lot of hinds with him and kept moving on. At last, late in the afternoon, when it was almost dusk, I got a shot and broke his foreleg. Toddles had been left with a ghillie about a mile away, but, much to our astonishment, she suddenly turned up within a few minutes of the shot being fired. We were standing at the place where the stag had been wounded, and the little dog, without being told and without hesitation, took up the scent of the blood and was off like a streak of lightning. I never imagined she would bay the stag, and, even if she did, I was nervous that she might be hurt. We followed after on the run and suddenly heard her barking. When we came up we found that this little dog had bayed the stag in a burn about a mile from where she had started, and thus enabled me to get him.

I had another amusing day's stalking at Invercauld after the South African War. One of the beats, known as ' the Lion's Face,' was only supposed to be good in a certain wind. I had been out stalking two days running, and it was my turn to stay at home, but when ' the Lion's Face ' was offered to two other rifles and they, knowing that the wind was wrong for it, chose instead to stay at home and play golf, my host, the late Sir Sigismund Neumann, asked me if I would like to take my chance. I jumped at it, and went out to consult Lamont, the stalker of the beat, who lived near the house.

" I'm afraid it is no much use," he said, " but we'll just try. Anyway, it'll be better than crawling aboot the hoose."

We went right up the steep ascent along the Balmoral March and saw stags, but they got our wind and went off the ground. On our way home I sat down to have a spy at some low ground overlooking the town of Braemar and also the golf-course, where the men who might have been in my place could be seen like ants. To my astonishment I picked up two stags below a large rock. Lamont had not seen them and, like many other stalkers, was annoyed at the idea of an amateur finding a deer before he himself had. He eventually had to admit that one certainly was worth a shot. It was an easy stalk, and when we got into them both were lying, one a very fine ten-pointer. It was getting late in the season, and this was evidently a case of a big stag travelling with his companion from Mar Forest across to Balmoral. I mention this day's sport as showing what a lot of luck there is in the game.

I have been lucky enough to have stalked a great deal in two of the best forests in Scotland: Strathconon in Ross-shire, belonging to Captain Christian Combe (known to his friends as ' Squeezer '), and the other Lochmore in Suther-landshire, belonging to the Duke of Westminster. The former is noted for its fine heads, the latter for the high average weight of the deer killed. Two days' stalking—one in each of these forests—stand out among the many others that I have enjoyed.

The first, at Strathconon, was on a beat called Schuir Vuillin (pronounced Scur Vullen), and the stalker's name was Rory Mackay, an old friend of mine, whose eyes were of different colours, but both equally good when it came to finding deer. The climb is a steep one, the mountain being three thousand feet above the sea. The view from the top is magnificent: on a clear day it is possible to see Dunrobin and the whole of Dornoch Firth, while to the south the best-known peaks of the Grampians can be distinguished. As is the case with most of the highest hills in Scotland, when one gets to the top the going is easy, and might be compared to a Turkey carpet. We sat down and spied. Sure enough at the far end of the plateau, and under the northern peak, about half a mile away, was a large herd of deer. After a careful scrutiny I said: " Rory, there are two of the finest ten-pointers in that herd that I've ever seen in Scotland."

" Mr. West is right, and those are the two we'll be going after."

I realised that a right and left was impossible, as the herd was a large one and the two big stags were some distance apart. After a good stalk I shot the first. The others went north on to what are called the Chaiseachain Flats and, eventually turning west up wind, settled on ground which was off our beat.

Captain Combe is the most generous owner of a deer forest that I know, as he allows his guest to shoot three stags, or more if he has ponies to spare. I had three ponies out that day, and a couple of hours later shot a second stag. At the particular point of the forest where we were there is an old right of way which comes up from Strathconon over the pass down to Achnasheen. Not once in ten years is this pass used, and even then only by wandering gypsies, or ' tinkers ' as they are called in that part of the country. Luck was with us that day. After we had had our lunch we sat looking with longing eyes upon the first herd we had seen, feeding peacefully off our ground about a mile away. Suddenly

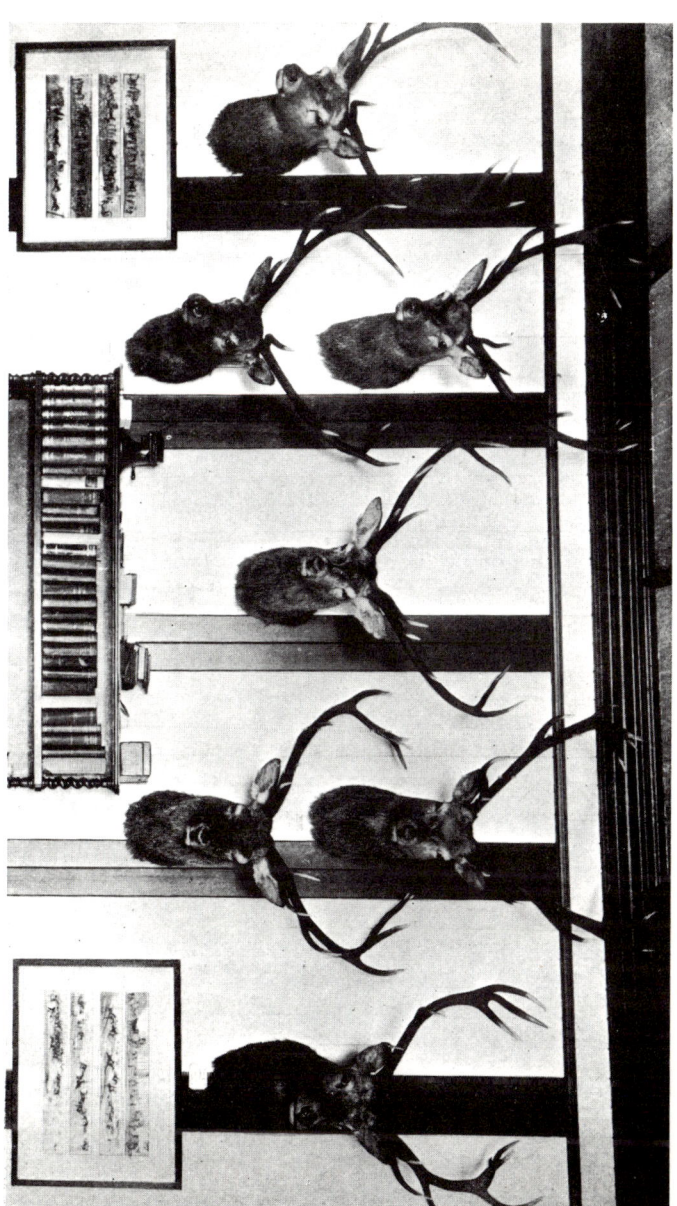

HEADS IN THE SMOKING-ROOM AT STRATHCONON

Rory said to me: "There's something disturbing them," and sure enough there was. Instead of working up wind, however, they seemed inclined to go straight back to their home at Schuir Vuillin. "There must be something coming up the right of way," said Rory. We started to run to a place we both knew which overlooked a pass the deer were bound to take if they continued in the direction in which they were moving. Getting myself into position, I waited patiently, and I admit I was trembling with excitement at getting the other ten-pointer. We hadn't to wait long. The whole herd came into sight a little below us, galloping madly. They were taking the pass.

"The big fellow's leading!" Rory whispered. "Take him as he passes yon grey stone—it's about a hundred and fifty yards."

I looked carefully. I always judge the distance of a stag by a golf shot, and this one looked to be a full iron shot—in other words, about a hundred and seventy-five yards. I aimed in front of the big fellow as he passed the stone. "You've missed him," said Rory. "Take another." I took what I considered to be the next biggest, and dropped him in his tracks. "Well done!" said Rory; "but I wish you'd got the first one."

I got up, saying as I did so: "I could have sworn I hit him, Rory."

While the last rites were being performed on the third stag I took out my glass and watched the herd galloping away in the distance. Suddenly I caught sight of a fork sticking out of the heather about three hundred yards away from where I was standing. "Rory," I exclaimed, "I didn't miss him!"

The old fellow took out his glass and saw that I was right. "But," he added with distress, "whatever shall I do? We've only three ponies out; we'll not get that stag home to-night, and the Captain will never forgive me!" I knew my host well enough to know that he would not find fault with the stalker when I had recounted to him the exciting day's sport, and I was right: no one was more pleased than he was. When I reached the second big stag I found that he was shot through the bottom of the heart, and only the pace at which he was going had carried him so far. He was a magnificent animal, his head being even finer than that of the one I had shot in the morning.

This was not the first nor the last occasion when I have seen deer come down wind in order to get back to their home ground. Hinds often do it, but it is, of course, far rarer with stags.

" Squeezer " Combe is a fine rifle-shot and a keen deer-stalker—so keen, in fact, that one of his guests was inspired to draw the caricature of him here reproduced, suggesting what might happen if he ran short of ammunition on the hill.

The second day referred to was at Lochmore. The night before, Westminster—or Bendor, as he is called—told me I was to go out on the Arkle beat. This meant a drive of about two miles to where Macaulay, the stalker, lived, whose habit it was to await one's arrival with the ponies ready saddled. When I got there I saw him working in his hay-field. He came running towards me and said: "I'm think-ing His Grace has made a mistake. I told him two days ago that I had arranged for the shepherds to gather the sheep on my beat to-day." I said it was too late to alter the arrange-ments now, and that if he would get the ponies saddled I would gallop up the path and see what could be done. After about three miles I got to what are known as " Lord Reay's Flats," where pandemonium reigned: dogs barking, sheep baa-ing, men whistling; and in the distance one could see deer galloping like squadrons of cavalry. Things looked hopeless. The shepherd in charge came up to the path, and I offered him a pound if he would gather in his dogs and undertake not to move from the spot for three hours. I knew my only chance was in one corrie some distance below us, which I hoped the sounds had not reached, as the wind was right. Macaulay came up about a quarter of an hour later, and off we started, at a jog-trot, to look into this corrie. Sure enough there were deer—and stags—on the far side, and absolutely unstalkable from where we were;

CAPT. COMBE ON THE HILL

THE BLOOD-LUST, OR

WHEN, SHOOTING NO LONGER SATISFIES.

it meant going round and coming in above them. There was no time to lose. It took us a good two hours to get round, and eventually, when we got into position, it was so steep that the stalker had to hold my feet as I was taking aim at the beasts below me. I shot one lying, and he never moved. The others got up, and I took a second, when, to my astonishment, the one I had shot at first, and thought dead, got up and moved slowly off. I gave him another and he fell. We were only just in time, as soon after this pandemonium raged again among the hills.

When we got down to the deer, I found that I had shot the first one right through the base of one horn. It had stunned him, but fortunately had not injured the antlers, and he was a royal. I started to walk back across the moor to Stack Lodge, and, if I had had a gun, could have shot three or four brace of grouse. My car was waiting at the lodge, where all the fishing-rods were kept, as it was close to the River Laxford, and I asked the stalker's wife whether anybody had been fishing that day. " Her Grace and the Princess (my sisters) have been flogging the whole day, and never a touch," she replied. Then I said to Price, my chauffeur, who was as good a ghillie as he was a mechanic : " We must have a try." It was then six o'clock in the evening. I got two salmon within the hour, and went home in triumph.

The only other places where I have ever killed two stags and two salmon in the same day were Morsgail in the Lewes and Glen Canisp, both of which had been taken by Minto Wilson. At the former I was lucky enough to do this two days out of three.

Many years ago at Lochmore I was out with a stalker, by name Willie Elliot, on a beat called Ben Owsket, not very far from the sea. I was stalking myself, and was after a very fine stag we had seen in the morning. We were within a quarter of a mile of the deer when suddenly, about two hundred yards away, we saw a huge bird sitting on a rock. I took out my little single Zeiss, and was certain that it was a specimen of the sea eagle, then the rarest bird in the

British Isles; now, unhappily, extinct. I could see the white on its tail, so there could be no mistake, and I made up my mind to see how close I could get to it, not, of course, with any intention of shooting it. Willie Elliot was furious, as he knew that by doing so the deer we were after would see me; he kept on muttering : " Eh, what a peety, what a peety ! "

We got within twenty yards of the bird before he saw us. The rock upon which he was sitting was not steep enough for him to take off from, and he flapped along for about fifty yards, making a hideous noise, to a ledge from which he could get on the wing. I told Willie Elliot that we had succeeded in doing what probably very few others had done, but he was very sulky, and kept saying: "Yon was a graand beast," meaning, of course, the stag. The deer were by now a long way off, but I comforted him by telling him we would now go after them, and eventually I got the stag. He was a magnificent eleven-pointer, and weighed seventeen stone. I still attempted to get Willie to appreciate the bird, but the most the old man would say was: " Weel, they're just twa graand beasts."

A friend of mine, the late Arthur James, was lessee of a very famous forest called Glen Quoich, where I used to stalk. I was sent out one day on a good beat and told to kill two stags. I got one in the morning, and late that afternoon saw another herd lying on a slope. The corrie where we were was a narrow one, and I could see it would not be a very long shot from one side to the other. After a successful stalk we found ourselves on the opposite side about two hundred yards away. All the deer were lying; a good stag faced us broadside and a smaller, but shootable one, immediately below him. We waited some time for them to rise. It was horribly cold, and I said to the stalker: " I'm going to take the big fellow lying down." I fired and, to my amazement, saw the stag immediately below him fall. " You've shot the wrong beast," the stalker said, with withering sarcasm. "That's not the stag I aimed at," I replied; " he must have got up as I fired and covered the other one." The big stag, meanwhile, had gone slowly round the corner out of sight.

198

I thought it curious that he should move off so slowly, and followed him up, to find him lying a hundred yards away, stone dead. The same bullet had killed both stags.

A friend of mine, Eric Fullerton,* who was staying in another lodge with me on one occasion, was sent out stalking and shot a small stag. His host asked him, when he returned, what luck he had had. " I got a stag," he said.

" Good one? "

" No."

" Good head? "

" No." Then, after a pause, he added: " But he was very well bred."

In the early days of motoring another friend, who shall be nameless, had a forest in the far north of Scotland thirty miles from a railway station. He had a powerful Mors car, which used to dash along the road at what was in those days a terrific speed, so much so that it excited the ire of the few people who lived there. A complaint to the police ensued, which resulted in a letter from the Procurator Fiscal (or Public Prosecutor) of the county, intimating that a summons would be taken out if this furious driving continued. My friend, anxious to propitiate the official in question, decided to send him a haunch of venison, but, being unfamiliar with Scottish legal terms, he addressed the label to ' The Official Procurer.' Curiously enough, the haunch reached the person for whom it was intended.

There is nothing more amusing than sitting on a hill on a fine day watching the deer. Where there are one or two big stags in a herd they seem to scent danger during the stalking season, and you seldom see them without outposts, mostly hinds, at all vantage points. I had a very interesting experience at a place called Ledgowan in Ross-shire (also let to Minto Wilson). I was out by myself with one ghillie and spied a magnificent stag with about thirty hinds, in what looked like an impossible place to stalk. I decided that the only way to get in was to crawl up a shallow burn, which necessitated a detour of nearly a mile. It was getting late

* Rear-Admiral Fullerton.

in the evening when, leaving the ghillie behind, I started. When I got to the point near where I believed I should be within shot of the stag, I saw the ears of a hind lying, knew that further progress was impossible, and retired without disturbing them. I recounted my adventures that evening, and my host generously said: "As you found the animal you had better go after him again to-morrow."

The next day the stag and his harem were in almost the same spot, and his outposts appeared in the same positions. I decided to try the same stalk again, and this time I was more successful. The hind was there right enough, but she was about four yards nearer the stag. I must have been within twenty yards of her as I crawled past to eventual success.

It is admitted that a deer's power of smell is phenomenal, but I doubt whether his sight is better than a man's; for it is amazing what it is possible for one man to do by himself right in the face of deer. On many occasions I have slid down a hill a few feet at a time, within three or four hundred yards of deer, remaining motionless directly a head looked up, restarting when the head turned or the deer began to feed again.

Once at Lochmore I was on the hill after a very wet night, when all the burns were raging torrents. I had killed two stags and was watching the herd disappear in the distance, a small stag leading, a big stag second. They came to what looked like an impassable torrent, nothing but brown foam. The small stag hesitated; he wasn't for it, until he received a prod in his haunches from the stag following him, which sent him flying into the water. After waiting to see that his junior crossed successfully, the big stag stepped in gingerly and got over, and the whole herd followed.

STALKING ABROAD

I once received an invitation from the old Duke of Pless (my brother-in-law's father), a true ' grand seigneur ' of the old school, to go and shoot a stag in what was then part of Prussian Silesia, at a place called Promnitz, not very far

GOOD SCOTCH HEAD FROM STRATHCONON

GERMAN HEAD

Dimensions : (*a*) antler spread, 37″; (*b*) base of skull to tips of
horns, 38″; (*c*) circumference at base of skull, 8½″.

from the town of Pless. It was a great honour, as only twelve stags were shot in the year, and were usually reserved for the Emperor, the Crown Prince, Archdukes, Grand Dukes or other German princelings. The forest was a forest in the true sense of the word: about sixty thousand acres of magnificent pinewoods, a certain amount of oak scrub and, here and there, broad openings of reedy meadow-like land through which there often flowed a sluggish stream. Stags were only stalked during the rutting season, a shot being obtained through following up the roar. It is exciting to hear a big stag roaring, to go through dense forest following the sound, sometimes nearer, sometimes getting farther away; very often, when a view is obtained, all that can be seen are the antlers or the haunches, but no vital spot to aim at. In the very early morning and evening the deer come out into the meadows to feed, and can be stalked up the side of a wood. The third method is by driving down the rides in a curious-looking vehicle with the seating accommodation, like that of an Irish car, back to back, but, instead of being over two wheels, is slung low between four. So much timber is felled in the forest that the deer take no notice of timber wagons, and the carriage described is a sort of copy of these.

The day after I arrived at Promnitz I was called before daybreak, about 4.30, and after a scanty breakfast I found one of these curious-looking affairs waiting for me. I was sent out with the head-stalker, a man named Reich, who wore a *Kaiserlicher* moustache and looked the part of a sergeant-major in a Guards regiment, in which, as a matter of fact, he had served. In my best German I told him that I thought it was very unfair to the stag to take advantage of his simplicity by allowing him to mistake our carriage for a timber wagon, and suggested that it was rather like shooting a bullock from the side of a road. He was a true sportsman, was Reich, and, somewhat to my amazement, he entirely agreed with me; so when we got to the beat which had been given us we left our sham wagon behind and started on foot.

I should mention that before the stalking season starts

every stag to be shot is known to the stalkers. Reich said that the Duke had allotted to me an exceedingly fine one, that the local watcher knew he was with hinds in the forest, and that he was roaring, but that he had not actually seen him for some weeks. We heard him that morning, but did not see him, and I returned home about ten o'clock and lay down until one, at which hour a huge meal was served. At four o'clock the Duke told me that I had to go out again after the same animal. I did this for three days in succession and, except for a glimpse of a huge head between some trees, which disappeared in a flash, I never saw him. During one of the unsuccessful days when we were following up a roar the stag evidently made off at a fast pace, because the next time we heard him the roaring was a long way off. A few minutes later a Polish charcoal-burner happened to come down the path. It was evident that he had given the deer the wind, and I never heard any man receive such a torrent of abuse as that wretched man got from Reich. I think he thought he was going to be shot on the spot; he got down on his knees and clasped the stalker round the legs, imploring mercy. It was not an edifying spectacle, and caused me to think furiously.

On the fourth day Reich was told that he had to get me *a* stag, and I shot one that morning, a fine animal with what appeared to me an enormous head. I was due to return that night to Fürstenstein, and about four o'clock that afternoon Reich came in with the news that my stag—the original one —had been seen in the open. Having already got one I did not expect to be allowed to shoot another, but my kind host insisted upon my going out, and this time I was more fortunate. We had a most exciting stalk up the edge of a wood, and I got him: a twelve-pointer, with the most magnificent head I have ever seen. He weighed no less than thirty-six stone, clean. The head subsequently won the first prize at the Sportsmen's Exhibition that winter in Berlin, and I give a picture of it here.

The red-deer stag, in this part of Germany at any rate, is not the same as his Scottish relations, as, in addition to his

PROMNITZ, PLESS: A GERMAN SHOOTING-LODGE

WILD BISON AT PROMNITZ, PLESS

being more than twice the size—which may be attributed to the excellence of the feeding—his nose is distinctly Roman.

Two years ago when stalking at Strathconon with the head-stalker, Cameron, the mist came down so badly that we were only able to see about fifty yards in front of us. Several stags were roaring near, and I asked him if he had ever tried to stalk a stag by sound, explaining to him what I had done in Promnitz. He became eager to try and, with the wind assisting us, we started off in the direction of what seemed the nearest stag. Suddenly the roar sounded quite close to us. We both flopped down, and a few seconds later what looked like an enormous stag appeared over the skyline. The mist was my undoing. He looked so large that I felt I could not miss him, but I did: he was nearer than I imagined, and I shot over his back.

On another occasion when staying at Pless I took part in a combined wild boar and bison (*Auerochs*) drive in Promnitz Forest. Before the War this herd of bison, with the exception of those in Russia, was the last in Europe. The animals were very like American buffalo to look at. During the trouble in that part of the world after the Armistice was signed this herd was almost exterminated by the Poles.

On the day in question we made an early start on the twenty-mile drive into the forest. We were eight rifles and were each given a butt. These butts looked like pulpits made of brushwood and were raised about six feet from the ground and faced a stockade about three-quarters of a mile in length, which was built in the form of an obtuse angle. On the side of each butt certain trees were carefully splashed with red, and one was supposed to shoot only outside these marks. The drive started about six miles in the rear of the butts in the form of an exaggerated crescent. Very soon the wild boar began to arrive, galloping past us, and directly they got to the stockade started running down it. Those who got to the end escaped. The butts were about a hundred yards from the stockade, and a galloping wild boar is not the easiest thing to shoot with a rifle. Towards the end of the drive I heard what sounded like an elephant coming along behind me: it was a bison, and Pless had told me that I might shoot one if it happened to come near me. I did so, and this time I really did feel as though I were shooting a cow! Three bison and thirty-eight wild boar was the bag that morning.

In 1912 I did a cure at Carlsbad, and as an after-cure was invited by Count Larisch to stay with him in the Tyrol, at a place called Spittal Ampern, for some chamoix shooting, a form of sport in which I had never before indulged. I and another man went by train to Alt Aussee, and from there we motored through some most gorgeous scenery. The house where we stayed had been an old monastery. On the evening I arrived I went for a walk round the building, and was suddenly confronted with not one but hundreds of grinning skulls looking at me from the bars of what appeared to be a basement window without glass. On a closer examination I saw rows and rows of thigh-bones and other parts of the human skeleton, all carefully stacked, and was told that they were the bones of the monks who had died there. How they came to be so beautifully stacked and docketed, like the stores in a workshop, I never discovered. There was something very sinister about that monastery, and I never slept comfortably any night I was there.

We made an early start the morning after I arrived, and rode for about six miles on ponies, and then began a very stiff climb. The going was bad, and at times the path overhung steep *glacis*, where a false step might have proved disastrous. We eventually arrived at the butts, constructed of loose stones, as the chamoix were to be driven towards us. After a wait of about three hours I was able with my glasses to see these beautiful little animals approaching over the skyline. Anyone who has never see a chamois can form no conception of its marvellous acrobatic feats and the apparent ease with which it does them. Exquisite little creatures, it seemed a pity to shoot them and, except that it was a novelty, it was not a form of sport that particularly appealed to me. We were six rifles, and the total bag was over forty chamoix.

CHAMOIS SHOOTING, TYROL
Centre figures: Author, Count Larisch and Lady Houston-Boswell

Chapter XVI

FISHING

THE person who has never caught a salmon still has something to live for. A well-hit half volley to square leg at cricket, a fine drive at golf, or a brilliant stroke at tennis all inspire feelings of satisfaction, but they do not necessarily thrill. From the point of view of sport, there is no thrill in the world like the first pull of a salmon, and when the fisherman realises that he is hooked, there come all those moments of intense excitement as to whether he will remain on; the steady boring upstream, then the rush across the pool, the reel screaming, and, maybe, a leap or two out of the water; finally the gasp of relief when he is safely landed on the bank, and, after the last rites have been performed, his beautiful silver sides and rainbow sheen to be studied and appreciated.

It is true my first salmon was anything but silvery. He was caught late in September when I was staying at Guisachan many years ago. Still, he was my first, and I experienced all the thrills and excitement I have attempted to describe. Like most novices, I was lucky, and caught three that day, while three more were lost owing to my inexperience. After that I used to go every year in March or April to stay with my friend the late Colonel Hugh Warrender, who had a beat on the Naver, a Sutherlandshire river, and one of the best in Scotland. Hugh was a very methodical person, and on the occasion of our first visit he, having preceded me by several days, announced that he had looked up Bettyhill (the nearest village) in the *Encyclopaedia Britannica*, where it was stated that the place was noted for the beauty of its women. We agreed the following Sunday to walk the five miles there to test this statement. Accordingly we set out, and when we got within half a mile of the place saw two women approaching us.

" Now we shall see! " he said.

And we did. When they got near us, I well remember his intense disappointment, for they were quite the ugliest pair of females either of us had seen in our lives. We returned home wiser and sadder men.

Whether it is the coldness of the water, or the fact that he is fresh up from the sea, the fish caught in the Spring is a totally different creature from the one caught later. He fights like a madman. Whenever I went to Rhifail, which was the name of the lodge where we stayed, I always had the same ghillie, who went by the name of Black George. He was an inveterate gossip. One day he announced to me that the Skelpic rods had been taken at last, as in those days salmon-fishing was not so much sought after as it is now. He went on to say that an old gentleman was the lessee, but that he did not expect he'd do much good, as he would find the fishing too difficult: " and indeed," he added, " they're telling me he cannot get about; they say he has not got a pair of feet that could walk upon a Turkey carpet! "

There is something extraordinarily attractive about these north-country rivers in early Spring. March is often a very fine month, with just sufficient sunshine to melt enough snow to keep the river up. The upper beats flow through moors, and one can hear the old cock grouse crowing everywhere, and even see deer near by, for at that time of the year they appear quite tame. The top of the Naver is dominated by Ben Cleibriach, one of the highest hills in Sutherlandshire. On a fine day he looks like some huge white pyramid against a brilliant blue background. The river which I have fished most in Scotland is the Helmsdale, also in Sutherlandshire, the only one where I have ever got more than ten salmon in a day. Fishing on this river some years ago, I hooked a big fish in the pool called ' the Chancellor '; after having had him on for several minutes he rushed to the far side, gave a prodigious leap, and landed on the opposite bank, where he struggled, eventually slithering back into the water.

I made certain that I should lose him, but he was finally landed.

The Helmsdale is divided into two series of beats, those above the Falls and those below. The latter fish best in the Spring, the former in Summer months. The lodge where I have stayed for many years belongs to General Hickman, whose wife is a keen and very good fisherwoman. It is the custom on this river, if the rods fishing the upper beats happen to come home before those fishing the lower, for the latter to signal to the cars containing the returning fishermen what their catch is, and to receive a corresponding answer. Sometimes it is done by waving a handkerchief, at others by holding up fingers, if the road happens to be near enough. On one occasion when Mrs. Hickman was fishing and had caught five fish, a car passed her along the road which she took to be coming from one of the upper beats; she held up five fingers just in front of her. The car, however, belonged to a total stranger, who imagined that he was being insulted, and, not to be outdone, put the fingers of both hands to his nose.

The Helmsdale is an amazing river. In a good year, late in the season, there is hardly a square yard which does not hold a fish. You see great waves as they dart away from the shallow places which the ordinary salmon fisherman would never imagine deep enough to hold a fish.

Much has been said and written about the use of a greased line and small flies when fishing for salmon late in the season when the river is very low. I have tried it on many occasions in the Helmsdale, and, while it is true that you rise a great number of fish—many more than in the orthodox way—it is extraordinary how few of them seem to take hold.

The best day's fishing combining salmon and sea-trout that I ever had in my life was on the Laxford, the river mentioned in the preceding chapter. I had been stalking every day and had got rather stale, so I asked my host whether I might be allowed to go out for a day's sea-trout fishing on the river. He recommended the loch as being the better chance, but I am not one who cares much about loch fishing, so I was permitted to go on the river. It was in September, and the day was brilliant, not a cloud in the sky, and a fairly strong east wind; from the point of view of the fisherman a less promising day could not have been imagined. True, there would be a ripple on the pools, but the river was gin clear, and I was obliged to use the finest tackle and a ten-foot trout rod. I put on a fly which I had never before tried. It was a Blue Zulu, and the fish took nothing else the whole day. That evening my bag was thirty-five sea-trout, several over three pounds and one of five, three big brown trout, one nearly four pounds—a most unusual occurrence in that river—two grilse, and one salmon of eleven pounds; and I was broken by three other salmon.

I have fished a certain amount in Ireland, and in 1920, during the troubled times, took a rod on the Bandon river, which was so poached as to become useless. One would go down to the river in the morning, and at each pool it was possible to see where nets had been dragged during the night.

The Irish method of fishing a prawn, or shrimp as they call it, is very deadly, especially in low water. A single hook is used, a very light rod, with the line coiled in front. The actual cast is a sort of hybrid affair between a fly and bait cast. A fly rod is used and the prawn is worked like a fly.

The other day when fishing in Ireland I had a most delightful ghillie. I started fishing a place which looked to me likely to hold a salmon, although he said it was no use. I hooked a fish, and when he had gaffed it he turned round to me and said: " Oi haven't seen a fish hooked in that shpot for tin years—and the last one Oi saw caught there was lost!"

For his size, the sea-trout is the gamest of his species, and probably that is what makes the catching of him so attractive. Many years ago Moreton Frewen had the Inver fishing in Connemara and invited me to join him there for ten days in August. The fishing consists of a chain of three lakes, overlooked by the Pins of Connemara. The scenery is very wild. The lodge was one of the most attractive places I have ever seen, built on an island which was a glowing red mass of fuchsias. The fishing was wonderful, and it was quite easy to get a bag of forty sea-trout in one day. It was when I was there that I made my first acquaintance with an illegal still, for this part of Ireland is one of the strongholds of the distillation of that fiery liquid already referred to—potheen. I saw smoke rising one morning on the shore of the loch, and my ghillie explained whence it came. As the fish were not taking very well I thought I would go and have a look. There were two men at work, who had not noticed me, so I stalked them and came upon them suddenly, thinking to startle them. However, the joke did not answer. I didn't look like either an excise officer or an R.I.C. man, and was met with two broad grins and the offer of a drink, but I knew too much about the stuff already.

Many years later I revisited Connemara in company with two friends, where we had taken some salmon and sea-trout fishing together. There were three beats, and we changed every day; the ghillies, however, remaining on their respective beats. On one of these there was an old fellow who, like many of his countrymen, as well as being an ardent politician, possessed even more strongly that Irish characteristic of wishing to please everyone. It was in 1912, and the Home Rule Bill had just passed the Commons. I suggested to him that he could not fail to be delighted that at last the Irish were to get their own way.

" Glory be to God ! " he answered, " and to Mr. Asquith and Mr. Redmond and the like, for having given the ould country what she'd been wanting these many years. Only last night at the hotel " (every pub is an hotel in Ireland) " we were giving thanks and drinking their health . . ." and he went on in this strain even so far as to praise the other English politicians for what they had done in the matter. That evening I said to one of my friends, who was going the following day on the beat I had been on, " I want you to say to old Murphy what a terrible thing it is for Ireland that the Home Rule Bill has come, and see what he says." He did so, and the result was exactly as I had anticipated, as the old boy started off: "Bad cess to 'em—Mr. Asquith and Mr. Redmond and the loike! Shure we're deshtroyed entoirely . . ." and so on.

One year I went to stay with some friends at Biarritz, and they advised me to bring out salmon tackle to fish the Gave d'Oleron, so I put a tin box full of flies in my portmanteau. I reached Paris late one night, where the heavy luggage was examined. Something had evidently happened to upset the Customs Officer, and he did not believe me when I told him I had nothing to declare. After rummaging in my portmanteau he produced the tin box and, giving me a fierce look, said: "*Ah ha! Qu'est-ce que nous avons ici?*"

"*Ce sont des mouches.*"

"*Comment? Mouches?*"

"*Des mouches pour pêcher le saumon.*"

He opened the box and gave a gasp of astonishment; he had evidently never seen a salmon-fly before in his life. All he said was: "*Ces mouches doivent être bien sauvages!*"

Salmon flies seem to exercise a fatal fascination over salmon fishers, as well as over the fish themselves, thanks to the wiles of the tackle-makers. For when they display their wares, dilate upon the advantages of such and such a fly on a certain river, emphasise the necessity of having different flies in different lights—and all the usual salesman's blarney— the customer, if he is a novice, buys a whole heap of totally unnecessary flies which he will probably never use. The old hand knows that, provided he fishes with the right size, the variety of flies in his box need never exceed half a dozen at the outside. Salmon take a fly because it attracts their attention and probably annoys them; if it is too big it frightens them, if it is too small they cannot see it.

Once when I was staying with General Hickman at Kildonan, we were discussing, while having lunch on the hills, the sort of fly suitable to the Helmsdale. The head-keeper there, Robbie Murray, who is a very fine fisherman and an expert fly-tier, backed himself to make a fly with the material on the spot. The only stipulation he made was that he might use a little silver tinsel. The challenge was taken

A TYPICAL ENGLISH TROUT-STREAM AT LONGPARISH

A TYPICAL SCOTTISH SALMON RIVER, THE HELMSDALE

up by one of the guests, and Robbie proceeded to pull some hairs out of the coat and tail of the General's old dun shooting pony and to cut off a lock of hair from a flaring red-headed ghillie. The next day he produced a fly with a red hackle, the body made of the short hairs of the pony bound with silver tinsel, and the wings and tail a combination of red and black hair, and sure enough he caught a fish with it.

There is a bridge over the Laxford at Lochmore, below which is a salmon pool where, in clear water, many fish can be seen lying. On one occasion Herbert Cairns * and I went down armed with a fly, a minnow and a prawn, our object being to see exactly the effect upon the fish of the various baits offered. I stood on the bridge while Herbert fished. The fly caused several fish to come up and look at it without taking it. Not one paid the slightest attention to a small Silver Devon, but when the prawn appeared in the water it might have been an otter from the fright it seemed to give the fish: it practically emptied the pool. It seems curious, therefore, that a salmon ever should take a prawn.

I was fortunate enough one year to be invited by an old friend of mine, Archie Morrison,† to the River Aurland in Norway, one of the finest sea-trout rivers in that country. We arrived one morning about nine o'clock, and, after changing and breakfasting, went to have a look at the river, the ghillies having previously told us that fishing was useless except between five o'clock in the evening and eleven at night. The Aurland is a glacier-fed stream, and its water is the most lovely turquoise-blue in colour. It was a hot morning, and after sauntering along the bank we sat down to admire a pool about half a mile from the Fjord. To our astonishment we saw a huge trout rise and take a dry fly. We rushed back to the village and put up our trout rods. We fortunately each had a few large sedges and alders, and started out full of hope. The big fish took what we offered them readily, with the result that during our stay we were fishing nearly sixteen hours out of the twenty-four each

* The late Earl Cairns.
† Colonel J. A. Morrison, late Grenadier Guards.

day. Never have I seen fish play as these did. They ran up to fourteen pounds in weight. They did not bore upstream like a salmon; directly they were hooked, their one idea seemed to be to get back to the sea as quickly as possible. The whole river was only about five miles long, and a ten-pound fish on a dry fly, on a ten-foot trout rod with light tackle, can do pretty well what he likes, and even take one down half a mile and more. Naturally we lost many more than we landed. Towards sunset we got out our salmon rods and fished wet. We had marvellous sport, but not the same excitement as with the dry fly.

The following year Archie Morrison had a special rod built, and unsinkable flies tied with cork bodies, and in one day he caught, to his own rod, using a dry fly, two hundred and twelve pounds' weight of fish.

I caught my first brown trout in the River Clwyd at Ruthin, at the age of nine. I had an old reel and rod of my father's, minus a top, and had constructed the latter out of a piece of bamboo used for tying up carnations. The cast and flies I borrowed from Bolton, the butler, who was a keen fisherman and was my first instructor in the gentle art. It was on the 1st of May, and May Day, in those days, was a recognised holiday in the schools. My father promised me five shillings if I caught a fish, and, thanks more to the tuition of Bolton than to my own skill, I earned the reward. True, the trout was only about three inches long, but it counted.

All my life I have been an enthusiastic trout fisherman, though not, like some of my friends, wedded to the dry fly. Fishing upstream with a wet fly is the most killing method in small Welsh rivers; and I have often descended to the worm in low water, with deadly effect.

After my grandmother's death in 1887, we spent all the summer months in Hampshire, the paradise of dry-fly fishermen, although it was many years later that I had my first days on the Test and Itchin. Bill Craven,* who invited

* The late Mr. W. Craven.

PIKE FISHING, LAKE WINDERMERE

me to the former, was a member of what I believe to be the oldest trout-fishing club in the British Isles: the Longstock Club, on the Test just above Stockbridge. It was founded by a Yorkshire parson well over a century ago, and he and two or three cronies used to drive all the way from the north country for what they called ' THE fly period,' the fly being the Mayfly, which in those days was the only artificial fly that was fished dry. At the time of which I am writing the records of the Club were in the little house used by the members—not only their fishing records, but also those of the amount of claret and port consumed. The quantity of wine that those old gentlemen apparently got through was prodigious; during their three weeks' visit, twenty times as many bottles were drunk as fish caught! The walls of the sitting-room were adorned with rough wooden models or plaster casts of huge trout. There was an old-world atmosphere about the place which almost constrained one to wear high leggings with buttons all the way up the thigh, and a tall beaver hat, like the fishermen in the old-fashioned prints. Plus fours and waders seemed out of place. Judging by the accompanying illustration, the costumes worn in 1892 when pike-fishing were equally odd, and not so picturesque.

The late Wynne Corrie, who had a good stretch of water on the Itchin, was also most kind to me, and often gave me permission to fish. The first time I ever went there I had caught two or three fish in the morning, all about one pound—in my opinion not sufficiently large to keep, although I had been given no limit. The keeper came up and asked me what luck I had had. I told him.

" Oh, you mustn't put any back," he said. When I asked why, to my amazement he explained: " Mr. Wynne Corrie believes that they go and tell the others."

A small stretch of the Candover brook, which runs into the Itchin, was included in this fishing, and had been stocked with rainbow. I had always heard that the right way to catch a rainbow trout was to offer him a small salmon fly, and as I happened to have some tiny Dusty Millers in my box, I used them with considerable success, and subsequently wrote to my host telling him what good sport I had had and how I had caught his rainbows. He wrote back saying: " I am glad . . . but what a pity! I have been trying so hard to educate them to take their meals dry ! "

The biggest brown trout I ever caught was at Panshanger in Hertfordshire, which belonged to Lord Cowper, the river being the Mimram. Just below the house is a lake through which the river flows; at the end of the lake it slides out over a water-fall—not a sheer drop, but at an angle of forty-five degrees—and for about fifty yards runs between a high brick coping, rather like a canal lock. On either side of this coping were dense blackberry bushes. Lord Cowper had given me permission to fish, and I went over one afternoon from Salisbury Hall. I looked upstream from below the bushes, and saw some enormous trout cruising in the pool below the fall, taking something which was coming down it. As I could see no fly I realised that they were probably feeding on nymphs, and before doing anything else, I tied down the wings of one or two Iron Blues. The difficulty was to get at the fish. It was impossible to throw a fly, on account of the bushes. The only way in which this could be done was to crawl through them to the edge of the brickwork. This I proceeded to do, a painful business, but I eventually got there, my chauffeur—the same faithful Price—passing the rod over the bushes into my hand, which was extended above me. Only my head and shoulders were free, and I still found it impossible to cast. Peering carefully over the edge, I saw one monster feeding greedily, but directly I put more than a couple of feet of the rod over the side he saw it and went down, only to return again to his meal after an interval of a minute or so. I decided to attempt to flick the fly out by using the rod as a bow, and after many unsuccessful efforts I saw my nymph land in the middle of the fall —which, at that time of the year, was merely a trickle, and roll down it over the big fish. He took it at once. The line was so short that I hardly dared to strike, but he was hooked right enough. Then the question arose how to play

A GOOD DAY IN SCOTLAND : AUTHOR AND COL. HEYWORTH-SAVAGE

HUMP-BACKED TROUT FROM THE REA

him. I could not get up; dipping the point of the rod towards the water, I let the fish take out the line downstream and hoped for the best. Without raising the rod, I yelled to Price to dash through the blackberry bushes, catch hold of it wherever he could get it, and guide the fish below the coping where the bushes ceased. It was an exciting moment, but after ten minutes' careful playing we landed him. He was just over four and a half pounds.

Another river where I was given *carte blanche* to fish was the Pang, which runs into the Thames at Pangbourne. This had been taken by Sol Cork,* who himself hardly ever fished. I once said to the keeper there, a man by the name of Lake, " Why does his Lordship keep this river on? He's never here." He answered: " He comes down here two or three times a year, sir; in my opinion to let off steam. He starts to fish and he gets caught up on the opposite bank, and I've heard his Lordship let off the finest flow of language it's ever been my pleasure to listen to. Then he goes home."

Big Thames trout come up this river to spawn, and sometimes, going there early in the season, I have seen what must have been monsters, evidently dropping down to the main river.

One of the best streams I have ever fished was the Rea, on the borders of Worcestershire and Shropshire. It was here that I caught a curious humped-back trout, a photograph of which is reproduced. It weighed about a pound, and was otherwise in first-class condition.

Last year I took a stretch upon a tiny chalk stream in Hampshire, near Andover, and it was there that I learned more about the habits of trout than I ever knew before. The stream, which was full of fish, was so narrow and shallow that it was impossible to stalk a rising trout: he was put down long before one arrived within casting distance, by the numbers of fish which had been disturbed. The only thing to do was to get into the water and stay perfectly still until the fish one was after started rising again. So long as one remained

* The late Earl of Cork.

motionless, the trout took no notice—in fact many a time they began to rise a few feet from where I was standing. The big trout who takes up his position between two banks of weeds, which he knows is good feeding-ground, will spend an enormous amount of energy, not in feeding himself, but in chasing away possible poachers from the claim he has staked. They reminded me of a stag with hinds chasing off small stags. There is a dog-in-the-manger attitude about a feeding trout: many more flies than he can eat come over him, but the mere approach of a smaller of his species is sufficient to infuriate him. In fact, after many weeks' study, I came to the conclusion that trout are as unkind to each other as domestic servants, or motorists who try to pass one another on the road.

I once had some wonderful sport in America fishing in the rivers of the Californian Sierras, which had been well stocked by that state with rainbow trout. It was late in August, and most of the fishing expeditions had already started, but a friend of mine in San Francisco undertook to arrange matters. Leaving that town over-night, I arrived at a place called Lemon Cove the following morning. Here I had a day's drive in a Ford car, climbing over five thousand feet to a camp known as Giant Forest. Near it are the finest trees in the world: the famous giant redwoods, the biggest of which is known as General Grant. With my left shoulder touching the trunk the whole time, I paced it round the base; the distance was just under thirty-seven yards.

After remaining in camp for thirty-six hours to get accustomed to the height, which they told me was necessary, though I doubted it, we started off with a guide and a cook (so called), three saddle-ponies, and two mules to carry provisions for some days. I took with me a dozen eggs, but, beyond flour, the rest of the food was tinned, as we expected, of course, to live on trout. The first night out I told the cook to scramble some eggs. He said he had never heard of such a thing, so I suggested that he should allow me to scramble the eggs while he made the cookies in the Dutch oven. As he was kneading the flour I noticed that the more he did so, the blacker became the dough and the whiter his hands. Finally I asked him if he'd ever cooked before, and he told me only for himself. " What are you by trade? " I asked.

" A traction-engine driver," was the answer.

" Well, what the devil do you mean by taking four dollars a day from me to cook? "

" I guess I just thought I'd enjoy the trip."

I consulted with my guide, and we agreed to ship the cook back the following morning. He tried to make trouble, but we were two to one. As there was only one path back to Giant Forest, and one forward, which we were taking, he could not possibly go astray, so the guide and I proceeded alone.

The fishing was difficult, and necessitated casting over logs and under boughs and bushes, and one was often broken, but the sport was wonderful, and although the fish did not run as big as they do in New Zealand, I doubt whether the rivers could be more interesting or the scenery more beautiful. On one pass we went over my barometer showed ten thousand feet, and we came down into a land which might literally be described as flowing with milk and honey: great open green spaces upon which were grazing innumerable cattle and sheep, sent up to the mountains for the summer months; and, growing wild, a profusion of flowers such as one sees in every herbaceous border in England : delphiniums, lupins and others; masses of flowering shrubs; the whole air laden with perfume and the sound of droning bees. The climate was perfect: tents were quite unnecessary, and we slept under the stars.

I had a long talk with an old shepherd, who told me he had been up every summer for forty years and gave me an account of a river some ten miles away, where, he said, the trout were golden, and embroidered his story by adding that this was due to the amount of gold in the river. I determined to visit it, not for the gold, but for the trout. In one respect I found he was right—the trout were pale yellow underneath, with light copper-bronze backs and wonderful red spots. I panned several handfuls of the sand in the bed of the river, however, but found no gold.

During this trip in the mountains I was fishing a river upstream when I saw another fisherman approaching me. Who should he turn out to be but Birnham, the raiser of the famous Birnham Scouts, who did such good service on the side of the English in the South African War. I had not seen him since we dined together with the rest of Lord Methuen's staff the night before the battle of Modder River.

On the whole, I have little doubt that the dry fly is the most killing method for trout. I once found myself in a small summer camp near a lake in the Rockies, which many enthusiastic fishermen flogged with a wet fly without success, though it was full of that most beautiful fish, the American brook trout. I instructed my American acquaintances in the use of a dry fly, and no matter how calm the water was, provided the line was sufficiently greased and the fly allowed to float on a surface like glass, sooner or later a big trout would always come and take it. The inmates of the camp were thrilled, and gave what is called a ' Pink Tea ' in my honour and to celebrate the advent of the dry fly. That is many years ago, and this form of fishing is now, of course, well known in the States.

Quite the most exciting way of catching trout is by dapping for them under trees and bushes. The Kennet flows through the grounds of Ramsbury Manor, a lovely old Jacobean place belonging to Sir Francis Burdett, and here I have often indulged in this form of sport. It is essential to have the sun shining in the right quarter and to wear clothes of a good neutral tint; then, armed with the smallest trout rod, a short cast and preferably a Coch-y-bondhu (a Welsh fly supposed to represent a small beetle and pronounced Cokybundoo), mark your trout feeding, approach him with the utmost caution, placing the point of the rod a few inches at a time over the reeds or bushes until he becomes accustomed to it, and drop the fly gingerly over his nose. For me the excitement is so intense that I get trout fever and my hand invariably trembles, which gives the desired effect of an insect struggling on the surface of the water. If you are lucky, an enormous mouth appears; if you are foolish, you strike at once and nothing happens. Give him time to take it, and then, the merest touch—and he is hooked and the fun begins. Trout feeding under trees are often cruisers, but they return along their beat with the greatest regularity, generally feeding close into the shore.

For many years King Edward made a point of spending the week-end after Cowes visiting my father and mother at Newlands. The lake there is full of carp, and I used to amuse myself by ground-baiting certain portions of it and catching these fish. One morning His Majesty came and sat on the bank with me, and grew quite enthusiastic, as they were taking well. We had two rods, one baited with paste, the other with small, carefully prepared worms. The gong for lunch sounded and he said: " Let's peg the rods down and come back after luncheon and see if we have caught anything." About an hour later the whole party went down to the lake, where I noticed a wild duck swimming about in an odd way, but did not realise what had happened. The King took up the rod baited with a worm, and immediately he did so the wild duck flew up in the air and took out the line, which, of course, it eventually broke, much to the King's disappointment.

I agree with the man who said that there is an element of poaching in the character of every true sportsman. I am rather inclined that way myself. On the day of the Khaki Election in 1901 I found myself at a place called Braemore, one of the lodges in Langwell Forest, belonging to the Duke of Portland. As it was twenty miles from the main lodge and motor-cars were not then in general use, I had been sent out there to spend ten days by myself. On the morning in question the stalker had to go and vote, and I was left to my own devices. A little salmon river ran past the lodge, and I strolled down it with a rod, fishing every pool without success. Presently I came to a slab of rock over which the water was trickling slowly into a pool a few feet below, from which every now and then a fish would jump, land on the slab, and slither back. This was too much for me. I cut the feathers off a big fly, attached it to the line and made a sort of whippy gaff out of the rod. After several attempts I foul-hooked and landed a fish of about ten pounds. In a novel of mine published last year I recorded this incident (about the only one in the book which was not fictitious), the only variation being that the man in the book was accompanied by an attractive girl whom he instructed how to commit this atrocity, whereas I was alone. The sequel was unfortunate, as instead of saying nothing about it and eating the fish myself, I dutifully sent it to Langwell, and when I returned there the Duke made a few caustic remarks. I was never asked again: whether it was on this account I do not know, but I am not aware of having done anything worse.

The year before the South African War I was at Invercauld, and from the bridge over the River Dee on the main road between Ballater and Braemar I had seen several salmon lying. The river was low and they would look at nothing. Without saying a word to anyone, I made a nicely leaded triangle and sauntered down one evening to the pool. It wasn't exactly the spot to choose for an attempt to poach, but youth is careless. I lay on my stomach on a big rock and peered over cautiously. Sure enough there were two or three salmon lying below me, one of which I eventually succeeded in foul-hooking. The rod screamed as the fish made towards the bridge, and I was busy playing it when my sixth sense told me that somebody was watching me. I looked up, and whom should I see but Queen Victoria sitting in her carriage, which was drawn close up to the coping. Also looking down on me were Alec York, a gentleman-in-waiting, and a Highland attendant—for all I know, John Brown. For the moment I was in a panic; at the same time I did not wish to lose the fish and dared not try to land it. My having no gut on the line would have given the show away. The only thing to do was to let it get down under the bridge, where I followed it, up to my waist in water, pretending that I was unaware of the spectators above. I remained there for the best part of ten minutes, with the fish still on, until I heard the carriage roll away, when I proceeded to gaff it.

One night at Lochmore, Westminster came in very late for dinner, saying that he had just lost the biggest fish he had ever seen in the Laxford. He was furious when we suggested that he had foul-hooked it (not necessarily on purpose), and declared that he had seen the fly sticking in its mouth at the moment when he had nearly succeeded in gaffing it; and that if we didn't believe him he would show us, by having the pool dragged the next morning. The following day none of us were sent out stalking, but we were all " put in orders " to assist in dragging the net. The whole party and about half a dozen ghillies arrived at the top pool at eleven o'clock. There were no less than a hundred and twenty salmon in the net, and goodness knows how many sea-trout. The biggest salmon was about thirty-five pounds, and we found Bendor's fish—one of twenty-five pounds— with a Blue Doctor sticking right at the end of its nose. This one we kept, in a spirit of revenge, and also a couple of clean fish; the rest were returned to the water none the worse for their adventure on dry land.

Our old keeper at Ruthin was the first to instruct me, when I was a boy of twelve, in the art of poaching trout by means of night-lines. These he used to prepare with the utmost care. Instead of using gut with the hooks, he used twisted horsehair, which he would pull from our old pony's tail. Worms as bait he rejected, saying they only attracted eels. He and I would go down to the river, where we would take off our shoes and stockings, and, each armed with a three-pronged fork, would carefully lift up the stones in the shallows and prod at gudgeon and miller's thumbs—bait that no trout can resist. I only used this form of catching trout when the river was dead low and a fly was impossible. My father had his suspicions, but as he was very fond of eating trout he said nothing about them. I have never been fond of early rising, but I used not to mind what time I got up in order to take up these lines, stimulated by the excitement of wondering whether or no there was a trout on.

Chapter XVII

GOLF, CRICKET AND MOTORING—EARLY RECOLLECTIONS

ONE of my earliest memories of cricket is being struck violently on the shin, when I was about thirteen, by a ball hit by a gardener at Newlands, and then told not to " pipe my eye " (the equivalent, in Hampshire dialect, of being told not to cry), and getting perfectly furious at the mere suggestion.

Every summer holidays, after I went to Eton, I used to play on Saturday for the local village team against neighbouring villages. The pitches were almost invariably bad, the out-fielding worse; but the lunches, although they never varied, were always good: cold salmon, cold beef and ham, apple tart and custard and bread and cheese, the whole washed down with shandygaff. We all sat at a long table. The parson of the village always presided, said grace, and umpired for his own side at the match with the most religious partisanship. Each village had its own fast bowler, calculated to inspire awe in the opposite side, but he never did, as, except when he laid one of them out with a bumping ball, the fast bowler of my young day was usually of the shut-eye, windmill type who kept no length and soon tired, even though he would never admit it and resented it if he were taken off. With a few exceptions, such as the curate or schoolmaster of the parish, or perhaps some public-school boy who had been taught the rudiments of the game, the batting was not of a very high order either; but there were always some marvellous sloggers with eyes like hawks. I was a bowler, and have a vivid recollection of good length balls on the middle stump being sent hurtling to square leg.

Once, when I was sixteen, I got up a team against Lymington, the best side in the district. Their crack batsman was a little pot-bellied fellow called Fisher, a general outfitter in the town, who was of the stone-wall type, and in this particular match was well set. Lymington had three wickets in hand and required eighteen runs to win. Matters looked desperate. I had on my side a stableman in my father's employ called Allen, who was a marvellous bowler of fast underhand grubs, or ' daisy-cutters '; the ball used to travel between the wickets rather in the manner of a flat stone thrown along the surface of a pond; and, much against the advice of the more experienced members of my team, which included Harry Scobel,* I determined to put on Allen. The first ball somewhat bothered the general outfitter, who twirled his enormous moustaches and put his funny little cap even more on the back of his head. The next ball bowled him, as he disdained any attempt merely to block it, and tried to play it. Allen bowled all the three remaining batsmen in his first over.

Hordle, a village near Newlands, possessed a fast bowler, Hillyer by name, one of my father's tenants. When it was a close match and every run was required, the batsman at the bowler's end was naturally on his toes ready to back up his partner. It was on an occasion like this that Hillyer would apparently deliver the ball, but, instead of letting it go at the proper moment, would bring his arm round and dash it into the wicket at his own end, thus getting the man who was backing up run out. He was not popular.

Hinton Admiral, belonging to Sir George Meyrick, possessed a really fine cricket-ground: beautifully kept, it was more like a county ground than that of a village club. Sir George was an enthusiastic but indifferent cricketer. He was a rich man, and kept a professional named Dible to look after the ground and bowl for his side; and the mere idea of being bowled at by a ' Pro ' used to inspire most village cricketers with fear and trembling, and resulted in Dible obtaining many more wickets than his bowling justi-

* The late General Scobel.

fied. The man who umpired for Hinton was the village postman, whose decisions were strictly in accordance with the hopes of his own side. On one occasion I was captaining the Milford team, and it was agreed to draw stumps at six-thirty, but to go on till seven o'clock if a definite result seemed probable by the extra half-hour's play. At half-past six Milford required thirty runs to win, with five wickets in hand. I was in and, together with my partner, we looked like making the runs. As the clock struck the half-hour, however, the postman pulled up the stumps and walked into the pavilion, saying as he did so that he ' wasn't going to see his own side beaten ' !

I once played for Austen Mackenzie in a village match near Henley. The other side had roped in a queer little Cockney as their umpire, who happened to be staying in the neighbourhood on his holiday. A ball hit my pad violently and was caught by the wicket-keeper. " How's that? " asked the latter.

" What for? " said the umpire.

" Leg before wicket, of course ! "

" Not aht. But," he continued, " 'e *is* aht—caught at the wicket ! "

I was proceeding to retire, when the captain of the opposing side called me back, at the same time saying, " How could he be out caught when the ball hit his pad? "

" Orl right," said the umpire, " *not* aht ! " Strictly against all the rules of the game, I continued my innings, and we won the match. When it was over the little Cockney came up to me and said :

" Sorry abaht that little incident, guv'nor. As a rule I 'ave a hye like a heagle ! "

What fun village cricket was in those days ! We all met on an equal footing, yet there was always just the right amount of deference, without obsequiousness, shown to a man who was entitled to expect it ; such a thing as class hatred or jealousy was never thought of.

Many large country houses in Edwardian days had private cricket-grounds in the park, and cricket weeks in

CLARE FREWEN, AFTERWARDS CLARE SHERIDAN, AT SALISBURY HALL

August after the London season were most amusing. Invitations to them were eagerly accepted by those with any pretensions to playing the game. At some places the cricket was taken very seriously, and teams of Free Foresters, I Z., Hampshire Hogs (I used to play for the last two) and other well-known amateur clubs were in great demand to play against the local team. At other places the cricket was not taken quite so seriously. We used to dance half the night and try to make runs or get wickets during the day.

I spent many a happy cricket week at Frampton Court in Dorsetshire, the beautiful place belonging to Squire Sheridan, the direct descendant of Richard Brinsley Sheridan. I and the sons of the house—there were four in those days—started in the morning by marking and rolling the pitch, the old squire superintending. At eleven o'clock the game began. One of the two daughters of the house, who are now Lady Wavertree and Lady Stracey, usually scored. Open house was kept, and every afternoon there was a sort of informal garden-party, many neighbours turning up. It was there that I made the acquaintance of Thomas Hardy, a man who knew more about his own county and English folklore generally than anyone I have ever met.

Cricket over for the day, the fishermen among us rushed to the river, the Frome, a first-class trout stream, and spent the hot summer evening trying to induce the fat, lazy trout to take what we offered them. After dinner we would dance. Our hostess, a daughter of the famous American historian, Motley, understood young people, and we all adored her. During one visit there, I went into the library to look at the famous Sheridan Manuscripts, and read " The School for Scandal " in Sheridan's own handwriting. What astonished me was the surprisingly small number of corrections in it. His pen must have flowed.

There were one or two private grounds round London—in fact there was one *in* London, at Holland House (now the practice ground of a golf school)—where I often used to play. Another was at Sundridge Park, Sir Samuel Scott's place near Bexley, now a private hotel. Bertie Tempest * once took a team down there to play against the Blues, in which regiment Sammy Scott was serving. We went down in two coaches, one driven by the late Lord Londonderry and the other by the late Georgina Countess Howe. One member of the team was Ronnie Moncrieffe, who, when he was feeling fit, was a very good bowler. Ronnie was once described by a friend as being " one of the most delightful fellows in the world, but a martyr to D.T." The first part is true, but I don't believe things ever got as bad as D.T., though he certainly could put away more kummel at a sitting than any man I have ever come across before or since. He was *persona grata* everywhere, despite his one failing, from which he had an extraordinary power of recuperation. I remember meeting him at a dinner given before a ball when he was distinctly suffering from an overdose of kummel, but he appeared an hour later at the ball perfectly well and dancing with Princess Victoria.

To return to the cricket match in question: we were all expected to stay to dinner after it, and the Blues Band played to us. We were a merry party, and the climax came when Bertie Tempest insisted on conducting the band. He was so funny that the musicians themselves were in fits of laughter and quite unable to play, and this resulted in the most extraordinary and excruciating sounds that were ever heard coming from a famous band. At about one o'clock in the morning the two coaches started to return to town. Their progress to Sundridge had been most decorous, but on the homeward journey they raced the whole way, and arrived at Londonderry House in well under the hour, and there the fun began again.

The best cricket story I ever heard was about an habitual toper, who had seldom played the game, but who at the last moment was impressed into playing in order to make up the side. The opposing team had a fast bowler, and in order to

* The late Lord Herbert Vane Tempest.

fortify himself against this attack the toper had drunk innumerable whiskies and soda during his side's innings. The match was exciting, only ten runs were required to win with one wicket to fall, and the other batsman was well set. As the semi-inebriated one started out from the pavilion his captain told him that all he had to do was to put his bat in front of the ball.

" I know all about that, ole boy, but what if I see three balls ? "—" That's all right, my lad, you aim at the inside one," was his captain's reply. Two minutes later the match was lost—our friend was bowled first ball. " You d—d fool ! " said the irate captain, " I told you to aim at the inside ball."—" I did, ole man, I shware I did, only I hit it with the outside bat."

" You're never going to learn that rotten game ? " This remark was made to me some thirty-five years ago, when, having left Eton and Germany, I found myself at the crammer's in Jersey, longing for exercise and without, apparently, any opportunities of taking it. " What do other people do here ? " I had asked several public-school fellows at the same crammer's. They answered, with withering scorn : " Oh, some of the old Anglo-Indians play golf ! " However, I did learn it, and never regretted it. There was only one golf course in Jersey in those days, that at Gorey. Tom Boutel was the ' Pro ' there—at least he combined the capacities of golf professional and fisherman. A wonderful natural golfer, he had taught the Vardons, Renouf, and many other distinguished professionals who hailed from there. Harry Vardon had just left to take up a position in England when I arrived, but Tom Vardon was then a caddie and a fine golfer.

These were the days of the gutty ball and straight-faced driver. A new club had just come into vogue called a ' bulger,' which was the ancestor of the modern wooden club. After about a fortnight's use of one driver, its face— to use a modern expression—had to be lifted and a leather substitute inserted, such was the deteriorating effect a gutty ball had on it. The head and shaft were glued, spliced and bound, and it was quite a frequent occurrence, when you hit a ball violently, to see the head hurtling through the air with a tail of string about two yards long attached to it.

When I joined the army no one else in the battalion had even attempted to play golf, and I practically gave it up. When I was quartered in Ireland I used occasionally to play with the ' Pro ' at Dollymount, near Dublin, or Kilmarnock, but even then I had to do it surreptitiously, for fear of invoking my brother-officers' scorn upon my head. A few years later Cecil Hutchison,* who in addition to being a fine cricketer was an enthusiastic golfer, joined the Coldstream Guards, and he and Grant,† known as " the President,"—also in the Coldstream—and myself may be considered to have started serious golf in the Household Brigade.

One summer before the South African War, when I was Acting Camp Adjutant at Pirbright, some of my brother-officers and those of other regiments became so keen about the game that we used to play at Woking every afternoon, and never went near London for weeks on end, much to the annoyance of London hostesses, who then, as now, were always in a fever as to how to obtain young men for their parties.

Soon after I was married we were invited to stay at Whitley Court, Lord Dudley's place in Worcestershire, for Easter. There was to be a big golf tournament, and all the best-known professionals of the day had been invited, including James Braid, J. H. Taylor, Harry Vardon, Ben Sayers and Andrew Kirkcaldy. The amateurs included an ex-amateur champion, the late Muir Ferguson, both his sons, who were almost as good golfers as their father, and several others. The amateurs drew for their professional partners, and I drew Kirkcaldy, and am therefore able to testify to the accuracy of the famous story of how he prevented snow sticking to our ball. It was about the third

* Major Cecil Hutchison, runner-up in the Amateur Championship.
† Now Major-Gen. Grant.

day of the week, and there had been a slight fall of snow, of which a little still remained on the greens. I noticed when playing that, whereas our opponent's ball was covered with snow and therefore impossible to putt with, ours always remained free. I also observed that on every tee Kirkcaldy carefully rubbed the ball on his caddie's head. He afterwards admitted that, foreseeing the difficulties of putting under the weather conditions, he had poured a bottle of salad oil over the caddie's hair—with marvellous results! He was a great character, " Andra."

Ben Sayers was even more so. He started life as a clown in a circus. He was a marvellous acrobat and, in addition to being a fine golfer, what he didn't know about card tricks—especially the three-card trick and games like ' Pea in a walnut '—wasn't worth knowing. On the occasion of the golf at Whitley James Braid subsequently admitted to me that Sayers had practically cleaned out the lot of them while playing cards in the evening. It was he who once tried to teach me chip shots at Floors Castle, the seat of the Duke of Roxburghe. As I never would keep my arms to my sides, he produced two newspapers, which he placed under my armpits, stipulating that every time I dropped one when making a shot I should give him a shilling. He grew quite rich that morning, but it certainly taught me how to play a chip shot.

To anyone who knew the late Lord Darnley, better known as Ivo Bligh, the story of Harry Vardon attempting to teach him golf at Sandwich will appeal. Ivo Bligh was a long, loose-limbed man, a fine cricketer and eventually quite a good golfer. When he took up the game and first swung his clubs, his arms and legs and back all seemed to be acting together like a windmill, and Vardon in desperation was heard to say: " If only your lordship would try to be a little more compacter! "

Like most golfers I have often played a match for a ball, or even for ten shillings, but only once for big money, and then not for myself. It happened this way. I went to stay one week-end with Sir Abe Bailey, who had a house near

Forest Row golf-course. Abe Mitchell was at that time his gardener, and already was a magnificent golfer. Amongst the guests were the late Colonel Frankie Rhodes, a brother of Cecil Rhodes, and Ludy Neumann. I had often played golf with the last-named and he knew my form to a T. Golf was the subject discussed at dinner the first evening, and Abe Bailey said: " I've got a man working for me that I'll bet could give a stroke a hole to anybody at this table."

Ludy Neumann at once said: " I'll name one man he can't, and back him for twenty-five pounds."

The bet was taken and doubled, and I was nominated. Frankie Rhodes, who had never seen me play, but felt there must be something in it, proceeded to back me for fifty pounds. Eventually there were a good many hundred pounds on the match, although I personally hadn't a six-pence on. It was arranged for the Sunday afternoon, eighteen holes, Abe Mitchell being, of course, the man I had to take on. He knew the course well, while I had played on it only once, and he started by winning the first two holes. A stroke a hole is a lot to give a man with a handicap of eight, as mine was then, and I succeeded in pulling myself together and winning on the seventeenth green, but registered a vow that I would never play golf for big money again: it was altogether too nerve-racking.

As it turned out, I indirectly broke my vow, because, soon afterwards, White's Club Golf Handicap was started. It took the form of a selling sweep, and the names were auctioned after a big club dinner, after which many of those attending imagined that they had a bigger bank balance than was actually the case, as exorbitant prices were bid for men who had really very little chance. One year I bought Oliver Martin Smith, by no means the worst golfer of a well-known golfing family. He got into the final, and I stood to win some fourteen hundred pounds. Unfortunately for me, the attractions of Paris during the *Grand Prix* week proved too strong for him, and he scratched.

I believe that in some years the value of the stakes of the White's Golf Club Handicap has been the highest ever played for at golf. The competition was always held at

Princes Golf Club, Sandwich, and on one occasion Freddie Menzies, who had just become a partner in Knoedler's, the picture-dealer's, made his famous remark concerning the course. He had suffered a severe defeat, and, when he came in, announced that he didn't consider it a golf-course at all; it was merely an exhibition of bunkers.

One or two of the starters employed on the more fashionable Scottish courses are well-known characters, the starter at St. Andrews being one. The Grand Duke Michael and his wife, Countess Torby, intending to play there one day, sent a friend to arrange a time for them to start the following morning. The friend in question explained definitely to the starter that he had to allot a time to a Russian Grand Duke and his wife, but the man was not in the least impressed, and when the time came he shouted out at the top of his voice: " Michael and Torby! "

The starter at North Berwick refused to have anything to do with the name of Paravicini, and when asked for a time by a gentleman of that name replied: " We no ken yon names up here, and ye'll just start at ten-fufteen in the morning under the name of Thompson."

Mrs. Walker, the Scottish lady champion, told me once of an Irish caddie she had when playing at Kilmarnock, who invariably produced the wrong club. Eventually she lost patience and expostulated with him, and he answered her: " Oi've been caddying for thirty years now, an' Oi've only brought out the right club onst—and then it was the wrong one."

I heard a funny story, which I hope is not too old to repeat, of a Jew and a Scotsman playing golf. The former drove his ball into the rough. The Scotsman, after looking for it for a few minutes, proceeded towards the green, when, to his astonishment, a ball played from behind him landed near the pin. The question was, what was he to do, as, unknown to his opponent, he had found the lost ball and put it in his pocket.

The starter at Mandelieu Golf Club at Cannes was once an officer in the Russian Imperial Guards. I was sorry for him, as he was a very cultured man, and I used to lend him books on various subjects. I often wondered whether he got the job on account of his name, which was Popoff!

On another foreign golf-course I saw an extraordinary thing happen. I was playing with Colonel Alanson at St. Jean de Luz, where the fifth hole—I think—is a long iron shot. It was rather a misty day, and I saw something brown on the green, but could not distinguish what it was. Alanson drove a ball which landed plump on the brown object, and when we got up to it we found he had killed a thrush, which, considering how few birds there are in France, was all the more remarkable.

I did not actually own a motor-car until 1900. I was taken for my first ride two years before that by the late Lord Montagu, and although we never went at more than twenty-five miles an hour, I thought it a thrilling experience. Almost the funniest part of motoring in the early days was the costume in which people dressed themselves for it: hideous goggles, almost like a gas-mask, extraordinary contraptions like divided skirts which men wore to keep their legs warm, the ladies swathed in chiffon scarves over appalling flat cloth hats, not to mention the stiffened canvas sails which stuck out in the rear of the car and acted as a protection against dust. It all sounds ridiculous now, but in those days such costumes and contrivances were most necessary. Wind-screens had not been invented, there were no side doors for the driver's protection, the cold was often intense and the dust beyond all conception. Tarred roads had not been heard of, and after a long journey, despite their veils, ladies' hair, eyebrows and even lashes would be white with it. The difficulty and horrible discomfort of passing a car raising clouds of dust beggar description. Early motors were odd-looking affairs, as may be seen from the photograph, here reproduced, of a Motor Meet at Southport in 1898.

In those days of motoring it was ten to one against your getting anywhere within ten miles without some minor mishap. To have said that you would arrive at a certain place by a certain time by car would have been a fool-hardy

prophecy. Many makers did not appear to realise that steep hills existed, and the petrol tank, generally placed under the seat and fed by gravity to the carburettor, was of no use if the gradient exceeded a certain angle. Thus it was that one constantly saw cars going uphill backwards in order to overcome this difficulty.

The gentleman who allotted the lettering to the various counties and boroughs, when the Motor Car Act came into force in 1904, either had too much sense of humour or none at all. The letters B.F. were given to the county of Dorset, but the late Lord Alington, a magnate of that county, so strongly objected to being B.F.1. that the lettering was altered to XF.

The first car I ever owned was a single-cylinder de Dion, where the engine was under the seat and the steering-gear was an upright pillar upon which was a small handle that had to be turned at least three times before any result on the steering-wheels was obtained. I was still with the British Thomson-Houston Company when I had this car, and took it with me to Glasgow. One day it completely failed to function. I understood nothing about it, nor, apparently, did any man in Glasgow, so I wrote a frantic letter to the makers, calling the car by every opprobrious epithet, and received a polite reply to the effect that if I would send it up by passenger train, and they found anything the matter with it, they would pay the cost of carriage. Still fuming with rage, and determined not to miss the opportunity of telling them what I thought of them, I travelled all night on the same train as the car, instead of going comfortably by the express in a sleeping compartment. When I arrived at St. Pancras I was met by a smiling young man, who, after three minutes' inspection under the seat, drove the car out of the station under its own power! I never felt such a fool in my life, and determined that it should not happen again. To ensure this, I arranged, two months later, with a firm in Paris, to go through the repair shops of their big garage, where, under the name of Smith, I learned as much as it was possible to know about a car in three weeks' tuition, a course which I have never regretted.

It was in the de Dion car that I invited Joe Laycock to come with me to see the new power-station of the London United Tramways, which had just been opened at Chiswick. Snow had fallen and was being melted with salt, with the result that the roads were full of slippery slush. We waltzed the whole way down the Bayswater Road without hitting anything, and eventually, ignominiously putting the near-side wheels to the curb and hugging it, arrived at the power-station in well over the hour.

The next car I had was the eight-horse Panhard, already referred to elsewhere. Jennie and I once went down in it to spend the day at Knole, intending to return after dinner. We had two acetylene lamps, which when we started on our homeward journey worked very badly; and when we got into Sevenoaks one burst into flames and was put out of action. A few miles further on the other did the same thing, fortunately without setting fire to the car. We had nothing left but a very small electric torch, with which Jennie, with arm extended in front of her, did her best to throw a feeble light on to the road. All went well until we came to a corner which we ought to have turned but didn't, and instead went up a small bank. Fortunately, we were going very slowly, but I never shall forget my feelings when I saw my wife fall slowly out, the car remaining perfectly upright—there was, of course, no side door to hold her in. However, she was not hurt; we reversed, and arrived home about two in the morning.

I had another amusing experience with the same old car in Scotland the following year. I attempted to drive from Invercauld to Lochmore in a day, a distance of about 150 miles. In order to shorten the journey I went by a place called Cock Bridge, which is at the head of Strath Don, where there is a road—one of General Wade's roads—which goes over the mountain to Tomintoul. General Wade made roads rather as the Romans did: he did not bother about going round hills, he just went up and down them. The ascent from Cock Bridge is about one in four, and the car refused to take it either backwards or forwards. There was nothing to be done but to get it towed up by horses, as to have gone back again would have meant a detour of over fifty miles. It was then about half-past nine on a Sunday morning. I woke up the man at the inn, who at first refused to do anything on the Sabbath, but by dint of heavy bribery I induced him to get out two post-horses. They were led out, snorting with terror when they saw the car standing at the foot of the hill. There was hardly room for them to pass it, and we had to put sacks over their heads before they would do so. The road at the bottom is very narrow and lies between two steep banks. As soon as I started up the engine, the horses began to run away uphill. In those days every car was fitted with a sprag to let down in case it slipped backwards downhill, and as I was not sure that the ropes would hold, I let mine down before we started, which added to the general clatter. Towards the top, however, the horses began to slacken speed, and we reached it safely.

I once took a chain-driven car over the Spittal of Glenshee, one of the steepest ascents in Scotland. We got to the top of the pass and started to coast down the other side, when I heard a clang, but took no notice of it, and went on for another two miles, where the road ascends for a few hundred yards before its final descent. In the middle of this ascent, which necessitated once more the use of the engine, the car stopped, and started to go back. Down went the sprag, which pulled it up with a jerk. I got out, and found that the chain had come off, and had to walk back two miles uphill to fetch it. I had a chauffeur in those days whose only qualification for the job was that he had been a stoker in the Navy. We began to mend the chain: my rivet worked all right, his was too tight, so the chain would not function, and it had to be done all over again. Eddie Stonor,* who was with me at the time, always declared that in my rage I sacked the chauffeur on the top of the Spittal and told him to walk back to London! We got to Perth, having taken ten hours for a journey of some eighty miles. Motoring in those days was full of excitements and uncertainties.

* The Hon. Edward Stonor.

Chapter XVIII

TRAVELS

THE first time I ever left England was when I went to Freiburg. The following summer, after my elder sister's marriage, the whole family were invited to Fürstenstein, and, as I was supposed to be able to speak German, it was taken as a matter of course that I should act as courier. Two days before we were to leave, I fell off a bicycle, which so infuriated my father that he almost suggested I had done it on purpose. A true Victorian, the prospect of visiting Germany with his wife and daughter and servants, not one of whom could speak the language, filled him with alarm. However, he eventually plucked up courage to embark upon the expedition, relying on the schoolroom German that my younger sister knew. I followed a week later, going by sea to Hamburg, where, unknown to me, cholera was raging; the Press had been allowed to stay very little about it.

A few days later an expedition from Fürstenstein was arranged by my brother-in-law. We were to drive in a coach and four to a place at the foot of a pass in the Riesengebirge, where we were to lunch in a woodman's hut and were then to walk over the pass. The coach was to be dragged by oxen to the other side, where a fresh team would await it. When we reached the hut, a man, evidently in great distress, came out and said a few words to Pless, and we were immediately hurried on up the pass for a mile or two and had our luncheon picnic fashion. We were told nothing of the reason for the change in the arrangements, but I discovered some days later that two people had been lying dead in the hut from cholera.

One of the principal amusements at parties at Fürstenstein was to "dress up" for dinner, and many were the weird and wonderful costumes invented. On one occasion, when the Grand Duchess of Hesse, now the Grand Duchess Cyril of Russia, was staying there, my Uncle Pat (whom she had never previously met) was also a guest.

As Royalty was present, medals and orders were worn by those who possessed them. Pat hadn't any, so he turned up at dinner with a row of old Race Club badges on the lapel of his coat. The Grand Duchess was intrigued, and asked him what orders they were. Pat, not in the least abashed, took off one which had been issued by the Leopardstown Club in Ireland : " That one, Ma'am," he told her, " is the Order of the Leopard, and is worn only by those who can claim direct descent from the last of the Kings of Ireland."

She quite believed him, but was not in the least annoyed when she was subsequently told that he had been " pulling her leg."

I once found myself at Fürstenstein for what were called the " Kaiser Manœuvres," as apart from the other military manœuvres held in various parts of the empire during September. In these, the Emperor always commanded one army, and one of his most distinguished generals the other. I believe on this particular occasion General, afterwards Field Marshal, von Mackensen—whose campaign in Roumania was one of the most brilliant achievements in the late war— was opposed to the Emperor. Again commandeering Pless's horses, the whole party rode out to watch the field-day. It was fairly obvious to anyone with the slightest knowledge of military tactics that the Emperor was completely out-generalled; nevertheless, at the end of the day, it was his army which advanced, while von Mackensen's retired.

The latter turned up that evening at Fürstenstein for a hurried meal before rejoining his force, and one of the guests asked him why, since he had been victorious, he was the one to retire ?

He answered: " The umpires value their jobs too highly to risk giving a decision contrary to His Majesty."

A certain British officer, now a famous general, who was once staying at Fürstenstein, was taken over to see the ancestral home of the Blüchers, not far distant. His hostess pointed out with pride the portrait of the celebrated Field Marshal, whereupon the officer remarked: " Ah! I remember, that's the old boy who turned up late for the Battle of Waterloo."

Fürstenstein itself is so fully described in my sister's memoirs * that I will refrain from repetition. Although much more modern, Pless was equally fine in its way. It was here that the Emperor had his headquarters on the Eastern front during the War, and here that he eventually signed the order permitting the sinking of merchant vessels by submarines without warning. It would appear, from what one of my nephews has since told me, that von Kühlmann arrived with the document and that the Emperor refused at first to sign it. The former then returned to Berlin, and within two or three days Admiral von Tirpitz himself arrived and was closeted alone with his master for several hours. He may have made it a matter of abdication: in any case the Emperor finally signed.

I have told elsewhere how it was necessary for me to visit Spain sometimes in connection with a copper-mining company of which I was a director. On one return journey I spent a day in Madrid with the Duc d'Alba at the Palazzo Lyria. It happened to be the Thursday in Holy Week, and my host asked me whether I would care to attend the Maundy ceremony at the private chapel of the royal palace and see King Alfonso feed, and wash the feet of, twelve poor men. I pointed out that I had no clothes with me suitable for the occasion, as a tall hat and frock coat were *de rigueur*. D'Alba had a secretary, who was also a personal friend of his, Luis Erazzu, and suggested that he might be able to fit me out. Señor Erazzu's frock coat and waistcoat fitted me admirably, but the tall hat was far too small and the trousers would not fit at all; but as I was to go in the Duke's coach and nobody was likely to look at my legs in the chapel I took the risk and attended the ceremony, immaculately dressed as far as the waist, but with a pair of brown tweed trousers and brown

* *Daisy Princess of Pless*, by Herself.

shoes to complete the costume. The Duke had made it clear to me that I would have to make my own way home, as he had to remain in attendance on the King, but the Palazzo Lyria was less than half a mile from the Royal Palace. The chapel was dimly lighted. The gallery where I was was filled with Spanish notables. The ceremony began, the twelve old men, dressed in black, being seated at a table. Each plate of food was passed up a row of Grandees until it reached the King's hands, and was placed by him before the old men in turn. The recipients, however, were only able to glance at the contents, as it was whisked away almost before it had been put in front of them. This happened with the three or four courses of which the dinner consisted, after which dessert was served. Included amongst this were walnuts, and these caused a *contretemps*—the King dropped the dishful on the floor. Immediately, all the grandees were down on their hands and knees, despite the tightness of their costumes and the rotundity of the figures of some, painfully picking up the nuts as they rolled in all directions. Incidentally, I was told that the twelve old men did subsequently eat their dinner in peace and quiet.

After the ceremony was over I left the Royal Palace to make my way back to the Palazzo Lyria, and then my troubles began. Directly I got out of the Palace I put my hat on my head, trying to look as if it fitted me; but as no wheel traffic was allowed in Madrid on this day, the streets were full of the inhabitants, including many small boys, who at once took notice of what appeared, even to them, an extraordinary costume. They started by pointing, they went on to jeer; finally they began to run after me. Then I ran too, as far as the gates of the palace, where I arrived breathless, pursued by a yelling crowd of street urchins. Fortunately the porter recognised me, let me in, and slammed the gate in the face of my tormentors.

On another occasion when I was in Madrid I went, for the first and only time, to a bull-fight. I had a good place near the barrier, and found myself seated next to a pretty, fair woman, who did not look in the least like a Spaniard, although she was dressed as one, with a mantilla. The procession began in all its pomp and circumstance, and with the same ritual that has existed for hundreds of years. A famous toreador named Machiquito was the great attraction that day, and he was received with cheers by the spectators. Twice the procession went round, and the second time Machiquito stopped opposite to where I was, and took off his embroidered gold cloak, which he handed to me, making a sign to give it to the lady next to me. I did so, and to my astonishment she thanked me in perfectly good English. " You are English? " I exclaimed. She told me she was, and that was she Machiquito's wife.

It is impossible for the ordinary person who goes for the first time to see a bull-fight to understand all the technique and finesse of the proceedings—one cannot call it sport—so my good fortune in finding myself next to the wife of the most famous toreador in Spain can easily be understood, as she explained everything to me. I asked whether she was not nervous for her husband, but she would not admit that she was, saying that he was by far the finest bull-fighter in the world, and that he would never be killed by a bull; nor indeed was he.

The skill of the men engaged in a bull-fight is amazing: the agility of the banderillos in getting out of the way of a frenzied bull just entering the arena makes one gasp: they seem as if they *must* be caught on the points of those evil-looking horns; the way in which the toreador gives the *coup-de-grâce* is a feat of skill requiring the coolest nerves, but the horse part of the business is revolting beyond words.

It was not until 1910 that I considered it was time to visit some countries outside Europe. Two friends of mine, Robin Duff * and Bertie Paget—both, alas! victims of the Great War—were at Tampico fishing for tarpon, and I decided to join them and combine a little business with pleasure. Tampico was the nearest town to the Pearson group of oil wells, and consequently there were many English and Americans there. There was not, however, a single decent

* The late Sir Robin Duff-Assheton-Smith.

hotel in the place, and we were obliged to take all our meals in a little restaurant called " The Two Parrots." I confess I was disappointed in tarpon fishing, as although the sport the fish give when caught is wonderful, it seems to me a pity to kill such beautiful creatures, which are quite inedible; not even the Indians would touch the flesh. The biggest of the tribe of herring, no fish fights more gamely than a tarpon, but to have to shoot him through the head with an automatic at the end of his gallant fight, tow him ashore and leave him there, except for a few scales as a memento, seems to me a poor form of sport. After catching one or two I decided to turn my attention to the yellow-tail, which is the second biggest of the mackerel tribe, and very good to eat. These fish run up to fifty and sixty pounds, and are caught in the same way as tarpon, by trolling a bait behind the boat, but are met with nearer the mouth of the river. I had a salmon rod with me, and had great fun with many of these fish, until one fine day a tarpon took the bait, and that finished the salmon rod.

From Tampico, incidentally the finest place in the world to see cock-fighting, I went on to Mexico City, where I had letters to the Governor, Señor Escandon, who was descended from an old Spanish family. He was kindness itself, and showed me everything there was to be seen, including the jail. Before arriving at this institution he explained to me that there was a man incarcerated in it who had committed several murders, whom he said he would show me, referring to him rather as to a species of wild animal. The prisoner in question was, however, a meek, mild, sad-looking individual, and the last person in the world one would imagine capable of murder. His only utterance during the interview was to complain of the quality of the beans provided. I asked Señor Escandon afterwards why he had been reprieved, and he answered me in French: " *C'est difficile de vous répondre. Moi-même je ne sais pas, mais je crois que j'ai une faiblesse pour cet homme.*"

The English-speaking Club in Mexico City is an old Spanish house with most lovely tiled floors and walls. It was there that I met one of the Duvals whom I used to know in Paris. Both he and his brother were great polo-players, and were at one time rich men, but misfortune had overtaken them. Duval offered to drive me to Taluca, stopping on the way to have a look at one of the old sixteenth-century monasteries, from which the monks had been recently ejected by the Mexican Government. The road, a fairly good one, led through the mountains, and I remember remonstrating with him about the pace at which we were going down a long steep slope. " There's usually a plank missing from the bridge across the river at the bottom," he replied, " and if we don't go fast we shall get in instead of over ! " My suggestion that we should pull up and see was met with scorn, and we went for the wooden bridge at about sixty miles an hour— far too fast to see whether it was whole or not! The monastery, when we reached it, was most interesting. Still in the same state as the monks had left it, it reminded me of the monastery of the Grande Chartreuse, which I had seen a few years before in a similar condition.

The old part of Taluca is attractive. The biggest brewery in Mexico is there, and made itself famous by a certain advertisement. A brewery in Milwaukee, U.S.A., advertised its beer as " The Beer that made Milwaukee Famous "; Taluca capped it with " The Beer that made Milwaukee Jealous."

From Mexico City I went to stay with my friend Captain Ernest Bald in the state of Michoacan, where he was managing director of a big timber forest. On the way we stopped with some friends of his at a place called Acambaro, and from there made an expedition to another old monastery, where there was a very famous Murillo that had been given by King Philip of Spain to the bishop of the see. We started early one morning in a motor launch down a lake, and arrived at the monastery about mid-day. It was a wonderful old building, with groves of oranges surrounding it. The picture was magnificent, and was hung in a certain position where, soon after mid-day, the effects of light were beautiful. For some reason or other this monastery had not been suppressed; the monks were still there, and the atmosphere of the place did not appear to have changed since it was founded some three hundred years before. From inquiries I have since made I understand that the picture is now removed to Mexico City.

I decided to return to England via New York, and on my way back the train was four hours late in arriving at Laredo, the border town on the Rio Grande between Mexico and the United States.

In the former country there is a law that no one other than a Mexican subject is to be employed by the Railway Company, and the consequence was that at the start the Pullman car was in charge of a little inefficient, chocolate-coloured creature, mainly of Indian blood. When we got over the border, the car was taken over by a full-blooded negro with a set of teeth as white as the coat he was wearing, who grinned at me as he said: " 'Morning, sah! Yuh sho must be mighty glad to get rid o' that black nigger what's been looking after yuh " !!

We had to wait at Laredo until the next day, so I took a stroll in the town, a comparatively new collection of streets. I became friendly with the bar-tender at the hotel, and asked him, in the course of conversation, what the local industry was. To my astonishment he replied, " Onions," and proceeded to explain that the sandy desert of that part of Texas, if irrigated by the waters of the Rio Grande, produces the most marvellous onions. " Yes, sir," he continued, " and the man who discovered it made a mighty big fortune— not only in onions, but in real estate. This city has grown up on onions."

At that moment a smart turnout, drawn by two mules with bells jangling, passed the swing doors of the bar. In it was seated an exaggeratedly-dressed, much-bejewelled and painted lady. I asked him who it was. " That, sir, is the Onion Queen, the relict of the Onion King! "

On my way to New York I was taken ill with the first symptoms of what afterwards necessitated a very serious operation. I had to leave the train at a Middle-West town, go to an hotel and send for the doctor, at the same time wiring to my bankers in New York for some cash. I was obliged to remain in bed, and the following evening one of the local papers announced, with big headlines, that a member of an old English family was staying at the hotel. The next morning when the nurse who was looking after me answered a knock at the door, two journalists, without waiting to be asked, made their way into my room, and greeted me with the question whether my ancestors had come over with the Conqueror or not. It was my first experience of American journalistic methods, and I was furious at their intrusion, and answered that as a matter of fact they had not: they had come over with Julius Cæsar. To my horror, the next issue of the paper announced that " West Refuses to Acknowledge Conqueror; Claims Ancestors came with Julius Cæsar! " When I eventually arrived at New York my friends never let me hear the end of it. It was the first and only time I attempted to pull the leg of an American journalist.

The following summer I again visited America with a friend, Dick Fenwick. It had been our intention to go into the state of Wyoming and shoot wapiti (or elk as they are called in America), but unfortunately I was again taken ill on the way, and found myself in a small hotel on the Canadian side at Sault Ste. Marie. This time the conditions were more serious, and, as I did not appear to mend, the local doctor threatened an operation. As his nails were a quarter of an inch in deep mourning, the mere suggestion revived me sufficiently to get up and board a lake steamer for Buffalo en route for New York. Dick Fenwick and Ernest Bald, known to his friend as " Nosey," had a violent quarrel in whispers one evening in my room as to which should sleep on the sofa, in case I wanted anything. Poor old Dick— he's dead now, alas!—claimed that as he was my companion on the shooting expedition it was his right. " Besides," he added, " with a nose like that you couldn't help snoring." " Damn it, man! " Nosey replied, " I was in the same house at Eton with him. Of course I shall sleep here."

They thought I was too ill to know what was going on, but as a matter of fact I was in fits of laughter. Eventually they tossed for it, and Nosey won. Unfortunately for me, Dick's deduction was correct.

I remember, too, when I was in bed at that hotel, a bell-boy coming into my room and asking me if I was interested in real estate, adding that there was a boom going on in the city—" the city " consisted of about two hundred wooden houses—and that the hotel in which I was had changed hands three times in the last twenty-four hours.

After the operation which I was compelled to have when I reached New York, I was in the Mount Sinai Hospital for more than seven weeks. The heat was intense and the city was nearly empty. When I was convalescent my American friends in Long Island, many of whom had visited me in hospital, showered me with invitations to go and recuperate there. I stayed at the beautiful home of young Mrs. W. K. Vanderbilt, and there met Judge Jimmy Gerard, afterwards American Ambassador in Berlin during the War. We had many walks together, and his knowledge of the European situation amazed me. The Agadir incident was fresh in the minds of everybody, and he was a severe critic of England's unpreparedness for what he felt was bound to come sooner or later.

In 1913 I visited Brazil and the Argentine in company with my elder sister. My first impressions of the harbour of Rio are unforgettable: the huge sugar-loaf (Pan d'Azucar) rising out of the sea, the mountain of Corcovado to the west, and the points known as " the Fingers of God " to the north, gave the impression of a vast setting for the last act of the *Götterdämmerung*.

Determined to revisit Brazil later on, we continued thence to Buenos Ayres. The German Ambassador had been warned of my sister's visit, and we were royally received. A gentleman, whose name I forget, but who was known as " the Lonsdale of the Argentine," had volunteered to look after us during our stay in the city. Except that he smoked large cigars, wore side-whiskers and was passionately fond of sport, he was not in the least like " the Red Earl " ; but he certainly did his best to give us a good time.

We were taken to visit the *Estancia* of Señor Martinez de Hoz, probably the greatest breeder of pedigree cattle in the Argentine. The railway company ran us a special train, and we were met at the station by the Señor's agent—he himself was absent in Europe—who conducted us to the house, where an enormous luncheon had been prepared. The meal over, we sat in the loggia, and the bulls, short-horn and Hereford, were solemnly paraded before us. After one had seen a few short-horns, unless one was an expert judge of cattle, they all looked alike, and their pace was about two miles an hour ; and when I explain that about three hundred short-horn bulls and half that number of Herefords were marched past, the time taken for the performance can easily be calculated. Daisy and I nearly became hysterical, neither of us had ever before taken the salute at a bull parade.

Afterwards we witnessed some Rodeo performances given by the cow-punchers. It was the first we had seen and we were enthusiastic, but those I saw some years later in the United States were far finer exhibitions of horsemanship.

After leaving Buenos Ayres we wandered through the Argentine, arriving finally at Corrientes and thence to Assumcion, where we were met by a motor-launch belonging to the Forestal Lands Company. This took us up the Paraguay river to one of their stations, where we spent three delightful days and were able to see how tannin is prepared from Quebraco wood and sugar from the cane. I never shall forget the terrible stench of the latter, and have often wondered why sugar is free from it.

I was taken out alligator-shooting one day, not a very exciting sport, as unless you shoot the animal in exactly the right spot, about the size of an egg, behind the eye, he just wriggles into the water and is lost. The most interesting part of this trip was the sight of the two mighty rivers, the Paraguay and Parano, one a perfect limpid blue, the other a dirty mud-colour, flowing side by side for many miles before their waters finally mingle.

The manager of the station told me of an incident which had happened a few years before when he had rescued a half-starved Scotsman dressed in a sort of comic-opera naval uniform from a boat coming down the Paraguay river. It transpired that there had been a revolution in Bolivia, and that the Scotsman was in charge of a small river steamer, which was seized by the revolutionaries and armed with one or two machine guns, he being given the choice of becoming admiral of their fleet to fight against the Government or being shot. He had preferred the former, but had eventually escaped.

The Argentine, though no doubt a prosperous country, is ugly. The impression left on my mind is one of rolling plains of pasture land, huge flat expanses of corn-growing country with nothing to break the monotony except a few groves of eucalyptus—even these originally came from Australia—and many hideous spider-like windmills used for pumping water.

We now determined to return to Brazil, where the scenery had so strongly appealed to us. Accordingly we got off the steamer at Santos and went by motor-launch across the estuary to the island of Guaruja.

Separated from the mainland only by a narrow belt of water on the two sides, Guaruja is unique, inasmuch as, while there is a luxurious hotel with gambling rooms built on the Atlantic shore, about two miles from the little pier where we landed, the rest of the island consists of either sub-tropical virgin forest or open spaces which are a mass of heath and flowering shrubs. A few Indian half-castes live on it, but beyond these the only inhabitants are those who live in or around the hotel. This was built by the Brazilian Railway Company, and was much frequented in the summer by rich coffee-planters and their families from the state of San Paolo. We were there in September, and the place was almost deserted.

Willie Holbeach, an old brother-officer of mine, and another victim of the War, was one of our party. We realised the possibilities of the place, and were fortunately able to obtain ponies upon which to explore. It seemed amazing that within twenty minutes of ultra-civilisation we should find ourselves in a tropical forest profuse with orchids and other rare flowers, every sort of palm, and trees on which monkeys jabbered in the most orthodox fashion and multi-coloured parrots screeched. Willie and I were struck by the brilliance of the butterflies, and we there and then determined to amuse ourselves by making a collection. We were fortunately able to obtain nets from the manager of the hotel, himself a keen naturalist. The slower-flying butter-flies were easy to catch, but it was quite a different matter with the fast-flying hawk moths and butterflies, especially as these invariably seemed to aim at the highest points of the flowering shrubs. Thus it came about that we organised butterfly drives. We got two or three intelligent native children, and by dint of signs and a few words of Portuguese explained that they had to beat the bushes in sunlit glades with long bamboos, while Willie and I took up our posts one at each end. I have already remarked that shooting a driven grouse or partridge going down wind is not an easy thing to do, but it is child's play compared with catching a driven hawk moth with a butterfly net. However, we managed to obtain some very fine specimens. One moth, which came into my sister's bedroom one night and fright-ened the life out of her, as she thought it was a bat, had a wing expansion of over ten inches, and the feathers at the base of its body were like those of a small bird. (In case I am not believed, the moth is still in my possession and can be seen!) It was not until I had shown some of my speci-mens to a gentleman at the Natural History Museum that I realised that Guaruja is a famous place for bug-hunters.

Although I could never bring myself to shoot a parrot— I was so afraid it might curse me with its dying breath—I made up my mind to try to get one or two toucans, of which there were many on the island, with the idea of using the plumage for tying salmon flies. Accordingly I set out one morning at daybreak, with a guide. I shot two toucans, and on the way home was walking under some low boughs when my guide violently pulled me back, and I found myself flat on the ground. Just above me he pointed out a snake about to strike, one which he informed me was of a particularly poisonous kind. It was the last attempt that it ever made, as I blew its head off.

We tried our luck on several occasions at the gambling table, but the odds were all in favour of the bank, as Roulette was the game played and there were two zeros. The principal punter was a little wizened Portuguese who, I was told, was chief Customs Officer at Santos. The story went that when his losses were considerable he recouped himself by making a small addition to the export duty on coffee— *si non e vero.* . . .

When we were not riding in the forest, we used to bathe, and it was here that I had my first experience of surf-riding on a plank.

We left Guaruja with many regrets; it was a divine spot. What a place for a honeymoon!

Our next stay was in San Paolo, where we had been invited by Gordon Leith,* who was then representing Spier Brothers' interests in Brazil in connection with the Brazilian Railway Company. While there we met many charming Paulistas, as the inhabitants of San Paolo prefer being called to being known as Brazilians. The centre of the greatest coffee industry in the world, San Paolo is probably the richest state in Brazil, and is as big as France. Its people are a race apart; unlike other states, they do not countenance mixed marriages between true-blooded Portuguese and Negroes, and it is uncommon to see half-castes in the city of San Paolo, whereas in Rio, the capital of the country, they seem to constitute the major part of the population.

While we were in San Paolo we received an invitation to visit a famous coffee *hacienda*, and arrived one evening in time for dinner. I have never seen a greater display of wealth and luxury. The glass used at dinner was richly decorated with gold; gold, in fact, was apparent everywhere, even every article of toilet ware in my bedroom was

* Colonel Gordon Leith, C.B.

glittering with it. The next morning we were taken out on ponies to witness the harvesting of the coffee berries, bright little red fellows like the hips and haws one sees in England. On the way there I noticed, winding up the sides of the hills, what looked like long white streaks all joining at a common centre, where another white streak came down to the court-yard of the *hacienda*. These were little concrete aqueducts. The berries were opened and the contents thrown into them, and a tiny trickle of water provided just sufficient impetus to carry them down to the drying floors near the main building. Once dry they were put into winnowing machines —the first process of grading the bean.

No article in general use passes through more hands before it is actually consumed than does coffee. The grower sells it to a coffee-grader in Santos, who sells it to a coffee-shipper. It then goes to a coffee-broker, who sells it to a wholesale merchant, who, in his turn, passes it on to the retailer before it is finally purchased by the consumer; and each of these has to make his profit out of the article.

When in San Paolo we paid a visit to another very interest-ing establishment, run by the Government of that state, where antitoxins are prepared against snake-bites. It was in charge of a distinguished Brazilian professor with a numerous staff. In front of the building was a large sanded arena of the same material as an *en-tout-cas* tennis court, in which were a number of what looked like different-sized beehives. Each beehive had allotted to it a small space surrounded by wire-netting. We saw the whole process of the extraction of the alkali poison from the snake's fangs. A man went behind one beehive and tapped gently with his foot: so soon as the snake appeared through the opening on the other side, a two-pronged fork was placed over it to prevent it from wriggling back. With his finger and thumb behind the prongs the man slowly drew the snake from its lair, and as it emerged other hands held its body taut. The professor then appeared with a small china paten in one hand and a kind of tuning-fork in the other. Another man opened the snake's jaws, by pressure at the back of the head,

250

and inserted a wedge such as dentists use, while, with the instrument that looked like a tuning-fork the mucous membrane on the poisonous fang was forced back. This had a pump-like action, and, holding the paten below the fang, the professor caught a few drops of yellow liquid in it. The operation was then repeated on the other fang. In a few seconds the secretion crystallised and looked like sugar candy. The snake was then carefully returned to his home.

Horses and mules are inoculated with small doses of the poison until they become immune, and a serum with anti-toxin properties is made from their blood. There are depots all over Brazil where this serum can be obtained, and the lives of many people bitten by snakes are saved annually.

We were afterwards taken into another reptile enclosure in the main building, and there we saw a collection of medium-sized snakes which, we were told, devoured small poisonous snakes from whose bites they themselves were immune: numbers of these are bred every year and turned loose in the country. We were then shown a practical illustration of what happens. One of the larger snakes was placed on the sanded floor of the room and two small poisonous ones were let loose; the bigger animal was inclined to be lethargic, but as soon as the smaller ones saw him they recognised their enemy and bit him mercilessly. This woke him up, and he proceeded to kill and swallow both of them. Before leaving, my sister was presented with two perfectly harmless and very small snakes, one green and the other a brilliant coral in colour.

After we had spent three or four days in Rio, Mr. Regis de Olivera, who was then Foreign Minister and had formerly been Brazilian Minister in London, took us to Petropolis, the Versailles of Rio. We also ascended the funicular railway which runs to the top of Corcovado, whence a magnificent view is obtained.

Late in September we sailed on the *Princess Mafalda*, the Italian liner which sank a few years ago on a journey between Rio and Buenos Ayres. I was not surprised when I heard its fate, as I had never been on a ship which rolled so badly. Amongst the passengers to Genoa was a certain lady who is now a famous prima donna; several other members of an operatic company which had been travelling in South America were also on board, and they and others, including my sister, did their best to make the time pass pleasantly; the prima donna, however, refused to sing a note and kept herself entirely aloof. After leaving Barcelona the last night out before landing at Genoa, I said to Daisy: " If we haven't persuaded her to sing, I'll bet I'll make her yell! " and that night at dinner I surreptitiously let loose one of the tame snakes in the restaurant. The effect was marvellous. Her table was next to ours, and when she saw the creature crawling towards her we heard for the first time what her top notes were really like. If we had not been friends with the Captain I might have got into serious trouble, as I at once became suspect.

I have visited many watering-places in Europe, but naturally I do not consider this as travel. I must, however, recount an amusing conversation I had at one of these places, with the late Ralph Nevill, the well-known author. We found ourselves together at Brides-les-Bains, where the waters are noted for reducing weight. Consequently the place was full of the fattest people it is possible to imagine: twenty-stoners were common. An amusing companion, Ralph Nevill used to invent stories about the various Colossi whom we met on our morning walk. One was a Turkish lady of stupendous proportions, who must once have had a very beautiful face.

" You see that poor woman there? " my companion said. " Hers is a very sad story. She was the favourite wife of a distinguished Turk, but he caught her *in flagrante delicto* with her lover. Instead of divorcing her or having her quietly put away, he caused her to be forcibly fed on Turkish delight—and that is the result! "

Another story from a French watering-place. I was at Vichy a few years ago, and made the acquaintance of an amusing little French actress whose dog I saved from being eaten by a chow. She confided in me that she was the mistress of a rich American who, except for the three months in the year when he visited Europe, gave her complete liberty. " *Vous êtes toujours fidèle, ma chère?* " I asked her. " *Mon ami,*" she replied. " *C'est parce que je suis si chère que je suis presque toujours fidèle.*"

Once, when I was returning from France, I arrived at Calais by the first boat-train, and as it was blowing hard and there was every sign of a bad crossing, I went down and took a bunk in the saloon of the steamer. Soon afterwards the second train arrived, and the saloon was invaded by a number of English tourists, amongst whom was a small Cockney with a very fat wife. From their conversation I appreciated, for the first time, the truth about a ginger nut.

She: " I sy, dearie, it *is* goin' ter be rough. I know I shall be sick."

He: " Yer'd better 'ave somefink, won't yer? How about a drop of champagne and a ginger nut? "

She: " I don't mind if I do—but not a ginger nut; they do 'ang about the gums so! "

Chapter XIX

THINGS SPOOKY AND PRACTICAL JOKES

ALL my life I have been supposed to be what is called ' psychic.' Perhaps I inherit the quality from my mother, for it is certainly true that when I was taken into hospital in South Africa suffering from sunstroke, she told my father that she had seen me that night in a hospital with a bandage on my head, but that I was not wounded. My father himself repeated this to me, and on comparing the dates we found that it had actually happened on the first night I was in hospital.

Personally, until some years ago I was very sceptical about anything to do with ghosts or ' manifestations,' until the evidence of my own eyes forced me to modify my views. One evening at Salisbury Hall (see Chapter XI), just as it was getting dusk, I came down the staircase which leads into the old panelled room that we used as a dining-room, and there, standing in a corner, I saw the figure of a youngish and beautiful woman with a blue *fichu* round her shoulders. She looked intently at me, and then turned and disappeared through the door into the passage. I followed and found nothing. She looked so exactly like a former nursemaid of ours, called Ellen Bryan, an exceptionally lovely girl whom we, as children, for some quaint reason used to call ' Old Girlie,' and who was then my mother's maid, that I felt certain she must have died and that I had seen an apparition of her at the moment of her death. Jack Churchill was living with us at the time, and I called him into the passage and told him about it. At his suggestion I rang up my mother at Newlands and after some conversation asked how ' Old Girlie ' was; she replied that she was perfectly well, and was going to marry

254

DINING-ROOM AT SALISBURY HALL, WHERE I SAW THE GHOST OF NELL GWYNNE

a Quarter-master in the Artillery, so that disposed of my theory about the ghost. I thought no more about the matter until a few weeks later, when my sister Daisy came to visit us. As Salisbury Hall had been inhabited by Nell Gwynne, I had made a hobby of collecting prints of this lady, most of which were in the library, and, taking up one, Daisy said: " I never realised before the truth of what people used to say about Old Girlie." I asked her what she meant, and she replied: " Don't you remember they used to say she was exactly like the pictures of Nell Gwynne?"

For the first time I realised the possibility of my having seen the apparition of the former mistress of Salisbury Hall. A few days later I mentioned it to a friend who was a member of the Psychic Research Society, who begged me to write a letter which she could put into the hands of a medium, in order that some light might be thrown on the mystery. I was still sceptical, but, after some persuasion, wrote the letter. Three weeks later I heard from my friend that it had been placed in the hands of a medium, who had stated that the writer had seen " an apparition of Mistress Eleanor Gwynne, who had come to warn him against an impending danger."

I knew of no impending danger at the time; but within six months of my having seen the apparition, a solicitor by the name of Bloomer, to whom I had entrusted a large sum of money to pay off some mortgages, absconded, and let me in for over ten thousand pounds.

I had a very uncanny experience when staying at Fürstenstein long ago. It is a very old house, and the moment I entered the room I had been given I was aware of something sinister about it, without being able to explain what it was. That night I was awakened by a distinct, rhythmical tap on the window, Rat-a-tat-tat-tat-tat. I assumed that one of the outside shutters had become loose, lit the candles (it was before the days of electric light) and opened the window, to find that everything was secure and it was a perfectly peaceful night. I got back into bed, and was just dropping off to sleep, when the tapping was repeated, this time at the back of my bed, close to my head. Lighting the candles again, I sat up and listened. All of a sudden, they went out.

Bertie Paget was sleeping down the passage a few doors from me and, remembering that he had a sofa at the foot of his bed, I determined to spend the night there. Anything was better than remaining where I was. I lit the candles again, seized my bedclothes and made my way to the door. As I reached it the tapping came again, on the door itself, right in my face. I fled. The next morning, when I insisted on changing my room, Daisy asked me why, but there was a twinkle in her eye, and I got her to admit that she had put me in the 'haunted' room on purpose; she wanted to see whether I would notice anything, as apparently other people had, and the room was hardly ever used. I told her I thought the joke a rotten one.

When staying at Blenheim once, half a dozen of us, including our hostess, Consuelo Duchess of Marlborough, turned the table one night. It was just before the Derby, and we asked the table what was going to win the race. It spelt out " Kroonstad." We at once rushed to the newspaper and looked down the probable starters, to find that this horse wasn't even entered; so we proceeded to tell the table what we thought of it. It then spelt out " You are all fools." A fortnight later the horse it had named did win the Ascot Derby.

Just before the War I had an unpleasant experience at the village of Pangbourne, where I had gone for the week-end to fish. I usually stayed at the Elephant Hotel, but on this occasion it was full up and the proprietress had engaged a room for me at a public house lower down the road, which overlooked the churchyard. There were two beds in the room. Early in the morning I woke up with the uncanny feeling that I was not alone; something prompted me to turn over. The moonlight was streaming into the room through the inadequate blind, and there, on the other bed, I saw the distinct outline of a coffin covered with a sheet. I gazed spellbound, and the hallucination, or whatever it was, remained for quite a minute. I could not sleep again, and got up and dressed. The next morning I made discreet inquiries, and was told that a relation of the innkeeper had died in the same room a few days ago and had been buried just before I arrived.

Personally I believe in reincarnation, and in connection with this belief a rather curious thing happened once at Versailles. I had, of course, read about the wonderful palace, but had never visited it—at least, not in this life—until one day soon after I was married when I went there with a friend from Paris. We found ourselves in the gardens, and suddenly I seemed to recognise my surroundings, and began to explain to my friend what path we must take in order to arrive at a certain statue. " I thought you said you'd never been here? " she asked. " Neither have I, but I'm going to take you to that statue," and I did.

Many of us have a constantly recurring dream. I have one which I have dreamt hundreds of times. In it I am a small boy standing between a lady and gentleman, possibly my parents, dressed in sixteenth-century costume. We are at the end of a bowling-green : to the right there is a sunk fence looking over a park. Several figures are on the green, one always prominent : a small man with a huge head dressed in green and red.

Except in the case of the guest-room at Fürstenstein, I have never minded practical jokes being played on me, as I have often played them on other people, one of the earliest and most successful being played on Mrs. John Brooke, my mother's widowed sister, who at that time lived in Elm Park Gardens and had become engaged to Colonel Guy Wyndham. It was a standing joke in the family that if ever there was a queer person to be met, or a lunatic escaped, she was sure to encounter him. When I came home, after leaving Eton, I heard how she had shaken hands in Hyde Park with a strange man whom she had mistaken for somebody else, and how, covered with confusion—she was of a very shy disposition—she had fled home. This was too good an opportunity to be missed, and I wrote her a letter in a feigned hand, which ran something like this:

> " DEAR MADAM,
>
> " At last I have discovered where you live. The sight of your beauty is for ever with me, and I still feel the clasp of your hand in mine! Life is impossible without you—will you not see me again, or must I haunt the pavement outside your house on the chance of getting a glimpse of you . . .? "

The first thing she did on receiving this epistle was to telegraph for her mother, old Lady Olivia Fitzpatrick, and for her brothers, Hugo and Heremon Fitzpatrick, to come at once! The latter two took turns to do 'sentry go' outside the house. It was some days before I heard of the state of siege that existed, and as my aunt was on the verge of a nervous breakdown, I wrote a very apologetic letter explaining the joke. It was quite a considerable time before I was forgiven.

When I was first quartered in Ireland I spent one winter with Bob Dewhurst and his wife at Clonsilla near Dublin, hunting from there. Mr. J. J. Maher, the famous breeder of bloodstock, lived about a mile away. He had always been considered a confirmed bachelor, but one day, to the amazement of his friends, he announced that he was engaged to be married; and everybody weighed in with a wedding present. A few days before the wedding, Mrs. Bob said to me at dinner one night: " Let's go and burgle J. J.," and at midnight we started out, each carrying a sack. As it was an Irish house it was pretty certain that we should find all the windows off the latch—and of course they were, in spite of the wedding presents being displayed on the dining-room table. Wrapping them carefully in straw, we took as many as we could carry in our sacks and hurried home again. I never dreamt that burglary was so easy.

The following morning J. J. came over in a terrible state of excitement to tell us about the burglary, adding that he had called in the police from Dunboyne. Mrs. Bob was a marvellous actress, and was full of sympathy. In the afternoon we went up and interviewed the Sergeant of the R.I.C., who, looking hard at the lady, said: " It's my belafe there's a woman in it! "

" Oh, Sergeant! Do you *really* think so? " she asked, with an innocent drawl.

" Oi do, Ma'am," was the curt reply. " Oi've seen a heel-mark outside the window."

There was nothing for it but confession. J. J., who was one of Mrs. Bob's oldest friends, was very magnanimous, and it was not difficult to square the sergeant.

My Uncle Heremon, otherwise " Pat," once played a horrible joke on a distinguished person who was staying at Eaton as my sister's guest. It was a wet day, and Pat had been amusing himself by looking at things under a microscope, including some cheese-mites. The distinguished visitor came in, and my uncle suggested that he might be interested to see one of the roots of his own hair—of which he had not a great quantity—under the lens. Accordingly, one was pulled out, and Pat, when fixing it, surreptitiously dipped the root in the cheese-mites. He then looked at it himself and, horror-stricken, turned and said: " My dear sir! I don't think you'd better look at this. You ought really to consult a doctor! " The guest, who was known to be a valetudinarian, insisted on looking, and was perfectly aghast at what he saw. Pat tried to comfort him by assuring him that it was a disease which could easily be cured with time.

The most successful—almost too successful—practical joke I ever played was also at Eaton. The victim, I am rather ashamed to say, was my father. We were both staying there for a shooting-party, and among the guests was Miss Emily Brooke, now Mrs. Atty Persse, wife of the well-known trainer. Emily Brooke, a cousin of mine by marriage, was, as she subsequently proved, a brilliant actress, and we conceived the plan of appearing one evening at dinner disguised as a Mr. and Mrs. Lorraine, newly arrived from America via Liverpool. My sister Shelagh was told of the project, and during lunch, out shooting, she announced that a Mr. and Mrs. Lorraine, who were friends of Minnie Paget,* had arrived at Liverpool that morning and had telephoned to know whether they might pay their respects and at the same time see Eaton. She added: " As they are friends of Minnie, I have asked them to dine." I said at once that I should not be able to meet them as I had to go to Stoke on business; the excuse was a good one, as I was then chairman of the Potteries Electric Traction Company.

Disguise has always been a simple matter for me: I have only to put on a black wig, darken my moustache and eyebrows and wear a monocle with a heavy guard attached, and the disguise is complete. Emily Brooke, who after tea had said she had a headache and was going to bed, appeared as the sweetest little French-Canadian young married woman it is possible to imagine: and we were duly announced as Mr. and Mrs. Lorraine, Mr. Lorraine speaking with a strong American accent and Mrs. Lorraine in broken English. My father, who always had an eye for a pretty woman, fell for her at once. He took her in to dinner, sat opposite me, and had the most open flirtation with her, to which I was careful to let him see I strongly objected. This, of course, may have stimulated him to further efforts; anyhow, I distinctly heard him say, " This is quite a modern place, dear lady, but if you would like to see the ruins of a really charming old place I will take you to Ruthin in the morning! "

Everyone at the table was taken in, though Guy Wyndham and Lady Jane Combe began to be suspicious. Dinner over, my father came and plumped himself down next to me. I thought now, of course, that the game must be up. Not a bit of it! He proceeded to cross-examine me as to how I obtained my wealth and why I had come to London. I explained that my wealth was a matter of luck, that I had struck a silver mine in Montana, where it was not a question of treating the ore, all one had to do was to carve

* The late Lady Paget, née Miss Stevens, of New York

COL. CORNWALLIS-WEST, FROM THE ORIGINAL OF
A CARICATURE BY "SPY" IN *VANITY FAIR*

it like cake. Even this did not make the dear old man realise the truth, though by now most of the other men had their suspicions. I gave as my reason for coming to England the fact that I collected pictures and was anxious to obtain some good specimens of the Barbizon school, of which I happened to remember there was a big sale the following week at Christie's.

" I cannot understand you Americans," my father said. " Why in the name of fortune should anybody be such a damned fool as to give a hundred and twenty thousand pounds for a Rembrandt! " It was only lately that Mr. Joseph Widener had given that figure for Lord Lansdowne's Rembrandt, " The Mill."

Some mischievous sprite prompted me to ask him : " Are you a fisherman? "

My father replied that he was, but he did not see what that had to do with the matter.

" Waal, Colonel," drawled Mr. Lorraine, " it's this way. If you were fishing in a pond for carp and you knew there was one there with a wall eye, I guess you'd be mighty anxious to get that one? "

He looked at me in astonishment, and said, " I still don't see what that has to do with it."

" Waal," I continued, " Rembrandt was the greatest portrait-painter who ever lived, but he painted mighty few landscapes, and that landscape to Joe Widener was like a wall-eyed carp to a fisherman! "

Soon after this we joined the ladies. My father once more made a bee-line for ' Mrs. Lorraine,' and I, affecting jealousy, suggested that it was time we took our leave. The bell was rung, and the butler, having been previously instructed, announced Mr. and Mrs. Lorraine's car. Emily Brooke retired upstairs to her room and did not appear again. I, after a decent interval, appeared as myself, and was greeted by my father : " My dear boy, you ought to have been here for dinner. We've had the sweetest, best-looking little French-Canadian I've ever met in my life, with the most boring cad of a husband! " He continued in this strain, and concluded by saying: " And she's promised to come to Ruthin with me in the morning! "

I saw that the joke had gone a bit too far, and consulted with Shelagh, who agreed that it would never do to let him know of the hoax, as it would hurt his feelings terribly. We knew it was highly probable that he would ring up the Grosvenor Hotel in the morning to find out at what time he should call for Mrs. Lorraine, so the porter there, who was a friend of the butler, was told to say, if this happened, that Mr. and Mrs. Lorraine had already left for London. Our anticipations were fulfilled, and at breakfast next morning the old gentleman bitterly complained of the fickleness of the fair sex. The next person whom we had to put wise on the subject was Minnie Paget, to whom Shelagh and I indited a long letter; and for months afterwards my father continued to write to this lady asking her if she knew what had happened to the Lorraines. To his dying day, some five years later, he never discovered.

Colonel Chris Elliot, who, until a few years ago, was in charge of the Passport Department, was always fond of practical jokes. He once heard that a great friend of his, a lady, was giving a dinner-party; and, happening to meet her in the street, asked why he had not been invited. He was told that she was very sorry, but there was no room. " I shan't worry about that, I shall turn up all the same," he replied. She rashly bet him a fiver that he would not, and he took it. On the evening in question, having previously bribed one of Gunter's waiters to be allowed to impersonate him, Chris appeared complete with the most beautiful side-whiskers and knee-breeches. All went well until he solemnly handed round the mint-sauce tureen with a fork instead of a spoon. Each guest, after unsuccessful efforts, glared at the waiter, who eventually arrived at the hostess. She did more than glare, and said a few words under her breath. Also in a whisper, he reminded her that he had won his fiver, and disappeared. He always said that it was quite a long time before she forgave him.

A very successful practical joke was played on me not

long ago. I was staying with a friend, Colonel Henry Porter, in the country, and he casually mentioned that he had had to give notice to a very excellent nursemaid they had engaged for the children, on account of the idiotic jokes she played on the other servants. On the Sunday, when we came in from a fishing expedition cold supper was laid out, and I asked permission to make myself a salad. I noticed that the oil in the cruet seemed rather pale, but I continued the operation, and finally sat down and began to eat. " Good God ! " I exclaimed when the first mouthful was in my mouth, " how awful ! " The nursemaid's Parthian shot had been to replace the salad oil by castor oil !

Chapter XX

SECOND MARRIAGE AND OUTBREAK
OF WAR

IN the winter of 1909 I took Mrs. Asquith's * house in
Cavendish Square, and it was there that I first met Mrs.
Patrick Campbell. Jennie had written a play called
" Borrowed Plumes," and was anxious for Mrs. Campbell
to produce it and to play the principal part; consequently
the latter became a constant visitor to the house. Besides
being a very beautiful woman, she was a brilliant conversationalist, and had a keen sense of humour and a ready
wit. Many are the stories told of her *bon mots*, one of the best
of which was *à propos* of the War. Someone asked her how
long she thought it would last. " You never know, when
once you start quarrelling with your relations," was her
answer. It will be remembered that, during King Edward's
reign, Buckingham Palace was refronted, but that the rear
portion was untouched, at any rate architecturally. Some
one asked Stella what she thought of it. " I should describe
it as Queen Anne in front and Mary Ann behind," was her
reply. She worked hard at Jennie's play and, with
Henry Ainley, did her best to make it a success. Had the
original intention been adhered to, and only four matinees
given, these would have paid for the whole cost of production, as people flocked to see a play written by one
brilliant woman and produced by another. But it was kept
on and, alas, being an indifferent play, it was another
instance of an unsuccessful enterprise.

Much has been written by others about the creative genius
of Mrs. Patrick Campbell. Impulsive to a degree, at times
her criticism of people and plays was inclined to be harsh.

* Now the Countess of Oxford and Asquith.

She confided in me, and I remember well receiving her first opinion of " Belladonna," which had been sent to her and which she had refused, describing it as trash. I had read Robert Hichens' book, and appreciated the possibility of its adaptation as a play admirably suited to her talent; after reading the play I realised that my first impressions were justified. We motored one Sunday to Burnham Beeches and read it again together, and I told her I felt certain she would make it one of the biggest successes of her career, as of course she eventually did, her creation of ' Belladonna ' being almost as famous as that of ' Paula Tanqueray.' I remember her saying to me with almost childish petulance: " How can you suggest my playing such a horrible part? People might think I am like that." I mildly remonstrated that the success she had had as ' Lady Macbeth ' did not necessarily stamp her as a murderess. It was only after much persuasion that she wrote to the late Sir George Alexander, and agreed to play the part. Incidentally, she once described its author, Hichens, to me as a man with " the eyes of a devil and the voice of a curate."

Some have said that she is better in comedy than in tragedy. In real life she possesses the characteristics of both, and that explains, I suppose, why she plays both parts equally well on the stage. Those who saw the first night of " Pygmalion " at His Majesty's Theatre in 1914 will remember how, despite the brilliancy of the play, it was her personality which carried it to success. The late Sir Herbert Tree, never famous for remembering his lines, forgot many of them that night, and this made her task the more formidable.

The first use of the word " bloody," in the modern sense, on the English stage was in itself an event—and how the audience yelled! By the applause every person present seemed to be expressing his delight that at last an author had been found who was willing to risk shocking them, and how much they enjoyed the process of being shocked.

I met many interesting people at Stella's charming little house in Kensington Square, including Mr. Bernard Shaw and Sir James Barrie. The former especially appealed to me, quite apart from his brilliance, by reason of the Irish in him and, above all, his extraordinary, unobtrusive kindness. How little the public realise the numbers of lame dogs that G. B. S. has helped over stiles! If there is one thing he hates it is being gushed over. One day at a small luncheon-party, where we all knew each other very well, there was one lady of a particularly gushing type, and Shaw shut up like an oyster until she literally forced him to speak. The subject under discussion was ' what constitutes true happiness in life.' G. B. S. having offered no opinion, the lady leaned forward and asked him, in her most alluring manner: " *Do* tell us what *you* think, Mr. Shaw? "

He looked at her with a stern eye, and replied, with just that *soupçon* of a brogue which is natural to him : " There are two things in life without which happiness is impossible."

The lady continued to gush. " Oh, do-oo tell us what they are ! "

" Easy boots and open bowels, Madam," was the reply.

Stella and I were married in April, at the Kensington Registry Office. I almost became hysterical during the ceremony at the sight of the two witnesses, who looked exactly like mutes at a funeral, except that they wore white ties.

Having always loathed publicity, my feelings turned to rage when I noticed two camera men attempting to snap us as we came out. I saw red, seized their cameras and, before they had time to recover from their astonishment, stuffed them into the dickie of my car and dashed off to Stella's house, where she had preceded me in her own car. We were followed to Crowborough, where we went for a few days before the first night of " Pygmalion," and the next morning, when out motoring, we were deliberately held up by a car placed across the road, so that we had to stop, and there were two other camera men. I repeated the performance—fortunately they were very small and offered no resistance. That night they visited us and capitulated, pointing out to me that snapping well-known subjects was their means of livelihood, and on condition that they undertook not to publish any photographs they had taken I returned their cameras. They kept their word.

During the Spring and Summer of 1914 my endeavours were concentrated on pulling together the shattered fortunes of my firm. In the last week in June I went to stay with some friends in Hampshire to fish, and on the fatal Monday morning of the 28th of June the news of the Sarajevo murder was published. I had always believed that war with Germany was sooner or later inevitable. The previous year I had been staying with my brother-in-law, Pless, at his villa in Cannes, and we had many discussions on the European situation. Once he went so far as to agree with me that if Germany and Great Britain were allies they could dictate to the rest of the world: " but," he added, " it's no use, my dear George, you can't have two top dogs in the same kennel."

Unfortunately, instead of returning to London immediately, I stayed on ; the lure of a Hampshire trout-stream in midsummer was too great. When I did return, it was with the most pessimistic forebodings. My partner's state of mind was the reverse. " A European War because of the murder of an Archduke? " he said. " Nonsense! " I found that the efforts he had made in my absence to justify his optimism were of a very expensive nature, and were the direct cause of the ultimate failure of Wheater, Cornwallis-West and Co.

So certain was I of the immediate outbreak of war that I fitted myself out with a khaki uniform, and when that calamity did happen I was one of the few older reserve officers who were not in plain clothes when they reported themselves at the School of Mines in Kensington, which was the temporary headquarters of the reserve battalion. After thirteen years it seemed odd to start soldiering again at the age of forty, as a lieutenant, and to find one had forgotten the little one had ever known and that the old methods of drill were practically obsolete. It was rather like going back to school.

Within three weeks of the outbreak of hostilities, Winston Churchill, who was then First Lord of the Admiralty, conceived the idea of the formation of the Naval Division. He considered that the existing first- and second-class regular reserves were sufficient not only to bring the fleet up to war strength, but also to fill up all casualties. He had at his disposal a considerable force of naval volunteer Reservists, many of whom had never actually belonged to the regular Navy, but were drawn from the crews of merchant vessels. It was unlikely that this force would be called upon to serve at sea, for the very excellent reason that there would be no ships to put them on, at any rate for some time. The material was good, and he decided to form an infantry division, comprising two brigades of these volunteers and a third brigade of reservists of the Royal Marines; this last was, of course, an efficient fighting unit. The War Office agreed to lend certain officers to assist in the production of the two brigades of trained infantry, and the First Lord was anxious to obtain, if possible, the services of ex-officers in the Brigade of Guards who would know what discipline meant. As there seemed every prospect of my remaining a subaltern indefinitely, I volunteered my services in this capacity, and was fortunate in being given command of the Anson Battalion which was then encamped in Lord Northbourne's park at Betteshanger, near Deal, and formed part of the Brigade under Commodore—now Rear-Admiral—Backhouse, R.N.

My recollections of taking over the command are vivid. I had hardly been in camp ten minutes before two very young officers in naval uniform came and solemnly asked me for permission to go ashore. I politely asked what was the matter with the ground they were standing on, and was informed that, as we were part of a naval force, the camp was considered as a ship, and therefore permission to leave it was equivalent to being allowed to go ashore. A few days later I came across a bunch of disgruntled-looking men standing at the guard tent at the entrance to the camp; they were being gravely told by the petty officer in charge that as they had failed to appear at four o'clock they had missed the boat, and would therefore not be able to leave until five o'clock! My sympathies were entirely with the men and, contrary to all orthodox naval ideas, I and other infantry officers who had taken over this somewhat complicated job of trying to turn the back-stair part of the Navy into the front-stair part of the Army, arranged that in future terra firma should be considered as such, and that where a man could use his feet to walk ' ashore ' he should be allowed to do so at any time after his leave started.

It was easier to train the men than to train the officers. I was sorry for the latter, who, in civil life, had given a considerable proportion of their time towards making themselves effective naval officers in case of war, and had never for a moment imagined that they would be called upon to act as foot-slogging platoon leaders.

Amongst the officers who subsequently joined my battalion was Rupert Brooke. How he slaved to become efficient, and yet how everything to do with the humdrum, sordid part of soldiering must have jarred his sensitive mind. But he never showed it, and was loved by everyone who came in contact with him.

I had as my orderly—messenger, it is called in the Navy—an old naval rating by name Simmons, whom I once had occasion to send with a message to Colonel Quilter, who commanded a battalion in the same brigade, but whose camp was situated about half a mile from mine. To my astonishment he returned with the answer within twenty minutes, pale and out of breath—he was well over fifty. When I commended him for his speed he replied to the effect that everything was done at the double on board ship, and seemed quite offended when I suggested that a battleship half a mile long had not yet been built, and that if he did it again he might have a heart attack.

Another amusing incident happened, this time concerning an officer of very high rank, no less a person than Admiral of the Fleet the late Sir Arthur Wilson. With the object of inspiring *esprit de corps* in the new force, it had been decided to appoint distinguished naval officers as honorary Brigadiers —or I should say Commodores—to each brigade. Thus it was that Lord Charles Beresford became honorary Commodore of the first brigade and Sir Arthur Wilson of the second. The latter announced his intention of visiting us, and as my battalion was encamped nearest to the entrance I was instructed to tell off a sub-lieutenant to look out for him. As it happened we had also been informed that on the same day Mr. ——, a Wesleyan minister, would be attached to us for messing and quarters. Not unnaturally, the lieutenant expected that an officer of Sir Arthur's high standing would appear in full uniform to inspect his brigade, and when, therefore, he saw an individual in a black Inverness cape, with a soft hat, elastic-sided boots, and badly-rolled umbrella, enter the camp, he treated him somewhat brusquely, walked him down the lines of the Anson Battalion to a tent with a few odds and ends of furniture intended for the use of the Wesleyan minister, and said: "This will be your quarters. The mess tent's over there." The stranger mildly pointed out that there seemed to be some mistake, as he was only down for the day. At that moment I appeared on the scene, recognised Sir Arthur and hastened to apologise for the manner of his reception. No one laughed more heartily than he did when I told him whom he had been mistaken for.

About a month after training began there were undoubted signs that some sort of shape was being given to the various battalions, and that there was every chance of their becoming a really efficient fighting force, provided that the necessary time was given to the completion of their training. Discipline was improving, company officers had begun to realise their duties and the men seemed to have entered into the spirit of the thing. One part of the training, however, was sadly lacking. Service rifles had not been issued until October 1st, so there had been no chance of musketry training. Most of the men had shot a few rounds with a miniature rifle on a short range which had been specially built, but practically none had fired even a recruit's course on a service range. In addition to this, the training of signalling corps and machine-gun sections in battalions was only in its infancy. Of entrenching there had been none, for the simple reason that no implements were available for carrying out this work.

The first Friday in October I was given forty-eight hours' leave to go to London to see Stella off to America, where she was due to open in New York the following month with " Pygmalion." Bernard Shaw was at the station on the Saturday morning, and we had a long talk on the general position, I having received from him, the day before, a priceless letter on the subject of German atrocities, which I give in full:

> 10, *Adelphi Terrace, W.C.*
> *2nd October,* 1914.

" MY DEAR CORNWALLIS-WEST,

Since you expect to go out soon, I really refuse to leave you troubled in spirit by that man with his eyes gouged out. I have been on his track for quite a long time now. A chauffeur who came to Torquay actually saw him; but on that occasion his wife did not go mad: she exclaimed, ' I know now that there is no God.' He was in the City of London Hospital until one of the governors went to see him there. But he had escaped; and the staff denied all knowledge of him. He is hiding with the baby who had its fingers cut off by the Uhlans. Both are believed to be with the Russian army we shipped to Belgium through Scotland from Archangel.

Ponsonby, just back with a wound, denies that there are any atrocities and sets up an opposition story of the remarkable kindness of a German officer to a Tommy whose elbow was smashed.

I have spoken with Miss Boyle O'Reilly, who was present at the sack of Louvain but returned intacta. She saw the nurses whose fingers and hands had been cut off. They had grown new ones and were in prime condition. One had her wrists burnt. She had fooled with a spirit lamp of explosive construction. Miss O'Reilly also interviewed the outraged women. They had all heard of outrages in the next village to theirs,

271

but had not actually witnessed them, and were, personally, virgins.

The atrocities committed by our troops fill the Berlin papers with copy and the Berlin soul with patriotic fury. We kill the wounded; we poison the wells; we toss babies on the points of our bayonets; we burn field hospitals full of German wounded; we chop off Belgian babies' heads in their mothers' arms, having previously put on the helmets of slain Uhlans; we make collections of breasts and eyes; we never venture into battle without driving crowds of women before us; we mock the Kaiser's grief for the death of his thirty-seventh and last of his six sons; our men shoot their officers (who persuade them that they are fighting the Russians instead of the universally popular Germans) and surrender with tears of joy to their kind captors; and the Tsar's mother is Sir Edward Grey's mistress.

As you know, the truth about war is always bad enough; but there really isn't a solitary scrap of evidence that the Germans, apart from their obsolete usage of hostage shooting, are behaving worse than we should behave in the same circumstances.

Stella will think that I write this for the sake of arguing. I do so because war is horrible when one does not respect one's enemies, and there is no reason why you should be depressed and disgusted by expecting more than the regulation horrors which are all in the day's work. I hope the very worst that will happen to you will be capture by Pless and imprisonment in his best bedroom until the war is over. But probably you will come back a Lieutenant-General.

Yours ever

G. B. S."

I was due to return to camp on the Sunday afternoon. On Sunday morning about eleven o'clock my second-in-command telephoned through to me from Deal, saying that he had been trying for the last hour to get at me, as orders had come from the Admiralty that the whole Division was to prepare for immediate embarkation at Dover on active service, and that the battalion was actually parading at that moment to march to Dover. I knew it was useless to try to catch the eleven o'clock boat train, so I rang up the Railway Transport Officer at Victoria, explained the position to him and asked if I could have a special. " Certainly, if you pay for it," was the answer. I told him I would, and within twenty minutes was at the station. The railway officials must have been duly impressed with the urgency of my journey, as, after passing through Ashford, I noticed the boat train standing on a side line to allow me to pass, much to the obvious annoyance of several ' brass hats ' who were peering out of the windows wondering why they were being held up. As it turned out I should almost have been in time had I cycled from London, as we hung about at Dover all day and only sailed at night. A kindly lieutenant-commander of a submarine alongside took pity on me and invited me aboard for a meal—the only time I have ever been on a submarine : what a box of tricks !

I was told how the Division had marched in grand style to Dover, bands playing and drums beating, but it did not take a military eye to realise how sadly lacking the men were in all necessary equipment—no khaki, no slings to their rifles, no packs, mess-tins, water-bottles or ammunition pouches, not even greatcoats: everything, in fact, was lacking. A few naval volunteers had leather gear; the majority of the men carried their bayonets in their gaiters or in any odd place they found most convenient.

The Division embarked. On board the ship and at Dunkirk greatcoats and water-bottles were issued—about one of each to every two men, also haversacks to each man; these were the only things in which emergency rations or ammunition could be carried. The spirits of the men were wonderful, but we military officers could not fail to realise the situation and the terrible risk and possible waste of sending a Division of fine men on active service in a half-baked condition.

T   273

Chapter XXI

ANTWERP

WE arrived at Antwerp after a ten hours' crawl, and marched through streets lined with an enthusiastic populace to one of the suburbs, where we rested for two or three hours. The Marine Brigade were already there and, with some Belgian infantry, were in occupation of the trenches in advance of the second line of fortifications. The two Naval Brigades marched thence to Vieux Dieux, another suburb of Antwerp, on the Lierre road; it was already under shell fire and the guns of the forts were answering.

That evening officers commanding battalions were sent for to attend a conference at the municipal hall. Winston Churchill was there, and was apparently in charge of operations, although General Paris, a distinguished marine, was supposed to be in command of the Division. We were informed of the military situation, which was certainly precarious, and were then told that it had been decided that the naval brigades should advance, occupy the positions in the rear of the Belgians and dig themselves in during the night. It was pointed out, with proper respect to the First Lord, that the men had never used an entrenching tool by day, let alone by night, and that their officers were not sufficiently advanced in their training to know how to lay out a trench, or even what it looked like. Another person present was the late Minister for War, Major-General Seely; he, too, was apparently taking a hand in this bit of amateur soldiering. All the military officers present were ex-officers in the Brigade of Guards, and there could have been no question in Winston's mind that, whatever the orders given us, we should do our best to carry them out, but it was obvious, in view of the untrained condition of the troops we commanded, that we could not be held responsible for any disaster that might happen. After further discussion we were told to return to our units and await orders.

The men were eventually given a small entrenching tool as used by the Belgian army, about as effective as a toothpick. Water was supplied to them in bottles which had been requisitioned from the local brewery, and the remarks which were made when it was discovered that they contained water and not beer can be left to the imagination.

Early on the morning of the 7th October orders came that the naval troops were to occupy the entrenchments between the forts and redoubts of the second line of defences. This meant that the Germans must have forced the passage of the river and that the shelling of Antwerp was only a question of a few hours. These entrenchments had been made on old models, and were practically useless against the German artillery, with the result that the men, already tired out, had to start to improvise dug-outs as best they could.

I well remember my impressions as we left our billets in Vieux Dieux. It was early dawn and things were not clearly visible, and as we neared the trenches I saw what looked like huge mill-stones placed at regular intervals along our line of front. I was reminded of Randolph Caldecott's illustration in " The Three Jovial Huntsmen." These objects turned out to be Cheddar cheeses, and very acceptable they were.

The bombardment of the forts began early on the Wednesday morning, the Germans using big 42-centimetre Howitzers, the huge shells of which made a peculiar, wailing dirge as they travelled overhead and fell on the doomed city. The reply was, as expected, feeble. The Belgian guns could not possibly reach the German positions; many of these guns, most of which had been supplied by the Germans themselves, were put out of action by a breakdown in their hydraulic machinery after a few rounds had been fired.

I visited the redoubts in my sector, one of which was commanded by an old Belgian Warrant-Officer. He showed me his ammunition in the magazine, pointing out those shells which had been supplied by a Belgian firm and those supplied by Krupps, which, he said, were quite useless. It seemed to me amazing that at the time of delivery no tests had been made to prove them effective or otherwise.

The first night in the trenches there was a false alarm. All manned the parapets and started blazing into space, and it was with the greatest difficulty that the men could be persuaded to cease fire. As they had not been previously issued with rifles it did not seem possible to inculcate in their minds any idea of fire discipline. As a result, a terrible thing happened. Hearing this persistent firing, the Belgian gunners who were manning the enfilading guns in the fort on my left flank were under the impression that there had been an attack and that the Germans had captured the redoubts, and they therefore opened fire on these, which were of course still occupied by their own troops. I tried to ring up the fort and explain what was happening, but it was some time before I could get an answer, and when I did it was too late. One redoubt became a shambles, a sight I shall never forget.

The day before this false alarm I had noticed hundreds of Frisian cattle which had been driven into the fields about four hundred yards from the trenches. The following morning, as things were quite peaceful, I and my adjutant walked out, more out of curiosity than anything else, to see whether the night firing had caused much damage. We expected to see the field strewn with beef. To our astonishment we found the animals grazing unconcernedly; it seemed incredible that not one animal should have been hit.

The accuracy of the German artillery was something marvellous. They systematically worked down the line of forts, putting each one out of action in turn. A shell must have fallen right on the magazine of the fort on my left flank, as about mid-day on the third day of the bombardment it blew up. As there was not a breath of wind, the effect was extraordinary. It looked exactly as if tons and tons of cotton wool were suspended over the ruins, and it was quite a considerable time before the dense smoke eventually cleared away.

Another wonderful sight was the attempt made by the Belgians to burn the Pontoon bridge which the Germans had thrown over the Scheldt. They emptied some oil tanks on to the water and set light to the oil, and this caused three huge black columns of smoke to move majestically upstream with the tide. Unfortunately the tide turned just as the first column neared the bridge, and all three, burning lower, retraced their course.

On Thursday evening the order came to retreat via a bridge of boats to a place called Bruight, the intention being to march to S. Nicolas, where it was hoped to find trains which would take us back to Ostend. For the most part the way lay through the narrow streets of Antwerp. We passed by the outskirts of one of the railway stations, which had been heavily shelled by the Germans, with the curious result that some of the locomotives were on their side, others standing up like dogs begging—the whole effect was like the nursery of some giant who had grown tired of his toys and cast them aside, letting them fall as they would. Before arriving at the bridge, the Division had to march through two huge oil fires. The road itself ran on a causeway between two sunk fields, upon which the contents of oil tanks had been emptied. They were probably set light to accidentally, and there was a fearsome grandeur about the scene which reminded one of Dante's Inferno; the heat was intense, but by no means unbearable. Fortunately, what wind there was was blowing from the smaller of the two fires; had it been stronger and from the opposite direction, it is doubtful whether the troops could have left the city that night. As it was, the fires contributed to the success of the retreat, as the smoke rendered it impossible for the Germans to see where their shells were bursting. It was obvious that they realised that if any retreat were to be made it could only be by this bridge, and they were doing their utmost to destroy it. An attempt had actually been made by German spies earlier in the day to blow it up; fortunately they were caught and dealt with.

After crossing the bridge I received instructions from General Paris to throw out an advance guard, as my battalion was leading. It was getting dusk, and I knew that an advance guard of infantry to cover infantry would be of little use against enterprising cavalry unless it were a long way ahead; we, of course, had no cavalry; field officers had not even been permitted to bring their chargers. I felt that the best thing to do in the circumstances was to go ahead myself, and with this idea I commandeered a Belgian bicycle and rode on about a kilometre in front of the Division. Many were the poignant sights I saw. The people of Antwerp, imagined that they were fleeing to safety by going into the country, and the people in the country believed that they would find safety in Antwerp: and when these unfortunate refugees met, and appreciated the true situation, and realised that it was equally useless to go forward or to go back, the scenes were truly heart-rending. After I had gone about half a mile beyond a village called Beyeren, I came across a Belgian officer legging it for all he was worth towards me. I asked him what information he could give, and explained to him that I was in advance of an English Division who were making for S. Nicolas.

" Then you're going into a hornet's nest," he replied, " as the Germans occupied it this afternoon."

He seemed so certain of his facts that I rode back to the head of the column and on my own initiative halted it. A few minutes later Commodore Backhouse turned up, and I gave him the information I had acquired. After another few minutes who should appear on the scene but the ubiquitous Jack Seely, who, when he was told, said with disdain: " I don't believe it." Even if inclined to over-estimate his own importance, Jack Seely is certainly a brave man, as, when I curtly suggested that as he had a motor-car and I had only a bicycle it would be quicker for him to go and see for himself, he did so at once, and the Division was told to take what rest it could meanwhile. The men simply fell like logs, so exhausted were they, and even a donkey cart running away over cobblestones, which sounded like a distant machine gun, failed to rouse them.

After a lapse of two hours, the information which the Belgian officer had given me was confirmed. The Division now had to retrace its steps, going back as it were along the centre line of the figure 3 until it turned left-handed on to the second curve. (It was here that I discovered that my bicycle was out of action, and had to leave it by the way-side.) This time St. Gillies Waes was the point to be made. The spirits of the tired and footsore men were raised by their being told that trains were waiting for them, but that those who did not arrive there would probably be cut off and captured. Thus commenced the second stage of that long night march; it could hardly be called a march, as from this point it deteriorated into a rabble. The road was narrow, and the Belgian forces, whose retreat from Antwerp had been covered by the Naval Division, were met with. An indescribable confusion of soldiers, marines, Belgian Artillery, Cavalry and Foot, thousands of refugees, and many motor-'buses blocked the narrow way. Winston had arranged for sixty L.G.O.C. motor-'buses to be taken to Antwerp for speedy conveyance of troops. It was odd seeing the huge advertisements on them—" Kitchener wants a million men," etc. It was not the fault of the men that they were strung out over so many miles: march discipline was impossible on a road where all this turmoil reigned. There were no staff officers to direct the transport along another road. By the mercy of Providence—I can find no other explanation—most of the marine brigade and one naval brigade arrived at St. Gillies Waes at about seven in the morning, having marched continuously, except for the two hours' rest mentioned, since six o'clock the previous evening. A glance at the map will show that nearly fifty kilometres were covered during that ghastly night.

Owing to the pig-headedness of its commander, the 1st Brigade were placed in billets in Beyeren during the night, and, tired as the men were it was hours before they could be got to fall in again. Their retreat had been cut off and they were marched into Holland, only to be interned for the rest of the war.

We were delayed for one night at Bruges, where I took the opportunity of snatching an hour to have a bath and a meal. I found General Byng * at the hotel, and was taken in to see him by one of his staff, Cavendish.

" Where the devil have you come from? " he asked me. Covered with mud and with a week's growth of beard, I must have looked a pretty sight.

" From Antwerp, sir," I replied, " and incidentally a German Army Corps is let loose, as the city has fallen."

He was kindness itself, and refused to hear any more until I had had a meal, after which he listened to all I had to tell him—how two-thirds of a division of infantry, entirely unprovided with cavalry or artillery, had made good their retreat from the besieged city, where they had undergone heavy shell-fire. He seemed amazed that, considering the Germans' known powers and practice of pursuit, we had been allowed to escape.

Two days later what was left of the Division was sent back to England to complete its training.

I admit that at the time I and many others who had taken part in this business, while proud of the way the men had behaved in such circumstances, were incensed at having been sent on active service with entirely untrained troops. In fairness, however, to Winston Churchill it must be said that the sending of the Naval Division to Antwerp may have altered the whole course of the war. Two years later I discussed the affair with the late Sir John Cowans, who thought likewise, saying that those ten precious days gave Sir John French sufficient time to move the British Army

* Lord Byng of Vimy.

on to the coast of Flanders and thus stay the advance on the Channel ports. The Germans, who always acted by rule of thumb and with very little imagination, refused to take the chance of leaving a hostile city, known to contain troops, on their right flank; therefore it had to be reduced. I doubt if their secret service could have given them any intelligent information as to the number or class of troops sent into Antwerp by the British. The two brigades of the Naval Division could easily have been accommodated in comparatively few trains; but numbers of trains of incalculable length—entirely empty—streamed over the bridge into Antwerp before the siege actually began, and for all the enemy knew there might have been twenty thousand troops in the city. It was a game of poker. Winston held the worst hand, but he won by sheer bluff.

Chapter XXII

ATTEMPTS AT PROPAGANDA WORK IN AMERICA

AFTER their return to England, what were left of the Naval Division were given ten days' leave. Their old camps had been broken up and the new hutments which the Admiralty were building on the Downs above Blandford, in Dorset, were not yet complete. At the expiration of their leave, the battalions were drafted to various naval depots to complete a course of musketry.

During my leave I was in London, and there I heard two interesting stories about myself. The first was that I had left my battalion in the lurch during the retreat from Antwerp and had biked like fury ahead of it to a place of safety. This libel I treated with the contempt it deserved. The second story, though more fantastic, was even more serious; but it had its comic element. I was supposed to have been shot in the Tower as a spy. It will be remembered that, after the outbreak of war, 'spy mania' was rampant in England: not content with accusing loyal British subjects with German blood in their veins, popular prejudice caused everyone with even a German in-law to be looked upon with equal suspicion.

I was walking down Pall Mall one morning when I met Victor Churchill,* who greeted me with a broad smile: "Hallo, George!" he said. "I heard yesterday that you'd been shot in the Tower as a spy."

"Well, now you'll be able to contradict it," I retorted. I was not feeling in the least amused.

"Oh, I contradicted it all right at the time," he assured me. "I said that no doubt you might commit many crimes, but not that one."

* Viscount Churchill.

To be congratulated on having got out of a nasty mess like Antwerp was all right; but to be congratulated half a dozen times in two days upon having escaped execution in the Tower by a firing squad became monotonous. It may have been my imagination, but I felt convinced that several people I met in the street started as if they had seen a ghost, and were subsequently overcome with confusion. It was at least a novel test of friendship. It was also said that my father had a hidden store of rifles in the cellars at Newlands, which had been deposited when the German Emperor was at Highcliffe a few years previously and had come over for the day to visit my parents. These rifles were supposed to be destined for the use of German waiters still living in England after the outbreak of war, who were miraculously to mobilise themselves at Newlands when the great day of the German invasion arrived. However improbable it may sound now, it was very real at the time, and not at all pleasant.

Early in December I went with my battalion to Bland-ford. The huts themselves were dry and comfortable, but the position chosen for them was one of the bleakest in England, and the cold was intense. Most of the naval ratings had been taken away from the Naval Brigade for service at sea, and we were supplied with recruits from all parts of the country, so it was a question of beginning the training all over again. The winter of 1914-15 was a severe one, and I was down several times with bronchitis. The last attack, in the early Spring, nearly finished me. My firm in the city had meanwhile become a complete wash-out, and what with illness and worry I became so unfit that a medical board was insisted upon, and I was given six months' leave of absence.

On the top of all this, I received evidence that the spy story was actually in print in America. So highly respectable a paper as the *New York Tribune* published the statement that I had been shot as a spy—but the Press Cutting Association, to which I subscribe, presumably did me the compliment of disbelieving the story, as they sent me the cutting! The most disgusting libel was, however, sent me by an unknown friend in Utah, who signed himself Stevens. It was taken from the Salt Lake City Something-or-other and consisted of the whole of the front page of the Sunday edition. Anybody who has been to America knows what a Sunday edition is—more like a magazine than a newspaper—and this was no exception. On the top were the headlines, in red:

HIST! THE SPY!

It then went on to give the most lurid details of my arrest, trial and conviction; and of my family history, stating that both my sisters and my mother, and even my poor old grandmother, Lady Olivia Fitzpatrick, who was then aged ninety-one, had been more than friends with most of the crowned heads of Europe. So far as I was concerned, the only redeeming feature in this scurrilous diatribe was that during my last moments I had " shown considerable fortitude."

This was a bit too much. Something had to be done. I went to Sir Francis Lloyd, who was then commanding the London district, and showed him these charming samples of American journalistic invention. I also explained to him that I had been invalided out of the Naval Division and given leave of absence, at the expiration of which I should in the ordinary course return to the reserve battalion of my regiment. It was he who suggested that I should join my wife in America, at the same time taking what steps I could to dispose of these lies once and for all: " And," he added, " you can do a bit of propaganda work if opportunity arises, and come back and report to me when you are fit."

Before leaving England I paid a friendly visit to Sir John Cowans at the War Office. He was much amused at the lurid libel, but quite appreciated that something ought to be done about it. He was in full agreement with Sir Francis Lloyd's idea of propaganda, and suggested that the best way I could serve my country while abroad would be by giving every possible interview I could to American news representatives. This I knew would not be a difficult matter!

Opportunity arose almost immediately I arrived in America, where Stella was playing in Boston. Like nearly all whom I met in New England, Bostonians were almost entirely pro-British. I was invited as a guest of honour to the Tavern Club, and the president informed me at the time of my invitation that a Dutchman was coming to lecture on the Capture of Antwerp by the Germans, adding that he believed the supposed Dutchman was a German himself. " We ought to have a bit of fun," he said, " as I don't suppose he has the faintest notion that anyone who was in Antwerp is likely to be listening to him, and may himself be able to add a few remarks on the subject."

The president was right. The Dutchman, if indeed he was one, was purely a German propagandist. Throughout his speech he belauded the feats of the Germans and belittled those of the English. According to him, the Germans succeeded by sheer dash and bravery in overcoming a huge force of English and Belgians in Antwerp. He made free use of maps and a blackboard. When he had finished, the president called upon me to make a few remarks, announcing for the first time that I had commanded a battalion of the besieged garrison. I shall never forget the look on the Dutchman's face; I must say he was horribly unlucky to have run up against me, as I was probably the only man in America at that moment who had taken part in the siege, so the odds were about a hundred million to one against his being shown up. This I proceeded to do with the greatest joy. After having politely asked him for the loan of his maps and blackboard, I explained to my audience how a small force of English—I did not give my country away by saying they were untrained—and third-line Belgian troops had held up a whole German Army Corps for ten days, and showed how that Army Corps might have been much more usefully employed elsewhere.

One or two German sympathisers in the room slunk

away with their Dutch friend, while the rest of us remained to spend what turned out to be more than " a pleasant evening." A delightful club, the Tavern Club. It reminded me rather of the Garrick in this country: a lot of thoroughly good fellows representative of every profession, many very well-read, all hard-working and capable of enjoying a good joke, especially the one just played on the Dutchman.

A curious incident happened when I was in Boston. I was walking through the older part of the town, looking at the Colonial houses—relics of a time when New England was still an English colony—many of which still stand, when I noticed one (I think in Market Street) which looked like an old corn exchange and might easily have been the tea exchange where the trouble first began. On it, beneath one of the eaves, there still was the British royal coat-of-arms, complete with lion and unicorn; the only thing that was wanting was the crown surmounting the whole. I asked a friend at the Tavern Club, to which I had been elected an honorary member, whether he was aware that it still existed. He assured me that it did not, and offered to bet me several dollars that I was wrong. Having seen it with my own eyes, I did not take the bet, although some of the other members offered to lay me a shade of odds. Instead I asked several of them to lunch with me next day, and took them and showed them what I had seen. They were all amazed, and agreed that it always takes a stranger to find out the most interesting things in one's town.

We next visited Philadelphia, where I again had the good fortune to be elected an honorary member of the best club in the city. One evening I entered its portals, and was met on the threshold by a man whose features seemed dimly familiar. He knew me at once and said: " George Cornwallis-West! My name's Scott, and we were at Farnborough school together." I then recollected an American boy of that name. It was obvious that he had been doing himself very well, and I was not enthusiastic when he came

286

upstairs with me, stood me a cocktail and insisted upon sitting at the same table for dinner. It turned out to be a good example of *in vino veritas*. The more he imbibed, the freer became his tongue, and the gist of his speech was this: "You English think we Americans like you. We don't *dis*like you, but we're damned jealous of you—we hate your superior manners and your straight noses and your precise way of speaking your own tongue," and then he leaned across the table and added confidentially, "And I don't mind telling you that you've married the second-best actress in the world!" His brain was too fuddled to answer my question as to whom he considered the best, and at that moment some other members, who had over-heard part of his conversation, came and took him away by main force. He afterwards wrote me a long letter of apology, to which I replied that I wasn't in the least offended, as home truths never did anybody any harm.

Another club in Philadelphia where I was invited to dine as a guest of honour, on Washington's birthday, was the Fish Club, one of the oldest in existence. Its head-quarters were at an old colonial house on the banks of the Delaware River, where members met on national fête days and whenever the spirit moved them. Every member had to produce some sort of food or drink, and no servants, other than the caretaker, existed. Everything was cooked and prepared by the members themselves, and I must say I never ate a better dinner in my life. When it was over, I was called upon to return thanks on behalf of the guests. Considering that we were celebrating the birthday of Washington, it was rather a delicate matter for an English-man to make a speech at all. I started by saying that I considered the American Revolution to have been the best thing that could have happened to the British Empire. Had it not happened, we might have lost all our colonies: it was the Revolution which taught us how to govern those that remained. It went quite well. I then introduced a little propaganda on behalf of the Allies.

Stella was very popular in Philadelphia and had many

friends there, having been there often before. On this occasion we attended a tea-party given in her honour. Anybody who has been in that city will realise that the name of Biddle, though ancient and highly respected, is fairly common there, and Stella, taking a delicious-looking cake rather like a Richmond maid-of-honour, asked innocently: " Is this a Philadelphia Biddle? "

American hospitality is proverbial, and we experienced it everywhere, even to the extent of being lent a house and servants at Washington by Mr. and Mrs. Stotesbury, who were quite indignant when we endeavoured to pay the tradesmen's accounts for the week we were there.

Bearing in mind my promise about propaganda work, I made a point of giving interviews to American journalists whenever they wished. I did not realise then that the opinions I expressed were in any way prophetic, although owing to my German connections I possibly realised more about the European situation before the war, and the strength of Germany, than most laymen; but, looking at the press cuttings in the light of after events, I am surprised to find that they were so. I had already got into hot water with some of my friends in England for saying that the war would go on for many years, and, as the stock question of the journalists in America was how long the war would last, I always gave the same answer: that I believed it would be a war of attrition, and that in the end the side who had the most men available would win, and that I did not believe it was a question of money, for want of money had never stopped any war. I was also asked if I thought America would come into it. That, I responded, was an impossible question to answer, but I did feel that, when it came to settling terms, the American President would be called upon to act in the same way as he had at the close of the Russo-Japanese War.

I made the stipulation that I should see the proofs of anything I was supposed to have said before it was published, and I must say that, with one exception, this condition was adhered to. The exception was at a small town in the Middle West, where a newspaper not only let its imagination run riot as to my views concerning the European situation, but suggested that Stella had been co-respondent in my divorce case, which of course was quite untrue. I was very angry, and stalked into the editor's office next morning and told him what I thought of him. He was a little man, and the more angry I became, the more frightened he grew, until eventually he rang up the police station and told them to send a constable, as he had a lunatic in his office. By this time I did not mind if the whole police force arrived, and continued my abuse. A few minutes later a policeman came in, announcing in the richest Cork brogue I have ever heard that he was " Constable Michael Cassidy." Instantly I went up to him, shook him violently by the hand, and said, with an equally rich Cork brogue : " Michael ! Shure I haven't seen you since we last met in Cork city all these years ago," and taking him by the arm I walked him firmly out of the office, leaving the editor in open-mouthed astonishment. The constable was so flabbergasted that he said nothing until we got into the street, when he bethought himself of his official duty and asked : " Who arre ye, annyway ? " I enlightened him, and explained why he had been sent for.

" The dirrthy dog ! " he exclaimed. " But Oi'll tell ye how ye can get the better of him. There's another newspaper in the town, and they're at daggers drawn. Now if ye were to go to that fellow and tell him of the dirrthy trick played on ye by this fellow, he'd have two columns cursin' him by to-morrow morning ! "

I thanked him for the brilliant suggestion, and went to the office of the other newspaper, where I poured out to the editor my grievance concerning the opposition paper. Sure enough, the next morning, a long article appeared on ' the honour of the Press,' etc. In the evening the other paper took up the cudgels, and so the fight went on. We were only making a two nights' stay, and we left the next morning, so who got the best of it in the end I have never known.

I was glad of the opportunity to visit San Francisco and that wonderful country, California. Although it was some years after the earthquake, it was curious to see several residential houses still in ruins alongside of those newly erected. There seemed to have been no plan made for the general reconstruction of the city and, appreciating American methods as a rule, I was rather surprised at this. The exhibition was in full swing, and some of the pavilions were truly magnificent. It was while I was there that ex-President Roosevelt sent me a polite invitation to visit him at his hotel. Although it was a hot day in July, I found him in a thick black frock coat. He began talking excitedly about the war, but asked me very few questions. Marching up and down the room, he explained vehemently that America ought to lose no time in coming into the world struggle; that the sinking of the *Lusitania* was sufficient justification for an immediate declaration of war on her part; that it was his ambition to command an American division in France. He struck me as a forceful and active personality, but not as particularly clever. He simply expressed his own opinions, without caring to hear the views and experiences of his listener, who, after all, was fresh from Europe and had seen some active service.

At the end of our stay in San Francisco I was taken seriously ill with the same trouble that I had had when in America before. On the doctor's advice, I went into the Californian Sierras, and it was there that I enjoyed that delightful fishing trip described in another chapter.

To return to the spy libel. When I had arrived in New York, the first person I had consulted was a Mr. Davidson, a well-known attorney in that city, who advised me to take no action against the *New York Tribune*, pointing out that as I had suffered no material injury he doubted whether an American jury would award me damages in the case. He succeeded, however, in obtaining me an ample apology. As regards the newspaper in Salt Lake City he admitted that he was not on very sure ground, as he did not know what the law of libel was in the state of Utah, but promised to make inquiries. Before leaving San Francisco I heard from him that an apology had also been made by that paper, but I certainly was not prepared for what actually happened. When, on my return journey, I arrived in Salt Lake City itself, I was met on the platform by the editor of the opposition paper, who shook me warmly by the hand and told me that I had done him the best turn of his life, as the rival paper had gone out of business and his own was flourishing! He went on to explain that according to the law of libel in Utah, if a statement published by a newspaper was proved to be untrue the paper was obliged to print an apology for seven consecutive days, *occupying the same amount of space as that originally filled by the libel*, " and," he concluded, " the folk of this city got so durned sick of reading an apology to you on the front page of their newspaper every day in the week, that they gave up buying it!" I remember wishing that my friend W. S. Gilbert had been alive, so that I could have passed on to him this perfect example of the punishment fitting the crime.

On the way to New Orleans we stayed three nights at Birmingham, Alabama. I loved the South, with its niggers—real ones, not the pale brown half-casts one sees in the North—cotton fields, quaint colonial houses and the blue-green haze of the horizon. Nothing in the Southern states seemed to remind one of the Northern, unless it was the hotels, many of them up-to-date and comfortable, but somehow not in keeping with their pulseless, yet attractive, surroundings; there were no ' hives of industry,' no huge factories throbbing with life and machinery. There is a certain melancholy about the South, which, in some odd way, reminded me of Ireland.

At Birmingham we were shown up to our rooms by a Negro bell-boy—boy in name only, as he was about twenty, tall and well-made, and, unlike most of his race, he walked and did not shuffle.

" Yuh belong to de troup?" he asked.

I was not certain what he meant, and he saw my hesitation. " De theatrical troup what just come to de town."

I told him we did. "I'm sho pleased to meet yuh!" he continued. "We coloured folk are mighty interested in theatricals. We have a troup of our own—yes, sir, we certainly have! We been studying ' Hamlet ' ! "

"Who is playing the lead? " I asked, wishing to be polite, and also interested, as he was so much in earnest.

With his hand placed theatrically on his heart, and grinning from ear to ear, he answered: "*I* am to play Hamlet."

And then to New Orleans, that flat, steaming city of contrasts. Fine wide streets and high modern buildings meet the eye, and then, turning up a byway for a few yards, you might imagine yourself in the slums of Paris or Marseilles: the same French houses, mostly flats, each window with outside shutters and a verandah with fancy iron balustrade, behind which, of an evening, the women-folk sit and gossip with their next-door neighbours. One even heard a curious sort of American-French *patois* spoken. It interested me to think that at the extreme north and south of this great continent—at Montreal and New Orleans—after the passing of more than a century, the French still retain their individuality in an English-speaking country.

New Orleans is nothing if not damp, even in summer, when we were there: consequently every sort of unwished-for insect throve. One night I heard a piercing shriek, a really effective off-stager, from the bathroom of the suite we had at the hotel. I rushed in, to find Stella apparently hypnotised by what looked like a huge slate-coloured Egyptian scarab. I hastily took off a slipper, and then—*plunk !* A sort of mild explosion resulted, followed by the most appalling stench I ever remember. Pulling herself together, my wife remarked: "What a pity they aren't found at home! One could have such fun with them at a Suffragette meeting."

Chapter XXIII

SOME EXPERIENCES AS AN A.P.M.

On arriving once more in England I reported myself to Sir Francis Lloyd and returned for duty with the reserve battalion of my regiment. It felt strange to go back as a somewhat antique subaltern after having commanded a battalion, but there was no help for it: my sole idea was to obtain military employment of some sort. I saw Sir Wyndham Childs at the War Office and asked to be appointed to a Division proceeding to France. I had not long to wait, and was offered a job as Assistant Provost-Marshal to the 57th Division; but I was fated not to see further service overseas. Just before the Division went out, the whole of the staff were medically examined, and I was again passed as unfit. Indeed, the dear old gentleman presiding at the Board shook me sympathetically by the hand and suggested that I was suffering from an incurable disease. I consulted my own doctor, and found that, although it was a recurrence of the trouble I had had in 1911 in America, things were not so bad as I had been led to suppose, but it was essential that I should remain in London for a course of treatment. The War Office were kind, and I was given the job of A.P.M. for the counties of Surrey and Middlesex, with headquarters at Hounslow, where I was to spend the next two and a half years.

If the Military Police were unpopular with soldiers, the same could be said of an A.P.M. with officers, especially the young ones. It certainly was a thankless job, but there was no need to make it a combination of ' Old Man of the Sea ' and General Bogey Man, as was apparently considered necessary by some of the A.P.M.'s one came across. The chief occupation of some of these gentlemen seemed to be in finding fault with the dress of unfortunate officers on leave from overseas, who, after going through hellish times, certainly did not want to be bothered by what they naturally considered unwarrantable interference. There were matters of a far more serious nature for an A.P.M. to attend to, without wasting his time over trivialities; although, of course, there were occasions when fault had to be found with young gentlemen who insisted on wearing yellow ties and mauve socks with uniform. My practice was to ask them whether they were colour blind, adding that, if they did not trust my opinion that their colour schemes were not only irregular, but ugly, they had better consult their sisters or their best girl. I found that a little good-humour usually succeeded.

For drunkenness in public, of course, there was no excuse, and taking it all round I came across very few instances of it. One of the disadvantages of being an A.P.M. was that one was always on duty, at all times and places, even outside one's own area. On one occasion in 1918 I had taken an evening off, and was with a friend at the Alhambra. George Robey had just started one of his inimitable songs when a young Australian officer, evidently intoxicated, plumped himself down in a stall just in front of me and, after making himself comfortable and everybody else uncomfortable in the process, slowly rose to his feet again and in a loud voice addressed the stage:

" You'll excuse me, Mr. Robey, and I apologise for being late, but as I've come to see you I should be obliged if you'd kindly begin all over again."

George Robey never turned a hair (he merely lifted one of *the* eyebrows), but the management were very much exercised, and a few minutes later I saw a gentleman in evening clothes beckoning me to come out of my seat. I knew what I was in for, and sure enough was requested to remove the officer in front of me, who, after the turn, had gone out to get another drink. He was too far gone to offer any resistance, and, much to my annoyance, as I lost most of the evening's performance, I had to cart him off to Old Scotland Yard, where a number of cubicles had

THE AUTHOR WHEN AN A.P.M.

been installed to furnish accommodation for recalcitrant officers. It was in charge of an ex-Sergeant-Major of my old regiment, who had a wonderful way with them. With a look of unutterable disgust he would say: " Take off your belt and spurs " (if they had any). He would then remove any instrument with which they were likely to harm themselves, and gently but firmly push them into a cubicle. In this particular instance, I was rung up the following day by the Adjutant-General of the Australian forces, whose headquarters were in Horseferry Road, and asked to go and see him. He told me that the officer in question was both brilliant and courageous, and did I want to take any further steps? I naturally did not wish to ruin his career, and felt that one night in a cubicle would probably be a sufficient lesson for him. He was brought in, abjectly apologetic. Poor boy, I have often wondered whether he survived.

I had some queer places to look after, including Tag's Island at Hampton Court, upon which was situated a dancing hall and restaurant known as the Karsino, considered high-class, and Eel Pie Island at Kingston, where a similar establishment existed, not so high-class. Another famous river resort was also in my area: I refrain from mentioning its name, as, if I did, I could not tell this story, which goes to show that local as well as metropolitan police are capable of corruption. Certain parents had complained to the authorities that their sons had been mulcted in considerable sums of money at a gambling-hell at the place in question. With this meagre information I was instructed to take " the necessary action." I happened to know the proprietor of an hotel there, who, though strictly honest himself, knew many of the shady characters who were habitues of this place, and I asked him one evening if he had heard of any gambling going on.

" I suppose you know Mrs. —— is here? " he replied, mentioning a well-known person who had already been in trouble for selling liquor on unlicensed premises. He then told me that she had taken a house-boat, where all sorts of funny things were supposed to go on.

I next visited the head of the local county constabulary, and asked him whether he was aware that gambling was supposed to be taking place in his district. I suspected the man immediately, as he tried to put me off by saying: "Don't you believe it, Major. It's nothing but hearsay."

There were one or two very good men in the Military Police who used to do C.I.D. work, and I instructed one of these to keep an eye on the house-boat. He reported to me a few days later that certain officers had been seen to enter and leave the boat, and that he had often seen women on board it, but that it was now empty. I felt certain that the lady would not leave the district, where she was evidently coining money, and that it was only a question of time before she would crop up again. I next heard she had shifted her activities to a small house on the river; and felt convinced that she had been warned by the head of the police to change her headquarters and that it was useless my consulting him again. Accordingly, one night, I went down in plain clothes, and crept through the shrubbery of the house to a window through which light was shining between the partly drawn curtains. The window was open; I opened it still further and peeped in. There I saw the woman and a number of young officers playing chemin-de-fer, with drinks going round merrily. I hastily made my way back to my car and drove to the police headquarters, where I said to the same officer: "If you don't believe there's gambling going on, come with me and see for yourself," and told him what I had seen. He made some ridiculous excuse about not being able to leave the office, and said he would attend to the matter later; and with this I had to be satisfied, as, in a case of this kind, I was powerless to act without the aid of the civil police. Two days later the house on the river was raided, and of course nothing was found.

I took the matter up with the Provost-Marshal of the Home Forces, who assisted me in every way; and I personally wrote to the acting Chief Constable of the county concerned, but received a snub from that gentleman to the effect that I had no right to make so grave an accusation against a man with five-and-thirty years service to his credit. I believe the matter was even put before the Home Office, but nothing was done, and the lady escaped, only to pay the penalty for her misdeeds some years later.

This was the only case during the whole of my time at Hounslow where I found the civil police unwilling to work with the military authorities. Much of my work was with the metropolitan police outside the county of London area, and I invariably found them active in assisting me.

In 1918, when every available man was called up, every possible subterfuge was used by a few, mostly of alien extraction, to avoid conscription; and it became necessary to have occasional raids on music halls and cinemas, hold up the audience and examine the men's papers. I had to undertake one of these at Edmonton one night, and when, towards the end of the performance, I appeared on the stage and requested the ladies to leave, uproar ensued, and the remarks yelled at me were not complimentary. The bag that night was considerable. When the house was apparently empty, we proceeded to search it. It was like a game of hide and seek: men were discovered hiding under furniture and behind odd bits of scenery, and every lavatory held at least two.

Another of these raids took place on Lingfield Racecourse, where, after the last race, the public found every exit barred by military and civil police. Rock Cholmondeley * was one of those held up, and I found him, foaming with rage, involved in an argument with a stalwart red-cap, who was telling him he didn't care if he were the Marquess of God-knows-where, he had to obey orders. Thirty-seven ought-to-have-been soldiers was the bag that afternoon.

Another case of this kind, and far more interesting, occurred in the Spring of that year. I was informed by the C.I.D. of the Home Forces that there was believed to be a leakage of men, who should have been conscripted, to Ireland, most of these being the sons of naturalised

---

* The late Marquess of Cholmondeley.

aliens in the East End of London. Forged railway warrants
had come into the possession of the military police at Euston,
and it was believed that the book from which they had
been extracted was one issued in the Hounslow district.
A great many officers of various departments in that district
had powers to issue railway warrants. In Hounslow
Barracks itself there was a big recruiting centre, one of the
biggest in the United Kingdom, and I first visited the
senior Recruiting Officer and asked to see his warrant
books. They were shown to me by a young corporal, a
sleek-looking individual, who appeared perfectly fit, and
to my mind should have been in France. The books
appeared to be in order, but I felt pretty certain that the
leakage complained of could only be carried out through
the instrumentality of someone in the recruiting office,
and my suspicions fell on the corporal, whose obsequious
efficiency I mistrusted. I made inquiries and discovered
that he himself was of alien origin, had changed his name
and came from the East End. There was in the Military
Police at Hounslow a man who had once been an actor,
and another excellent fellow, by name Fairservice, who
used to play cricket for Kent; and these I told off to watch
the corporal, instructing them to get into plain clothes and
leaving their make-up to the actor. I realised the hope-
lessness of examining every warrant book in the Hounslow
district; even if it were possible, such a course would have
excited suspicion, and it was therefore necessary to find
out who the corporal's friends were. A third military
policeman discovered that he was in the habit of going
into the office of one of the army veterinary surgeons and
appeared on friendly terms with a non-commissioned officer
in that department. I arranged with the veterinary surgeon,
unknown to his clerk, to examine his warrant books, and
there, sure enough, in some of the unused books, I found
that warrants had been torn out and the counterfoils not
filled in. Meanwhile, my two military detectives had
tracked their man down to a public house called the 'Vine
and Grapes' in the East End, and had seen him pass

something and receive something in exchange. It was necessary now to obtain evidence, so I communicated with Detective-Inspector Collins of the C.I.D. of the Metropolitan Police. He arranged for a man to impersonate an alien tailor, who was to get in touch with the corporal and find out on what terms he could be supplied with a warrant to go to Ireland. The corporal fell into the trap, and agreed to meet the pseudo-tailor at the same public house, where he sold the warrant for three pounds. These he received in marked notes, which were discovered upon him when he was arrested coming into Hounslow Barracks the same night. He was tried by Court Martial and sentenced to a long term of imprisonment, which was subsequently commuted to six months on the understanding that he was immediately sent to the Front.

One of the principal duties of an A.P.M. was to discover the whereabouts of absentee officers. It was a distasteful business having to arrest some wretched man, perhaps recently married, who wanted to spend a few extra days with his wife, not knowing what might happen to him in the future; but it had to be done, although my sympathies were often with the culprits. There was one case, however, where I had no sympathy with the individual in question, as he was actually quartered in England. I was informed that he was absent from his regiment, and was given an address in Croydon where his wife was supposed to live. I visited the house, and the door was opened by a pretty woman who appeared to realise at once why I had come, as, before I could say anything, she asked if I was looking for her husband, saying that she had not seen him for weeks, that he had deserted her—all the old story, in fact, of having been infamously treated. Her flow of language seemed so carefully rehearsed that I became suspicious, and asked her if she had any idea where her husband was likely to be found. She promptly gave me an address, right at the other end of London, in Tottenham, where she maintained that he was living with another woman. I decided to follow up the clue, but left a plain-clothes military policeman to keep an eye on the house. When I arrived at the Tottenham address, I found a tousled middle-aged lady, who informed me that *she'd* like to get hold of young so-and-so too, as he'd been living there with his wife, and owed for a fortnight's rent and washing—she emphasised the washing. Her description of the wife tallied with that of the woman seen earlier in the day. On my return to Hounslow I was rung up from Croydon, to be told that an officer had been seen that afternoon entering the house I had visited. I arrived there shortly before midnight, and for a long time could get no answer. Eventually, however, the wife opened the door and, despite her remonstrances and abuse, I went upstairs and found the husband under the bed.

It was amazing to what lengths certain types of men who still remained would go to escape foreign service. The military police at Epsom reported to me that a young officer covered with medal ribbons was seen on a motor cycle leaving the town most days, and that he had taken up his abode at a villa on the outskirts of the town. As it was known that no officers were given more than a certain number of days' leave from the front, and it was unlikely that one would live in a villa instead of being attached to a unit in the district, suspicions were aroused. I interviewed the owner of the villa, who informed me that Lieutenant X was such a nice young man, and had done so well in the war that he was billeted on them as a favour, and was attached to a machine-gun section in the neighbourhood. He admitted that he had been paid nothing for having fed and lodged him, but did not appear to think that unusual. I waited until the return of Lieut. X, and the account he gave of himself was so unsatisfactory that he was arrested, and turned out to be a private in a line battalion at Dover. He was wearing no less than seven medal ribbons, including that of the South African War, and as he could not have been more than twenty-three this alone should have excited the suspicions of his host.

A funny thing happened at the Savoy on Armistice Night. About ten of us dined there to celebrate the occasion, and, long after closing hours, the manager came to me in desperation to ask whether I would assist him to clear the restaurant. I was not attached to the London district, but I did what I could. One officer in a Highland regiment was obstinate. He had been celebrating lavishly, and was now sitting dourly at a table with a far-away look in his eyes and the table-cloth wrapped tightly round his legs. I suggested that he had better go home, and he looked at me and said: " Mon, I canna move. Some —— has stolen ma kilt! "

One of the last jobs I had as A.P.M. at Hounslow was to attend Ascot Races in 1919, when I received special instructions from the Eastern Command to make a note of the names of all general officers who appeared in plain clothes, as an order had been issued that uniform was to be worn. The first Generals I saw there were two old brother-officers, Sir William Pulteney and Sir Cecil Lowther, both in plain clothes. Sir Noel Birch and many others whom I knew were dressed in the same way. When, however, I saw that the general officer who had issued the order was also in plain clothes, I ceased to take any interest in the instructions, and proceeded to enjoy myself. My report to the Eastern Command was to the effect that as I had seen the G.O.C. himself in plain clothes I had taken it for granted that the order was either a mistake or had been cancelled.

Soon after the Armistice the managements of the various race-courses round London, most of which were in my area, were kind enough to allow officers in uniform to use the members' enclosure on payment of a reduced entrance fee. This privilege began to be abused, and officers who had been demobilised, and others who had never even been mobilised, appeared in uniform and got in on the cheap. I received complaints about this from the managers of Sandown and Hurst Park. On the morning of a meeting at Sandown, the first person I saw on arriving was an old gentleman with a long white beard, clad in a prehistoric greyish-blue braided uniform smelling strongly of moth-ball. I asked him politely whether he was still on the active list, and he replied that he had left his regiment—some Indian Volunteer Corps—in 1881. He was prosecuted under the Defence of the Realm Act at Kingston for wearing uniform when not entitled to, and was fined ten pounds and costs, and this, for the time, put an end to the privilege being abused. The *Evening Standard* and one or two other papers attacked me furiously for what they considered unwarrantable interference on the part of the A.P.M.

The summer of 1919 was a hectic one for Provost-Marshals. Mutiny was in the air. The men could not understand, now that the war had been over six months, why they were not demobilised. Unpleasantness occurred at Kempton and Osterley Park, both occupied by the Mechanical Transport of the A.S.C., and one night in Barracks I received a frantic message from the station-master at Hammersmith to the effect that a train had been boarded by a number of soldiers who threatened that they were going to Hounslow to burn down the Barracks. I jumped into a car and drove to Osterley Park station, where I told the station-master not to allow the train containing the men in question to proceed beyond his station, and that I would accept full responsibility. I was only just in time, as it happened to be the next one in. Most of the civilians got out, and I went into the carriages where the men were, explained to them that the train was not going any further, and ordered them out. I fell them in on the platform and re-formed them again outside the station, where I addressed them on the folly of their ways, adding that I intended to take no names, but counted upon their common sense making them behave themselves. I then marched them into camp and dismissed them, when, to my astonishment, they gave three cheers for the A.P.M.! A 'Red-cap' to a soldier was like a red rag to a bull; fortunately I had brought none with me, otherwise things might not have been so easy.

Another source of trouble were the unfortunate patients

at Addington Hospital, who were 'carriers' of enteric fever. Feeling perfectly well, they could not understand why they were treated as social outcasts, and no amount of medical instruction could convince them that they were not being unjustly detained.

One day during this summer I received a communication to the effect that a complaint had been made about indecent behaviour of soldiers and women in Richmond Park, and more especially in the enclosures, concluding with the usual instructions to " take the necessary action." I mustered a force of military police at the Ham Gate and told them that we were to spread out in a line, like beaters, and walk straight through the park, omitting the enclosures. I had often been in the park myself, and, although there were many soldiers and their sweethearts about, I never saw any signs of indecency, nor did we on this occasion. If anything of that kind did occur, it must have been in the enclosures, and could only have been discovered by prurient-minded people who were deliberately looking for trouble and rejoiced when they found it.

In August 1919, instead of being demobilised, I was sent as A.P.M. to the south of Ireland, with headquarters at Cork. It seemed odd to go back to Ireland, after a lapse of five-and-twenty years, in a military capacity, and I rather looked forward to it. I felt certain that life would be both interesting and exciting in view of what was happening in that country.

When I arrived at Dublin I had to report at headquarters, and instead of going by the mail to Cork could only catch the evening train. There was no restaurant car, so I telegraphed to Limerick Junction ordering a dinner basket and mentioning a whisky and soda. When the train reached the junction, a boy duly handed me the basket: I opened it and found a soda-water bottle with a button stopper and only a corkscrew to open it with—this would happen in Ireland. I pointed out to the boy that the corkscrew was useless. His reply was characteristic: " That's all they do be giving us, annyway, your Honour,"

303

and then he added, in confidential tones: " Ye'll find the latch of the lavatory'll fit foine ! " and it did.

My district was a large one, and comprised no fewer than seven counties. I was allotted a Ford car with a woman driver belonging to the Women's Legion, and together we covered more than ten thousand miles in the four months I was there. She was Irish herself, and came from Mallow, and knew many people in the district; consequently I was often accommodated in private houses, though nobody thought it in the least odd if we stayed together in an hotel. Which reminds me that I only came across one instance of an officer making improper advances to his lady driver. She happened to be exceedingly ugly, and whether it was that she wanted her fellow-drivers to know that somebody had made up to her, I cannot say, but she reported the officer in question, who lost his commission.; and she herself was put in Coventry by the other girls for the rest of her service.

Looking back at those troublous times, I am convinced that never was there a greater proof given of the English incapacity to rule the Irish. If, instead of treating the whole matter as a rebellion, the British Government had treated it as civil war and had allowed the army a free hand to re-establish order, it is my firm belief that none of the terrible atrocities would have been committed. The thing the Irish resented more than anything else—and I had plenty of opportunity of talking to Irishmen—was the fact that their army was not taken seriously. One man in Cork, whom I know was a Sinn Feiner, although he naturally would not admit it to me, asked me this very pertinent question: " It's a hundred and fifty years ago since America gained her independence; do you believe that if Cornwallis and the other British generals had treated the American rebels in the way that the British are treating the Irish now —using a lot of dirty scallywags like the Black and Tans— America would have fought on the side of the English in this last war? No, Major," he continued; " the bitterness created would, even after a hundred and fifty years, not have been forgotten. The two sides fought like gentlemen : why should not the English and the Irish do the same? We don't mind the army, but we can't stand the riff-raff employed."

In 1920 I visited Ireland in a civil capacity on a fishing holiday, and stayed with my dearest friend, John Peacocke. A few days after I left, he was murdered in cold blood in his garage. His life and the lives of other loyalists were a sacrifice to the use of the Black and Tans, the most glaring example of the misrule of the British Government.

Chapter XXIV

THINGS LITERARY

WHENCE my elder sister and I obtained our literary aspirations I have no idea, unless it was from our Grandmama West, the lady mentioned in the first chapter. When she was about sixty, Mrs. West wrote a three-volume novel, the best part of which was the alliterative title, for it was called " The Doom of Doolandour." I once tried to read it, but was forced to agree with the reviewer of *The Scotsman*, whose brief notice I found among her papers. I give her credit for a sense of humour for having kept it, as it ran: " ' The Doom of Doolandour,' by Mrs. Frederick Cornwallis-West, and the doom of anybody else who reads it ! " Daisy's first effort was a novel written, at the age of fourteen, which she called " Don Juan di Bastellano." It was never finished, as my younger sister and I killed it by ridicule, calling it " John Jones he-busted-long-ago."

My own first serious attempt was made perforce when I had to write an essay on military music in my literary examination for the army. I had just returned from Freiburg, where I had been in the habit of listening to a first-rate military orchestra which played three days a week in the square. After dilating upon the use of the sackbut and the psalter in the Bible—instruments which I took for granted were used in a military connection—I made an invidious comparison of the use of military bands in this country and in Germany. As my crammer pointed out to me afterwards, it was treading on dangerous ground to criticise army methods, seeing that I was endeavouring to pass for the army. However, the examiner, whoever he was, bore no malice, for he awarded me 90 marks out of 100.

MRS. FREDERICK CORNWALLIS-WEST, THE AUTHOR'S LITERARY
GRANDMOTHER

I had an extraordinary stroke of luck in this exam. I had been reading for my own amusement Zola's " Le Débâcle." I was much struck with the beauty of a certain paragraph, where the passage of a river in the early dawn by a squadron of German Uhlans is described; so much so that I read it three times, and took the trouble to look up some words of which I was not quite certain. The actual paragraph was set for translation in the French paper.

When I was in San Francisco I was persuaded by an American lady to have my horoscope told. I merely had to give the date and time of my birth. When the document arrived, I remember feeling distinctly sceptical at its fore-cast that " the life upon entering middle-age will devote itself to literary matters." At that time the symptoms of this complaint had not made themselves apparent.

When I was at Aldershot in 1916, I amused myself by writing a one-act play called " Pro Patria," which my wife produced at the Coliseum. One or two papers described it as " the best one-act war play yet written," the rest as " the worst." Personally I agree with the rest, despite the fact that it was afterwards turned into an opera. When the gentleman who composed the music asked my consent to this transformation, I readily gave it, making the one stipulation that he did not ask me to sing in it.

Having experienced the delight of spending money earned by my pen, I decided to attempt something more serious, and wrote a four-act play called " The Mousetrap." It was never produced, and I still shudder when I remember that I had the temerity to write to Bernard Shaw and ask him to come and listen to it. The wonderful part of it is, that he came, and, still more amazing, did not go to sleep during the recital of the four acts. A few days later he wrote me four pages of advice upon play-writing, some points of which might serve as a guide to all aspirants to that difficult art. In order that the letter may be fully understood, it is necessary to give, as briefly as possible, the plot. A very charming lady violinist lives with her husband in the country; she has social aspirations, and longs to go to London. Against his better judgment, the husband agrees. The lady is an immediate success, and becomes the prey of a professional lady-killer, who imagines that the seduction of a country mouse will be a comparatively easy task. He nearly succeeds, but is foiled, partly by the badly constructed lies of the husband's best friend, Jack, and partly by the fortuitous aid of an old servant, Larry. A couple of *nouveaux riches* are also introduced by way of stuffing. Here is the letter :—

"... Its most serious dramatic defect is that there is only one point of view in it. Now every play ought to have as many points of view as there are characters in it. This defect brings the play to an absolute standstill at the crucial moment in the third act. The ladykiller, when the lady repulses him, walks off the stage without a word. This is impossible, both technically and dramatically: to walk out and take no further notice of her would be a victory for him if it were taken as part of the play; and if it were not, it would suggest either that the theatre was on fire or that the actor had succumbed to premonitions of a sudden and violent attack of cholera.

"His part in the scene must be played from his point of view. He might be genuinely surprised and say, ' What an extraordinary woman you are ! ' Or, if he had Irish habits of speech, he might say brazenly, ' Well, you can't say but you were asked.' Or he might cry, and implore her not to tell her husband, and offer hush money. Or he might be virtuously indignant and threaten to complain to her husband of the way she had led him on. Or he might say that he only did it because he naturally thought she expected him to pay her that compliment, and assure her that her refusal did not break his heart and that he was quite ready to go on being a brother to her. Or, perhaps best of all, he might tell her quite seriously that seducing married women was his chosen occupation in life; that he liked it and was generally successful; and that now that he knew she was not that sort of woman they had better shake hands and be friends. The offer of his hand might provoke her to break the Strad over his head; and he might go out laughing on, ' You'll have to explain that broken fiddle, dear lady. So long!' In short, there are a dozen ways of getting him off the stage with an exit speech, but not one really effective way of getting him off like a puppet being shovelled back into the box when he is done with.

" The last act as a whole is open to the objection I mentioned: there is no fresh invention in it: only a harping on what the audience has already seen, with a very unexciting reception of it by the husband. When Geoffrey fails so completely to share his wife's indignation with Jack, he not only becomes a sort of walking sugar stick of kindness and sentimentality; but he fails to do what he would do in real life: that is, exasperate her by taking his male friend's part against her, a thing which maddens all wives. Why not follow this up and involve them in a good stiff quarrel, ending in such a dispute as to what actually occurred that, when Jack comes in, it is referred at once to him by both parties? Jack, under cross-examination, would of course break down miserably, because he is an impostor who has really seen and heard nothing. Geoffrey would become more and more suspicious; she would become more and more furious; Jack would become more and more involved and more and more hopelessly convicted of lying; and in the end he would have to confess the truth, and the climax would be the summoning of Larry as *Deus ex machina* to bring about the happy ending. Larry might even be driven into declaring that he was drunk and invented the whole story; and the two men might accept this with such relief that Molly might decide to pretend that she only kept up the pretence to punish them—what for, God knows; but the audience would take a very thin excuse. There is plenty of material here for a first-rate comedy scene. The act would be tremendously enlivened, and you would get rid of that rose painting of your favourite characters which makes the present version too sentimental. Also you would give your leading man and woman some real acting to do in the last act, instead of sitting there and being too good for this world and talking about what happened in the previous act without giving it any fresh turn.

" Another point to be borne in mind is that if you want to preach from the stage, as all great dramatists do, you must have a devil's advocate, or you will inevitably become sententious, like Joseph Surface or the traditional stage sailor who announces that the man who would raise his hand to a woman, save in the way of kindness, is unworthy the name of Briton. This applies to your point about smart society having only one criterion: money. If you want to make that point effectively you must have a scene in which Jack, very sore about it, reproaches somebody for giving him the cold shoulder, and finds that the somebody is quite prepared to defend his position. Zimmerman might be used for this purpose; for as he stands in the existing version he is not a very definite character and would bear further development. His line is obvious enough. ' Well, my dear chap, what other criterion can Society apply? It would be only too willing to be sentimental. It is always talking sentiment, adoring sentiment, playing at sentiment: it asks nothing better than a practicable set of Arcadian rules. But the Arcadian rules won't work. The one indispensable qualification for society is to have plenty of money to spend. It is not only disagreeable to know people who are in difficulties, but unkind to themselves to invite them to take part in a routine which they cannot afford. Of course you must not only have money, but be free of unpresentable relatives, and of the cruder vulgarities: that is why I, Zimmerman, being a foreigner, and therefore having neither relatives in England nor English vulgarities, am accepted where an English manufacturer of my income and standing would find it hard to get in. But now, frankly, would you know me if I had £150 a year? Would you have tolerated me for a moment? you, who have come to my house and drunk my champagne and smoked my cigars and had your whack out of the monstrous sums my wife makes me spend on you and your class? If not, why should I know you now that you have not even £150 a year, but, as I guess, are a good £15,000 to the bad?' That is the way to do it. No conflict: no drama.

" Such comedy conflicts will give you a chance of using your wit and humour, which are too much smothered in your version. Also, you will be able to give yourself away, which is the essence of fine comedy, and is indeed the only excuse the playwright has for lecturing or ridiculing his fellow-creatures. There must always be that sort of fair play between the castigator of morals and his audience.

" I think the references to kicking and duelling should come out. Suppose we two discovered Carpentier and Jack Johnson offering assignations to Stella and Charlotte, could we do anything but assure them with abject politeness that the ladies were already engaged? Even Othello did not venture to tackle Cassio. The kicking is a melodramatic convention; and a woman has a perfect right to be left open to offers and trusted with her own defence. . . ."

After that I hardly dare further confess that I also had the cheek to send the play to Sir James Barrie. He, too, was kind enough to read it and wrote to me about it:

" DEAR WEST,
        " I have read the play, and return it, and I

think it is a very good play. It grows in interest very much, but I question there being much cutting to do in the first act, as it sets the characters on their legs in a leisurely pleasant way. Here and there are ' asides ' which are the only amateur's thing about the piece, and they are so unessential that a few minutes' work would get rid of them. The lady who comes into a room at midnight and finds the man is a complication as old as the hills on the stage, but it is so because of the drama in it, and you seem to me to treat it in a way that makes it your own. I don't myself know everything about the kind of people you treat of, and wonder if there are ' persons in Society ' to whom money means so much as to swallow up all else, but it may be, and at any rate you make them live and move, and have lots of shrewd things to say about them. I am sure it would all act well.

" Are there butlers who drop their h's etc. in this way? I believe you say there are because he is funny, and he is.

" I hope you will have a great success with it.

" Yours,

" J. M. BARRIE."

It is curious how many people, myself included, take pleasure in reading a novel where the principal character is an impossible person. I remember reading with delight " Tante " by Anne Douglas Sedgwick, which was afterwards dramatised by Haddon Chambers as " The Impossible Woman," the principal part being played by Miss Lillah McCarthy. Nothing daunted by my first effort, I conceived a plot on lines somewhat similar to " Tante," where a man falls a victim to the fatal fascination of an irresistibly charming, but temperamentally difficult, woman; and wrote a three-act play. Shaw was again kind enough to read my work and wrote to me as follows:

" . . . The play is not at all uninteresting as a char-

312

acter sketch; but I should not produce it if I were a manager, not because it is in any way unpresentable as a piece of work, but because the attempt to present that particular character on the stage has been made, by Haddon Chambers and others, even including lately St. J. Ervine; and it has never been successful, for a reason that ought to be obvious enough though somehow it escapes notice until too late.

" That reason is that if a person has an entirely peculiar, idiosyncratic unaccountable fascination, as a result of which she becomes hopelessly spoilt, and unbearable in all the ordinary relations of life, the only thing you can put on the stage (unless she plays the part herself) is the unbearable part, with the fascination omitted. One contemplated Haddon Chambers' lady and said, ' This is an odious woman : why the devil don't they kick her out of the house? What interest is there in her vagaries? And why do they go on pretending that she is charming and irresistible and that we must forgive her everything she does, when, as a matter of fact, she is neither charming nor irresistible nor have we the slightest disposition to forgive her anything : quite the contrary? '

" I think that is the whole case against the play. . . . But in fact its real centre ought to be the hero, not the heroine; it is the comedy of his escape rather than the tragedy of his capture which offers the real material for an attractive bit of work."

In view of this letter the play has been relegated to the limbo of unsuccessful enterprises, but some day, perhaps, it may reappear in the shape of a novel.

As most of the plays I have written seem to come under the same category, I thought I would amuse myself by attempting to write ' Movie ' plots; and went out to Nice some eighteen months ago armed with letters of introduction to Rex Ingram. The first plot offered did not appeal to him, but he was extremely kind, and we dined together

several times in an Arab Café, which he insisted on patronising, and there he told me that he was anxious for a plot
which dealt with supreme sacrifice on the part of the principal
character. As an indirect result of this suggestion, I wrote
" Two Wives," which was published last year as a novel,
and seems to have broken the spell of bad luck, as although
" The Life and Letters of Admiral Cornwallis," published
in 1927, was favourably reviewed, the publisher went bank-
rupt.

Rex Ingram, apart from his extraordinary good looks,
is one of the most interesting men I ever met. An Irishman
by birth, he has all the curious fascination of his race.
Although probably the finest living producer of spectacular
films, he certainly gave me the impression that he preferred
sculpture to anything else. Amazingly clever with his
pencil, he drew for me in about five minutes the sketches
here reproduced, of types round us in the Café.

A propos of the novel, a lady friend of mine went into a
bookseller's shop in Cheltenham and asked the respectable
old gentleman behind the counter whether he had " Two
Wives." " I have not, Madam," he answered indignantly.

Not the least interesting part of writing a novel is to
read the criticisms, which prove more conclusively than
anything else that ' one man's meat is another man's
poison.' Although, presumably, the aim and intention of
a critic is to educate the public mind to appreciate the
difference between what is good and what is bad, how
can this be achieved when few of them ever agree? All
the same, I maintain that the public does not make nearly
enough use of its critics, who are, in their way, an admirable
institution. As they so seldom agree, obviously the only
safe course is for individuals to discover the critic whose
taste accords with their own, and to follow his advice.
What Mr. Hannen Swaffer says is true—that the public
and not the critics make or mar a play, but it does not in
the least follow that the public should make intelligent use
of its critics.

In conclusion: this book deals with the past, therefore I

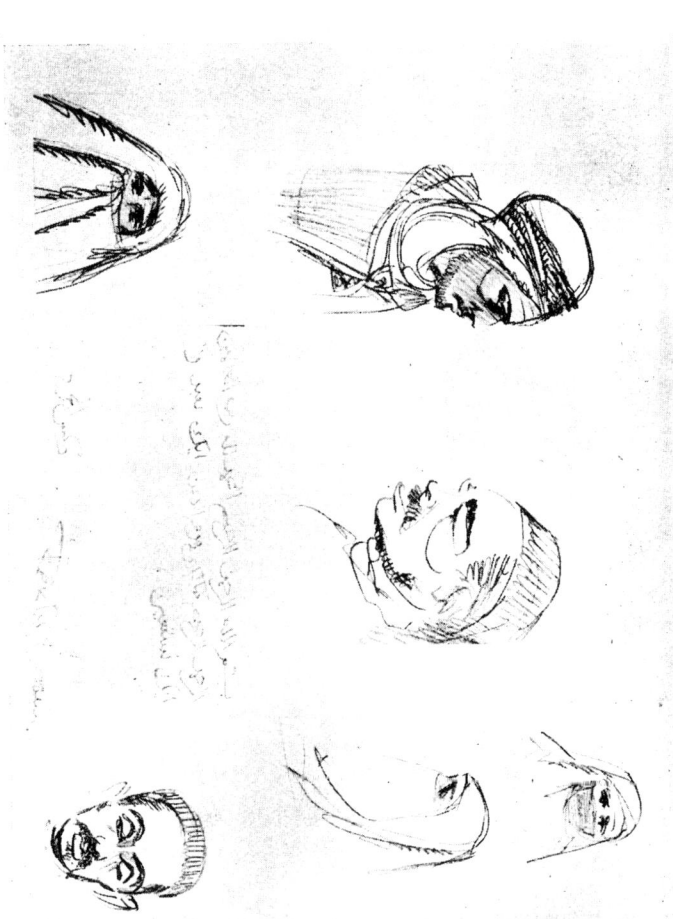

SKETCHES BY REX INGRAM

do not propose to inflict upon my readers any views I may hold about the present. It is an accepted mistake to compare them. There doubtless has never been a past generation which has not looked askance at the present, which has not wondered what was going to happen next, and felt that the country was going to the dogs. If I do hold any views, they are admirably summed up in a little symposium which I heard in a 'bus one night not very long ago. It was nearly midnight, and there entered a gentleman who had obviously dined well but not too wisely. There was plenty of room for him to sit down, but he insisted upon strap-hanging at the far end, facing his fellow-passengers, whom he proceeded to address, rather thickly:

" Ladish and gen'elmen, I'm not a politish'n, although I've just come from a political dinner. I hate politicsh— and I don't like Mr. Lloyd George, who said he was going to make thish country fit for heroes to live in. What I say is, what with the Income Tax at four-and-sixpence in the pound and whisky at twelve-and-six a bottle, you've got to be a blinking hero to live in it 'tall!"

INDEX

317